WITHOUT A CHAIR

WITHOUT A CHAIR

David Schel

ISBN-13: 9781978018181
ISBN-10: 1978018185
Library of Congress Control Number: 2016906558

Printed in the United States of America
www.davidschel.com

DEDICATION

To dedicate this book to my daughters seems trite. Every breath I take is dedicated to them!

Acknowledgement

THERE IS NO SUCH THING as a fair-weather friend. This person was never a friend. One person stood by me during my difficult days and to say I could never have accomplished this without you, a foul weather friend—a true friend—is beyond an understatement. You have driven me across the finish line, figuratively and literally, and I am forever grateful for your wisdom, guidance, understanding, and compassion!

AUTHOR'S NOTE

———◆———

Musical Chairs: *"A game in which players march to music
around a row of chairs numbering one less than the players
and scramble for seats when the music stops.* Also: *a
situation or series of events suggesting the game of musical
chairs (as in rapid change or confusing activity)."*

— MERRIAM WEBSTER DICTIONARY

DIVORCE, ALONG WITH THE BLENDED families created in its wake, has been
interwoven into our culture as an accepted standard; a dysfunction
viewed as "normal" in the timeline of life. However, social dynamics,
along with the unique way each person is affected by divorce, create
a catalyst leading away from black & white thinking. My hope is that
you will experience a full range of emotions, and together we may
resensitize ourselves to the far-reaching and everlasting collateral
damage divorce can cause.

PART ONE

PROLOGUE

———◆———

ACROSS THE EAST RIVER FROM Manhattan lies Brooklyn, where modern-day America has roots, George Washington's army amassed upon its shores in 1776. When he saw the overwhelming number of British ships in New York Harbor, General Washington led a retreat across the Hudson River all the way to Valley Forge and on to victory.

Ellis Island is at the mouth of the East River and was the immigration station through which both sets of my grandparents entered the United States from Eastern Europe around 1900. During this time, many immigrants, as well as my grandparents, would come to settle in Brooklyn, developing communities that lent to this city the moniker of "The Center of the World."

Brooklyn's Jewish districts were home to both of my parents, resulting in firmly rooting their Jewish heritage. At a time when Brooklyn could just as easily have been called the capital of Israel, as was Jerusalem, is when I came to be.

At the same time, the famed Sandy Koufax (an alumnus of the same high school my parents attended) made a decision that would not soon be forgotten by sports fans and Jews alike. He refused to pitch in Game One of the World Series, because it fell on the day of Yom Kippur—the holiest day on the Jewish calendar.

My parents left Brooklyn's Jewish enclaves and traveled east to Long Island shortly after the Dodgers headed west to Los Angeles. While Brooklyn and Queens, two of New York City's boroughs, are geographically located on the western end of Long Island, the eastern counties of Nassau and Suffolk are what are commonly referred to as "Long Island."

The affluent environs of Nassau County would become the location of a distinct brand of Judaism and the dominion of my lifestyle.

General George Washington bravely led his troops in 1776 from Brooklyn westward to what eventually became liberating independence. This ensured his standing as the hero of a revolution that brought freedom and national pride. I would soon discover, however, that this was not always the outcome of conflict. For, fewer than two hundred years later, my father would lead his family east from Brooklyn and into a personal civil war.

CHAPTER 1

———◆———

YOU CAN DO THIS!

The voice screams in my head but I don't believe what it says. I reach my hand toward the knob but my fingers won't obey.

It's too far...too much to ask!

My shaking hand drops back down to my side. Beads of sweat surface upon my forehead but I cannot wipe them away. I am unable to do anything but stare at the expanse that calls me to pass through it. Suddenly, my lungs will not expand. Tiny tubes in my chest suck air into lungs that will not expand.

Just breathe.

I hear the command and my chest rises forcibly. I guess this is how it's done. Just force everything to happen the way it's supposed to.

You know you'll never make it out. You know you're trapped inside this place. You might die here.

I shake my head to silence the voice but it only laughs at me. My breathing continues, faster and with greater force, but it doesn't feel right and my head begins to swim against it. I lift my hand and catch the sweat with my wrist as it drips from my cheek. My other hand follows and wipes my forehead with the back of my sleeve. The expanse widens and my heartbeat pounds in both ears. The skin over my chest begins to burn.

You know you'll never do it. You'll just die instead.

I refuse to let this beat me, so I urge my feet to move. First, one step…then the next. I've moved forward at least two inches but it's not enough. The expanse is overwhelming. My heartbeat quickens and the air becomes heavier. I'm not going to make it. The voice was right all along. Perhaps I will die here. Perhaps this is my destiny. My eyes shift and I blink back tears that have found their way to the surface. I catch a glimpse of a man out of the corner of my eye. He's frozen, unable to move. He is a worthless effort to make something of himself. I turn my head to stare at him and he does the same. Our eyes meet and I see the sorrow buried there.

I say nothing, staring at myself in the mirror. Indeed, there is sorrow there—sorrow for having failed another day, sorrow for being here in the first place. I blink the tears away and the man in the mirror does the same. Is this the culmination of my life? Am I looking at the best I will ever be? My image shakes his head.

Try…just once more.

The voice snaps my focus away from the mirror. I stare at the doorknob once again and notice the expanse is deeper. I will never make it. My hand lifts toward the brass knob but I cannot make my feet follow. The realization that I'm going nowhere breaks something deep inside of me and my knees buckle in response. My cheeks are chapped from tears the day before. This has happened so many times that I cannot count them. I bury my face in my hands and allow the grief to rise.

You're a failure and you know it. You never were going to make it outside today. You'll never leave your room. You're a prisoner in your own life.

"Stop it." The words pass through my throat and choke me. "Please stop."

Yet I know there is truth to what the voice says. I'm a victim of my own fears, unable to function in the world outside of this room. It's true. I cannot leave today. The sun will peak and eventually drop behind the horizon and I will spend the whole day within these four walls, just like yesterday.

I surrender to what I've become. My body curls into a ball on the floor. This is where I'll be for the next hour or more. This is my destiny for today.

How did I get to this place?

Though I've asked this question for years, it remains unanswered. I don't suppose today will be the day I discover the answer. But I remember days when I was not so damaged, days when I could place my hand on the doorknob and step over the threshold. Those were days I could enter the world outside, and life held hope. Panic was not my companion then.

You've always been here.

The voice would not let me be.

"Perhaps you have always been with me, you and your angry twin, fear. But once I could control you. Once, I had a life in spite of you."

I glance around the room, searching for refuge, a place just to sit and rest where I can feel safe, but there was no chair in sight. So, I close my eyes and try to remember how I got here and just for that one moment, the voice is silent.

CHAPTER 2

———◆———

SUMMER HAD REACHED ITS APEX, bringing with it the promise of swelter-
ing sunlight, cooled by an afternoon swim or an ice cream from the
truck that magically appeared every evening just before supper was
ready. It was a typical day for any little boy but instead, it was the day
my dad left.

Streamers and broken balloons peppered the back lawn, waiting
for Mom to pick them up. Such things would be considered trash to
most people but to me, it was a happy reminder that I had celebrated
my seventh birthday the day before. Life was great, a time when little
boys dreamed of bugs and bicycles.

And then he left.

"Forever," Mom said.

I used to think a lot about the simplest things, dreaming of super-
heroes and baseball. But today, my mind wouldn't stop thinking
about my dad. He didn't even look back when he walked to the car.
He just tossed the brown tattered suitcase into the back seat and then
climbed into the driver's seat next to my sister. I think his eyes moved
my way just for a moment because I saw them but he wouldn't turn
his head, not even when I ran toward the car and called out his name.

"'Bye, Gil," Deb called to me. She stared out through the back
window and waved but I couldn't wave back. I was too stunned. The
car pulled away from the curb before I could reach it, and then they
were gone. I stood alone in the street for the longest time watching,
waiting for him to come back, but he never did.

My birthday was done and so was my dad. All I could think about was why. Why would my dad leave? Why would he take my older sister with him and not me? A sudden overwhelming loss fell over me and tears welled up in my eyes, spilling onto my cheeks.

"Gil, get out of the street," Mom shouted.

I started to run, down the street to the corner, just in case dad stopped the car to turn back. But he was nowhere in sight. I saw only the stop sign and a man mowing his lawn on the other side of the intersection. My stomach growled and I headed home, knowing dinner would soon be on the table. Mom was nowhere to be found when I walked through the door. I guessed dinner would be whatever I could find to eat.

It wasn't always like this. It wasn't perfect, but it wasn't like this.

Two cars were always parked neatly in the garage flanked by a perfectly manicured lawn. The exterior had been painted with colors that smacked of happy family life. Inside, a dusky mood colored what most would call "parental nurturing." I just called it home. I sat and dropped my head in my hands as I stared down at the table. *If we could go visit Grandma, it might be different.* The thought was fleeting.

Things were always better at Grandma and Grandpa's house. They didn't live far from us. Upstate New York and the Catskill Mountains were only a few hours' drive. Those mountains held wonders for me. Thick cover within the deep woods and crevasses folded in craggy hills were perfect hiding places. No one could find me in the Catskills. It was magical.

There were many people at the bungalow colony my grandparents ran. They all kept calling it some kind of Borscht Belt. I never quite understood what that meant. I tasted the beet soup they called borscht once. It wasn't good, but the Catskills sure were.

My sister was eight years older than I was, a teenager. They all called her a jap. I didn't know what that was. I had learned about Japan in school, but Deb didn't look Japanese. She looked just like the rest of us. Mom said Dad spoiled Deb and Dad said Mom was overbearing. I didn't know what any of this meant. Mom wasn't a bear.

I also didn't know what Dad meant when he said Mom couldn't cut the cord with me. Then Mom would say Dad treated me like I was a Prince of Entitlement. I didn't have a cord attached to me. So, I didn't know what they were talking about.

Dad was supposedly some Captain of Industry but everyone said he answered to Mom, that she ruled our home. We didn't have a boat and I never understood what everyone was talking about when we were in the Catskills. They talked about stereotypes but didn't listen to music from the stereo when they talked. It seemed to me that what everyone called the American Jews of the 1970s were pretty complicated. I wasn't. All I loved and cared about was in the Catskills. In that place, Dad couldn't leave.

I crossed the kitchen and took an apple from the basket, then glanced through the window above the sink. He still hadn't come back. I returned to the table, took a bite, and sweet juice ran down my chin. The sound was so crisp, it echoed in the empty kitchen. I glanced up instinctively but Mom didn't hear it. I didn't think she'd care if I ate an apple since there was nothing for dinner that night, anyway. I took another bite and felt grateful for its flavor. I sure needed something to sweeten the bitterness of the moment.

Apples always did that for me, because happy memories were attached to apples in my life. I would sit for hours in the highest branches of Grandpa's apple trees, camouflaged by the leaves, surrounded by apples, any one of which I would pick and nibble on as I watched what seemed to me a myriad of people below. There, I would hide, remaining invisible until I decided when to descend and join them. That was my haven, and sweet apples, my companions.

Blueberries peppered the bushes below and I would eagerly help myself on the way to Grandpa's barn. I could spend hours exploring the farthest corners and the hay traps that made up the magic inside that barn. Here was my province and I could be anything I wanted in it: a cowboy, a spy, Superman, or even an astronaut. Anything! But, all too soon, Grandma would ring the dinner bell.

At Grandma's house, we always ate dinner together. And there was always a place for me at the table too. I sat with the rest and helped myself to piles of rolls, bowls of mashed potatoes, and corn, and nobody said, "Your eyes are bigger than your stomach, Gil." I could be myself and eat what I wanted, or disappear in the barn, or hide out in an apple tree and no one bothered me. I was free.

Even Dad sat at the table. He never got up and walked away like he did at our house. Eating together was different at Grandma's house. I liked it best there.

I glanced out the window again and saw the empty driveway. *Now that Dad's gone and taken Debra with him, I don't suppose we'll ever return to the Catskills.* I didn't know if I'd ever climb the apple tree again. I bit into the apple and tried to forget the angst clawing at my stomach.

Every day for nearly two months, I walked to the end of the street to look for Dad's car. After a few minutes, I would shuffle back home, my eyes studying the lines in the sidewalk until I reached our driveway. There I would sit with my feet in the gutter and wait for him to come back.

He never did.

Across the street, I noticed the neighbors loading their car. Baskets and blankets were thrown haphazardly inside but I never saw any suitcases. Isn't that what families usually did when they went somewhere? Load up their suitcases? But the neighbors never did. Where could they be going without them? Each one of the kids, even the ones smaller than me, would carry something in their hands and put it into the trunk. The mom always had a basket of some sort filled with food. The dad would carry soda pop and sports equipment in both hands at the same time. Finally, they would all pile into their car and drive away. They would be gone for the entire day. I would still be sitting on the curb when they returned, almost at sunset, everyone falling out of the car, grabbing at the stuff in the trunk, and carrying it inside the garage. They would all be smiling, tired, and very happy. I always wondered what that family did, because I'd never helped put stuff in our trunk and driven away for a day.

Maybe that's what Dad was doing with Deb. Maybe he was just staying away a little longer than the neighbors did. I decided to wait for another hour or so at the curb that night.

The moon had risen by the time I made my way inside. Mom had gone away somewhere and the house was dark, her car still not in the garage where it belonged. I don't remember her leaving but I do remember her shouting something to me just before the back door slammed shut. My stomach reminded me I hadn't eaten much during the day. The cupboards were high, too high for a seven-year-old to reach. Dragging the stool across the floor only exaggerated the silence of the empty house. Finally, the cupboard was within reach as I stood on top of the footstool.

Making sandwiches was something I was good at and I didn't really mind eating them for dinner either, so I made two, peanut butter and jelly, my favorite.

I carried my sandwiches to the table, pushed aside the papers gathered there, poured some juice into a glass, and sat down to dinner. Glancing at the empty chairs around the table reminded me of the dinners when everyone was at home: Dad, Mom, Debra, and me in the house at the same time. The chairs were still empty then, our table still cluttered with paperwork and Dad's projects. We never ate dinner together like most families I knew. This was how we ate, alone, one by one.

I think that's because no one really wanted to eat with anyone else in the family. I did, but Dad was always distant, disappearing whenever he could. Mom seemed too busy with other stuff. Dinner was whatever I could throw together. Usually it would be sandwiches or soup that I occasionally would share with my sister when she wasn't too busy with her friends. I mostly stayed out of the way. I could remain invisible and sneak out to feed, like a wild animal. I could be anything I wanted—lion, wolf, bear—whatever I felt like at the moment. It was a good way to stay hidden, a good way to be safe.

CHAPTER 3

———————

I THINK ALL ALONG, I was meant to stay hidden. Mom had problems being pregnant, or at least that's what I was told. She couldn't have babies after my sister and someone said the eight she did have died before they were old enough to be born. But she had one more baby, and that was me. I was the last, and I'm not sure why. It doesn't make sense that she would keep trying to have more babies when so many died. I couldn't understand it. Perhaps that's why she and my dad were always fighting.

The shelf was just high enough for my body to squeeze under and just low enough that grownups couldn't see me underneath without bending over. Here, I would hide and eavesdrop on my parents as they fought night after night when my dad finally got home. Mom would cry and Dad would eventually stomp out of the house with nothing resolved between them. I kept listening for my name but never heard it from either one of them. Still, I was certain that the fights had been all my fault.

I'm pretty sure my dad didn't want me. I would have accepted a general fondness, but that was not meant for me. It was okay, though I don't know what it looked like to have a dad who loved you. Dad really loved my sister. He would spend time with her. When I climbed into my bed and lay very still, his voice would filter through the heater vent. Stories of castles and ponies belonged to my sister. I would listen in as he told her tales of make-believe. The stories about dragons were my favorite.

Dad seemed to be very busy, absent from home most of the time. I wanted to learn how to ride a bike or throw a ball but he always seemed to say, "Not now, Gil. I've got too much to do." For some reason, Deb knew the times when dad wasn't busy. He taught her to ride a bike, took her to the movies, and once even took her to get her nails done after lunch. I guess dads have more time for their daughters. I guess they figure boys just grow up and don't really need dads around. I was okay with it because I found other things to do.

Mostly, I would hide and watch other people. I had lots of hiding places around my yard, some in my house too. From where I hid, I could watch my parents, my dad mostly, when he was around. He always had something on his mind and his hair seemed messed up a lot. He rarely looked anyone in the eyes anymore, except Debra. But that was only for a minute; then he would look away. He never looked at me. There wasn't anything behind his eyes. They were dark, vacant, and stared too much. I think he was turning into someone different because I almost didn't recognize him.

After Dad left, Mom wasn't around very much. Fear became my constant companion when she would close the door, jarring my little spirit into survival mode for the long hours as I curled up into a ball next to the window, waiting for my mother to come home. It was dark, I was a child, and terrified to be left home alone. It was the way families were. They lived in the same house, sometimes there and sometimes not.

It was hard for me to watch day after day go by and feel the house empty because my father wasn't there anymore. He was with his new family. Every day, I would try to forget about dad and his new family, but I still looked down the street for his car.

I overheard Mom's friend say she wasn't coping with divorce well and she should go speak to some lady. I guess my dad was "coping with divorce" because Mom kept talking about some kind of woman he was seeing. Mom called her "his trampy girlfriend." Mom's friend kept talking about how outraged she was that my dad had met her while he was away at the temple men's vacation when mom and dad were still married.

Pretty soon, Carole became his "wife" and my mom was called "the X." I wasn't sure what that meant, but I knew it means they weren't married. Supposedly, I had two moms now, my real mom and a stepmom. There were two other kids who came along with my stepmom and I was a little jealous of my sister because, unlike me, she was able to live with her new siblings, who were my age. I was still alone with Mom and she wasn't around very much. My reality *was* in chaos.

One day, I left my house to catch the bus for school and my stomach hurt. I couldn't eat breakfast and remembered that I hadn't wanted to eat very much the night before. Mom wasn't there and I only had a little soda for dinner, then watched TV until I was tired.

I stared at the sidewalk that morning, counting the cracks as I walked to the bus stop—twenty-three of them. Only a few of the kids were waiting at the bus stop when I stepped over the last sidewalk crack. I stopped walking and stood still for a moment, staring at the back of my neighbor Jason's head. A stubby tuft of straw-colored hair stuck straight up through a hole near the top of the scraggly black ski cap he wore. My eyes wouldn't leave the hay tuft on his head. Just then, my stomach lurched. The bus was close but I had to get away. No one else knew I was there so it was easy to make an escape. I ditched into the bushes and hid. Within moments, the bus pulled to a stop just in front of the boy with the straw-hair. He stepped onto the bus along with the rest of the kids gathered there. I stayed where I was, silent, an animal hidden, unseen by predators, in the bushes. As the last kid climbed on board and the doors closed, my heart leaped. *They don't know I'm here.* A sense of triumph rushed over me as I realized I was safe.

Three days later, I watched from the bushes as the bus pulled away from the curb and for the third time in a row, I decided to stay instead of going to school. There really wasn't any reason to go to school every day and no one had called my mom to tell her I was missing. The bushes were safe and I could think and pretend all day long. I liked being there.

In the bushes away from the schoolyard, I had friends. No one played with me at recess and most of the time, the bigger kids would shove me around. I would get tears in my eyes, which only made the bigger boys tease me more. In the bushes, no one made fun of me. No one knew where I was except the roly-polys that would crawl over my hands when I let them. There were a few birds that landed in the tree overhead. I think they were trying to tell on me because they chirped louder when there were people around, but they always grew quiet in the middle of the day when the sun was overhead and it was a little too hot for people to walk on the sidewalk. No one looked at my bushes. I was well hidden and could watch the sidewalk without being discovered.

I started to take snacks with me. Sometimes, I would leave crumbs from a sandwich along the sidewalk just in front of me. The birds would drop down and stare at me, then snatch a crumb and fly away without any loud chirping. I think we made friends that way.

A week after I started hiding in the bushes, something wandered through the area. When I caught sight of the buttery brown cat, it didn't appear too worried about me at first, and mostly watched the birds pick at their crumbs. I watched it for a while but lost interest and began the task of looking for roly-polys for my collection. Within a minute, I felt something staring at me. I'd been discovered. Icy claws of panic ran down my back and I couldn't drag my eyes from the dirt before me, afraid of what I'd see. The heat of the other's stare bored through me, forcing cold chills up and down my spine. I sat there with my eyes downcast for the longest time, studying the patterns traced in the dirt by the birds from the night before. Unable to stop myself, my gaze wandered up.

Yellow and black marble eyes stared directly at me through the branches. The feline's ears lay back slightly and her body crouched, ready to leap at the least provocation. I didn't know what to do so I stared right back at her. I could hear a low growl coming from her and thought for certain she would scratch my eyes out. But I held her stare and slowly inched my hand to the snack bag that rested alongside my thigh. With two fingers, ever so gently, I pulled a chunk of tuna from the sandwich, then lifted it out to her. Her ears moved forward but her body remained still. I dropped the fish onto the dirt in front of the bush. It landed on a branch before falling to the ground. The cat shifted her gaze. Suddenly, she nipped at it and carried it away, leaving a piece of tuna wedged on the branch, undisturbed. I watched as she skittered away and wondered if she would come back for the rest tonight, when there was no one peering from the other side of the bush. I couldn't wait to find out.

The next day I was forced to return to school. Mom had barely said a word to me and I'm not sure who told her I'd been missing from school because no one said anything when I returned. Not even the big kids who were mean to me, and especially not my teacher. I don't think anyone missed me because I never had anyone ask, "Where were you all this time, Gil?" It had been two weeks of hiding in the bushes, two weeks free from the bullies, two weeks to make friends with the only real friends I knew—the roly-polys and the birds.

I never saw the buttery-brown cat with the yellow-black eyes again. I guess he didn't like me much either.

CHAPTER 4

———•———

"GIL, THIS IS BRUCE," MOM said one day, taking hold of a very tall man wearing a polo shirt and jeans.

"Hi," was all I could muster. I didn't know who this guy was or what he was doing in our kitchen but Mom acted like he belonged there. Bruce stuck out his hand to shake mine. I didn't know what to do so I took it and gave the best handshake I knew how to.

"The little squirt needs some muscle, Eileen," he said, laughing and squeezing my hand so hard I flinched. Then he slapped my back and I lost my balance, tripped over the chair and landed on my backside. Bruce laughed even harder. "He needs to learn how to walk too."

I just stared at him.

"I'm just teasing you, Gil," he said in response. "We're going to be buddies."

"Bruce has three grown children, Gil. You'll have brothers and sisters now," Mom said, smiling, then turned to face the stove. She was baking something. She hadn't done that in a while but I guess with Bruce standing in our kitchen, today was different.

After that, Mom called him my "stepdad." I didn't know what that meant exactly but since my real dad rarely called and only showed up once in a while to take me for a quick dinner or a movie, I figured he'd be better than nothing. I never knew when my dad would spend time with me. There was no schedule and I'd learned not to count on him. The only constant in seeing my father was the feeling accompanying our random visits, that I didn't matter. Maybe having Bruce around wouldn't be so bad after all.

"Grab a mitt, Gil. Let's throw the ball for a minute while your mom's getting supper ready," he said as he pushed through the screen door to make his way outside.

"Okay...I'm hurrying," I called back over my shoulder as I ran to fetch my baseball glove and meet him on the front lawn.

By the time we both made it outside, Mom had the meal almost ready. Bruce threw a pitch directly into my mitt, which promptly bounced out. I chased after it and threw it back as hard as I could. It wasn't far enough and Bruce had to walk up the lawn a ways just to pick the ball up where it stopped in the grass. I positioned myself for the next throw that he lobbed, like a girl, so I could catch it.

"Maybe you should stick to reading books or catching bugs," he said.

"I can do it. Let me try just one more time... and throw it the right way"

He tossed the ball overhand, not very hard, but it went way over my head. I jumped, missed again, and had to run after it. For a while, I couldn't find it. I looked everywhere, even crawling on my hands and knees. Finally, the dirty white leather ball caught my eye deep inside a sumac shrub. Dropping back to the ground, I carefully crawled to the edge and reached with one hand as far as I could. My fingertips touched the ball but I couldn't grasp it. There was only one way to get that ball. I would have to crawl underneath and get it. That's just what I did.

"Got it," I shouted with the ball held victoriously overhead in one hand as I spun to face Bruce. He was nowhere to be seen. My hand dropped to my side and the ball rolled from it bouncing along the grass. I didn't see where it went even though my head dropped. I was alone on the grass with a stupid mitt on my hand. It fell too and I left it there as I walked slowly toward the house.

"Be good, Gil, and don't forget to turn on the porch light when it gets dark," Mom called from the passenger seat of Bruce's car as she adjusted both her seatbelt and the casserole she was holding in her lap. "We'll be home late so just go to bed."

I watched them from the top of the driveway as Bruce and my mom drove away and left me home alone. *It's hard to be alone and be eight at the same time.* The thought brought tears to my eyes. I brushed them away and stepped into our empty house. The kitchen still smelled of melted cheese and chicken, a supper made for someone else, not me.

That night I went to bed hungry and cried myself to sleep. I'd done that a lot lately, especially as I wondered why Mom didn't get me a stepdad who had kids my age so I could have a family like Dad and Deb. They seemed happy with Dad's new wife and her kids.

Who is Bruce and why did his wife kill herself? What does that even mean? Is anyone thinking about how this works for me? But I had little choice and definitely no place else to go. An alternate household had been created and I was a part of it. This would be my "family" now.

Bruce's other kids had moved away…far, far away, from what Mom said. Only one son lived nearby but he was too old to play with me. He was married too, so I didn't see him much, except when Mom decided it would be a good idea for him and his wife to babysit when she and Bruce traveled. I didn't think I needed a babysitter. I'd done all right by myself up until then.

"People will talk, Eileen," I overheard my new stepdad say once.

Eric and his wife Elizabeth seemed kinda cool. I heard Mom and Bruce talk about them as "screw-ups" but they seemed fun to me.

"We will be gone a few days and Eric is coming to stay with you," Mom said one day.

I ran to the living room window, my eyes glued to the front curb waiting for Eric's car to pull up. The sun started to drop into a bright orange and gold sunset just as Mom made her way into the kitchen. I was still looking out the window waiting for Eric.

"We've got to get on our way, Gil. Eric should be here soon. I don't know where he is but he said he was coming. Isn't that right, Bruce?" she said, and her voice sounded excited.

"Yes, dear. I'm sure he'll be here," Bruce answered from the hallway. 'The kid hasn't left that window in hours. I doubt he'll be leaving anytime soon as it is."

Mom grabbed a suitcase and waved as she walked out the door, followed closely by Bruce. I waved back and watched as they backed out of the driveway and drove off down the street.

I stayed at the window and watched the curb until my stomach growled. *Perhaps a few minutes won't matter.* The thought urged me from my post and carried me into the kitchen. A pot of chicken noodle soup had been left on the stove for me to heat up. Mom had made dinner for me! *It is a very good day today.* Quickly heating up the soup, I ate dinner seated at my post in front of the window. It was dark outside by then and a little tricky to see who made their way down the sidewalk. Fortunately, Eric would be driving a car so all I had to watch for was the headlights.

Finally, a set of lights appeared in the distance. I watched, as they grew brighter, drew closer to my house, and finally stopped just in front of the curb. Eric and Elizabeth hopped out of the car and walked to the back porch. In a few moments, another car pulled up behind theirs, then a third that parked in our driveway. I wasn't sure who all these people were, but they seemed to know Eric, so I guessed it was all right.

"Gil, buddy," Eric called out as he walked in through the back door. He carried an armful of grocery bags and a large box filled with cans and tall bottles. Those were set on the counter. Then he pulled out a bag bulging with something that looked like the grass clippings from Bruce's lawn mower. I couldn't see why everyone in the room got excited when he set it down on the table, as if it were some big thing.

"Hi, Gil," Elizabeth said and bent down close to my face. She smelled funny and her eyes were sleepy. "You ready to party, big guy?"

"Uh huh," I answered and watched as a group of strangers walked into my house.

Elizabeth lifted a can out of the box and snapped the tab. It fizzed over the top a little but she ignored that.

"This is for you, buddy. Party on!" Eric said and handed the can to me.

I'd always liked soda pop so I didn't hesitate and took a great big swig. Immediately, I started choking and wanted to spit it out because it was bad, but I didn't want to hurt Eric's feelings. My face must have shown that the soda tasted funny because they all started to laugh at me.

"It's malt, Gil."

I didn't know what Eric was talking about and looked at the can, confused. I'd never seen a chocolate malt in a can before.

"Beer, buddy," he said and laughed again.

Elizabeth made her way to a chair and almost fell onto it. "How sweet, little Gilly's tasting his first beer and we're here to watch."

I took another swallow and this time it wasn't as bad. Beer didn't taste anything like I thought it would, nasty stuff in my mind, but I wanted to be cool with the older guys here. So, I drank more. In fact, I drank all of it even though my stomach felt sick. My head felt funny after a minute or two, and I couldn't walk very well. Everyone laughed, especially Eric. I made my way into the living room toward one of the big chairs no one was sitting on but it kept moving…or maybe I did. I couldn't tell. It was pretty funny and I started laughing about it and couldn't quit. Finally, my butt hit the soft cushion and I sank into the over-stuffed chair and laughed hysterically.

Elizabeth made her way over to where I sat and bent down looking into my eyes, our noses inches from each other.

"I think little Gilly is inebriated," she said. "And he likes it."

I didn't know what else to do but smile back at her. She grinned at me and lifted a strange looking cigarette to her mouth and inhaled. I watched the end blaze bright orange and black embers. Just then, smoke swirled around my head as Elizabeth blew the smoke into my face. Then she put it to my lips and told me to breathe in...

I don't remember anything after that.

◆

"Happy birthday, buddy," Eric said the day I turned nine and handed me a beer. We were celebrating again. This time it was for me because it was my birthday. I was cool with that... I was just cool. I chugged the beer without any problems; I could do that now. Jim, one of the guys who came over nearly every time Eric and Elizabeth stayed with me, handed me a joint. I took it and got the hit, then handed it back.

"No, Gil, buddy. It's yours all night long. A birthday present," he said and sniffed something off his wrist. His eyes always watered whenever he did that, but then he smiled so I guessed it was okay.

Mom and Bruce seemed to be traveling more now that they had someone who could watch over me for a few days. It was their "break," as Mom put it.

Eric was always partying, and they made me feel like one of the older guys they'd invited. Jim always showed up late and left early. I wasn't sure why. Once I made my way into the kitchen to get something to eat and I saw Jim hand Eric a big wad of dollar bills. It must have been a lot because Eric tucked it into his pocket really fast. He handed Jim a bag of white stuff and another lunch bag filled with something. Then Jim left. Occasionally, I would see Elizabeth hand out bags just like Jim got, but these were to people I had never seen before. They usually didn't stay for the party, and most of the time I never saw them again.

The next time my stepbrother and his wife stayed with me, they decided that I was old enough to go into one of the back rooms with one of them. Most times during the parties, one of the guys and a girl would go down the hallway into one of the back rooms for a while. Eric and Elizabeth disappeared down the hallway once in a while, sometimes with another person. Today it was my turn. I stood up really tall so that the others could see that I was older too. Elizabeth handed a pipe to me that the other guys had been sharing. I sucked on it for a minute and felt the hit, then handed it back. She smiled and gave me a glass with some gold-colored liquid in the bottom.

"Drink this, Gilly. It's got something special in it to help you enjoy what's going to happen next."

"Okay," I said and stood a little bit taller. Only the older guys drank out of these glasses. The drink burned my throat and made me cough. Everybody laughed. I figured that was okay so I smiled and took another sip. Just then, the walls began to blur and I could barely feel my fingers.

"Whoa...don't drop the fine crystal, boy." Elizabeth took the glass from me. There wasn't much left in the bottom so she finished it off.

"You'd better help him walk," someone said from a chair to my right but I couldn't make my head turn fast enough to see him.

"This way, Gil-buddy," the voice was familiar. "Sweet Elizabeth is going to make a man out of you tonight."

I'm pretty sure it was my stepbrother speaking because I heard him laugh from somewhere behind. A hand went to my back and another grabbed my arm. I started moving but my feet could barely feel the carpet. I'm not sure if I walked or was dragged down the hallway. It didn't matter because it felt like I was floating. The walls seemed to move, pulling closer toward one another as if they were going to squeeze us.

"Hey...the walls..." My voice didn't sound the same.

"Almost there," Elizabeth said and Eric opened a door on one side.

"In here, buddy," he said and moved me to a great big bed. "Just relax and let Elizabeth take care of you now."

They pushed me backward and my head settled onto a pillow. I stared at the ceiling. Little dots in the tiles circled each other making swirled patterns that never stopped moving. It was beautiful.

Suddenly, I felt her hand stroke my thigh and the room spun.

When I awoke the next morning, I was naked. Dark spots matted the sheets in places and my privates hurt. I looked around and didn't recognize the room. The bed was tousled as if there had been a lot of people sleeping in it but there was only me this morning. A marshmallow-puffed pillow lay to one side on the floor and next to it, my jeans. I looked around for my briefs but they were nowhere to be seen. My socks and shoes had been discarded in a pile next to some towels, stained with the same dark spots as the sheets. I decided to gather my things and slowly slid off one side of the bed.

"Ow!" I couldn't help but cry out. Every muscle in my body ached and my head pounded. I stood slowly and the room spun again. It ached "down there" and my hand dropped inadvertently, seeking the cause. Something crusty met my fingertips and pulled at the skin inside my thighs. "What is this?"

A wave of nausea rolled over me as the room spun again. I fell back against the bed and saw blood where I sat. In fact, all of the dark spots were just that—blood. It wasn't a lot but I was afraid to find out where the blood was coming from. "Eww, gross!" my voice said out loud as my hand brush past my butt and surfaced with a bright red streak. I was bleeding from my rectum and I didn't know why. I didn't know what to do, so I made for the towels and covered up the blood spots, then sat on top of one of them. Hopefully no one would see them.

"Gil, buddy...you're up! Good!"

The voice was familiar. My limbs started to tremble. It was cold in here without any clothes on and I didn't want the person shouting my name from down the hallway to see me naked.

"Yeah," I called out feebly and threw the blanket over my legs, then pretended to be half asleep. My stepbrother stepped into the doorway and leaned against the frame.

"Hey, buddy," he said casually, "whaddya say we go get something for breakfast? Elizabeth said there's nothing in the fridge and I'm starvin'."

I threw up onto a towel.

"Okay…well, I guess you're not up for it. Go back to bed then," he said and walked out of the room.

I laid my head back into the pillow and pulled the blanket over my head. If I had to throw up again, no one would see me. Squeezing my eyes tight, I prayed quietly that the blood would go away…and so would the morning.

"Gilly honey." Elizabeth's voice sounded tired. "Gilly, are you still asleep in there?"

I stayed quiet as a mouse under the covers and prayed with my eyes closed that she wouldn't find me.

"Oh-ho-ho! I see you nestled up tight in that bed waiting for me to join you," she said as she entered the room.

Please go away…please make her go away. I would say that about Elizabeth and Eric so many more times over the next few years.

"The cat's away and we can play now. Just like we did last night, remember?" She lifted one corner of the blanket and climbed in beside me.

CHAPTER 5

———◆———

DEBRA PUSHED HER HAIR BEHIND her ears and leaned against the car door. I stared at her for a moment, wondering if the metal door was hot enough to burn her backside. The sun had been shining down for hours and July heat was relentless at this time of day.

"You need to come in and get something to eat before you leave, Debra," my aunt shouted from inside the house. My sister didn't budge. I wondered why no one seemed to worry about whether I had eaten lunch yet or not. *Typical.* I shook the thought out of my head and took a swig of the grape soda that had grown warm in my hand.

"So why did you do it?" I asked her.

She turned her head and studied the street with vacant eyes. I could sense she didn't want to tell me the truth but it didn't matter. I was going to get an answer out of her, even if it meant we would stand there all day in the heat. She pushed her hair behind her ears again and kept her eyes glued on the street.

"They made me," she whispered.

"How the heck can anyone make you pick sides? It's your choice. You're living in the USA and have rights too," I spouted off. Purple sprayed as I spoke. I wiped my mouth with the back of my hand. "I mean, they can't *really* make you say what you don't want to say…not really."

"You don't know anything, Gil," she snapped and her eyes flashed. "They took me into a tiny room and made me stand there, my arm up in the air, and swear to tell the truth, the whole truth, and nothing but the truth, so help me God. You weren't there so you wouldn't know."

"I know they wouldn't make me say anything I didn't want to… especially about Mom and Dad," I said.

She dropped her hands onto her hips and studied me for a minute. "Yeah, well, that's because you're still too little to get how it works in the world. Things aren't as easy for the rest of us as they are for you, Gilly." She said my name singsong, sarcasm in her voice that reminded me of Elizabeth. My gut wrenched. I studied her for a minute. Something had happened to Deb. She'd been pulled into the courthouse to testify and that put her in a safe place, a place far away from me.

"How can you say that, Deb? You weren't the one left behind!" I swallowed hard against the lump rising in my throat. I wanted to be in that safe place too but realized that would never happen. I was left with Mom and whatever happened next. "I watched Dad fighting with Mom just so he could take you with him. He didn't fight for me like that. He didn't even say my name…not once! The truth is, he never even asked to have weekends or school vacations or summers. I never know when I'll see Dad and time with him has become so random, I never expect it anymore."

"How do you know? You think you know so much, Gil."

"Because I do…I heard them fighting all the time about things. Mostly Mom cried whenever they got into all the babies she didn't have, the miscreants—"

"Miscarriages, dummy."

"Miscarriages…she had eight of them and then had me, but I can tell neither of them wanted a boy. They wanted another girl or maybe one of the other babies but they didn't want me, that's for sure…still don't."

Debra lifted the back of her hand to her face and wiped a cheek. She was staring at the street again and I knew she didn't want me to see her cry. *That's too bad! I've cried a lot and no one saw me do it…maybe it's good to have someone watch!* I swallowed again and decided to wash the lump in my throat down with some more soda.

"Look, Gil…Dad doesn't want to be married to Mom any more. That means divorce and the kids split up. If I'd stayed behind with you, it wouldn't have been fair. If you'd gone with Dad, then you'd still be mad because I'd be with Mom."

"That's not true either! Dad didn't want me. He didn't fight to have me with him and I'm stuck here with Mom who only wants to be with Bruce." My eyes darted to the house. No one was listening to us from inside. I could hear Mom and Dad arguing through the closed kitchen windows and knew Dad would bolt outside in a minute or two.

"You think you know, Gil, but you don't know anything." She choked back a sob.

"Did Dad ever mess up your birthday?"

Debra lifted tear-filled eyes and gazed at me, confused. When she blinked, they rolled down her cheeks but this time she didn't wipe them away.

"I don't know what you're talking about, Gil. He didn't mess up anybody's birthday," she said.

"Oh yes he did. You wouldn't know because you weren't there… and neither was he. Jeff and Donald were waiting with me the entire time. Dad never showed up and we missed the game."

"What game? What are you talking about, Gil?"

"It was on my birthday. You weren't there. Dad wasn't around for almost an entire year and he promised to take a couple of friends and me to the Mets game for my birthday to make up for it. Only, Dad never showed up. We waited and waited for almost two hours but he never showed." My voice cracked.

"You're upset about a stupid baseball game?" She shook her head again.

"It *wasn't* just a baseball game, Deb, it was my birthday and my friends were counting on me just like I was counting on Dad. When he finally showed up, it was too late to go so Jeff and Donald just went home. I lost out on a game and I lost my friends."

"You're being dramatic, Gil," she said softly.

The voices inside the house grew louder and I heard something crash.

"It was embarrassing, Deb, and a lousy way to spend a birthday. I also had to have a separate 'Visiting Day' for Dad at camp because he couldn't come the same day as Mom. Do you have any idea what it's like to be the only kid there whose mom and dad are divorced? I already don't fit in, Deb. Now I'm the only one they said who's 'from a broken family.' Only me out of three hundred kids. I stood out like a sore thumb and got teased."

"Then why did you go there? Why didn't you go to a different camp that had 'broken families' in it?" Her sarcasm stung.

"Because you know I could only go to one where the Jewish kids from Long Island went and Dad said he'd only pay for camp if he got to be the one to choose it. I couldn't go if I didn't go where he told me to."

She cocked her head and looked at me, then blinked her eyes into slits. "Well, then, it sounds as if it's your *fault*."

"You're so stupid, Deb! You'll never understand. It's not just the camp. He didn't get involved in any way or even show up for my Bar Mitzvah! Got teased there again too. Lousy things to do to your own kid, don't you think?" I waited but she didn't answer. "You wouldn't know. Just wait...he won't even say good-bye to me when he leaves."

Just then, the door slammed open and Dad busted outside. Mom shouted something from inside and the door slammed again. Dad rounded the front bumper and yanked open the driver's door, positioning himself behind the steering wheel as if he would rip it from the dashboard any second, then laid on the horn.

"Get in, Debra, we're leaving!" he shouted from the driver's side.

Deb climbed in next to him without looking at me. Before she could close her door, the car was already backing down the driveway, heading away from the house...away from Mom and me.

"See ya, Dad," I said softly and threw my soda can into the bushes.

Deb did a lot of talking that day but she still never would tell me why she spoke to a judge—and why no one wanted to talk to me. My mind wandered off and wondered what it would be like to get to tell someone what my life was like. Maybe it was a good thing I didn't get to, though. I didn't feel like I could tell anyone about Eric and Elizabeth. Mom would protect at any cost the relationship that mattered most to her—Bruce—just as Dad had picked Carole over me.

I would do for Eric and Elizabeth's secret what they never did for me. I kept it safe.

I felt so much shame. *What's that, even? Why do I feel this?*

I've always felt like I could never tell anyone the truth about anything because my life didn't look like everyone else's. My family didn't look like all the others on our block.

I feel so alone. I feel so weird. I feel like I don't belong. I can't tell the truth.

What would it be like if I told someone just one thing—maybe about what happened one night around the same time that I was hiding in the bushes and didn't go to school? It was before Bruce, before Eric and Elizabeth, before Deb had gone to talk to the judge. I was a little boy and alone—and I remember too well how terrified I was.

——◆——

"The tuna can was harder to open that time," I said.

You fend for yourself too much. Now look what's happened.

Mom had been gone a lot, which meant I was home alone a lot more. She had stopped talking as much lately and seemed to cry a lot. I was afraid I had caused her trouble so I didn't say as much either.

I dropped my chin and peered at the blood on the counter. Without thinking, I clutched my injured thumb very tightly so that I could see the other knuckles turning white in some places. Panic began to set in so I rested both hands over the pounding in my chest, hoping I'd figure out what to do next.

See! the voice in my head said, apparently studying my handiwork. I knew it wouldn't be quiet, not when something like this happened. *And why would a young boy at your age open a can of tuna in the first place, especially with an electric can opener?*

"Well, I suppose I was hungry," I said aloud because no one was in the house. No one except the voice in my head and me.

You suppose? The voice sounded sarcastic. *Wouldn't most mothers be with their little boys at night?*

"Of course, but that's not fair!" I protested holding my injured thumb in the air. "She's busy tonight and just wasn't here when I opened the can."

I could almost feel my thoughts pick up the pace. *I see…and where exactly was she when you opened the can of tuna all by yourself?*

"I honestly cannot remember," I said and scanned the room for something to put over my thumb. "Does that really matter? I mean, it's really about all the blood and this cut, isn't it?"

Is that what you believe? Your injury is the issue here?

"Well, yeah…duh. Look at this!" I insisted and walked across the kitchen, leaving a trail behind me. "I'm bleeding all over the place."

I managed to pry open a drawer and pulled a towel out with my teeth. The blood dripped into the drawer, leaving crimson balls splattered across mom's clean linen. I swallowed hard, trying not to be ill. It was a long time before the voice said anything again. I caught myself glancing up at the clock several times as I fumbled with the towels.

The voice cleared its throat. *So, Gil. Let's talk a little bit more about what will happen when your mom comes back home, shall we? What do you think she's going to be most upset about?*

I thought the voice sounded sarcastic, but I wasn't sure. She was going to be really upset about a lot of things…the blood mostly, I figured.

"I don't want to think about it, actually. She's going to be awfully mad," I said and rinsed out a saturated rag. My thumb had stopped bleeding but the mess was overwhelming to my young mind.

Tell me exactly how she'll find you when she gets home. Will you be more worried about the blood? Is there anyone who will worry about Gil?

I glanced down at my thumb and traced the laceration with my eyes. Every time I wiggled it, the blood started up again. I held it very still, tucked away in a towel.

"Well, she'll probably walk in the door and see all this blood... everywhere..." I stopped talking and gulped again, then picked out another rag from the open drawer. I rinsed it with water and began mopping as best I could.

The blood is obvious. Where will you be, Gil? The voice in my head sounded a bit testy. My eyes surveyed the room, certain I had stepped in blood because it was tracked across the floor. It was everywhere!

Gil?

It was obvious I had been trying to clean up because there were towels strewn all across the floor.

"Anyone could slip and fall in all that blood," I said.

Yes, but what about you? You're the one who's injured, Gil. The voice was getting frustrated, I could tell. I shrugged my shoulders. *Someone needs to look after you.*

"I'll get it all cleaned up before she gets home, I promise. She'll be mad when she sees all the blood tracked into the bathroom. That's the most important thing. I mean, I have to find out where else it's tracked...there's so much of it."

Then, I saw it.

What? What are you looking at? You're missing the point, Gil. The voice arced in pitch along with its irritation.

"Oh no! The bloody white towel! It's the last clean one!" I began to collect them into a pile in one corner of the kitchen. "I must have used them all. It's a good thing she's not home."

I quickly realized there were no towels left and the carpets might already be ruined. I could hear the voice in my head shift uneasily.

The issue isn't a stained carpet, Gil. Don't you realize that?

"I do now!" I said glancing at the stack of dirty towels. "Thanks for the warning! She's going to be mad I've dirtied up all of her towels."

Forget everything else, Gil. What about her injured son? The voice was tense. I glanced at my cut thumb. The knuckles were white on both hands by now.

"Oh, well, I will be in the living room waiting for mom." Problem solved!

Won't you be crying when she finds you? the voice pried.

"Oh, gosh no!" I said. "I'll probably be asleep, I think." I looked in toward the living room bay window, the place where I always waited for Mom whenever she was gone late at night. I nodded my head, reaffirming my own supposition. "Yessir, I'll just wait for my mom to get home so she can help me with my cut thumb," I said and nodded again.

See! There…you said it. You must wait for someone to take care of you? The voice in my head was relentless and obviously couldn't see my side of things. I glanced at my padded thumb. The blood had stained through the towel but there was nothing dripping down my arm any longer.

Yes, I think I'm beginning to understand what's happening very clearly, the voice said. *There's really no one to look after you, is there, Gil?*

I refused to listen and stacked the towels in the laundry basket.

Fine. We'll talk about something else. Do you remember exactly where you usually wait for your mom when she is away?

I nodded. "I remember really well because I always wait for her there…every time she leaves me home by myself, I wait for her in exactly the same spot very patiently."

I think the voice in my head smiled at me but it wasn't sincere. *Where is that, Gil? Where is that special spot in your living room where you wait for your mother every time she is gone?*

"Right there by the window, where I can see her drive up into the driveway," I said and walked over to the exact spot. I must have been doing a great job remembering because the voice was smiling at me.

So you have a special chair to sit on that lets you watch for her out the window?

What games was the voice in my head playing now? "No," I said very politely. "I sit on the floor in the same place each time." I demonstrated the exact place and position, curling my feet beneath me as my back arched like a cat's.

One place to stay hidden, curled up in the fetal position until someone shows up to care for you. The voice sounded sad. *You're still bleeding.*

I could see a little blood on the place where I waited. "I don't mind waiting there. It doesn't get on me anymore."

Get on you?

I laughed nervously and shifted where I sat. "I guess I didn't get all of it up...there was so much of it, you know, and I can only do so much with a carpet and a little rag."

The house seemed unusually quiet all of a sudden.

"I had a hard time when I cut my thumb because the cut kept dripping on the carpet and I couldn't get it to stop. That's why I used the towel...but I guess it didn't help much because there was some blood that dripped on the carpet when I laid down there on the floor," I said and stared at my shoes.

You laid down there?

"Yeah," I said quietly. "I waited and waited for a long time and the cut wouldn't stop bleeding so I just lay down and curled into a little ball. I figured that maybe if I got small enough, the cut would get smaller and stop bleeding. It didn't work very well, I guess."

Neither of us said anything for a while. I didn't want to look up because I was afraid of the tears that filled my eyes. My fingers tensed around the cut on my thumb again, only a tiny souvenir of the scarring she left on my psyche, and I stared at the floor.

I think I've heard all that I need to hear for today. I couldn't argue with my conscience this time.

CHAPTER 6

———————◆———————

"SO...ARE YOU GOING TO GO or not?"

He was only a year older than me, in middle school, and he wanted to be my friend! I met him at the candy store. I didn't have many friends and he'd been eager to make friends with me for a few days now.

"Heck yeah!" I said and started running for home. "Let me get my bike and I'll be right back."

He stepped off his own bike, a shiny black Stingray with a cracked banana seat. It was cool even though the paint had been scratched off almost every part that showed metal. The rear fender was missing and I was pretty sure the handlebars were bent, but he looked really tough riding it. That meant I would look tough too...riding alongside my new friend.

I ran a little faster.

When I finally returned, he was still waiting for me, tossing rocks at a sleeping mutt that lived down the street. I don't think he ever hit the dog because it stayed curled up against the house and never moved. I even watched a rock hit close enough to dust its fur with dirt that exploded in all directions from where the rock landed.

"Let's go," was all he said as I rode up. I felt pretty good because my bike was new; the tires still had the little rubber nubs sticking out from the sides. Turning was easy and I could pedal fast on my new bike. It was easy to keep up!

"Where are we goin'?"

He nodded to a street up ahead of us.

"Cool," I said and passed him. I leaned to my right and turned the bike on its edge, carving a narrow turn down the street he'd indicated. There weren't any people along this street, a good choice because we could ride as fast as we wanted and no one would get in our way, no stopping us. I pulled up next to a fire hydrant and waited for him to catch up. When he finally made it to the hydrant, he hopped off his bike and kicked one toe at some gravel.

"Hey, um…let me try out your bike. It's pretty cool," he said.

"Okay, sure!" I said excitedly. My new friend really liked my bike and me. This was great! We were going to be great buddies. "It's brand new. Just got it a couple of weeks ago for my birthday. Here ya go," I said, my voice barely able to contain my enthusiasm as I tipped the handlebars toward him.

He wasted no time hopping up on the seat and literally peeling out on the loose asphalt as he took off down the street. I stood by watching, proud. It was obvious he really liked that bike. That meant he would really like me too.

Gravel sputtered as he skidded in a U-turn, heading back toward me. My lips curved into a broad grin.

"One more time," he shouted as he shot past me.

"Okay, sure," I shouted back.

His feet flew over the pedals, circling faster than I've ever seen anyone pedal a bike. He turned the corner and headed down the main street. *I guess he wants to show my bike off to everyone.* The thought made me whistle. I kicked the gravel at my feet and glanced down the street, waiting for him to circle back.

But he never did.

It was nearly an hour before I moved away from the fire hydrant. My feet moved slowly as I walked toward the main road and past the beat-up bike he had left behind. I felt my eyes sting and within minutes, my cheeks were wet. *Surely he's coming back.* The thought wasn't convincing. *My new friend wouldn't take my bike...that's not what friends do.* I couldn't face the idea that maybe he wasn't really a friend. That couldn't be it. He must be lost.

I walked around the corner but he was nowhere to be seen. My bike was gone and so was my new friend. Tears fell over my face that I didn't bother to wipe away, not this time. I didn't care if anyone saw me crying... I'd lost my friend.

By the time I made it home, Mom was in the kitchen fixing Bruce dinner. The door was heavy when I pushed against it.

"What on earth? Gil?" she said.

"My bike is g-g-gone and s-s-so is my new f-friend," I stuttered.

Bruce shook his head and stared at the plate of food Mom set in front of him. I kinda wished that Dad had been sitting there, but I didn't know where he was and hadn't heard from him for months now. Mom wiped both hands on an apron and stood there, staring at me. I guess it was the tears.

"What? You lost your bike? The brand new one Bruce paid so much money for?" Her voice started to shake.

"I think he got lost," I answered and glanced up at her, wiping my eyes with the back of my hands. "That's probably it. We should probably call the police and tell them to find him so nothing happens."

Mom's hands went to her hips and Bruce spun in his chair.

"You really don't get it, do you, Gil?" he said, then looked at my mom. "Can anyone be so dense? What an idiot!"

"Gil..." Mom stopped and shook her head the same way Bruce had done only a few minutes ago. "Please tell me you didn't just give it to him. Please tell me he beat you up or something to get it from you."

"There isn't a mark on him, Eileen. Look at him. He's bawling like a baby. Of course Gil gave it to him. He's too naïve to know when he's being conned...by a *friend*, no less!"

I cried out and started for the hallway.

"He's my friend. He wouldn't do that. Something happened," I shouted as I made for my bedroom, unable to face what I knew was true.

"Yeah, we should call the police because something *did* happen, Gil. You let some kid steal your bike!" Bruce stuffed a forkful of food in his mouth.

"So much money, Bruce, on a stupid bike." Mom's voice was barely audible by the time I got to my room.

I fell onto my bed and sobbed. They could never know the truth—that I had, in fact, handed over my bike and let somebody I trusted steal it from me without even a fight. I could never tell anyone what happened. Thankfully, I'd probably never see him again. I cried harder and pounded my hands against the pillow. *He was my friend!* I swallowed the truth and buried it deep with the rest of the secrets that lived there.

———◆———

"Bruce found a new bike for you!"

The fender was rusted and the paint was chipped off one side, but it was a bike and it was mine. Mom was elated and clapped her hands, waiting for me to hop on and ride away. I wasn't sure what I was supposed to do so I just stood there, staring at it.

"Well, aren't you going to say 'thank you'?"

"Oh." I jumped to and glanced through the glaring sunlight at Bruce, who stood with one hand on the bike while he shifted the sunglasses over his eyes with the other. "Thank you, Bruce," I stammered and grabbed hold of the handlebars.

"Do you even remember how to ride one of these things?" He laughed and moved to stand by my mom.

"Yeah." I took that as my cue. I hopped onto the seat and clapped my feet over the pedals. "Yeah, I think so."

I spent most of that summer riding my bike. It was the best way to get out of the house and be as independent as Mom apparently wanted me to be. She was always asking me, "Don't you want to go for a ride on your new bike, Gil?"

I wanted to go everywhere on that bike, but I felt safer tucked inside my room where no one would notice me. I could hide under my bed or in a closet if I heard Bruce walk down the hallway. Not that I minded if he was there, it was just that I liked staying hidden.

Riding a bike was fine, though. I could get away fast and turn down a street somewhere, then disappear where no one would know I had gone. I suppose that's like hiding…but more out in the open.

One summer evening, the sun was just beginning to drop behind the hills that lay to the west of my neighborhood. Ridges painted in dark green and sienna were illuminated with amber sunlight that melted into warm tangerine, just inches from where it dipped over the horizon. It was glorious. I had to take it all in before it was too late and the sun disappeared completely.

I pedaled as fast as I could to the top of Linden Drive—the highest place I could get to in a hurry. I made it, barely, and waited while the sun slowly hid itself behind the hilltops. *What would that be like?* I often wondered. I imagined myself following the sun as it played hide-and-seek with the moon. A flock of geese flew overhead, honking obnoxiously as they broke the silent majesty of the moment. *Tattletales!* The thought made me smile and I wondered again if birds could follow the sun wherever it went, even to China, where it must be rising now.

Turning the handlebars, I pulled my bike around and pointed it downhill. Shadows began blanketing the street, a sign that my mom would wonder where I was, if she was home tonight.

My bike sailed a little too fast for my comfort as it reached the bottom of Linden Drive, so I pushed my heels against the pedals to slow down. Just then, something honked at me, too loud to be one of the geese. I jumped a little on my seat. I never saw the headlights as the bumper made contact with the side of my rear tire. The impact threw me off the seat and I landed in a heap on the side of the road. The tires screeched for just a second and I heard a car door open.

"Are you okay?" The voice was shaky.

I glanced up to see a man's eyebrows knit together with concern. "Where's my bike?" I mumbled, and brushed the gravel off my palms.

"Don't move," the man said, and bent down to take a better look at me. "We should call an ambulance or something."

"No!" I shouted. "I'm okay, mister. Really… I just need to get my bike and go home."

The man stood up and scratched his head as he stared at me. After a minute, he put out his hand to help me stand up. My knee hurt badly underneath a big tear in my jeans but I couldn't see any blood and took that as a good sign.

"Are you sure? What's your name?" he asked.

"Gil," I answered and walked as casually as I could to where my bike lay. The wheel was turned up on itself but I was certain I could fix it without much fuss. Bruce had shown me how to do it once before when the front tire had slipped out of alignment with the handlebars. I was glad I'd paid attention while I held the tire between my knees and straightened the handlebars again. I didn't let on that my knee hurt even worse afterward.

"Okay, well, if you're sure," the man said and straightened his hat back onto his head. "I can call somebody…your mom or dad maybe?"

"No!" I said, not wanting him to discover they might not be there, and not wanting the man to get in trouble because of me. I just wanted to get back to my room, and to sit and be alone, where no one could see my torn jeans or the road rash on my palms. "Really, I'm okay but I gotta get home before it gets darker or I'll get into trouble."

I hopped onto my bike and rode off without looking back. I knew the man was watching as I rode down the street because I could feel his stare. It made me nervous so I took a different route home and turned down Birch Street instead. There were no streetlights, but there weren't any cars either. I pedaled faster and soon arrived in my own neighborhood. As I turned onto my street, I glanced down at my knee. Every time the pedal rose up and my knee bent, it stung. A dark stain had surfaced over the tear and I worried about what Mom would say. *At least my bike isn't broken.* I would have to keep my knee a secret for a while, and probably get rid of my jeans before Mom discovered them.

The plan hatched in my brain as I turned onto the driveway and pulled into the garage. There was only one kitchen light on. I didn't hear any voices and decided it would be safe to go in through the back door without being discovered.

Bruce's car was parked inside the garage and it was a tight squeeze with my bike between it and a stack of boxes that lined the garage wall. I hopped off and started to walk alongside my bike, both hands on the handlebars so that they wouldn't scratch the side of his car. Suddenly, a sharp burning sensation shot up my left arm to my elbow. A voice cried out and my hand dropped from the handlebar. I looked at it and saw the bend just above my wrist. I cried out again and grabbed hold of my forearm with my right hand.

"Oh no!" I said out loud. My left arm didn't look normal and the whole arm burned. I slowly made my way into the house, opening the door with my foot as my right hand carried the deformed left arm.

"Gil? Is that you?" Mom called from upstairs.

"Mom," I said, and panicked a little at what she would say when she saw what I had done to my arm.

She walked into the kitchen, wiping her hands on an apron. I stood to face her, waiting for what she would do next.

"What's going on—" Mom stopped and her jaw dropped.

"Mom, I think I hurt myself," I whispered.

She moved across the room and was on her knees, fingering my left wrist. I cried out.

"I think it's broken," she said and grabbed a cutting board from the counter. "Here. Lay your arm on here and ..." She stopped and eyed me. "What happened, Gil?"

My arm felt better almost immediately, lying stationary on the cutting board. I looked up at her with tears running down my cheeks. How could I tell her what really happened, after my other bike had been stolen? Bruce would never let me own another bike if he knew I'd been hit by a car, riding this bike—and I had let the guy go.

"I fell out of a tree," I lied and dropped my gaze to the floor.

"You did what?" she said, pulling off her apron with one hand. "What were you doing in a tree?"

I shrugged my shoulders and the burning shot up to my neck. "Ow!" The tears began to pour out of my eyes again. I couldn't stop them. Mom grabbed her jacket and took hold of the cutting board.

"Let's go," she said and led me by the cutting board she kept propped up with her palms, outside and into our car.

I said nothing as we drove to the hospital. Mom ranted about "being careful" and "not taking risks you can't handle," and said, "I'm going to find out where that tree is and sue the owners"…or something like that.

When we finally pulled up outside the big red sign that said EMERGENCY, my wrist was throbbing and the board didn't help much. I felt like I was about to throw up, but didn't dare tell Mom that. It would be one more thing for her to get upset over, so I swallowed hard and tried to concentrate on an ambulance pulling up in the circular drive.

We walked into the waiting room and were met by a nice nurse wearing a white hat. She smiled at Mom and glanced at me briefly, then picked up the telephone and called someone. Within minutes, Mom and I were ushered through two big doors and escorted down a long hallway to Room 15. There were people everywhere, some of them crying, others lying quietly while IV tubing dripped clear fluid from bottles into their arms. I wondered if they would do that to me. I decided my arm didn't hurt so much and dropped my eyes, focusing on my black sneakers. One of the laces with a big knot in it had come untied and dragged loosely along the floor. *You won't be able to fix that with a broken bone in your arm.* The thought made me feel worse and I made sure to watch where I walked so I wouldn't trip and fall.

Mom and I sat silently inside Room 15 with the curtain drawn to close out the rest of the ER. Occasionally, she would look at me and shake her head.

"I don't know what I'm going to tell Bruce," she said and I let my eyes go back to my shoelace.

There would be trouble for certain if Mom and Bruce knew what had really happened. I could never tell them the truth, never tell them that my knee was bleeding, or that the car that hit me had broken my bone. There are just some things that should be kept quiet.

"So, Gil. Tell me what happened to your wrist," a young dark-haired doctor wearing black-rimmed glasses asked as he fingered the place where my arm bent crooked.

I winced and looked down at the deformed appendage that rested on the cutting board. "I fell out of a tree," I said...and the pattern of lies and secrets continued.

CHAPTER 7

———◆———

"GRANDPA'S IN THE HOSPITAL AND we're going to see him now."

Mom's announcement hit me like a freight train. I barely remembered anything she said afterward, something about meeting Deb and Dad there. There would certainly be trouble ahead with Mom and Dad in the same confined space, not to mention Debra's inclusion in the mix. My mind wouldn't let me think about it… *Grandpa is sick*.

"What's wrong?" My voice cracked as the words crossed my lips. I was already halfway through the kitchen door with my jacket clutched in one hand. Mom was just ahead of me and had managed to jump into the car before I even made it outside.

"Your dad called for you and I spoke with him instead," Mom announced.

"Dad called?" I hadn't talked to my dad for nearly a year. "He called me? Why didn't you let me speak to him?"

"Because we were in a hurry, Gil. Don't forget to lock the door," she said and turned the key, bringing the car's engine to life. I hopped in beside her and slammed the door shut. "I don't know what's wrong and I'm not going to wait to find out either. Dale said it was urgent."

"What did he mean by 'urgent'? What does that mean? Why did Dad say that word?" I couldn't stop asking questions.

Mom pinched her lips together and drove the rest of the way to Brooklyn with a vise-like grip on the steering wheel. When we arrived, she screeched to a halt in the nearest parking spot and jumped out of the car muttering, "They're *my* in-laws, not hers!" Then she bolted straight for the front door. Fortunately, my legs had grown at least a foot within the past two years, and I could easily take long strides to catch up with her.

Sadly, those long legs did nothing to help me secure a place with any of my high school's athletic teams, even though I loved sports. I lived for sports! In particular, basketball and hockey. I remember watching the guys on the school teams with envy. Those guys were not only team-mates, they were friends. They had something I longed for: they had each other's backs. But I never had the confidence to try out. I guess I just didn't fit in. It shouldn't have surprised me because I've never really fit in...that was clear from the first day I sat in the bushes and watched as the bus drove off, leaving my seat vacant and unnoticed.

I shook my head and all thoughts of high school vanished. I was here for Grandpa and that was my focus right now.

"He asked to see Gil," Deb said.

Mom was incredulous. "But I'm here too," she insisted.

"That's what he said." Deb sounded older, more mature but with the same sarcastic lilt I remembered as a kid. "I'm not making it up, Mom. Ask Dad if you don't believe me. Dad called the house so he could pick Gil up and bring him here, but then you...jeez!"

I stepped through the doorway and faced my grandpa lying flat on an oversized hospital bed. His mouth hung open and his eyes were tightly closed. *Maybe I'm too late!* I glanced up at Dad and then at Deb, who just stared at me hard before tipping her head, a signal for me to step up to Grandpa's bedside.

"Go on, Gil," Dad said dryly.

I moved forward and took a place next to Mom. Deb and Dad stood across from us against the wall. All eyes stared at me.

"Grandpa?" I whispered. He did not move but gasped a deep breath through his open mouth. "Grandpa," I said a little louder, and his eyes opened.

He mouthed my name, then weakly said, "Sit me up."

Mom fumbled with the remote as Dad pressed a button next to a rail on his side of the bed. Immediately, Grandpa sat upright, his head propped by a pillow.

"Gil," he finally said. His voice was so weak that I could barely hear it. "Come sit here, boy." He dropped one hand to the edge of the bed, pointing.

I did as he asked, and he took hold of my jacket in both hands.

"Don't be shy, Gil. Say something!" Dad said.

"For heaven's sake, Dale, leave him alone," Mom snapped.

I glanced at both of them and decided I didn't want to cause World War III right here in Grandpa's hospital room, so I leaned forward and spoke in a rather loud voice. "Hi, Grandpa. It's me, Gil."

Grandpa nodded. I leaned forward again and shouted into his good ear.

"How are you doing? How's Grandma?" The words fell out before I could check them.

"Fine...she's fine. It's been a long time. When are you coming to visit us again?" he asked and closed his eyes for a moment. I heard Mom *harrumph* in the background but never took my eyes off Grandpa.

"As soon as I can," I responded. I didn't know what else to say and so I sat there, silently thumbing the snaps on my jacket.

Dad stepped forward and so did Deb. "We're all here, Dad. Me, Debra, and Gil, as you know."

Grandpa patted my hand but never opened his eyes. I looked up at Deb, who just stared at Grandpa. I could see tears welling in her eyes. *That's probably my fault because I'm the one holding Grandpa's hand and it's likely that she wants to.*

"Here, Deb," I said, lifting Grandpa's hand to her. "Your turn now."

She shook her head. I couldn't understand it. I could see the hurt behind her eyes but for some reason, she held back.

"We need to go now, Gil," Mom said and kissed Grandpa on the forehead.

"Me too," Dad piped in. "C'mon, kiddo." He motioned to Deb but she remained fixed against the wall, eyes glued to Grandpa.

I shook my head. "Can't I stay a little longer?" I implored.

Deb tore her eyes away from Grandpa and glanced at Dad. "I could drive him home. I brought the car."

Dad shrugged and made to leave while Mom stared blankly at us both.

"Okay, Pop," Dad said and patted Grandpa's head. "I'll check in on you tomorrow." He moved toward the doorway. "Don't be too late, Debra."

Deb nodded and moved to her side of Grandpa's bed. She sat down gently and placed her hand over Grandpa's. I held his other hand. We said nothing, just stared at one another in silence as Mom and Dad left the hospital room, separately of course.

The next day, Grandpa was dead and I knew, deep down in my gut, that seeing me was what had killed him.

I couldn't face the next month, knowing that seeing me had been the reason Grandpa died. The guilt was more than I could stand. He'd been fine for years, then suddenly, right after my visit, he died. My young mind couldn't let go of the images that filled it, of the many different ways he might have passed that night and how I was the cause. Days dragged on and I never felt better about it. In fact, I felt worse. Time alone hiding from everyone else seemed to bring the only relief from the pain in my heart. So I hid.

Over the next year, I spent too many hours hiding in my room, hiding from Mom, hiding from the guilt...until one day some news arrived that shifted my attention from Grandpa to my sister.

CHAPTER 8

———————

"DEB'S GETTING MARRIED!"

The announcement arrived serendipitously one afternoon via phone call. Mom was upstairs when I answered the phone, and I literally could not believe the words I heard broadcast over the receiver. I was ecstatic!

Ron was a great guy and I liked hanging out with him, the few times I got to. His six-foot-plus stature eclipsed my five-foot-ten frame but I never felt small around him. Even Deb seemed more amicable whenever the three of us were together.

A few weeks later, on a Saturday morning, just after Bruce had driven off to play golf, I made my way outside to collect the mail. The sun shone as brightly as my countenance and I heard myself whistle as I closed the lid to the mailbox and began to rifle through the stack of letters in my hand. An oversize envelope caught my attention.

"Look at this," I said, walking into the house. Mom made her way into the kitchen where I spread out the mail over the table, holding tightly onto the envelope. Its paper was pressed, used mostly for formal announcements, so I knew exactly what lay inside.

"What's that?" Mom asked casually.

"I think it's Deb's wedding invitation," I answered, trying to sound nonchalant. It did just the opposite.

"Well, give it to me then," she said.

I reluctantly handed it over.

She scanned the front of the envelope and anger flashed behind her eyes. She held the envelope as if it were dirty laundry.

"I guess you're the only person from this house who's been invited," she snapped and handed the envelope back to me. "It's addressed to you, Gil. My name isn't anywhere on that thing."

I hadn't taken time to study the pristine handwriting scrolled over the front and was rather shocked to see only my name written on it. I glanced up at Mom, who had turned her back on me.

"I'm sure there's one on its way for you and Bruce too. The mail-man just didn't deliver it yet."

That invitation never came.

Weeks passed and the reality of exclusion hit Mom hard. I found myself looking for ways to avoid her whenever possible, simply out of guilt. The departure from routine home life took me straight to Deb and Ron's side, and I found myself enjoying more and more time with my sister.

Mom's distress increased until one day when she could no longer contain herself. "Look at all your father and Deb have done to me! Now you are going to betray me just like they did." Her hands rested firmly on her hips.

I shifted in my chair. "That's not true, Mother. I would never do anything to hurt you," I said and dropped my eyes.

She began wearing a path in the carpet as she circled the living room. I followed her feet with my eyes, refusing to look at her face.

"You have no idea, Gil. There have been so many things…so many people who do things that hurt me. This is the frosting on the cake! My own daughter!"

"But Mother, you and Deb rarely speak. You never see her except when Dad comes by for something and that hasn't happened in years." I knew it was a mistake as soon as I said it.

Her eyes flashed and tears began to well. She blinked and imme-diately wiped them from her face. It was rather demonstrative but made her point. "Gil, that was a hurtful thing to say. I never sent your father from this house. He chose to go. Chose to chase some young blonde tramp and leave his wife and son behind. I never dreamed he would leave so quickly and take your sister with him," she sobbed and dropped into the chair on the opposite side of the room. "I haven't spoken to your sister because she chose sides."

"We were little kids then, Mom. There were no choices for either of us. Dad took Deb and you took me," I said.

She looked up at me with tear-stained cheeks. "I didn't get to choose. Your father chose everything, the divorce, which child he wanted. I was given the leftovers."

I swallowed and stared at her.

"Now I'm being handed this—a mother excluded from her own daughter's wedding when I should be there too, celebrating with her, part of the family," she said.

The familiar clench in my gut began and I swallowed again. *You can't do this to her.* The answer was clear but I couldn't bear to listen. *If you go, it'll kill her just like your visit with Grandpa killed him.* She sobbed out loud and buried her face in her hands once again. I had to say something.

"If it will make you feel better, I'll stay home with you. Deb will understand." I didn't know where those words came from and soon realized it was my own voice speaking. There was no way I wanted to miss out on Deb and Ron's wedding. I knew this but the vise around my gut said otherwise. I was the rope held in the emotional tug-of-war played by my mother and Deb. I juggled so much anxiety over this issue. I wasted months waffling back and forth, weighing the options and evaluating the consequences of my decision. *You can't live with the guilt of hurting her. Deb would be easier to betray than Mother. You know what you must do, even if it's not what you want.*

The day had arrived and the clock chimed its painful reminder that the wedding was only a few hours away. Mother sat with her face in her hands and I still needed to fix the mess Deb had created by inviting everyone but Mom. There was no question what I would do.

The voice in my head was right about today, as it had been all along, though I'd never found the courage to tell Deb.

I took off my jacket and pulled at the knot in my tie, my preparations undone. The effort to get ready was moot anyway. It was only a few hours before the ceremony and I would be late at this point. Mom had made certain there would be no way for me to make it on time. She glanced up and smiled. I could barely look her in the eyes. As I laid my jacket over the armrest of the chair, she thanked me for being such a good son, "unlike your sister." I didn't feel like a good son, more like a liar, but the guilt of leaving Mother behind had clenched my entire insides and wouldn't let go.

"Of course, Mother," I said and the vise released its hold.

CHAPTER 9

———◆———

THE HOCKEY HAWK HAD CAPTURED Northeast ice arenas and held captive sport fans for decades. He was also one of my heroes. Hours spent at the radio listening to Brett Carter's broadcasts between game periods had been time well spent, or so said my young seventeen-year-old mind. I rarely missed anything Carter produced and was most taken by the articles he wrote about the game.

So, when the opportunity to intern with Brett Carter presented itself in the newspaper, I jumped at it. My grades didn't support someone who would intern with The Hockey Hawk but I wanted to try. This was an opportunity that rarely happened, especially not for someone like me. It was such a random event. I had to do it! I don't know where I found the courage, but I did.

The day the phone rang, I could barely speak.

"Is this Gil Belmont?" The voice, thickly coated with a Brooklyn accent, reverberated through the receiver.

"Yes, sir," I said sounding weaker than intended. I cleared my throat and tried again. "Yes, this is Gil Belmont speaking."

"Congratulations, Gil. You've been selected to work in an internship position with Mr. Carter. Your start date is July 5. Will you be able to accept?"

I could hardly speak! A lump had formed over my vocal cords and I had to clear my throat again. "Absolutely! Yes, sir. Thank you, sir!"

I hung up the phone, my face plastered with a grin that would not go away. Mom was standing by and said nothing, but nodded her head as she watched me. I suspected she was okay with the idea, even though it meant a commute to Manhattan. It didn't matter at that moment what she thought. I had been selected and felt such pride that I was fairly certain I could make the sun rise just by thinking about it. I immediately dialed my dad's phone number.

"Dad! I got it! I got the job working for Brett Carter!"

His voice resonated pride—a new sound for my ears from my dad. The smile on my face only broadened.

"That's great, son. When do you start?"

"July 5. I have to go to the city but the train goes straight to there from here."

"How much are they paying you?" he asked.

My smile weakened just slightly. "It's an internship, Dad. They don't pay anything but I get trained and—"

"What do you mean, they don't pay?" Dad's voice had changed.

I swallowed. A new lump was forming, one that was all too familiar. He must have heard the silence because he continued.

"We don't work for nothing, son, not this family. If they don't pay, you don't do it. You hear me?"

My voice had vacated and the lump had taken its place. "But, Dad," I squeaked.

"Don't 'but dad' me! There's nothing more to say. You call that guy right back and tell him he'd better come up with a decent salary or you're not taking the job!"

My eyes began to sting. I glanced at my mother for support but found her standing with her arms crossed, lips pressed tight. I could sense the fear in her, afraid that I could amount to something and leave her behind.

"This is really important to me," I whispered through the receiver.

"It has nothing to do with what's important, Gil. It's about money. They give you zip. Zero...nada, and expect you to actually pay for train fare to get to Manhattan and work for *free*?" His voice was getting louder. "What kind of an outfit is it anyway?"

The decision had been made.

"Dad, this is a really great opportunity for me..." I tried to rationalize but he wouldn't listen.

"You can work for Joe. I'll get you on. He's paying nearly two dollars per lawn. I hear he's got work lined up for the entire summer," he stated, and that was the end of it.

Three hours after receiving the news of my internship award with the prestigious Brett Carter, I made a phone call that I would live to never forget.

"Mister Cooper, this is Gil Belmont. I can't take the position..."

And then it was done. I turned down the opportunity of a lifetime and went back to being dutifully average.

I guess that was the way things were meant for me—average. Kids at school seemed to think the same way about me as Dad did. I wasn't the nerd who was no good at anything, but I wasn't popular either. I never fit in with any group, and would never be on any of the teams. It seemed that sports weren't meant for me. That made it even more painful as I hung up the phone. Mr. Cooper didn't argue with my decision either. I figured he was on to the next guy.

It was a lot like my girlfriend...or at least the one girl at school that I had thought was my girlfriend. She was beautiful, an amazing girl with the most beautiful brown eyes. I couldn't believe she would be interested in me but she was. I always did things for her, and she seemed to like that. We had a great time together. That is...until she got a good look at some of the high school jocks. She'd never noticed them before and then one day, she stopped answering my phone calls and was too busy to talk with me in the halls. I could sense the shift in her attitude with me... I'd been this end of it before. Most call it rejection but I just figured that was how it was for me—that was my life.

"I can't see you anymore, Gil. I'm...well, I'm just too busy," she said, spun on her heel, then walked away. The ponytail she had tied up with a big white ribbon swung briskly as she hurried down the hallway. I stood there, alone in a hall filled with bustling students, and watched her until she met up with a guy who wore a letterman jacket. He put his arm around her shoulders and they walked off together.

That's the way it is with you, Gil, the voice in my head said as I strolled toward my next class. *You'll always be average. You'll never get the girl or be on the team…you're not meant to work with The Hockey Hawk either. You're just average.*

"Shut up!" I said under my breath. I took a seat at my desk in the back of the classroom.

———◆———

"Syracuse University would be good for you," Mom said and set a bowl of cereal in front of me. I began to eat, lost in my thoughts, oblivious to the corn flakes and bananas that automatically made it to my mouth. "Did you get the application done?"

"Yes," I muttered.

"What are your chances, really?" she asked, wiping her hands on her apron.

"Good," I said.

"Your grades aren't good. It's a miracle you will graduate from high school."

"I scored high on the SAT test, Mom." I swallowed a mouthful and continued, "That will get me into college."

She *harrumphed* from across the room, then joined me at the table.

"Dad said he would make a call."

"Wait…'make a call' … what does that mean?" She put down her coffee cup.

"Dad knows people. He said I would probably need a little help and he said he'd make a call…on my behalf…you know, to get me in."

She picked at a piece of toast and shrugged off my bravado. "Tell me that's not going to happen, Gil."

"Stop being so dramatic, Mom."

She picked up her toast and walked out of the room.

Less than a month later, I proved Mom wrong. Graduation came and I was part of the graduating class that would soon walk up to be congratulated with a diploma and some applause. I stood anxiously awaiting that moment and scanned the crowd of people assembling for the ceremony.

They'll be here! The reassurance didn't do its job. Deep in my gut, another voice kept whispering the truth. *They're not coming.* I adjusted my cap and gown and allowed my eyes to survey the audience again just in case they'd taken their seats and I'd missed them. My classmates decked in green and white gowns wandered from their families to the side of the auditorium, taking their assigned seats in turn. Moms and dads would kiss a cheek or pat a shoulder as their graduate prepared to walk in the ceremony. My shoulder remained without encouragement. While Mom sat quietly in her seat, her eyes wandered to the contents of her purse, disinterested in the immediate happenings. I stopped watching for them and turned my attention to the front of the massive chamber we were gathered in.

"Graduates, please take your seats. Ladies and gentlemen, welcome. We are about to begin the graduation ceremony," the vice principal announced through the speaker. Voices buzzed as family members made their way to their places.

They're not coming. I knew my gut was right and my heart sank. Staring straight ahead, I could hear my classmates whispering about the parties that would follow the graduation ceremony. I had not been invited to any such party and had no plans for after the ceremony, not even dinner with my parents or ice cream or anything. I wondered if Mom would surprise me. *You know she won't,* came the answer.

The band began to play the school song and we all stood for the Pledge of Allegiance. I glanced behind me into the crowd of faces just one more time, hoping to see them. No such luck. My heart sank again and my fingers fiddled with the edges of the dark green gown I wore. Several speakers later, my row was signaled to stand. We all made our way single file to the edge of the stage. As each student walked across the stage, the principal stuck an empty leather folder into an outstretched hand. The binder was representative of the graduation certificate that would be mailed. Finally, my name was called and I made my way across the stage. I didn't look into the audience. I didn't want to see who wasn't there. The folder was handed to me. I smiled for the camera.

"Congratulations," the principal said and nudged me off the stage before turning to the next student. I mustered a "Thank ..." but nothing else before I was ushered out of the way and pointed back down the aisle to my seat. In my peripheral range of view, I noticed Mom. She was staring straight ahead with glossy eyes. I wondered if she knew I had just crossed the stage. I wondered what she thought.

I took my seat and stared at my feet. *I guess this was it.* I was a graduate with no place to go, no plans, nothing to do—not even a party afterward. *This is as good as it gets for you, Gil,* the voice said. *Keep your head down and your mouth shut. This is how you survive.* I knew my inner voice was right this time, so I kept quiet and laid low for the rest of the evening, even as we drove. Mom said nothing and neither did I the entire way home.

Deb and Dad, of course, didn't say anything either. They never showed up.

CHAPTER 10

———◆———

Syracuse University, nestled at the tip of the Finger Lakes region of upstate New York, seasoned by architecture flavored with tall, colonial-style brick buildings, represented everything I believed the promise of "new hope" would be. Pillars were draped in ivy and trees displayed the colors of autumn. I could not take it all in. From the first day, it took my breath away.

"Let's put it on the card," I laughed. I held the rectangular blue plastic card over my head with one hand and lifted a beer to my lips. Cheers followed. I was sure I had made new alliances because as long as I was buying, everyone there was my buddy. I'd always been on the outside, watching my father be the life of the party as though that was the most important thing to be, and now I was the one in the middle, the one with the draw of plastic money.

Parties were more important than my education at Syracuse. In fact, I decided that completing classwork was optional. Dad seemed to agree because he took a carte blanche approach to funding my life at school.

"I can just write a check." I couldn't see any problem with this.

"Where did you get all of these checks?" my roommate asked. "This is really cool."

"My dad gave them to me," I answered and glanced at the signatures written on the bottom of about twenty blank checks.

"Cool."

I gathered up the stack of paper with dad's signature scrawled over the bottom right corner. My roommate's interest made me a bit suspicious. I didn't want to become anyone's next target.

"We should use the expense account your dad gave you and throw a bitchin' party, Gil," he said, eyes wide.

"Sure." I collected the last of the checks and tucked credit cards into my wallet. "We should…that would be totally cool!"

I put everything in a folder and walked out of the room, heading straight for the commons area. He didn't follow but I'm sure his eyes did. I made my way to the vending machine and bought a Coke. As the can toppled down the apparatus, I noticed a flyer posted on a nearby wall:

PARENTS WEEKEND
October 17-18

Next week! Time had escaped me. I hadn't told either of my parents about it yet. Grabbing the Coke from the bottom shelf, I ran outside to the nearest payphone. My fingers fumbled for a quarter and I nearly dropped the folder with dad's blank checks. Finally, I found two quarters and slipped one into the slot. The dial tone sounded and I quickly dialed my house.

"Well, I'll have to run it by Bruce to be sure but I think we can probably be there," Mom said. I thanked her and immediately slipped another quarter in the phone's slot and dialed my dad. Carole answered.

"You'll have to ask your dad," she said. "He's not here though."

"Carole, please give him the message. I'm out of quarters and the whole thing takes place next week!" My voice sounded frantic. I took a deep breath. "Please, Carole, just tell him for me."

"Okay," she said and hung up the phone. I wasn't sure if she would say anything but I figured I'd done the best I could.

I finished my Coke and went back to my room. My roommate was nowhere to be seen. I quickly found a hiding place for the checks and credit cards. Stepping back, I surveyed the hiding place and felt relatively good about it. After all, I was the king of secrets and hidden things.

Parents Weekend came and both sets showed up. I was shocked, but pleased. Providing a tour of the campus was huge for me. They all seemed interested and I felt proud of my new "home."

"Nice place you've got here, Gil," Dad said glancing at the century-old Math building.

"Yeah, I don't go in there much but…yeah, it's pretty cool here," I said. It sounded lame, like a kid in junior high. I hadn't gone to any of my math classes and didn't really know what it was like inside that building. I pointed out the Community Center.

"Is that where you study mostly?" Carole asked.

I glanced at her and caught my dad's eye on me as he put his arm around her, waiting for an answer. The Community Center was a place to meet up with friends. I didn't want to lie to her but I didn't want to disappoint her either. That would mean trouble.

"Yeah, we study a lot in there," I lied.

Mom smiled and patted my back. "Nice," was all she said and glanced at her watch.

We finished the day with dinner at an Italian restaurant, with the linguini taking a backseat to the linguistic food fight between my parents. At least there was no more talk about school and I didn't have to tell any more lies.

When we parted ways for the evening, I was relieved. I would have an entire night to think about what I would tell them tomorrow. There would be a program on the goals of the school, and then it would be on to the football game. I knew that would capture Dad's attention and hopefully draw the rest into something other than my educational experience, which was basically partying. I went to sleep content that my parents were settled in a hotel for the night and tomorrow's activities were taken care of.

The next morning, I discovered I was wrong.

"What? When did he leave?" I couldn't believe what I was hearing.

"I don't know, honey. Early. It was before the sun was up, before you were up, I'm sure," Mom quipped. She popped a forkful of eggs into her mouth.

I stared at her and Bruce, dumbfounded.

"It's no big deal, kid," Bruce said, biting into toast. "We're here having breakfast, be here at least another hour before we hit the road."

"You're leaving too?" This was unbelievable. "Dad didn't even say good-bye. I didn't have a chance to thank him or Carole for coming."

"Does it really matter?" Bruce swallowed the toast.

"You can thank us instead, honey." Mom smiled as she sipped her coffee.

I dropped my eyes to my plate.

"I guess it doesn't really matter." I pushed my plate away.

Mom reached her hand to mine and patted it.

"He did his duty as a father," she said.

My eyes darted up to hers.

Bruce stood. "Yep, and now it's time for us to get going too. Long trip home and you've got lots of homework to do, I'm sure."

Mom followed him, kissing me on the cheek as she walked from the table.

"I'll get this," Bruce said, snatching the bill. They both walked out, leaving me at the table. I stared at my plate, bewildered, and the waitress poured coffee into an empty cup.

I spent the rest of the weekend watching my friends with their families, knowing everyone back home had never left his or her usual roles. I settled back into what had now become mine.

Until what felt like a ton of bricks hit me.

———◆———

I was nervous walking across campus on that frigid January New York winter day. Still, I didn't fully understand the seriousness of having gotten four D's and an F in my first semester…until the day I walked up to the dean's office.

Burled oak rolled in knotted waves on the massive door. Midway down sat a bronze handle curved in a long ﺱ , a symbol for Syracuse. My eyes trailed along the grain, taking in its omniscient dignity. Perhaps its majesty embodied the formidable office these sentry doors sheathed. I swallowed.

"The dean will see you now," a woman in her mid-fifties said, looking over turnip-colored spectacles perched on the tip of her nose. She crossed the room with the fluid steps of a Barbie Doll in spiked heels. Her skirt was too tight at the knees to walk in customary strides. With the palm of her hand, she commanded one of the great oak doors to open. Smiling with pursed lips, she glared at me and waited.

I stood and brushed my hands against my thighs, straightening the creases in my khakis. It didn't help. I still appeared disheveled. *Daniel in the lion's den.* I swallowed the thought and stepped through the doorway.

On the far side of a subdued office, a desk laden with the same burnished oak as the doors was surrounded by bookcases filled with university tomes bound in the colors of the earth. A blue and green Tiffany lamp rested peacefully on one edge of the desk, illuminating the corner with prisms of color.

"Come in, Gil," a voice behind the desk echoed in spite of the volumes of leather-bound books overlaying all four walls. I padded across the plush red carpet and took a seat opposite the dean on a lush tapestry-covered chair. He smiled gently at me through stern eyes and shuffled some papers lying on the desk. I supposed my name was written on at least one of them.

"Hi," I mustered.

"You know we have standards of excellence here at Syracuse," he said.

"Yes…I…yes." I blinked a few times, trying to adjust to his unyielding stare.

"Our standards demand a level of responsibility from students who attend this institution, and not the least of these is an attendance policy. Your attendance has not met the minimal requirement to remain as a student here." He paused for effect.

I nodded. *You're so busted, Gil.* The thought made my palms sweat. "In addition…"

There's more? I shifted in my seat as he continued.

"Your grades do not support your continued status as a Syracuse student."

I'm getting kicked out? What will I say to Mom and Dad? I felt the familiar flutter of my heart against my ribcage. Reflexively, I began to wring my hands. "Is there anything I can do?" I asked meekly.

The dean studied me for a long time. Finally, he leaned back in his seat and took the black-rimmed eyeglasses from his face. He glanced down at the papers and then back at me. A long sigh escaped his lips before he spoke again. His voice was different, gentler, to match the eyes that met me when I first entered the office.

"Gil, how badly do you want to go to college?"

His answer caught me off guard. It sounded like a "for the record" type question and my heart began to settle itself.

"Really bad," I said and felt the lump rise.

He stared at me again, then leaned forward, pushing the papers to one side. "Your behavior doesn't reflect that intention."

"I…I guess not. But I do want to be here," I said.

"There are conditions, as I said before, Gil. Your actions are reflected in your attendance and grades. Your behavior suggests someone not interested in university study, someone who would rather drink, do drugs. Do you understand what I mean? Is that you, Gil?"

"No."

He smiled and stood, meandered around his desk and perched on one corner. "I didn't think so."

He smiled again and I could tell this was someone who actually cared about me—cared about my future as a student. "Just tell me what I need to do."

He stood again and walked over to where I sat. Dropping one hand on my shoulder, he spoke very softly. "You need to get your act together. Go to class and turn your grades around."

I nodded. "That's exactly what I want to do. I want another chance."

"I'll make a deal with you, Gil." He resumed his place behind the ornate desk. "I'm what they consider an Assistant Dean here, but I have a little pull in certain situations. I'll use my influence to give you that chance and in exchange, you give me one hundred percent. Does that sound fair?"

"Yes! Yes, sir!"

"You're accountable to yourself but I will have you answer to me," he said and replaced his glasses. Gripping a tapered black pen, he scrawled something over one of the papers. "We'll meet weekly for a while, then maybe push back to every other week. Is that acceptable to you?"

"Yes." I rose to shake his hand. "Thank you!"

He walked me to the door and rested one hand on my shoulder again. I knew this man cared, and I felt a surge of confidence.

I left his office a new man, mindful, for the first time, of the responsibilities that came with attending Syracuse. I was aware that my new mentor and advocate was an assistant dean of the university who was willing to use his influence on my behalf. I could do no less. Freshly motivated, a solid plan and direction was my newest companion that sat in a small window of opportunity, the opportunity to pull myself together. In twenty minutes, a total stranger had changed my focus from one of belonging to one of self-value, something I'd never received with eighteen years of parenting from Eileen and Dale.

I kept my end of the bargain and met with the dean every week to exhibit the accomplishments I'd made during the previous seven days. On several occasions, he seemed very proud and offered his chair for me to sit in during our conversation.

During the semester, I reverted to another habit though—one I was too familiar with. There were secrets that needed a protector again, someone who could keep them hidden far away. I was the best, and did it to protect myself because my mother had inserted herself and was running interference in my life once again.

"What do you mean, there are twenty unpaid parking tickets?"

I could hear my dad through the telephone receiver from arm's length, which was exactly where I held it, my arm extended. When the squawking stopped, I replaced the earpiece against my ear and tried my best to respond.

"I guess cars aren't allowed on campus for freshmen," I said. Immediately, the phone began to reverberate with his voice and I pulled it away again.

"When did you take the damn thing up there anyway?" he roared.

After a minute, I returned the receiver to my ear. "Mom insisted that I bring a car to school," I said calmly, knowing it had been my idea so I could remain popular. Mom had been an easy rubber stamp.

His voice lowered somewhat and I kept the receiver in place. "Look, Dad," I said with the most adult voice I could muster. "I had no idea there would be a problem. She never said you would mind and I didn't know it was against the rules."

It was a lousy excuse, but the only one I had.

"I'm not paying these tickets! It's a good thing you're finished for the year. I can't afford your tickets!" he snapped, and the conversation was over.

I hung up the phone, seething inside. Another setup from Mom and I'd taken the brunt of it. I turned to my bed and finished loading a heap of clothes into a box. In just a few days, I would be leaving for the summer after a chaotic, ultimately successful year.

Once the parking tickets had been paid—by Dad—and were out of the way, my grades were released and I proudly presented four A's and a B. These were more than enough to be able to stay at school.

"I knew you could do it, Gil," the dean said the final time we met. "Welcome to being a true-blue university student. Welcome to your future."

I'd heard those words before, but they took new meaning when spoken within the walls of the sophisticated office lined with books that I now appreciated. My life had changed and I was committed to its new course.

CHAPTER 11

———◆———

BACK AT SCHOOL IN THE fall for my sophomore year, my grades were at an all-time high. I seemed to excel at everything I attempted, including friendships and individuality. In this light, I caught the attention of Kimberly, with her long legs and glistening hazel eyes. For some reason, she picked me. I was with friends one night when out of nowhere she kissed me. I fell, hook, line, and sinker.

I was attached to a popular girl on campus, one of the top achievements of my life so far. I was proud to have Kimberly on my arm, knowing that she was an asset to my quest for acceptance. But I should have seen the "red flags," recognized the familiarity of my patterns with relationships. Sadly, Kimberly didn't work, not for me. Still, I hung on to her. I liked her.

"You're too busy with the eye candy to hang out with us," my roommate quipped one day.

"What do you mean by that?" I asked. My gut wrenched a little.

"Oh, you know, man. It always happens. Guy gets the girl and it's over for the bro's. You're too busy keeping her happy to do anything with your buddies. I get it," he said and he walked off, leaving me dumbfounded.

"I thought having a girlfriend would make you guys like me better." The words slipped out before I could stop them. Fortunately, he was long gone and no one else had heard. *You're so dense, Gil.* The voice inside my head had awakened to what I already knew. I'd spent every moment not only with Kimberly but doing everything imaginable for her.

Spending money seemed to make her like me and that made me happy. The sense of belonging was the feeling I'd been after all my life. So having this one beautiful female person actually like me gave me an overwhelming sense of belonging. I couldn't do enough. I also couldn't take the chance of losing that belief that I belonged. I even told my dad my laundry had been stolen and that I needed more money for clothes…only to use those dollars to take Kimberly away to Puerto Rico for the weekend.

Within a few months, the voice in my head had convinced me to take a second look at this beautiful woman who had made the choice to be with me. *How could someone like her want to be your girlfriend?* That question remained unanswered, festering inside my conscious thoughts every time I looked at her. One day, it slipped out as I meandered around the idea of us breaking up.

"But, Gil, you and I are meant to be. We're together now, isn't that all that matters?"

Maslow's Hierarchy of Needs kept popping into my head. It was all I could think about since I'd learned it in Psychology 101. That had caught my attention. That explained the lying, the secrets, and the unending drive to "belong."

The voice in my head was hysterical now. *No! I didn't choose this relationship,* you *did.* I couldn't get it to be quiet and let me think. What did I want really? It wasn't this relationship; that was certain. I was drawn more to the *idea of* her than *to* her. I needed to belong to someone but I wanted to make that decision, not have it made for me. *And yet, you're throwing it away. You think she's the best thing that's happened to you and you're throwing it all away.* I sat silently staring at her while the argument festered in my head. *I want to be part of a "we," an "us," something I didn't have with my family. I don't want to lose myself in my desire to just belong though.*

"Of course, that's all I want too," I said.

I didn't know where that came from. This *thing* we were doing wasn't working for me. She defined it with her decision to create whatever existed between us. I had no say.

"You're such a good boyfriend," she said and caressed my arm affectionately. I felt her body press against the part of my chest where, for as long as I can remember, I'd felt a certain pain. It began again—that pain, a shallow ache in my gut that told me "something's not right." I didn't listen. Immediately, as if to snag my attention from Kimberly, I felt the air being sucked from my lungs. I couldn't breathe and the more I tried, the harder it was. My chest hurt and I lifted a hand to it.

She watched me and smiled. "I love you too, Gil."

Did she seriously think that I was clutching my chest as a sign that I loved her? I had to get away.

"I'm glad. You're a sweetheart, Kimberly."

The voice coming from my mouth wasn't mine. Why was I saying these things? I dropped my hand and forced my thoughts away from my chest and the lack of air that accompanied it. Sweat coated my palms, so I tucked them into my pockets. She dropped her head onto my shoulder.

Now you're a boyfriend. What are you doing, Gil? And why out of this whole big university do you spend time only with Jewish kids from Long Island? The voice was incessant, but it was right. I had to get out of it somehow.

"I'm glad I make you happy," I said without thinking.

I don't want to hurt her, I argued with myself. But there was no way out otherwise. *She sees what she wants to see and she's dragging you along for the ride.* I wanted to get off this rollercoaster she called a relationship. I wanted out!

"We're good together," she replied.

I nodded, listening to my own voice, not to hers. She smiled contentedly. How could I tell her without hurting her? *You can't. She'll be hurt no matter what, but it's her or you. Are you going to let someone else decide your future?* No! *Then don't let her do what you've let everyone else in your life do: determine your likes, wants, your life's course.* Truth. I couldn't argue with that reasoning.

There was only one thing to do.

———◆———

"I'm transferring to Florida in the fall."

Truth was, the friends were gone, and that left me with the only two things in life that would have me: school and Kimberly. Neither of them knew my secrets. I had a newly found confidence that I was capable of more, and that I could choose what I wanted. The warm sunshine of Florida was where I would begin.

Kimberly and I had fun over the summer. We ran an ice cream truck together and ate most of the profits. But as soon as August arrived, I finally said the words out loud and told her of my plans. Her face dropped, followed by pleadings not to leave her. The voice in my head was right. There was no way to honor myself and prevent her from being hurt. Bailing out on Syracuse was, among other things, an escape from the girl I didn't want to be my girlfriend.

Two months prior, I'd put in transfer papers to the University of Florida.

"It's too late," I said. "I've already submitted my registration."

She sobbed, begged, pleaded, tried to guilt me into staying, but my resolve was firm…I had to run.

Fall and my junior year began as a new start in life, one that had no girlfriend around to take away my energy and feed my need to please. It was also the first time I wasn't amongst a lot of Jews. This wasn't Miami Beach. I was in Northern Florida. But three weeks in, something else swallowed my soul and I started to disappear again.

"What's wrong with you, man?" My roommate Brad asked as he made his way across the room.

I couldn't answer him. *He's going to do something,* the voice in my head said, and my heart pounded harder.

I was sure Brad could hear it.

"Gil, come on."

I pulled my knees to my chest and tucked my face between them, shutting out the light as my eyes squeezed tighter.

"Oh man, you're really wasted, aren't you?" Brad bent over and took a better look, then walked out. "Whatever, man."

The sun set and the moon spilled silver light over a caramel shag carpet when my heart finally slowed to its normal pace. I opened my eyes and glanced at the clock on my nightstand. It said 10:27. I'd been lying in a fetal position on the floor for nearly three hours. My other roommate Ray hadn't come back to check on me, which was probably fine. I took a deep breath and felt my lungs fill to capacity with air, warming my ribcage after hours of panting.

"That was a bitch!" I said aloud to no one. The panic attacks had come slowly at first, but then gradually increased in frequency over the few weeks I'd been at school. I hadn't suffered anything like that one before. Suddenly it hit me with the impact of a fully speeding semi. *Bad trip.* "I should never have smoked that joint," I said.

Uncurling my legs was painful but the stretch rejuvenated my aching muscles. Three hours on the floor did nothing to help my body stay functional. I reached for a bottle of water sitting on the dresser and drank deeply. My stomach rumbled, reminding me it had been neglected far too long. I grabbed a half-eaten bag of Fritos, then decided I'd better get something more nutritious.

I opened the door just a crack and peered out. Lights through doors that sat ajar illuminated the hallway. I could hear voices, but no one appeared on either side of the hall. Now was as good a time as any. My feet barely moved, paralyzed with the last remnants of anxiety. *Just walk.* Finally, they complied and within minutes, I was rummaging through the fridge. Moments later, a cluster of males rounded the counter, most likely looking for the same thing as me—food. I snatched a half-eaten sandwich, not sure who had the original claim on it, and slammed the fridge door, shutting out the merciless light. My gut wrenched and my heartbeat increased, as if to race against the new anxiety that filled my entire being.

They're not out to get you, Gil. I knew the voice was lying and the panic rose uncontrollably. My hand trembled and I dropped the sandwich I'd been eating.

"Hey," someone shouted from the cluster. "Hey, stop!"

My heart pounded even harder and bile rose in my throat. I knew I would never survive here. I had been carrying innumerable secrets with me for too long already. No actual danger existed, but that's all I could discern. A physiological response from a perceived threat is a false reality. I knew that from my psych classes, but it made no difference. I couldn't stop the anxiety attacks. I was in a perpetual state of panic and I could barely make it through a day. An unbearable sense of fear now controlled my life. I feared being in places where there was a risk of having a panic attack, or a fear of being alone. I feared that people might witness my uneasiness, and that getting away quickly might be difficult. I saw no end in sight.

I took off from the campus and left my university studies. I wanted to call my dad, but felt that I couldn't. That left Mom as the only choice.

———◆———

So there I was, back on Long Island in the home that had already caused me so much pain. My world now existed within the confines of my room. Bruce had been tolerant but I could tell that he was getting irritated.

"You can't stay in there forever, Gil," Mom would say from outside the door. Moments later, I would hear the echo of her footsteps trail off as she walked away in frustration.

You can stay here forever. You're safe here, I would reassure myself and double-check the lock on the door. The knock sounded again.

"Gil, your father sent another one this month. That makes two. The least you can do is come out and call him to say thank you."

I glanced at the crack under the door. A slip of paper slid underneath and settled on the floor. I stared at it blankly, waiting for her footsteps to trail off again.

My father's attempt to stay in my life culminated in that slip of paper. The check was always written for more than I would use that month. I picked it up and stared at it. Same amount, same standard paper, same colored ink with one exception. His signature was tightly scribbled this time, as if he didn't want anyone to be able to decipher his name. It felt impersonal. I set the check on the dresser and curled up on my bed.

There would be no sleep for me again tonight. The thought of going downstairs to face mom and Bruce was more than I could bear. Their faces would be pinched to match the syllables coming from their tight lips.

I had a bigger concern now, and an even bigger secret to keep. I had met Dawn toward the end of the summer before I went to Florida, right after Kimberly and I broke up. We stayed in touch while she was at the University of Colorado. How would I explain to her why I was back home? What about the people I still knew from Syracuse? What would I say to kids from high school who were still in the neighborhood attending community college? I couldn't explain what happened and why I was back home, not even to myself.

"Hello, Gil." Mom's voice shook a bit. "I'm glad you decided to come out of that room and join us for dinner."

That's a change. She fixed dinner and expected you to join her? What happened to the days when you were a little boy and no one fixed dinner, no one except for a hungry seven-year-old? My gut began to twist on itself.

"You've got to get it together, boy." Bruce's irritation went unchecked. "Can't expect to live here and do nothing but hide up in that room for the rest of your life. Can't expect me to pay for a full grown adult man that can't leave his room because he's scared."

"I'm not hungry anymore." I pushed away my plate and ran back upstairs to my room.

No, I couldn't face them anymore tonight. I had to leave...and quickly.

The next morning, a glossy handout caught my eye. It had been left conspicuously on the counter for me to find should I finally venture out of my solace. No one was home, and I was free to roam the house feeling safe. I picked up the pamphlet and sat down at the table with a bowl of cereal.

Je Maintiendrai

It was written on a blue scroll beneath a pair of yellow lions wearing crowns. The crest stared back, inviting me to unite with the other students only fifteen minutes away at Hofstra University. I missed being at school, so I immediately called the number listed and requested the admission application.

Soon after, I was attending class at Hofstra. It was a measure of hope because the radius from home in which I felt safe was beginning to expand a little, and I wouldn't fall any farther behind in school. Campus life indeed proved to be the escape I desperately needed from home. My schedule began to take an established form, and Mom left me alone most of the time. That lasted, however, only a few weeks.

CHAPTER 12

———•———

"GIL," MY SISTER'S VOICE FILTERED through the phone receiver. "You really should come by this weekend and spend time with us."

"I'd love that but Mom…"

"Forget Mom! Just come by for a few days. You really need to get away from there," she insisted.

I agreed, and left the next morning for Deb and Ron's house. We had a great time and I began to wander over there more often. With both my parents' continued focus on new spouses and stepkids, Deb and Ron felt like the only real family I had. Mom and Bruce made subtle comments designed to create a guilt trip tailored to press my buttons and get a reaction. My goal was to avoid them as much as possible.

Ron proved to be the older brother I longed for. We had great conversations and enjoyed each other's company. Dinnertime was my favorite, a time to feast on food and family.

"When was the last one?" my sister asked casually one night as she cleared an empty basket from the table. "It's been awhile, hasn't it? I mean, you seem much better since those damn things stopped happening as much."

"I honestly can't remember. I don't keep a running log of panic attacks, Deb. Maybe a month?" I grinned, shoving a forkful of mashed potatoes into my mouth.

"That's great, Gil. You deserve to be free from that stuff," Ron said.

"Yeah, I guess so." I changed the subject. "How's Dad? I only see him for a dinner here and there."

Out of the corner of my eye, I saw Deb shoot a sideways glance at Ron. He slathered butter over sourdough bread and bit a hunk out of it.

"Oh you know, Gil. The guy stays busy," he said.

I understood the attempt to cover for Dad keeping me at arm's length as usual. We didn't talk about Dad again that night or for the next three weeks.

———◆———

"I'm glad you asked me to go with you," I said, casually glancing out of the car's open roof. "You could have taken anyone to surprise Deb. I'm really glad you asked me."

"Yeah well, someone else wouldn't have been as much fun," Ron responded.

We boarded the plane chatting about sports and politics and were soon en route to Miami. Not once did I feel that familiar vise tighten around my gut, and I found myself relaxed nearly 30,000 feet above the ground. Fate had provided a welcome travel companion. *It's a good thing Ron is in your life now.* I had finally found a friend and confidant.

A few hours later, light escaped below the horizon. While the moon rose over Biscayne Bay, we made our way through downtown Miami to the world-famous Fountains Hotel. Darkness arrived, symbolic of what awaited us as we ascended within the elevator and found our rooms at the end of the hallway. I watched the moon's reflection glistening a warning from the water. The moon seemed brighter that night, secretly smiling as I keyed the lock and entered the hotel room. Darkness would keep me safe until morning, when the sunrise would divulge its daytime nightmare.

Trouble!

Silently, I faced the door with the number 201 tacked onto it. My hand was raised, balled into a fist, ready to knock, but the voices behind the door stopped me cold.

"How could you do this?"

It was Ron's voice, raw and as full of the emotions I could feel seeping underneath the hotel room door.

"Why didn't you call? You never just show up!" Deb was angry.

"I wanted to surprise you, Deb," he shouted back, a painful declaration. "Your brother's here too. We both wanted to surprise you."

"You brought Gil? How could you?" She trailed off and I heard rustling. "You should never have come, Ron, never! You should never have brought him here."

Silence. Perhaps this was my chance. I had heard my name and I knew there was trouble in that room. Maybe I was the cause and maybe I could fix it. I knocked.

Seconds later, Deb opened the door. Her face was mottled, red, and puffy. She had been crying. I stared at her with my mouth hanging open. Beyond her, sitting on a chair tucked away behind a small round table, Ron rested his face in his hands. I couldn't tell if he was crying or just angry. I decided this was a bad time to interrupt their argument and begged out.

"Hey, I'll come back later…at a better time," I finally mustered.

"No," Ron barked from the corner. "This involves you too."

Deb had moved away from the door and was throwing clothes from a dresser drawer into an open suitcase lying on the bed. She glared at Ron, then at me, her eyes tearing up again.

She isn't sad. Those are tears brought on by something else, something you'll never understand. I swallowed hard as the thought stuck itself into the voice in my head.

"Tell him what you've done," Ron said and lifted his eyes. They were swollen and red. He'd been crying. "Go on."

Deb swung around and faced me as I sat delicately on the edge of the closer bed. She put her hands on her hips and cast a dark look at Ron, then glanced at me, tears welling again.

"If you must know, which I don't think is necessary," she looked again at her husband in the corner, then dropped her gaze to the floor. "I'm not here alone."

I stared blankly at her. *Of course you're not alone, Deb. You're at a conference with your coworkers.* Ron seemed to pick up on my ignorance and stood.

"She's having an affair and we busted in on it, Gil," he said. "She's unfaithful to her husband, living a double life while she works." He choked on the last word and sat back down.

I stared at Deb, my eyes watering as I realized what was happening. "Is this true, Deb?"

She only nodded and threw another piece of clothing into the suitcase.

Silence passed among us for several minutes, no one able to look the other in the eyes. Finally, I raised my imploring gaze to my sister's face in silence. *It has to be a joke!* But my gut told me otherwise.

"Deb." My voice was a whisper. "Why?"

"That's what I want to know," Ron said and stood up again. He began to gather his things.

She only shook her head and wiped her cheek with the back of a hand, then walked into the bathroom.

"What are you going to do now?" I said to Ron.

He stared at me for a minute before answering. "I'm leaving."

Moments later, my mentor and friend was gone. The hotel door closed behind him, and Deb refused to come out of the bathroom. Sure enough, that vise found my gut again and I began to shake. Slowly turning to face my sister, I stared at the closed bathroom door and heard Deb's sobs coming from within.

"I'll be in my room," I said through the crack in the doorframe and left without waiting for her to answer.

The next morning, I flew home. I never talked to Deb again during the trip. There was nothing to say. Ron was gone and the flight home was empty. My sister had cheated on her husband and torn apart her marriage, interfering with someone else's dreams at the same time. I wondered if she understood the ripple effects. *Probably not*, the voice in my head answered, unsolicited. *She doesn't care anyway.* She fed her own ego with the decision to break her vows and it had an impact that changed lives: Ron's, her lover's wife, and mine.

———◆———

A month later, Dad and I drove Deb to JFK and watched as she boarded a plane that would take her to Los Angeles, into the arms of a man who would only know her as his mistress.

"It's a classic example of the pot calling the kettle black," Deb said over her shoulder as she walked away. I saw Dad's face flush and I knew he was angry with Deb. I didn't know what she meant exactly, but then remembered the decision he'd made when he walked away from Mom and me. *You're the pot, Dad.* I couldn't say the words aloud. *You're the one pointing fingers and you're no better than she is.* My stomach lurched as the vise grabbed hold.

"I need to go home now," I said, and he agreed.

CHAPTER 13

———◆———

WHY COULDN'T I HAVE GONE home to him? Why did he keep leaving me with her? Why did he watch me disintegrate emotionally and do nothing? I needed his help, and his money couldn't fix that. I was still a little boy looking for dad to step up and take me under his wing. My life was empty once again.

I gotta get out of here.

I had just stepped out of the shower, hoping the warm water would soothe my frayed nerves. It hadn't. The mirror over my bathroom sink was fogged, so I opened the door leading into the bedroom and waited for the steam to clear.

Where would you go, Gil? Going too far away is out of the question. That didn't work out well last time, remember?

"But I gotta get out of here," I said aloud. Stepping up to the mirror, I rubbed a towel over it to clear what was left of the mistiness. Almost immediately I wished I hadn't. The face that stared back at me was pathetic—empty eyes, full of a sadness so raw it was palpable.

I leaned in to the mirror and studied the reflection but saw nothing that brought reassurance. If anything, the face reflected an isolation that had become the foundation of my life.

My heart began to pound. *Not now! Not another one.* I closed my eyes and tried to will my heartbeat into a gentle tempo, to no avail. Almost immediately, the familiar pain hit my chest and I knew it would be hours before I would breathe normally again. I gasped and looked in the mirror at the man with knotted brows and the telltale face of a full panic attack.

"It hurts." I winced and looked at the place on my chest where I felt the pain. Then, I saw it...the mark of innocence lost, the mark of isolation, of someone forgotten or neglected. A scar began to appear, pale pink at first, then rising to a blistering white with each gasp for air that I took. Without thinking, my hand rose to meet it, but I could feel nothing under my fingertips. Still, I could see it—feel its pain as my heart pounded against my ribcage.

"Please stop," I said and could feel the tears well up in my eyes. The more I tried to fight it, the tighter my lungs clamped down to fight against the air I desperately needed to breathe in. Just then, the room began to spin, and I clutched the edge of the sink to keep from falling. The mirror mercilessly reflected my pitiful state, and though I tried to avoid its reflection, my eyes drifted to it.

SELF-ACTUALIZATION

ESTEEM

LOVE & BELONGING

SAFETY

PHYSIOLOGICAL NEEDS

I knew immediately what the words meant and where they had come from.

"Maslow," I breathed and prayed they would go away.

How can you expect to move on when you haven't mastered the most basic of needs, Gil? The voice sounded crueler than usual. *You are stuck. You'll never get higher than the basic needs.*

"Stop it!" I cried out and stared at the mirror. The words had appeared on the glass, magically positioning themselves into a pyramid to remind me of the truth I'd learned when I'd first heard of Maslow's Hierarchy of Needs. "Go away," I shouted again, but the words only mocked me.

Do you see it, Gil? Do you see the one thing that is keeping you down? Keeping you only one level above the beasts?

"Shut up!" Tears fell from my eyes, blinding me to everything but the scar. It was brilliant crimson, the same color as my blood, lying directly over my heart. I felt it break again and struggled for air.

Family...it's FAMILY that you will never gain. That's the one piece that's missing...the one part of this you'll never claim as yours.

"NO!"

My fist slammed against the mirror, shattering the glass into tiny pieces that carried the words into the sink along with the blood that dripped from my fist. The last one to fall pierced my consciousness as it formed and glared at me from the glass: *Family.*

———◆———

I awoke on the floor of the bathroom, shivering and covered in blood. While the cut wasn't deep on the palm of my hand, it had bled a great deal and had made a frightening mess. I quickly grabbed a towel and began to clean it up, remembering that little boy who'd cut his hand on the tuna can.

Nothing had changed for me.

"I've got to get away from here," I said again, remembering my thoughts just before the panic attack had consumed me.

Where will you go?

"You, I will not talk to. Not any more today." My voice sounded confident as it came from my lips. I turned from the bathroom and walked to the desk where a map had been spread out. "I thought that if I could just expand my radius a little, maybe I'd feel safer," I said, more to convince myself than anything. The words sounded good spoken out loud.

My hand reached for the map. I closed my eyes and let my finger drop. The idea of living in Washington, DC and going to American

University was enticing. It was only a four-hour drive, and the Eastern Airlines shuttle operated every hour on the hour if I needed to escape.

It was January when I arrived in our nation's capital. It was difficult arriving in the middle of the school year. Nevertheless, I was enjoying school and for the first time, began to think about what kind of work I wanted to prepare for. A few friends had come my way, but they hadn't come easily.

There's a reason for that. You know why. In truth, I couldn't explain why or what had happened in Syracuse, then Florida, then Hofstra, and finally here. The only thing that made sense was Dawn. She and I kept speaking over the phone, and conversation came easily with her, mainly because she didn't press me for information. So, it was easier to prop up the lie I had told her about what happened in Florida, as well as keep the other things from her. Even though our families were so different, maybe wanting to run from them was what bonded us. After all, wasn't a relationship somewhere on that damn Maslow chart?

One of four children, Dawn had decided to break away from the family unit and escape from Long Island all the way to the University of Colorado. In spite of the strain that sat between her parents, they had stayed together and forged a strong family unit. This impressed me, particularly as I watched my own family structure unravel at the slightest setback.

But, there still was one pressing matter that I had to deal with before I could give Dawn my full attention. I wondered if I could face it.

CHAPTER 14

———◆———

"She's making a huge mistake."

I never heard those words spoken out loud about Deb, but I'm sure they were said. Despite the condo in Brentwood and the stylish Porsche, she had been on the prowl ever since discovering right away that her lover would never marry her. She found Miles Fischer in less than eight weeks and it took him only a couple of months before he'd dropped to one knee in front of Debra. Desperate people do desperate things. That's exactly what it must have looked like the day Deb moved into Miles' house.

"You really need to come out here and stay with us. Miles wants you to visit too," Deb said. Her voice sounded rather animated.

I made the promise to try and ended the conversation. *You'll never go.* I brushed off the thought and glanced around the vacant room. My hand reached for the receiver and I began dialing.

"Dawn." I waited for her to respond. "Yeah, I'm great. Listen, I'm planning a trip to Los Angeles over the summer to visit my sister Deb and her new husband and was wondering if you want to come along?"

Dawn was more than enthusiastic and within a week after the semester ended, we'd booked our flights and were on our way to sunny California.

Dawn handled the introduction to Miles with more finesse than I was able to muster. Right away, the guy got under my skin. It wasn't the way he flaunted his multimillion-dollar house in Hollywood

Hills, or the way he made sure I knew there was a Ferrari parked in the garage, although that didn't help. Mainly, it was just...*him.*

"A pompous ass," I hissed one day as Dawn and I walked into a local grocery store.

"Maybe so, but he takes good care of your sister," she responded with her eyes glued to a pile of apples between pomegranates and tangerines. "He'd probably take care of you too if you asked him."

"I would never do that!" I snapped. "The guy is out for show and besides that, he bugs me."

"Why?" She plucked two apples from the pile and dropped them into a clear plastic bag.

"I don't know, he just does."

"Well, give him a chance. You might benefit from having him as a brother-in-law."

"No way," I said and moved to a bin of dried fruits and nuts.

Dawn stepped across the aisle and snatched up a watermelon. "I think this would be great by the pool," she said as she sniffed the rind, then smirked at me. "Gil, just be his friend."

I took the watermelon from her hands and placed it in the cart. "I don't need friends like that."

The topic never came up again. What did bubble up in our conversations was marriage; the pressure was on to include Dawn as a part of my family, a permanent member.

"I'd make Deb a great sister-in-law," Dawn said one afternoon, and the not-so-subtle hint hit me squarely in the sternum. I couldn't breathe. While I wanted to keep Dawn around for the duration, becoming my wife was not part of that plan right now. I'd gingerly avoided the M-word for months.

I'd spent every moment with Dawn that summer. I was already in *here we go again* mode. *My every thought was how to make her happy. I went through so much money doing that. I felt as if I belonged. I envied her because she had been able to run and didn't have to come crawling back. Why did she pick me?*

Lately, marriage was all Dawn talked about.

You're not able to run your own life, let alone a family, Gil. I brushed the thought away and came up with the best explanation I could. "But I do love her and she's the kind of girl I'd want to marry." My gut wrenched.

Gosh, you're not even out of college yet, Gil, much less into life. I knew the voice in my head was right. Toward the end of the next semester, I began to drift away from the phone calls with Dawn, and I avoided visits all together.

"I hope I don't regret this," I said one day. The voice didn't respond.

I didn't seem to feel much regret over the next few months, but as the cherry blossoms made their way into the background of all that encompassed our nation's capital, I should have known there was something inside me that would awaken as well. Spring was a potent season in my psyche.

The panic attacks hit with full force a month later.

Blue and red illuminated the space I occupied, glaring back at me from the mirror. The wailing siren made me jump, a reflex meant to propel my body into "fight or flight" mode. It worked only a little. I glanced down at my feet, only inches from where they stood on the rug moments before. Within seconds, the flash of red and blue light disappeared and silence soon followed.

She disappeared, Gil.

This time my feet moved as my weight shifted with the incoming thought.

"Who did?" I asked, but I already knew the answer.

She might have been The One, you know.

"Who? And why are you pestering me like this now about something that happened a while ago?" I glanced at the doorknob across the room. It seemed miles away, and an eternity would pass before

I could grasp it. My breath came in shallow gasps, the panic acutely centered around my soul.

Because Dawn was the last straw. She was the one person who would have changed everything but you only saw her as another weight to carry on your tired shoulders.

"Yeah, so why does it matter now? It's over and done with."

I blinked wildly to force back tears. My heartbeat ramped up a notch and the vise tightened. I knew the voice in my head was right. Kimberly was the catalyst that propelled me out of school because I had to run. I remembered too well the angst of that moment when I realized I couldn't take it anymore. I felt it again, but would running make Dawn the one that "got away"?

That moment was a shift in your life, Gil. You still cry from the pain it represents. You are the little boy who never made it out of the bushes to go to school because he was afraid, the youth who craved a father who didn't care, the child who was abandoned by a mother too busy with her own life to notice yours.

"Stop it! Stop saying these things!" I screamed and covered my ears with my palms. Tears spilled to run the length of my cheeks and I couldn't stop them.

You ran from the one person who truly cared about you, ran back to a life that consumed you in loneliness.

"I know, I know." I sobbed, my eyes tightly closed to squeeze out images that clawed through my brain. I remembered what my dad always said, "Don't let them see a grown man cry." I kept my eyes closed for a moment but that only made things worse.

One day you'll be able to see yourself for who you really are: a good person with toxic surroundings. It's not your fault, Gil. Life hasn't been fair. You played the cards you were dealt and hoped for the best. That's all.

Somehow, a tissue found its way into my hand and I blew my nose. The tears subsided, but with the mildest provocation, they spilled down my cheeks again. I knew there were happier times somewhere beyond Dawn. I tried to imagine them and force my mind in a different direction.

Your only option is to get away and hide. Otherwise, everyone will know. The voice was right. Shame was my only companion. Again, I was back where I started, living in my mother's house again, utterly debilitated and dysfunctional again. It was clear I would soon be completely disabled if the course were not changed.

I fought to regain control as I moved farther away from the vent until the sobbing had stopped. Mom and Bruce were downstairs, and I knew that if they heard me, I'd hear about it all week. "Breathe," I said aloud but the air wouldn't come. I began to pace. *Distraction! That's exactly what you need, Gil. Distract yourself by pacing the floor. Bruce will never hear you treading a line up here.* I stopped immediately. Bruce would absolutely hear everything through the vents and the creaking floor. I was doomed. There was nothing to do but wait it out…just as I'd done for so many years. *Surrender.* That was my life. *Complacency, the status quo, and give in to whatever makes everyone else happy and comfortable; that's what you do best, Gil. Just lie down on the bed and suffer through it. Keep your mouth shut and try not to die in the process.*

The voice in my head had become cruel. But it was right…again. There was nothing I could do except take care of the others in the house by swallowing up my own suffering. I lay down on the bed and curled into a ball. No one seemed to notice I was there as the sun disappeared and nightfall extinguished any existing light. In that moment, I wished that I could be extinguished too.

CHAPTER 15

———————

"It's the best money can buy," Dad said over the phone one day. I sat in silence, not believing him, but happy he at least seemed to care. "Gil, you have to trust me on this. It's going to make the difference," he insisted.

"I don't see how it can help," I said weakly.

A few days later, I was sitting in the office of a therapist at a prestigious mental health institute in New York City on the affluent Upper East Side. Dad footed the bill and I agreed to show up. There were six initial therapy sessions, which seemed doable for me since the most difficult part would be to make it through my bedroom door and out of the house. Fortunately, on the first day, I remained relatively at ease and made it to my appointment on time.

"Gil Belmont?" A broad grin accompanied the full alto voice. "I'm Irma Gold," she said and extended her hand. I grasped it and was amazed at the energy behind Irma Gold's handshake.

"Where's everyone else?" she asked, seeming surprised at the sight of only me standing there.

"What do you mean, where's everyone else? I thought this is for me because I have the problem," I said sheepishly.

"I specifically scheduled a family session. To speak with everyone involved. I told your father this when we spoke."

"Well, Dad's in Europe, Deb's in California, and Mom, well, she's wherever Bruce is."

"Hmm." The noise sounded more like a grunt than a hum, which is what I would have expected from her. Irma Gold pointed to an oversized leather chair and invited me to sit.

"Thanks for seeing me," I said, rubbing my hand, not knowing what else to say.

"My pleasure," Irma said warmly. "I understand you're having some difficulty with anxiety."

"I have panic attacks and they're bad ones," I said as nonchalantly as I could muster.

She made the "hmm" sound again and began her inquisition of my anxiety-ridden life. We talked for nearly an hour. It seemed possible that Irma Gold might be able to help me. Perhaps with her help I could get past the debilitation that ruled my days and nights. The session ended on a positive note, and I felt hopeful. However, three sessions into our meetings, it became clear that Irma Gold could not solve the problem.

"It's about your family's dysfunction, Gil," she said one day. "Their choices have left you conflicted, unable to move forward with your life, at least unable to move forward in a positive direction. Your job is to figure out what you can do in spite of their toxic behaviors."

Great! She's confirmed what we already know. I'm not sure who invited the voice in my head to the session, but it showed up.

"It appears…" She paused and looked around the empty room for emphasis. "… that no one takes these 'family' sessions to heart except for you. So, you have to decide what's most important and take steps to secure it."

"How do I do that?" I asked.

"Think about what makes you happy, what brings you peace. Follow those cues and take an approach of doing what's best for Gil, not what's best for everyone around you," she continued.

I told you so. You already know that's impossible. You've failed before you've begun.

I nodded because I didn't know what to say.

"Do you understand what I'm saying, Gil?" she asked. She was on to me. I couldn't lie this time because she'd know. I decided to tell her the truth…the whole rotten inflammatory truth of it.

"Look," I said. I couldn't believe the words were coming out of my mouth. "All I learned growing up was that nobody would choose me. I mean, I certainly wasn't going to do what was best for me because I had to protect everyone else. You know?"

Irma Gold stared hard at me. I assumed it was because she didn't know, so I continued. "It was my job to protect Dad from the responsibility for his choice to be with Carole's kids instead of me. I had to protect Mom from her choice to make Bruce more important than me. I had to protect Deb from Mom and Mom from Dad."

"Why?"

"Because, don't you get it?" My voice was getting loud but I couldn't control it. "Because nobody wants me even when I don't make waves! Can you imagine what they would do if I had?"

"Relax, Gil."

I uncurled my fists and took a breath. Irma Gold didn't understand. She never would understand.

"You don't get it, do you?" I lifted my shirt and pointed to my chest. The scar blazed and her face shifted to horror. I knew I had her so I continued, "I'm trying to explain it to you but you still don't get it!"

"Stop that, Gil! Please lower your shirt."

"No! You can't stand to look at it any more than I can bear its incessant burn into my skin." I was practically screaming and decided to pace.

"I don't know what you're talking about. Sit down and let's continue this civilly," she said.

I could hear the exasperation in her voice. "The scar!" I lifted my shirt again to show her again. It pulsed beet red on the skin just to the left of my sternum. I pointed to it just to be certain she hadn't missed it, although I don't know how she could. "There…see that?"

"What are you pointing to? I see a nice man with a lot of issues, that's all. No scar." Her brows knit as she stared at me.

"It's right there. That big red scar right over my heart…right *there!*"

The room fell silent and Dr. Gold just stared at me. I returned her gaze and let my shirt fall. Something was off. When she spoke again, it was nearly a whisper.

"Gil, there's nothing there. No scar. Nothing."

Tears filled my eyes as I realized what she was saying. She couldn't see it. Only I could. And I could *feel* it too. It was so very painful.

Maybe she's trying to work you over. The thought made my eyes narrow as I glared at the good Dr. Irma Gold, unsure what to say.

"Gil. Stop this…this pretense for just a moment and think about what causes your…pain."

"The scar causes it."

"Okay. Let's say that there really is a scar there. What have you discovered will cause it to…to…"

"To burn? From the inside?"

"Yes. What causes your pain?" She clasped her hands and feigned a smile.

I didn't buy it for a moment. "Do you really want to know what I've discovered? What causes the most pain?"

Dr. Gold nodded.

"Somewhere I learned that if I made others happy, like Kimberly and Dawn, they'd want me. I'd belong. Without doing everything possible for other people, I wouldn't belong. I'll never belong…anywhere."

Without doing for others, you'll never find your place, there will be no place for you in anyone's life, and you'll always be left without a chair.

I looked at her, the therapist, and felt pity. Irma Gold was the crazy one. Did she really think that I'd give it all up? *She wants you to change your plan of action, Gil. She wants you to give up the only formula for survival you've ever known.* I stared at Irma Gold and felt nothing… nothing but contempt for her ideas and pity for her lack of reality. I would never give up the only system in my life that kept me safe.

I thanked her for her help, shook her hand, and walked out of the office. Therapy provided one benefit to me: the validation I needed to confirm that my family was not a "normal" family.

I walked out of Dr. Irma Gold's office and back into my life as a student knowing that I only had one task: survive each day.

My class was about to finish college, on time in four years. I was behind nearly a full year and wouldn't graduate with them.

In order to move ahead, I'd have to leave the past behind. The bleak reality of another secret about my failure at school propelled the decision to end my education that spring. College was over. Four years spent running in circles, an endless cycle of failure and fear, had finally come to an end with no degree to show for it.

I picked up the phone on a sunny afternoon and placed a call shadowed in lies.

"What do you mean?" Dad's voice was incredulous. "How could you do this to us, Gil? I've given you every opportunity to make it through your schooling, and this is how you thank me?"

I had no response.

"You are an embarrassment to the family, Gil. So many people had their hopes built up for you."

I hung up on Dad and dialed Mom. *She'll say the same thing*, the voice in my head jabbed.

"You've let everyone down," she said.

It was true. I'd let everyone else down, but not myself. I had kept the lies intact...all except the one I'd told them over the phone: that I'd failed at school. But I had been the one to choose what to tell and what to keep secret. I would leave higher education without a degree but with my secrets intact and a plan of action.

I did leave with one other thing, though. Debt.

Competition between my parents had escalated during the years, unbeknownst to me. I found out soon after leaving college that I was heavily in debt. Dad's open-checkbook policy for my school years proved to be a challenge to my mother. Her method of "keeping up" with my father took the form of handing money to me, equivalent to my father's support, or so she thought.

The touchy part of this was that Mom and Bruce didn't have the kind of money my dad did. As a result, Mom found a way to take out student loans in my name without my knowledge, and defined the funds that she would then hand to me as a "gift." It wasn't for my support as much as it was intended as a tally to match my dad's contributions. I became the prize in their unending battle of wills.

The tally rose and debt was the trophy—awarded to me.

CHAPTER 16

———◆———

THOUGH I WAS GLAD TO be "back on track," looking for a job with my peers, in fact, I didn't have a choice. My mother's decision left me deeply in debt. I set out immediately to interview for a position with a big insurance company, a sales position where a degree wasn't required, even though I lacked the confidence to succeed in sales. Their office was located in a Park Avenue landmark building. I felt confident as I entered the interview.

"So, Mr. Belmont, I see you're looking for an entry position," the general manager said and puffed his chest out.

"Yes, sir," I answered.

"Well, then, let me ask you one question." He paused, mostly for effect. "What is your favorite food?"

"I'm sorry?" I stammered. Surely I hadn't heard him correctly.

"I said, 'What is your favorite food?' It's a simple question."

"Chinese."

He leaned back in his chair and smiled then stood, extending his hand. "Well, I'm looking for more of a meat and potatoes kind of guy." He motioned toward the door. It appeared I was dismissed; in reality, I was confused and remained seated.

"I'm sorry," I said. "Is this interview over?"

"Young man," he said and took me by the arm in escort out of his office. "There are certain kinds of people out there. We are looking for a rare breed. I call them 'meat and potatoes men.' You said yourself, you're not one of them. So, yes, this interview is over."

I left more confused than ever...and still very unemployed.

The next interview was just as unproductive. I remained keenly on the lookout for 'meat and potatoes men,' apparently my competition. I didn't see any of them as I walked into one of the new long-distance telephone carrier's offices, a company born from the Ma Bell breakup. Another sales position where no degree was required.

"The job is yours!"

Now things began to get really confusing. This interview didn't even touch on meat or potatoes. "Do you want to know what my favorite food is?" I asked.

The interviewer laughed. "You have a great sense of humor! I like that. You're going to be perfect here," she said and winked at me.

She didn't ask the right questions. I walked out of that interview even more perplexed than before. *Still, you got the job.* The voice in my head was right! I was now considered gainfully employed. Fortunately, the time had come when I could feel somewhat ready to pay back my mother's debt.

Life showed some promise. I began to enjoy the idea of being in an office. No one, except my employer, had any idea I had entered the workplace without a degree. Whenever talk of school would come up, I always just said I graduated from Syracuse. It would be too complicated to explain my lack of degree and quite frankly, I felt smart enough, having garnered a collection of A's and B's on my transcripts. *It's just another secret.* Right again! I could do this easily—keep the secret of my education skillfully tucked inside the silent gaps of my fractured life.

I walked the Big Apple with my head held high. I knew how to lie and hold onto information, and did it well. Learning to keep secrets was the best education I had received thus far, and I practiced it proficiently.

My father lived right near my new office. It made sense for me to live with him, since commuting from my mother's house on Long Island took three hours round-trip each day. Also, everyone I knew was beginning to move into Manhattan. But, I was petrified to ask. Dad had never wanted me to live with him before. Here was a crossroads and I almost didn't want to know which way Dad would send me. I dialed his number and used my best businessman persona, disguising my voice with confidence.

"I just need a place for a year, until I can get settled and make enough money to get a place of my own," I said.

He paused for just a moment. "Uh, sure, Gil. That should be fine," he said. "Of course, I'll need to run it past Carole first."

"Of course," I repeated. "Just let me know if it works for you both."

A week later, with the shock of him having said yes still not worn off, I moved in with Dad and Carole. Living in New York City proved less challenging than I thought. The panic attacks were less frequent and never debilitating. I was able to function in my job. I got into the routine at work, reconnected with friends from Syracuse, and connected with an old friend from Washington, Tina. Keeping secrets from her, my friends, and on my job proved exhausting though.

I'd devised a cover story a few years ago one night while I watched a program on TV about chemical imbalances. *You can use that, Gil.* I quickly decided self-ascribed "chemical imbalance" would be a great way to account for the past four years. I felt pretty confident that the whole medical-jargon diagnosis would make it sound as if I had a physical illness rather than an emotional one, something completely unacceptable for a man. *You just better make sure the day never comes that you slip up on your story. It seems you spend an inordinate amount of time focused on propagating the tale of your nonexistent college degree.* That was true.

———◆———

Tina began to take a bigger chunk of my time and focus. I'd been living with Dad & Carole for almost two months and sensed I was on a slippery slope.

One Friday night, I began to slide and it was a little too late to stop.

"Well, he can't stay here!" Carole's voice permeated the house.

I walked in quietly and tried to avoid the living room where Dad and Carole were having a heated discussion. Beneath my feet, the floors creaked and the pre-war building gave me away.

"Gil, is that you?" Dad's voice wasn't as loud as Carole's, but I could hear the irritation. Without waiting for an answer he said, "Come in here for a minute."

I turned on my heel, letting my briefcase and jacket fall to the floor where I stood, and ambled down the hallway to the living room. "Hi, Dad...Carole."

"Why are you so late?" Dad asked, irritation pushing a low pitch into his voice.

"I can't live like this, Dale," Carole said, refusing to acknowledge my presence.

I shifted my weight and tried to stand casually with one hand on the doorframe and the other in my pocket. "What's the problem?"

"You're the problem," Carole snapped. "I want my home back, my life back." She turned her back on me and walked out of the room. My eyes drifted to my father's face. It was red and the furrows between his brows had deepened.

"You can't just come and go as you please, Gil. You can't show up at three in the morning and expect us to change our lifestyle to accommodate yours," he said. He began to pace. "We've got a routine and things work well for us. Your decision to live here was supposed to be temporary. We had rules and we expected that those living under our roof would follow them, including the courtesy of coming home at a reasonable hour. It's turned into a three-ring circus in this house and I won't have it!"

I was dumbfounded. I had never been given a curfew or rules or anything from my mom, or my dad either, for that matter. Was he trying to parent me now after all these years?

"What do you want me to do?" I asked and I stood a little straighter. I could feel the tears begin to well.

"You need to make other arrangements. Go live with your mom or someone who's used to your erratic hours and spontaneous mealtimes."

I felt my face flush and didn't know what to say. Dad was kicking me out of the house? After less than sixty days? This was his opportunity to build a relationship with me, one that had fallen by the wayside for years and now he wanted out. *How can he do that? You're his flesh and blood. He's never been there for you...ever!*

The voice in my head was back, an unwelcome reminder of my dysfunctional life.

"Well, maybe we can fix that," I said aloud to the voice in my head.

Dad glared at me. "Nope. You need to make some phone calls and figure out what you're going to do. I'll give you a week."

I was becoming confused. Dad was speaking of rules and a curfew, it seemed, and at the same time, he was abandoning the opportunity to be a parent, for the first and only time in either of our lives. I could feel that familiar pain across my chest begin to pinch at my heart.

"But, Dad, I'm sure we can come to some kind of an arrangement. I've been here less than two months. What about me living in one of your apartments here in the city? My job will be affected if I have to move back in with Mom," I pleaded with him.

"Not my problem," came the response. It was apparent that he cared little about what became of me, particularly since the only option available to me now would be to move back in with my mother, the source of so many problems. I felt a stab of rejection and knew the pain I'd felt in my chest would only grow stronger. Instinctively, I raised a hand to cover it. Behind my dad, I could see Maslow's pyramid begin to materialize. The second level glared at me: the need for security. I was being thrown out and my safety was slipping through my fingers at the same time.

"Dad...please..."

"No, Gil!"

I shouldn't have been surprised. He'd never fought for me as a kid, never even fought to have a visitation schedule. He never fought for me during my college years when I was emotionally disintegrating, while Carole's daughters thrived with him. I was finally under his roof where he could shape my future and he was sending me right back out to face everything I'd failed at before. *My chest hurts.*

You're disposable. You always have been.

A week later, after quitting my job, I was back home with Mother and Bruce, hamstrung by my inadequacies, secretly torn up inside, directionless, defeated, discouraged, and riddled with guilt about so many things. I was grasping at straws. Panic settled in as a constant companion and nearly drowned me.

The voice in my head was on a rampage, berating me for past and present grievances. I didn't know how to stop it. The expectations for a young Jewish man from Long Island were well defined. Although only a figure of speech within our community, there was a ring of truth to the notion that I would be a doctor, a lawyer...or a failure. I was tremendously successful at failure.

Shame is the status quo. You live ashamed of the things done to you, the things you've done, ashamed of things that have happened to you, even ashamed of things that were never accomplished. You have no self-esteem and the life you're living is nothing but secrets.

I couldn't handle the voice in my head so I ignored it...even though it spoke the truth.

"Gil, are you available for lunch? I'd like to talk to you about something." Dad's call came out of the blue. I wasn't sure what it meant, but I wanted to assume good intent. *Maybe this is his way to make things right again.*

"I want you to work for me in my New York company, Gil," Dad said when we met for lunch.

"Really?" I was stunned. What would motivate a man who had spent his life running from his role as father to show an interest in his son now?

Dad was an accountant by trade. He began by working for his uncle and then took over. He parlayed that background into a lucrative career in real estate, as one of the first to turn New York City apartments into co-ops and condos.

Later on, he bought the London-based branch of a worldwide air courier headquartered in New York City. He also purchased a New York City-based facilities management company that transported documents for large companies. Just as with his London-based business, the primary clientele was Wall Street brokerages. His goal was to merge all these companies together. Dad was a visionary.

This was during the 1980s, an era of mergers and acquisitions, the heyday on Wall Street, and my dad was in the thick of it. All business in those days was done on paper and transported by postal mail so there was a market for courier companies that hand-delivered valuable documents the same day to a location across the country or around the world.

"Yes," he continued, "and there are perks that might interest you."

He had my attention. I sat forward and sipped the ice water in front of me.

"You'll rub shoulders with some of the big names. One of my partners is Daryl Erikson, the local football legend, the former starter with the New York Jets. You'll be going to football games with clients as part of the job."

The benefits certainly sounded appealing.

"When do I start?" I extended my hand across the table. Dad smiled and shook hands with me, a bond we had never shared before.

"Come into the office on Monday. You'll be introduced to the staff there."

This new accountability felt good—my chance at success. It was a done deal. I reported to work with Dad's company at the Fifth Avenue office. I began as a dispatcher. The job was a good fit for me and within a short time, I found myself climbing the corporate ladder. Life was positive and my relationship with my father improved. For the first time, I believed perhaps my dad had come around to accepting me as his son.

My responsibilities increased and carried my self-esteem along with them. I spent time with big-name clients and then worked out of our flagship World Trade Center office. I liked my newly acquired success. Interestingly, I garnered respect from the clients I worked with. I still had a lot to learn, though.

At my first ever business lunch, with a client from American Express, I concluded our meeting and pulled out my credit card to pay for our meal. My client noticed the Visa in my hand and, laughing, made fun of my choice of credit cards. Within twenty-four hours, an American Express card was delivered to the office with my name on it. From then on, the American Express card covered all future lunches.

The company grew, becoming even more successful, and I exceeded everyone's expectations, except my own. I had always known who I was, as my father's son, but I had never had the chance to show it. Now I could, and I earned real recognition from my father, as well as gaining a sense of accomplishment.

——◆——

It was a bright, sunny morning in early spring when my father arranged to have a meeting in his office. The air was crisp and the tulips had just pushed through the frozen earth in spite of the chill. I plucked a red one on my way into our giant headquarters and thought about how my life mimicked the tulips, pushing through impossible circumstances to bloom in spite of adversity.

"Come in, Gil. Take a seat," my father said as I entered his massive office. I dropped the tulip into a glass of water and carried it with me to one of the leather chairs that faced Dad's desk. Surrounded on all sides with floor-to-ceiling plate glass windows, my dad had a big view of New York City. He pulled up a chair and I handed his secretary the flower. She smiled and pulled the door closed.

"Gil," he said, using his business voice. "I want to start an air courier division right here in the US just like the one I have in London, and I want you to help me start it."

I was shocked. There was no reason for him to assign me to this division. It carried too much responsibility and I was not qualified. Quite frankly, it didn't make sense why he would start something like this when he owned the London branch of a company that was headquartered right here in New York City.

"Absolutely!" I said, accepting the offer anyway. Being part of this project was priceless.

It will be an opportunity to share an important piece of your father's life. I knew this without having to be told. *Not only will you be a part of his company, you will also work with him and do a great job for him.* My thoughts raced and I could not hide the grin that spread across my face. I was back to a childhood wish that had been spontaneously fulfilled, captured within this task. After all these years, he would finally be proud of me.

"You're doing great, son," he said and shook my hand, man-to-man.

My new assignment within Dad's company was born and I worked like a dog to help create it. I was determined and it paid off.

CHAPTER 17

———◆———

"For the first time, I feel like I fit in."

I said it out loud and beat a Tarzan fist on my chest. I was a member of a social scene that played into my father's. *Maybe so, but dating is still hard for you. You still lack the confidence to think a girl would choose you over others.* I hadn't asked for the reminder and begged the voice in my head to go away. It wouldn't listen. *Anyway, Gil, you're drawn more to a full-blown relationship than casual dating.* It was true. *You'll fall into your trap again.*

Ever since I was a kid, I desperately wanted a family of my own. Even though Dad and I were closer now, and even though I felt as if I was becoming more a part of his family, the bar had been set pretty low. I knew his first priority was Carole and her two kids came along with that.

But how are you going to have a real relationship? You don't trust anyone enough to share your secrets with. There will be no one for you. I couldn't listen anymore, so I did the only thing I could think of: met my friends and partied the voice in my head into silence.

We typically would gather at night in various Manhattan bars. One night, a friend of mine sat with me, talking as if she was interested. I appreciated it and told Laura that. All of a sudden, without warning, she kissed me. Immediately, I fell, hook, line, and sinker.

You'll have anyone who'll have you, Gil. Here we go again.

I had known Laura at Syracuse. I was taken by her confidence and simple air. She had a coolness to her but she wasn't stuffy like so many girls I knew there. Laura grew up in historical Oyster Bay on Long Island. She was raised in a loving home with her younger sister and parents who'd been married for over twenty-five years. Her father was a wealthy stockbroker and her mother spent her days at the Tennis Club. Laura worked in the fashion district and though she was a very bright girl, her goal was to secure an MRS rather than an MBA degree.

Laura was tall, willowy, with black hair, and piercing brown eyes. Her olive skin and thin Jewish face hid a stereotypical Jewish out-look on life. Achievement and status were of vital importance to her, but she had a lighter side, one that allowed her to laugh at herself and her friends. She didn't have to be on her best behavior every moment.

We went everywhere: Lincoln Center, Broadway, Madison Square Garden, Yankee Stadium, Central Park. We did everything there was to do. We ate at restaurants all the time. We traveled to Cape Cod, the Hamptons, the Jersey Shore, and the Caribbean. We were always on the go.

You seem to prefer each other's company to anyone else's. I paused at the thought and studied my image in the bathroom mirror. Maslow's pyr-amid was missing this time but its memory stained the glass anyway. I couldn't make out any level but one that blazed "Safety" across it.

"Laura and I never really 'click'," I said. "In truth, the spark isn't there." There was no answer, so I looked away and walked out of the bathroom.

My gut ached and I knew deep down that I should listen to it. She wasn't The One…or so I thought at the time. Laura never asked questions, so it was easy to keep secrets from her. Fortunately, our conversations never went much beneath the surface. We all hide our insecurities. Dating can be the most superficial of moments, particu-larly when one hides his deepest hurts and fears. Putting your best foot forward to win love is the status quo with dating, and I was an expert at that part, mainly because I did such a great job at keeping my insecurities to myself. In truth, I was terrified that she wouldn't want to be with me.

Do you love Laura? How could you love Laura if you don't accept yourself?

I wasn't "alone" when I was with Laura, but privately I was insecure and alone. I knew it, and so did my conscience. *You'll never create a more intimate, loving connection than the one you have now. Face it, Gil.* As if to prove my conscience wrong, she became more than my chum, more than my girlfriend. I allowed myself to think of her as the One.

There was one secret I couldn't keep through all of this, one thing about me that I couldn't hide. My family.

Winter had just come upon us and Laura rushed home from work to my apartment, where she'd practically been living, with the earnest intent to hit the sales at Bloomingdale's for a new coat.

She rounded the store's departments and caught sight of Carole's daughter Amy. It should have been the perfect accidental opportunity. But the chance meeting didn't happen that way because immediately she noticed Amy acting rather evasive, always glancing for an escape out of the store. After some prodding, Laura found out the reason. When she walked into the apartment later that night, Laura brought with her more than just a coat. She brought home news.

"They're all going," she said over dinner.

"Everyone?"

"Yup. Everyone. Your dad, Carole, her kids, Deb, Miles—literally everyone."

"But nobody's mentioned anything to me about it," I said, rather frustrated.

"I know. I thought Amy's whole demeanor seemed rather odd. Then she finally admitted it was because of their trip to Mexico."

I stared at Laura solemnly but forced a smile just to be polite.

The next day, I strolled into Dad's new Madison Avenue office and asked what was going on. He glanced up momentarily as I entered, then dropped his eyes to the paperwork scattered over his desk. Moving boxes lined the floor. I assumed he'd probably managed to hang a few pictures up on the walls, but I was pretty sure his plan was to let his secretary to do the rest.

"My schedule is full over the next two weeks, Gil. We'll have to get together next month sometime. I've got meetings out of town and Carole wants to go. It'll be boring but she insisted."

"Mexico? Is that where your meetings are, Dad? You're planning to take the family to Mexico for 'meetings' and manage to leave the one person out of the equation who actually works for the company?"

Dad stopped what he was doing and leveled a sharp look at me. He'd been caught in his own lie but it was obvious he wasn't going down without a fight.

"What are you talking about, Gil?"

"Cut the crap, Dad! There are no meetings in Mexico. Laura ran into Amy at Bloomingdale's last night. She told Laura about your plans, including the part that left me out of the trip."

"Don't use that sarcastic tone with me, Gil." Dad's voice grew as harsh as the conversation that followed. "Deb is coming and I don't want any conflicts. Your relationship with her has always been strained because of your mother and I don't want it to affect my family."

"*Your* family?" I was incredulous.

The argument lasted only about five minutes but it was enough. Dad had planned a family vacation, decided to leave me out, then lied about it.

How typical.

———◆———

There was nothing I could do about it, so I shifted my focus to the only part of my life that was constant. My professional life was flourishing and along with it, I had an amazing girlfriend. Everyone around us was pushing us to get married. My dad approved of Laura and with her by my side, he was accepting me into his family more and more. That meant a lot to me. I could fit into what was expected of me. I decided that marriage was the best route to take. My father was happy I was with a nice Jewish girl from Long Island, and I was looking for affirmation from my father, as much as for the love of a woman.

Laura was ready for marriage. It was obviously time to take the next step.

"Okay, I'll just do it then," I said the day I talked to my father.

I knew proposing to her would be a once-in-a-lifetime moment and I wanted to do something unique. So many missed moments had already passed by in my life—this wasn't going to be another. I spent long hours thinking of just how I would propose. I decided to rent an eighty-foot yacht, fully staffed with a six-person crew. It came with a captain, a butler, and chef.

When the big day finally arrived, we drove up to Port Washington where the yacht was docked, waiting for us. Laura was a little suspicious but I skillfully avoided her questions.

"What is all of this, Gil?" she asked as we strolled down the pier.

"Dad's got clients to entertain tonight and said we could use it this afternoon," I answered, casually masking my rattling nerves.

She bought it. A few hours later, in the middle of the Long Island Sound, with the Connecticut coast approaching and the waves as my orchestra, I dropped to one knee.

"Will you be my wife?"

She glanced askance and her hands dropped to her hips. I was certain the answer would be "no."

"You mean to ask, 'will you marry me?'," she stated and burst out laughing.

I joined her, more relieved than anything else. *She's a spitfire, that one is.* I had to agree.

A few hours later, her parents boarded the yacht, joining us for dinner. We spent the next two days blissfully at sea celebrating our engagement.

———————◆———————

I had been living in Greenwich Village and Laura in Midtown. We officially moved in together right away, in a doorman building on New York City's Upper East Side. Laura was not one to create her own style. She decorated in the popular style of the day. It was a magical time and my confidence blossomed. I even ventured to the famed NYC basketball courts after work and tested my skill against some of the best. Laura would go to the gym or the stores after work. Afterward, we would go out for supper and a peaceful walk home, relishing our life together, free from drama and dysfunction.

I had everything I ever wanted: a beautiful fiancée, a lucrative job, a budding relationship with my father…and a big Jewish wedding on the horizon.

I'd been engaged just about a month when the Jewish high holy day of Yom Kippur came upon us. Laura and I went to the prestigious temple on Central Park West that Dad and Carole belonged to. No sooner were we seated than my father whispered quietly into my ear. "Get up in ten minutes and meet me across the street in Central Park. I want to talk with you about something."

I knew instantly what that meant and my voice found its way to my stomach.

The setting was beautiful, warm, and soothing except for my gut instinct that there was bad news coming. I should have noticed the clues, walking to the lawn with Dad at the very location where the "corporate raider" decks the stockbroker who got in the way of his hostile takeover in that one iconic eighties movie. Indeed, our conversation was much like the movie scene where "Greed is said to be good."

"So, Gil," Dad began, his voice too composed for my comfort. "We need to talk about the company's future."

"Okay, what's your plan?" I hoped to divert the negativity permeating our discussion. "I'm all ears."

"Tomorrow morning everyone in senior management will be out. None of the upper level management will be employed with the company. The company is being taken over and sold off in parts. Of course, this is to be our little secret, agreed? I mean, none of the others know what's about to happen."

I was dumbfounded.

"What does that mean for me? I'm part of that management team, Dad."

"Oh, not to worry, son. Rest assured, you'll find something else and in the meantime, I'll take care of you financially, if that's what you're worried about."

Still stunned, I could only stare at him. This was my job, my future! Everything Laura and I had planned was based on moving forward with a solid career. That was the agreement I'd made with Dad when I signed on for the position.

"That's not the issue, Dad. You made a promise. Now you're changing it up and sending me off with no more than twenty-four hours' notice? Are you kidding?"

"Don't be so emotional, Gil. This is just a bump in the road for you." He turned to leave.

"A bump in the road? Dad, you just put me on a juncture to an entirely different course without a map. You can't do this! And what about Ned? He and Crystal just had a kid! His father's okay with this?"

"Mo made the negotiations real difficult. Ned will still have his job with the company."

"Oh, so it was unacceptable to your partner that his son get screwed while you guys make out like bandits? And you had nothing to say about me?"

It didn't matter what I said to Dad because he was finished with me; his only job that day was to deliver the news. I was left standing at a fork in the road with no idea where I was going.

"I have plans, Gil. There's a way around this but for now, it is what it is and you're going to have to live with it."

Dad walked off as if I had never been in the park with him. His gait betrayed uneasiness with each step, but to casual onlookers he was just a businessman in a nice suit taking a break from work. My pace back to the temple was entirely the opposite. I took a longer route than usual, trying to make sense of the blow just delivered. *And what plans does he have now? Are you a part of it? How do you tell Laura?*

I stopped at the merry-go-round and tried to answer the questions incessantly pounding my thoughts. Dad had let me down again, although I didn't want to admit that outright. Still, I would be unemployed by morning and needed to figure out what the next step was.

My father once again does what is best for him regardless of its effect on me. His abandonment of his family took an enormous emotional toll on me and limited my ability to achieve what was expected of me. This latest move threatens the emotional stability I've achieved. I restated the facts and the voice in my soul did not argue.

"Plans change," Dad said the following day. Dad ignored the glass barricade I'd put in place and opened my office door without knocking.

"Not now, Dad," I said and closed the lid to the first box filled with dreams of a relationship with my father, otherwise known as things from my office.

I couldn't bear to hear those words one more time so I closed the door and continued to fill the boxes that lay on top of what used to be my desk. Bitterness was not part of my nature but it crept up with an ugly foot and into my constitution this morning. I dismissed the thought and finished packing.

That evening, I met Laura at our favorite Chinese restaurant. It would likely be our last night out for a while, and hopefully it was a decent venue to break the news. She took it rather well, hiding the disappointment on her face skillfully.

"I suppose we can live on my income for a while until you can get another job," she said and forced a smile.

"You know this won't last."

"Of course it won't, Gil. You're industrious, I know that much," she said, but I didn't think she believed it.

I broke open one of the twisted almond cookies tossed onto the table after the plates had been cleared. Laura watched hopefully as I pulled out the paper announcing my fortune.

"What does it say?"

I read the words scrolled across the tiny slip, then glanced up as I handed it to her.

The world may be your oyster but that doesn't mean you'll get its pearl.

When she looked up at me, she had tears in her eyes to match my own.

———— ◆ ————

I struggled the next few months to keep my spirits up. Dad had given me another mystery to hide. To add one more secret to the stockpile I kept tucked away brought about an internal dialogue that made me uncomfortable.

I thought you worked for your father. He's loaded. How come you're out of a job? I had no answer. My hopes were sinking fast and just like he always did, my father summoned me to another meeting.

"There's an opportunity for you to buy an equity portion of the air-courier division being sold off by the new owners," he announced and closed the door behind him. "You should do it. You helped start it."

"I don't have that kind of money, Dad."

"Don't worry about that," he said, swatting the air. "I've made an agreement that it be sold off separately with an additional side agreement nobody knows about. It will be re-sold thirty days later to one specified individual."

"Let me guess…"

"You, Gil! You can buy it, keep the business alive and we'll merge it with my London company in a year or so when things quiet down."

I was incredulous. "Me? Didn't you hear what I just said, Dad? I don't have the money or the interest to buy any equity portion remaining."

"Of course you do. I'll give it to you…but it has to stay our little secret." He turned his head and looked through the closed glass door demonstratively, then placed both hands on the desk and leaned forward as if to whisper some clandestine piece of information. It was ridiculous.

"Of course, a secret between us." I couldn't hide the sarcasm in my voice.

"I can't allow a competitor to find out. A private arrangement, really, Gil, and I'll loan you the money."

"A loan?"

"Yes. The best way to do this, trust me." By default, I had just become partners with two industry veterans Dad had pieced together for this "arrangement."

Now what are you going to tell Laura?

The Mexico trip along with a termination had left us both with a bad taste for Dad's deals. When I left Dad's office that day, I wasn't sure whether my new title was "industrialist" or "sucker."

Fortunately, Laura was very understanding about the change of events. Laura's family was whole, functional, and supportive of each other. She had a fresh perspective on everything that seemed to emanate from the expanse of her character.

She dreamed of a simple but elegant wedding that made the stress of planning relatively problem-free, given the pressure we were under with my job and Dad's new expectations. I was grateful for her soothing influence on my chaotic life.

Laura's parents were planning a lavish wedding to be held on the opulent North Shore of Long Island. They spared no cost to give their daughter the best. It would be the social event of the year for the family, complete with a write-up on the *New York Times Social Page*.

During the months that followed, tension mounted between my family members. Mom wanted my wedding to look a certain way, which didn't include Dad's new family. Dad insisted that his step-daughters be brought into the wedding party, which didn't fit Mom's vision of her only son's nuptials. I was caught in the middle of an escalating war and dragged Laura in with me. I had no clue what to do until one day at lunch with Dad and Carole.

Columbus Day in the Berkshire Mountains, two hours north of New York City, is the most glorious weekend of the year, with fall colors in full display: every leaf turned a different shade of gold. Dad's hundred-acre country home was becoming a regular part of our social calendar and the perfect place to lure us in.

"Take this, Gil," dad said, and slid a check across the table. "Use it for the honeymoon or whatever you need."

I looked at it and my mouth dropped. Laura leaned over my shoulder and eyed the dollar amount, then glanced up at my dad.

"Really, Dale, we can't take this," she said and pushed it back toward my father.

"I insist! It's the least I can do and you need it. Besides, Carole wants me to give it to you, and you know how she can be if she doesn't get her way," he said, laughing at his own joke.

He doesn't realize how true that statement is, though you don't believe for a second it was her idea, now do you? The thought did little to appease my confusion about the scene playing out in front of me.

"We just want a simple wedding party, Dad, just Laura's two closest friends, my two friends, Laura's sister, and Debra. Things have been getting better with Debra. That's it."

"Hogwash, Gil. I know Laura wants the entire family involved. It's a big day for all of us," he said pushing the check back.

Take it. He owes it to you. And besides, why do you care who's in your wedding party? It'll be over in a day and you'll only be plagued with a pile of photos to show for it, which you can tuck away and never look at again if it bothers you that much. I couldn't argue the logic and glanced up at Laura. Her cheeks were flushed but she said nothing, just shrugged her shoulders in response.

"Okay, well...it isn't necessary but thanks." I tucked the check into my pocket.

It wasn't long before Mom found out.

"How could he do such a thing? He bought you out to insert those girls into *my son's* wedding? They're not even blood related!"

I hadn't told her how much he had given us, but it wasn't difficult to figure out that the sum was hefty. Laura wanted to go to Europe. I wanted a once in a lifetime moment to be a great memory. Mom realized too easily that the trip wasn't in our budget and put two and two together rather quickly.

"Mom, you've got to let this go," I said. "It's not about the money or who's in the wedding. It's about Laura...and me."

"The hell I do!" She marched to one corner of the kitchen and wiped her hands on a towel, then spun to face me. "If his step-daughters, who have no relation to anyone involved, are going to be included, then so are mine! I won't have him dominate this."

That was the end of it. Preparations were made to invite a conglomeration of people, unrelated and otherwise uninvolved in our lives. A Jewish wedding always seems much bigger than first imagined, snowballing until the event itself becomes the center of the community. Ours was no different.

The moment Eric and Elizabeth were included on the list, I checked out. This wasn't a wedding. It was payback. I had failed to protect Laura from the toxicity of my family's antics, even on our wedding day.

Instead, I opted to wave the white flag.

I could do nothing about my parents. I went back to the one thing I could control, my work. I poured myself into my job and watched as my air courier company took off again. We signed on with some big name clients and it appeared that the business was better positioned than it had been originally. My dad's priority remained the same, to eventually merge us with his European company. This is what my new partners expected when they signed on. I took the bait loyally, proud to be part of the process.

It should have come as no shock when word spread that my dad might not keep his end of the agreement with my new partners. Rumor had it he'd found it more profitable for his London company to do business with someone else in the USA. Less than a week before Laura and I were to be married, mutiny brewed within my new company, threatening my career.

———•———

CHAPTER 18

"I DIDN'T DO ANYTHING."

"Of course not." His mustache curled over a full lip that twitched as he stared at me.

"No, but I really didn't, honest."

He leaned over the metal table that separated us in the tiny room with only one door. His open palm landed a little too hard on the shiny surface, and the slap echoed against the tile that lined the walls.

"You know what's amazing? Every schmuck who sits in that chair there says exactly the same thing. And you know what? Every single one of them is a goddamn liar!"

I dropped my eyes to hands pressed against one another helplessly. There was no way this guy would believe anything I had to say... or let me go.

"Yeah but I'm telling the truth," I whispered, unable to raise my eyes to meet his.

"Sure you are. Just like the rest of them," he said and leaned against the wall.

Rapping on the steel door indicated that someone wanted his attention and quickly. The agent rose reluctantly and walked to the door, opening it a crack. A deep voice spoke in low tones from the other side and the agent nodded.

"He says the same thing."

The mustached agent's arrogance didn't help his image. I watched him as he exchanged secrets about my brother-in-law and me through a partially opened door. He caught my look and stepped aside, head cocked as he studied me.

"Your buddy tells the same story, apparently. You plan this, you two? Get your stories straight ahead of time?"

"No," I shook my head and dropped my eyes again. "May I please make a phone call?"

"No!"

Time passed as slowly as the conversation continued between the agent and the person behind the door. I would never get out of here in time.

"Please?" I begged for a phone.

"Why?" The agent seemed intrigued and walked back to the table, the door remaining ajar as a red-haired man in his early forties looked through and studied me.

"I'm supposed to be at a rehearsal dinner tonight," I answered weakly.

Laughter erupted from the doorway and the redheaded agent stepped into the room. The agents exchanged looks, amused at my precarious situation.

"A rehearsal dinner? For what? A wedding or something?"

"Yes," I responded, unable to meet their stares. "I've already told you that's what this trip was all about. A bachelor party!"

The redhead laughed out loud again. "This oughta be good. For Christ's sake, Bart, give the guy a phone. I wanna hear this one."

The mustached agent stared into the mirrored wall behind him and waved his hand. Moments later, a blonde woman arrived. She wore a dark blue vest with US CUSTOMS in gold lettering that did little to hide the curves beneath. She handed the mustached agent my cell phone. I stared at him, wide-eyed, my focus shifting between his smirk and the cell phone. Apparently, my reaction to finding these strangers in possession of my personal effects was not unusual and seemed to bring a great deal of amusement to everyone there, except me.

"Thank you," I whispered and flipped open the phone. The screen remained dark. The battery apparently drained sometime between the moment I got off the plane where my belongings were confiscated and now. "It's dead."

"Yup, so it is. Happens all the time," he said, and pulled open a drawer tucked beneath the tabletop. "What do you have?"

"It's a Motorola," I said helplessly.

He fished around inside the drawer for a moment, pulled out a long white cord, then plugged it into an outlet on the wall. I inserted the cord into the phone port and waited for some sign of life. Finally, the red hourglass appeared to indicate the charge had begun. I pushed the side and the familiar tones rang out loudly in the tiny room. My eyes drifted from the phone to the agent who was now leaning back in his chair, hands clasped behind his head, a broad smile plastered across his face. *I hate you! Hate this place!*

"Who ya gonna call, Gil?" The grin never left his face as he spoke.

"My fiancée."

I began nervously scrolling through the contact list, hoping to avoid the topic I knew was certain to become the next target. Pinging sounded as my search was interrupted by text alerts from hours ago. I stopped scrolling and glanced at the alerts. My message log was nearly empty.

"Somebody erased all my messages," I said unable to believe my eyes. "Who'd do that?"

"What? Your fiancée?" The agent ignored my question. "You gotta be kidding me! This is getting better each minute." He stood up and walked to the door, exchanging words with the redhead once again.

From the corner of my eye, I could see both of them stop and snigger for a moment before they continued their conversation in private. I pulled my attention to my phone again.

All of the texts between my sister and me were gone, deleted by a third party. So were the messages between my mother, my father, and my clients. Only three remained, all from Laura. What had they done? *Erased your entire life for the past few months, Gil, that's all.* I didn't want to believe my instinct but I knew it was true.

"Can I please make the call now," I asked.

"Oh, please…make the call," the mustache said.

"We can hardly wait," the redhead added and stepped alongside his partner, arms crossed over his barrel chest.

I scrolled through my contact list and noticed several contacts had been deleted too. Blinking back the tears that threatened to spill, I found Laura's photo and pressed my thumb over her name. Within moments, the image of a phone flashed on the screen and I held the receiver to my ear.

"Gil? Gil is that you?"

"Laura, I need to tell you what's happened—"

"Where the hell are you? Don't you have any respect for me? Do you know what this means?" she cut me off.

I swallowed against the lump rising in my throat. "Yes, I know this is bad…really, really bad but I can't help it. Something's happened and I—"

"I don't care what's happened, just get here fast. This isn't funny, Gil!"

"Laura, I'm trying to but it's out of my control—"

I didn't hear anything else because the agents were laughing too loudly. Laura's voice popped from the receiver in staccato bursts that rose in pitch with every "but—" that I interjected.

"I'll call you when I know more. I just have to talk with these guys about—"

"Guys! What guys?" she screeched.

"Some agents who have a few questions for me."

"About what? For heaven's sake Gil, what's happened now?"

I glanced at the agents who had moved deeper into the room. Cupping my free hand over the mouthpiece, I tried to deflect their laughter.

"Look, Miles flew us to the Bahamas for a bachelor party instead of Atlanta for a supposed meeting. I had no way of knowing that's what he was doing until it was too late. We're trying to get there in time for it but they're holding me here for questioning."

"Holding you? For what? I told you to stay away from Miles."

"I don't know. I mean, I don't have my passport but that's because I didn't know he was taking me out of the country. Miles never said anything and—"

"All I know, Gil Belmont, is that you'd better get your ass over here before this is over. People have been waiting all night and you're embarrassing me."

"Laura, you know I'd never do anything to embarrass you—"

Laughter pealed from the agents. I covered the mouthpiece with my hand and waited for a reprieve. It came in the form of a coughing fit from the redhead.

"What in the world is going on there, Gil? Are you at a bar? You'd better have a good excuse."

"Of course not, I'm in Ft. Lauderdale."

"Florida? What the hell, Gil? That's a three-hour flight back to New York!"

"They think I'm bringing drugs into the country," I blurted.

"They think *what!* Why would they think that? What have you done, Gil?"

"It's pretty obvious, Laura, two guys in suits, flying in and out of the country in a Learjet with no passports and no luggage."

Laughter blasted again and my head dropped as I realized my mistake.

"When did you go to the Bahamas?"

"Yesterday, instead of Atlanta. I told you that already." I felt her anger seethe through the receiver.

I heard Laura's mother in the background.

"Drugs! What are you talking about? You're doing what...with drugs? This is inexcusable, Gil!"

She hung up. I slowly flipped the phone shut, then looked up at the agents now hovering over the table only inches from where I sat.

"So, who's getting married tomorrow, Gil?"

"Me...at least that was the plan," I said and turned the phone off.

———◆———

CHAPTER 19

"I TOLD YOU SEVERAL WEEKS ago, Gil. I'm not doing it. It's not going to happen!" Deb's eyes pinched as her brows knit together. This was her immovable face, and I knew I wouldn't be able to change her position.

"Deb, please be reasonable. Mom's never even met the girls. You still won't let her meet them today? Can't you, just…this once?"

Her lips pursed to match her eyes. I'd crossed the line. Fortunately, a grip on my arm rescued me from what might happen next.

"Gil, we've got a problem," Dad said in the hushed voice he used for inside stock trading.

"No kidding," I said, trying to ease the tension.

"This is serious," Dad continued. "I'm not doing it! I simply won't walk next to that woman. I'll only walk next to my wife! I don't care what they say I'm supposed to do. I'm not doing it!" Apparently, there would be no changing Dad's mind either. This was getting ridiculous!

"Come on, Dad," I said and my hands dropped. "I've already agreed to your step-daughters being involved, against Mom's wishes, I might add. When she found out, she pushed me to bring in all her kids. It's a flippin' three-ring circus already!" It would be no use trying to convince him otherwise. Once Dad had made a decision, there was no turning back. As if to confirm his position, he shifted his weight and folded both arms across his chest. I decided to use my only weapon. "This is exactly what Laura didn't want!" I could cut the tension with a machete.

"Dale, this really is breaking with Jewish tradition. You know the parents are supposed to escort their child down the aisle together." Rabbi Yosef Eli Scheinbaum's pleading nearly dropped him to his knees. *The Rabbi's on the side of tradition, poor guy.* "The ceremony starts soon. Be reasonable, Dale, please! For the sake of your son."

The words of supplication had been issued, and there was no way he'd ever budge, not now. I'm certain I saw tears in the Rabbi's eyes. It was my turn.

"Dad, think about how it will look…for you." As soon as I said it, I knew it was exactly the wrong thing to say. A finger rose in the air and landed inches from my nose. "I mean, Dad, look, you're one of the most respected men in our Temple. How will it appear if you don't do this? Think of that. Think of me!"

I'd pulled out all the stops but it only deepened the lines of his forehead. His lips parted but his teeth didn't and I knew whatever was coming next wouldn't be pretty. I prayed Rabbi Yosef had a thick skin.

"I've told you already…I will not walk next to that woman. Not for Rabbi Yosef," he paused and cast the humble *I'm sorry but this isn't my fault* look directly at the Rabbi. "Not for the Temple." Another glance at the Rabbi. I was going to be sick. "And most definitely not for you, Gil!"

That was it. Dad wasn't going to do it. I figured having Mom as my only escort would be strange but not completely inappropriate. After all, widows escorted their sons alone, didn't they?

"Mom, I need you to…"

The remark never left my lips before I realized she was nowhere to be found, and neither was Deb.

Less than half a football field away, the battle had begun on turf reserved for invited guests and flowers. I rushed from the sidelines, intercepting a certain brawl about to take place in front of a photographer.

"What's going on?" I already knew the answer but didn't know what else to say.

"She is *not* going to take photos with my daughters! I've made that clear and she doesn't listen!" Deb's pace was difficult to match as she made her way to a flowered berm draped with palm trees and a lake in the background. It was a perfect background for a family portrait. Mom had positioned the girls around her and the photographer was in the process of setting a proper focus.

"*Stop!*"

Deb screamed so loud, the photographer dropped the lens cap he'd been holding. I rushed ahead of Deb to create a barrier between her and Mom and the girls. Blood would spill if Deb made it there first.

"Deb, think about it just for a minute," I started to say, but Mom pushed past me.

"You have no right, Debra! I am their grandmother and will have a photo with my granddaughters if I choose to."

Those kinds of edicts never worked on Deb, and I watched her pinched eyes nearly disappear. Once more, I tried to position myself but it was too late. Dad had followed me, talking the entire time with Rabbi Yosef. I decided to change the subject, hoping to distract Deb from throwing a right hook at someone.

"Mom, what about walking me down the aisle? Wouldn't that be just as memorable?"

"Who's *your father* going to walk with?"

I didn't want to answer because I knew the fireworks would ignite with one simple word. "Carole," I said, and Mom's face turned the shade of a cherry bomb ready to explode.

"Nope," she announced. "If he walks with that woman, I'm walking with my husband and that's final!" She folded her arms and turned on Deb again.

I looked helplessly at Rabbi Yosef whose eyes were cast heavenward, his lips moving in silence, fingers knotted into a ball at his waist. He finished the unanswered prayer and shrugged.

As if on cue, Miles marched up and immediately turned on my mom who was nose-to-nose with Deb. I stood there helpless watching as a very Jewish family escalated in fine Italian form while a rabbi prayed. There was nothing I could do, so I decided to try to find my soon-to-be wife.

"You can always do it by yourself, I suppose." Rabbi Yosef had stopped praying and the answer was for me to go solo. *How appropriate*, I thought. I turned from them all and took my place, waiting for my family to finish their quarrel, the photographer to collect his equipment and his wits, and the rabbi to signal that the ceremony would actually take place.

Just then, the music reached its crescendo—my cue to begin. My heart pounded in my chest, it refused to slow down as I made my way down the aisle alone...just as I had been my entire life. Jewish tradition was broken.

Ahead, the chuppah rested empty, welcoming. Perhaps there would be peace under that canopy. Perhaps it would bring a peaceful beginning to my new life as the husband of the sweet woman waiting to be escorted by her parents. Perhaps.

My eyes dared not deviate from the path I was taking, a much longer walk to the chuppah than I thought. I guess walking alone does that—makes the walk seem longer—but I could see smiles on the faces of family and friends out of the corner of my eye. The houses had been divided once again. My family was on one side, unwilling to sit by one another, leaving empty chairs to mark their differences. Many of them, I'd barely ever met. Apparently an invitation wasn't required for my bloodline to show up for wedding cake and free champagne.

Laura's family sat, side by side, without empty chairs or animosity. They were happy. This was what I sought; the peace and joy that comes with an intact family, and it would begin when Laura and I made our vows. I waited patiently and focused on her delicate face, walking toward me with a parent on each arm, and toward the future I wanted so badly.

No one walked beside me and it seemed to fit the path that led to the woman with whom I would create a new life, a peaceful life filled with love and purpose. Perhaps breaking Jewish tradition this one time wasn't so bad.

"Ahhh-main" sounded from both sides of the congregation as Rabbi Yosef finished another verse. He was singing now and my beautiful Laura stood on my left. The music started up again and Laura began to walk in the traditional circle around me. Seven times she did this, and each time she made a complete circle, "aahs" and "oohs" followed.

"May the Source of Life, the Fountain of all being, find living expression in the love between you. May you forever uphold the chuppah of peace that we see above you this day. And let us say, 'Amen.'"

"Ahhh-main."

I was supposed to do something. Laura stared up at me, her eyes soft and gentle. I knew she loved me and I loved her more than I knew was possible. Our life together would be perfect. I whispered to her, "I love you," and she replied in kind.

"Lift her veil, Gil." Rabbi Yosef was also whispering.

"Oh," I said, and immediately took the silky fabric between my fingertips and lifted it from her face. She was radiant. My eyes welled and I knew I would not be able to hold back tears. I was so happy.

Rabbi Yosef began to sing again. I didn't know what to do next and I didn't care. The crystal goblet in Laura's hand dulled in comparison to her beauty in my eyes. I blinked back tears once again. She smiled as the rabbi handed me a goblet. I took a sip and handed it back. Rabbi Yosef wrapped it in a cloth. He placed it at my feet and, without taking my eyes off my bride, I stamped on it, the crystal turning to dust under my foot. Our union was complete. After another blessing or two, I would face the world as Laura's husband.

"This way, Gil."

I heard music begin and my body led onto the dance floor. Laura rushed alongside me, her delicate hand gripped in mine. Somewhere between Rabbi Yosef's song and this moment, we had been introduced as Mr. and Mrs. Belmont. *I am married to Laura, sweet, beautiful Laura. Nothing will ever come between us.*

"Time to dance the hora," someone shouted from one corner of the room as he dragged my father into the circle. My mother came next but she refused to dance next to Dad and moved over to where Debra sat nursing a glass of wine, skillfully moving the chair sideways between them.

I waved at them and shouted, "Come, dance with us. It's the hora."

Deb shook her head and Mom leaned in closer to hear whatever she was saying. Mom then looked up at me and shook her head as well.

Someone began shouting from the bar. I recognized the voice and prayed to God I was wrong.

"You son of a bitch!"

Miles was calling someone out. Someone fell to the ground. I prayed it was the champagne to blame and not one of my relatives. Panicked, I glanced at Laura, who was smiling affectionately at her father and mother, arm-in-arm on either side of her, moving gracefully in and out of the circle. Laura apparently hadn't heard the fracas.

"Excuse me a minute," I tried to break out of the circle but chairs had already been brought into the center. "I need to go see what—"

I was pushed from behind onto a chair and hoisted up on the shoulders of a few of my friends. Laura was already up, bouncing up and down on her own chair, a handkerchief dangling from one hand. The vantage point was perfect to see our guests and the beautiful accommodations of the celebration.

As they spun me around to face my wife, I saw a look of horror spread across her face. She had pinpointed the exact location of the voices I'd hoped were only in my imagination. I followed her eyes and glanced at the same corner. Erupting in a tornado of tempers and broken loyalty, her new in-laws stood ready for combat. Mom and Deb had shown their true colors, even at my wedding, the most sacred event of my life. They were screaming at one another about everything and nothing, and no one was spared. Bruce and Carole, my so-called bonus parents, were the most demonstrative, save for my brother-in-law Miles, who quickly swung around to find Bruce. A tray of crystal glasses shattered violently against the wall as he missed his target.

The music rallied and I looked at my gentle Laura who simply mouthed, "Oh, Gil."

I took her hand, the one still clinging to the lacy white handkerchief, and lifted it overhead, a symbol of the Jewish wedding…

…and a symbol of surrender.

———◆———

We made it through the wedding in spite of the drama. Laura was a beautiful, dignified bride. She was my wife. We spent our honeymoon in Europe for two blissfully serene weeks. Time slowed down to a crawl. We traveled to the many cities peppered throughout the Bavarian Alps, sipped coffee in Italian bistros, and toured castles, forts, and museums built centuries before either of us was born. It was bliss. Most of all, it was freedom from my feuding family's theatrics.

Upon our return, life picked up right where it had left off. The first day back, I went straight to my office, at least the place where my office had been. The nameplate had been removed and the door was locked. My key wouldn't turn to open it.

"Jackie, what's up with this door? And what happened to my nameplate?" I asked over my shoulder as I pulled and jiggled against the lock. The receptionist looked up. "I just need some help," I said and forced a smile.

"Umm, let me get someone." Jackie bumped into an open desk drawer as she fled to one of the partners' offices down the hallway. "Wait here just for a minute, Gil," she shouted over her shoulder.

Moments later, I was joined by a flustered Jackie and a stiff suit who informed me that the locks had been changed more than a week ago. Apparently, the office was no longer mine. The partners had voted, assuming I was part of my father's disingenuous actions toward them, and fired me. I was devastated.

Now what are you going to tell Laura? Newly married and without a job, I was in a bad place. "I'll think of something," I said aloud to my thoughts and bolted for the door. Inside my chest, my heart began to pound its familiar brisk rhythm. On the surface, the scar seared. I knew it wouldn't be long before I lost control…again.

"Of course you will, Gil," came Jackie's response behind me.

I needed to get away, to someplace I could be alone with my thoughts and the rising panic that threatened to consume me once again. Solace was too much to ask for in the high-rise office building where I used to have a career. Everyone knew me there. I wanted to be surrounded by strangers. I bolted down the street and made my way several blocks.

You've done it again, Gil.

"Actually, *he's* done it again. Left me high and dry without so much as a warning or a prospect to fall back on." My voice wheezed, not so much because I was running, but more likely because my airway had already begun to constrict…or at least, that's how it felt. I lifted a hand to the burning scar that no one knew was there, except me and Dr. Maslow.

You should call him…talk to him about it. Stand up for yourself this once!

I agreed with the voice in my head but found myself unable to rationalize the next step. I dodged into a hotel on the next corner and found a bank of payphones tucked inside the lobby. Slipping into one of the open-air glass enclosures, I fumbled around in my pocket for a quarter. A moment later, the phone was ringing through the receiver. To my surprise, someone answered.

"Dad." My voice sounded stronger than I was accustomed to. "This is Gil. We need to talk."

"This isn't your father, Gil," the voice on the other end said. It was Carole. Why didn't I pick up the sarcastic tone in her voice the moment she said, "Hello"? I took a deep breath and willed my nerves to settle. It didn't work. "Can't you tell the difference between your dad and me?" she quipped.

"Of course I can, Carole," I said spitting the words into the receiver. "I need to talk with Dad. Is he there?"

"No."

"Well, can you tell me where to reach him? When he'll be back? Anything?"

"Don't take that tone with me, Gil Belmont! I don't have to take it from you, not after that ridiculous issue with the wedding announcements and the toasts," she snapped.

"Can we talk about this some other time, Carole? I really need to talk to Dad. It's rather urgent," I said.

"No. There are a few things I want to say to you and you're going to listen before I'll tell you where your dad is."

I could feel my face turning the color of tomatoes. The vise had returned to my gut and my hands began to shake. On the surface, the scar flared and burned with the anger I'd kept stuffed away for so many years. I couldn't hold it in any longer and blurted into the phone, "While your husband was being a father to *your* kids, instead of taking care of his own flesh and blood—"

"What are you talking about? Calm down, Gil!"

I couldn't stop myself. "Eric and his filthy wife raped me for three years. Drugged me, then used me as their little sex toy when I was only nine!"

Silence followed on the other end. "I don't even know who Eric is," she finally said.

"That's not the point!" I screamed.

The secret I'd kept for almost two decades was finally out, spilled through a pay phone in the middle of a hotel lobby, surrounded by strangers. Of all the people to reveal such tender wounds to, I'd chosen Carole. This was not the way I envisioned disclosing my most raw secret, but the dirty little story had finally been told, and for the first time, my father's wife was speechless.

Complete silence trickled through the receiver as I poured out my darkest moment to someone who didn't care.

Now you've done it. You're tied up in knots and the fire burning in your chest is witness that you've confided in the one person who will turn it all against you.

I needed to do some damage control and do it quickly.

No one knew what had happened so many years ago, no one except Eric, Elizabeth, and me. I had failed to say anything to Laura about this and knew it would only be a matter of a few phone calls before word got to her of her husband's dark history. She had to hear it from me first.

I bolted from the hotel lobby and observed sideways glances from observers who'd likely heard my exchange over the phone. So much for secrecy! The scar burned worse than I remembered from before. Things were out of control and I would be the one to suffer once again for it, even though I had been the victim. There was no place to go for solace…no place of safety for me. Maslow's pyramid flashed through my mind, but there were only two tiers: the higher one emblazoned with the word *Safety* and the lower, *Physiological Needs.* I still hadn't passed beyond the basic needs of human beings. Only one person remained in my life who might be my salvation, and it might be too late for that.

I rushed home, found my wife, and told Laura everything. Fortunately, she was rock solid, never shifting her emotions to pull the focus to her. I needed to feel understood and supported and Laura was champion at doing just that. She *was* my safety zone.

"We have to shut everyone and everything else out, until we can deal with this properly," I announced and Laura agreed.

"Do whatever you need to do, Gil," she said.

Moments later, the phone rang. My dad must have arrived home and received an earful from Carole. I couldn't talk to him now. I couldn't face him, couldn't face anyone at that moment except Laura.

Dad caught up with me around lunchtime the following day. We drifted into a diner at his insistence, a difficult venue to discuss sexual abuse in, but I accommodated him anyway. For the next forty-five minutes, we dodged the prickly topic that stuck its thorn into our relationship's side.

A few days later, Mom called and began by yelling at me because my dad had called to yell at her. It took everything I had inside to say the words out loud to my mother over the phone that day. It took nothing for her to throw it back.

"You can't blame me. I didn't know what they were doing behind closed doors. I only knew that they were drug addicts. I didn't know they were molesters," she said impassively.

"What?" I couldn't believe my ears! "What are you saying?"

Don't let her get away with this! How can she call herself a mother and allow you to go with drug addicts?

I felt the leg under my chair begin to give way at the same time the scar began to burn. I reached down one hand to catch myself but I was sitting upright. Suddenly, I knew that being off balance was an internal metaphor, just like the scar, just like everything else. My parental support never existed, and the missing piece had just fallen away.

The chair is your life and the scar is the resulting damage, Gil. It's broken and each leg represents someone of significance in your life.

"You're blaming me!" she said. "Your mother!"

I didn't hear anything else for a moment because she hit the nail right on the proverbial head. She was the support I'd leaned on but never found in place, always missing or crumbling. I felt myself letting go.

"Moms don't let their little kids go with drug addicts!" I heard myself shouting into the receiver.

Silence.

Don't let her off the hook now, not while you have her attention.

"I was a child, your little boy! Moms are supposed to protect their children, not purposefully put them in harm's way!" I was shouting.

She offered nothing else. She was a blank slate with no remorse. The conversation was over and she owned nothing from it. The last thing I heard as I slammed the phone down included the words, "… eight miscarriages and not my fault."

I didn't speak to my mother after that. Although she made several attempts to contact me, I wanted nothing to do with her as long as she was going to continue to defend herself. The chair had lost its leg and would never be repaired.

You should have told someone. How many others have there been? Countless numbers of innocent children taken into the back room by Eric and Elizabeth. If you'd told someone, perhaps you could have prevented another soul from suffering as you have.

I gagged and got up from the sofa.

"Gil? Gil what's wrong, honey?" Laura said.

I couldn't answer her question as I rushed down the hallway and closed the bathroom door behind me.

———◆———

CHAPTER 20

DAD NEVER FELT THE WEIGHT of his decision the way I did. Moving ahead without remorse seemed to be a talent my parents shared, something I didn't inherit and never would understand.

The next two years found me in a familiar place of inadequacy. I'd lost my confidence and I bounced around a few meaningless jobs. My emotional demise continued to spiral as I felt uprooted from what had anchored me: a job with my father, a career I could manage, and a relationship.

"He owes you something. He's the reason you lost your job in the first place," Laura said one day over dinner. I glanced up at her, astonishment coating my look. "Don't look so surprised. You know it's true."

"Yes, but I've never heard you say anything disparaging about my parents before," I responded.

"It's not disparaging, Gil. It's a statement of fact."

She set down her wine glass and clasped both hands in front of her plate, a sign that she wanted my full attention. I set my own glass down and dropped sweaty palms into my lap. If Laura had something that important to say, she was likely right about her position, which meant I had to act. I wasn't sure whether I was able to act on anything that would lead to confrontation with my dad.

"Fact: He caused you to lose your job. Fact: He hasn't bothered to apologize or even acknowledge his role. Fact: In addition, he hasn't offered to help you find a job anywhere else. Fact: He made certain that he and Carole are secure with a fat check from—"

"Points well taken," I said and wrung my hands where she couldn't see them.

"And furthermore, why won't he ever include you in his real estate business? That's where he's made his money to begin with! Everything else he does is a hobby!" Laura was furious.

The expectations for a Jewish man from Long Island were high, and my self-confidence was at an all-time low. I could barely look her in the eyes.

"You've got to start believing in yourself. It's the only way you'll get a decent job!"

Laura was right. I didn't believe in myself, so how could anyone else? I glanced up at Laura. Her eyes sparkled in spite of the uneasiness I knew she must feel inside, particularly with her husband unemployed. I felt nothing.

What's wrong with me? I asked myself silently, staring at my wife across the table. *I should be filled with gratitude, love, hatred...anything.* But there was nothing. Our life together had grown stagnant and mine alone was a cesspool.

You don't truly love her, the voice said.

But why? She's a good person, and we always have fun, I countered in my head, and took another sip of coffee.

Neither of you loves the other. Friends, yes, but lovers? Deep, abiding love? No, never.

I had no argument. Excusing myself from the table, I kissed my wife dutifully on the forehead, thanked her for a lovely meal, and went into the den filled with silent dread. My marriage was a sham.

I couldn't hide the vacancy in my heart. It was as though a glaring sign hung over a cheap hotel, blazing a neon message that flashed erratically from a broken light. That was my existence with my wife, Laura. I was certain I saw the same emptiness in her.

Over time, our conversations shifted and minor differences began to show ugly faces. Where should we live next? How many kids should we have? Where would we eat on our fiftieth anniversary? Such topics led to raw emotions and revelations.

With the fun drained from our once happy marriage, we quickly discovered different paths. It was clear that Laura and I knew exactly how to have fun, but the question remained: did we want to spend forever together? We had chosen to marry because that was the next big step in "adult life," a step neither of us should have taken. Of course, compromises could have been made, but there was nothing of substance holding us together at that point.

Did you ever love her at all, Gil? Or did you just feel that with Laura as your wife, you'd fit in with your dad's expectations? I couldn't face the answer.

Throughout all of this, Deb and Miles kept pestering us to move to California. Miles had a huge real estate company and offered me a job. Miles didn't interest me and this definitely was not what Laura wanted for us. She knew, in spite of any benefits that might come with creating a life in California, nothing could justify the dysfunction we'd endure by becoming a part of Deb and Miles' existence. Theirs was a whirlwind of chaos born of Deb's infidelity.

"How can you even consider it?" Laura asked one day.

I shook my head. Taking Miles up on his offer was not an option. "I don't know. I can't stand the guy."

A week before my twenty-ninth birthday, Dad called. He'd rearranged his schedule to meet me for lunch. My schedule didn't matter, but then it never did when it came to lunch dates with my father. I agreed, as always.

"Gil, you're making a huge mistake," Dad offered, unsolicited.

"No one asked you, Dad," I responded.

"Well, someone's got to point out the obvious. It's an opportunity, son! You have nothing else on the hook right now and Miles is literally handing this to you."

I glared at him. This was his "out" from feeling guilty about leaving me unemployed. I didn't want it to be so easy for him.

"It's not what I want," I said. "And besides, Dad, you hate Miles."

He waved it off. "You don't have any options, son. When a man has no options and a wife who's too stubborn to see a gift horse even when it bites her on the ass…well, you have to take it." He pounded a fist on the table for emphasis.

There was no point arguing. He was right that I had no options. No one stood at my door begging me to come work for them. But my wife insisted that California was not the place for us, and she had her reasons. I knew I had to listen to her. We had our differences but I always knew when Laura was right…and my father was wrong.

I glanced at Dad with a sour look on my face. *You've got to make a choice, Gil. It's your dad or your wife. One or the other…not both.*

I stared into the face that remained indifferent, concerned mostly about what he looked like to others. My well-being was never part of his plans. Still, I wanted to please him and decided to listen to my gut. After all, there really was only one choice to make.

"All right, Dad. I'll call Miles in the morning."

"Atta boy, Gil!" he said and slapped my back, then snatched up the check. I didn't have the money to pay for lunch anyway, so I didn't argue. Instead, I went straight home and dialed my brother-in-law.

You're acting in desperation…a most desperate act. I rubbed the place on my chest that suddenly burned again. *Do you really have such dire need for a new start in a new place? Are you really willing to move ahead, with or without your wife?*

"But it will mean more to my dad if I do. He advised me to go for it," I said aloud.

You're cashing in all your chips on a bad hand: your dad. Are you sure you want to do this? Choose him over Laura?

I shook the thought from my head as the voice on the other end answered.

"Hello, Miles, this is Gil and I'd like to talk to you about coming out to California..."

———◆———

Laura and I were over. I kept to my code of ethics, my *modus operandi*...and ran. Deep inside, I looked over my shoulder, hoping to see her close at my heels, but my family pattern had been well established. Get married, betray your spouse, and have Dad drive you to JFK to hop a flight to Los Angeles...and of course, get divorced.

You've succumbed to the one thing that we both hated most, the one thing that put your life on a crash course to despair, the very thing we both resented your parents and sister for doing.

As the plane backed out of the gate to begin its journey, I glanced down at the flight magazine and tried to ignore the sting of truth from the voice inside my head.

You chose your dad over your wife? Why would you do that, Gil? This decision is another nail in that coffin you keep building for yourself, all because you want to please your dad so badly.

My eyes stared blankly at the page. "I know, I know," I said softly, rationalizing that we had no kids so there really was no harm done.

But you're following in your father's footsteps. You've betrayed your own values and made a choice to be disloyal to Laura.

"I've done the one thing I swore I would never do," I whispered. The man sitting next to me gave me a dirty look. I guess he wasn't used to people who whispered to themselves, even when it was for a good reason. I looked up at him and shrugged.

"I'm getting a divorce."

"Congratulations," he said and turned away.

As the plane sped down the runway, I looked out the window at New York growing small in the distance. I remembered the Little League baseball game I had stopped to watch for a few minutes while walking through Central Park just the other day. There was a message in that for me, but somehow I ignored it.

You did ignore it and the symbolism was clear as a cloudless day. How could you not see its meaning for you, Gil? As the plane turned into the sun, I thought back to that sunny day only a week ago.

"He's out," someone said from the sidelines.

"Not moving," another observation sounded from deep within the crowd. The concern in their voices was palpable. Murmurs accompanied pointed fingers and bug-eyed stares at the injured ten-year-old on the field. Faces froze, filled with horror.

Hitting the batter with a pitch was something kids learned from watching the professionals. But there was always a fine line between a direct hit meant to intimidate and the impact that caused a serious trauma. Oftentimes, that line wasn't recognized and was easily crossed and then it was too late; the damage had been done.

The kid lay still on the ground. His limp hands spread outward, matching sprawled legs in a perfect spread-eagle. His immobility was creepy. As if holding still would somehow make the situation better, no one in the stands moved. This kid was in trouble and everyone waited—waited to see if he would prove the gut impression wrong.

Just then, a lithe female bounced onto the field, one hand raised in the air signifying a God-given permission to speak with authority. Her ponytail recoiled against her back as she jogged toward the motionless kid.

"I'm a nurse. I'm a nurse," she announced, as if that would make everything better.

A few onlookers shifted their weight. This didn't look promising. Moving two steps closer to the bubbly medical "expert," a man wearing jeans and a black T-shirt stepped forward to listen.

"Okay, okay. The nurse has this," someone stated, crouched near the kid. No one knew who he was either.

"We have to move him," she said and began waving her hands to call the oglers forward.

"Wait!"

The voice of the guy in the T-shirt reverberated, and the cluster of people and bodies instantly froze. The kid remained where he was for another moment, eyes closed, limbs sprawled. Blue eyes glared as the nurse stared up at the guy in the T-shirt.

"We *have* to move him off the field!"

He studied her for a moment. "Well, we're not moving this patient anywhere, not without a board and cervical stabilization." He knelt down next to the kid and began examining the little boy's eyes. "I'm an ER doc. We need to call 911 and do this the right way, for his sake." He glanced over his shoulder at the nurse, who had taken a few steps back, her eyes the size of sand dollars. "What kind of nurse did you say you are?"

She swallowed and whispered, "I work for a dermatologist."

Nothing more was said as she slipped out of the crowd and likely left the stadium. Medics were dispatched. From the gossip that followed, the kid suffered a mild concussion that kept him home from school and out of team sports for at least six weeks.

Just then, the stewardess made an announcement and I snapped out of my daydream. There was a strong message for me that day; perhaps the "experts" really aren't. Perhaps those who voice too loudly their opinions to interject a narrow view into someone else's life are to be avoided. Perhaps I shouldn't have taken my dad's advice and gotten on this plane.

That memory lingers when I think of his bad advice given for the wrong reason, even when given under innocent pretenses. The most important role the so-called nurse played in her own mind was as the hero, something she had hoped others would have remembered too, but with little thought given afterward to the young kid or her ability to offer adequate assistance. It was all about *her* in that moment. Her deficit of skill was irrelevant, as was the potential to cause harm with the wrong decision. Serious consequences in order to be a hero.

Dad didn't wear a ponytail but his intent was the same.

Decisions can be that way, and the innocent are usually the victims of a less-than-moral objective. I learned this early on but never seemed to recognize it until after that fine line had been crossed.

CHAPTER 21

———◆———

THE BRICK SHATTERED HIS CHEEK, transforming the truck driver's face into a pulpy mush. Ten seconds later, the scene changed as another brick tore through a large plate-glass window, shattering it into tiny pieces that rained on a local Los Angeles street. Fire exploded in a building and seconds later, the newscaster announced, "...the California National Guard was called in to help assist police. Apparently they failed to reach the city in time..."

This was the city I had chosen, the place I landed in the day before, where I was going to make my new start. *What have I done?* The question surfaced over and over again as I watched the live news feed of the Los Angeles riots on TV. *Surely this can't be for real.* I couldn't peel my eyes away as I watched for the next four days while Los Angeles heaved, imploding upon itself, destroyed from the inside by its own citizens.

Welcome to Los Angeles, City of Angels. No shit! People are dying everywhere in this city and they put it on TV for the rest of America to watch!

I knew in that moment that Laura had been right. She had made the call and I had refused to listen to her.

"Uncle Gil," the tiny voice called from behind my chair. I quickly snapped off the TV so her innocent eyes wouldn't see the angry rioters.

"What, sweetie?" I answered and spun in my chair.

Blonde curls the color of honey bounced as Jessica skipped up to where I sat. Her arms were stuffed with a fluffy giraffe nearly twice her size.

"Sugar wants to play with you," she said and pushed the giraffe into my face.

"Okay, okay," I said, laughing, and slid to the floor.

For the next twenty minutes, I was transported into a magical jungle filled with fairies, dragons, and giraffes. Sugar twisted and swayed as Jessica lifted her stuffed giraffe high in the air on the back of an imaginary dragon, then plummeted it straight for my back, which had fairy wings, I was told.

The outer reality of life was lost in the moment as I played on the floor with Deb's little girl. She had four children now, and all of them loved their time with "Uncle Gil," a title I wore with pride. I found joy with my nieces and nephew. I wondered what my father's life would have been like if he had spent that kind of time with me. Maybe this was the family I had always craved?

Miles hadn't changed much since the first day I'd met him, but he was decent to me. I had taken up residency in his house, so the decision to tolerate my sister's husband was easily made. Family time was precious and I wasn't going to allow his personality quirks to get in the way.

Deb and Miles lived an extremely lavish lifestyle, a clear sign that Miles had become very successful financially. Located in prestigious Beverly Hills, their house was unbelievable. Artwork valued at a price simply stated as "several million dollars" hung on every wall. Imported Italian marble floors supported a collection of antique kaleidoscopes, their appraised value more than most homeowners' lifetime collection of houses. Top-of-the-line cars filled the garage, with extra cars kept at the ready. Two Mercedes and a Porsche Carrera were parked snugly alongside a private jet housed in an airport hangar.

I'd never seen such extravagance and began to wonder if this was how everyone lived in southern California. The maid interrupted my thoughts as she brought a rich assortment of cheeses and chocolates to an ornate sideboard set alongside the dining room wall. I watched her move gracefully around the room, dusting rare collectibles and adjusting knickknacks. The bulk of her sixty-hour week was spent cleaning Deb's massive home.

Independent artists were brought in to paint the children's bedrooms while four full-time nannies minded them, one for each child. I was fascinated by the attention each child received from a dedicated adult, even if it wasn't the parent. That was something I'd never experienced. I thought of how precious just a few minutes alone with my dad would have been. *He was too busy, Gil.* The voice in my head was right. Dad never would have found time like that for me.

Winter weekends were spent in the house in Vail where Miles and Deb skied with their kids. They thought the locals fawned over them as though they were celebrities, but in reality, they saw them as a payday. Once in a while, I'd peek through Deb's office door and see her sitting behind the elaborate mahogany desk, talking on the phone. She'd smile and wave but I never could figure out what she did there. An enormous staff managed the home here as well. In addition to the nannies, the kids had individual all-day ski instructors. Sven waxed everyone's skis. Elise made certain the parkas and hats matched the skis. The list went on and the ostentatiousness and snobbery was embarrassing at times.

Miles was never around so I had the honor of doling out piggyback rides, deciphering New Math homework, and cheering from the stands at soccer games. Through it all, my account overflowed with bedtime hugs and "thh-ank you's" from little people who could barely say their "th's," spoken as they were through gaping holes where baby teeth once lodged.

Miles owned a low-income housing real estate development company, a sharp contrast to the luxury estate he called home. In order to build properties, he secured federal and state tax credits and then sold them to investors. While there were bigger public companies doing this, Miles was the largest private company in the country to raise cash for developments in this way.

"It's compact, affordable housing without the high-pressure sales pitch those other guys give 'em," he said to me one day. My title of

Wholesaler did nothing to bring me anywhere near the image that Miles had managed to create for himself. He was the 'poor man's do-gooder,' a real estate icon that provided housing to the poor.

I was just happy to have a job and a home filled with family. Surrounded by such joys, I considered myself a wealthy man. In spite of these "riches," I still had difficulty making friends. *You've just got to get out there and meet people, stop hiding behind your emotions. No one likes a grown man who is as shy as a seven-year-old.* The voice in my head was relentless but I couldn't muster the courage to do anything about it, so I went to work and returned home to hide, inside my sister's estate with my nieces and nephew as companions.

"There's a letter here for you, Miles," Deb announced one day. She carried a stack of envelopes in one hand, turning a larger, certified letter over in the other. The green sticker stood out against the white paper as she moved it back and forth.

"Who's it from?" he shouted from the next room.

"It says The United States Attorney's Office on the return address. I had to sign for it," she answered.

I glanced up from where I was sitting in the studio and saw the black, block letters written on the upper left corner. The fact that the letter had been sent certified mail was not a good sign, I guessed. Miles walked into the room just then and took the letter from Deb. My eyes remained glued on him as he tore into the top of the envelope with a bronze letter opener in the shape of a broadsword.

He peered inside and his face went white. The "target letter" had come from the United States Attorney's office.

"It means I'm a target of an investigation." He threw the letter on the table.

"Why in the world is anyone investigating you?" Deb asked, picking the envelope up and eyeing the return address again.

"The Federal Bureau of Investigation."

She stared at him blankly. I swallowed and tried to appear smaller than my six-foot frame allowed.

"The FBI," he said.

"I know who it is," Deb finally answered. "Why would the FBI make you a target of an investigation, Miles?"

"I don't know," he said, and I could tell it was a lie.

After that, we parted ways for the night. I wondered if "parting ways" would be my future now that the FBI was after Miles.

Too soon, we found out that he faced prosecution for fraud, embezzlement, and commingling of company funds. To say it simply, Miles was a crook. In spite of his countless denials of the accusations, the moment I saw that "target letter," I knew he was as crooked as the day is long. I also knew I was in trouble if I continued to work there.

The next day I went out and found a good attorney.

"I don't think you'll have anything to worry about, Gil," he said, seated across a well-worn conference table. He wore a designer suit with a cinnamon-red tie that lay easily against his white, starched shirt. The guy was dynamic. I scanned my own khakis and blue polo shirt and realized he was the attorney I needed, in spite of his fees.

"That's a relief," I answered.

"The timeline doesn't fit your starting date. According to the complaint, Miles is alleged to have committed these acts for years before you went to work at his company."

"I wasn't even in California then. I got here six months ago."

He nodded and smiled, a toothy grin that exposed teeth too white for the black coffee he had sitting in front of him. I suspected my attorney didn't skimp on any cosmetic enhancements he deemed necessary for his professional appearance. That was fine with me. He exuded power.

"I want to keep my job," I said, cutting to the chase.

"The issue isn't keeping your job, Gil," he said, resting both hands on the table. "The issue is keeping you out of jail if you were to stay."

My eyes must have gone vacant, mirroring the voice that suddenly went mute. He took my silence as proof his comment had hit home and exposed his teeth once again in a smile that I knew had been well practiced.

"It's like this, Gil. You need to get as far away from this company as possible. Resign before you're forced out when an indictment occurs, which it most certainly will, and cut your losses now."

Our meeting ended soon after that, my head spinning with empty options and no idea what to do next. I called my sister.

"Deb, this is serious," I said, trying to sound as direct as my attorney.

"I know it is, Gil. You're not telling me anything new and I'm doing everything in my power to keep it together, so give me a break," she snapped.

For the next twenty minutes, she explained how it had all been a setup, that Miles was completely innocent and the corporate hierarchy simply picked him as their fall guy. By the time I walked through the front door of Deb's house, I'd made her believe I'd bought her story lock, stock, and barrel.

She met me in the entryway, hands on hips.

"Besides, Gil," she continued as if the conversation had never shifted from phone to in person. "If you leave now, it'll make Miles look guilty. How could you do that to us, after everything we've done for you?"

"I...I..."

"You cannot bail out on us during our time of need and leave the impression that he did something wrong. You simply can't do that!"

I did not want to lose my sister. Tears softened her ultimatums but I knew what stood behind the words. She was the only family member left in my life and I couldn't squander our relationship after so many years of separation. I decided the only recourse available was to continue to work for Miles. After all, I hadn't done anything wrong. I did need some space though, so I moved out of Miles and Deb's home and into an apartment near the marina.

Within weeks, I was promoted to a high-level position in the company.

Does Miles really think I don't know what he's trying to do to me?

My rise to the top of the corporate ladder accompanied massive scrutiny going on daily within the office walls. The investigation extended lengthy arms throughout the company. Change within the company had taken on steam and was about to explode. I was constantly doing a two-step to stay on the right side of the line.

Deb was also hard at work to keep me in place. She put her networking skills into overdrive at the temple. Soon enough, Stephanie and I had gone from the blind date that the rabbi's secretary had orchestrated into an intimate relationship. It was obvious that I needed to keep her in the dark about what was going on at my brother-in-law's company. Nevertheless, Stephanie was Laura all over again: the nice Jewish girl designated for me and with whom I had tons of fun, but didn't trust enough to share my secrets.

At that point, I caught Miles in a bold-faced lie. He was cheating on Debra with a female pilot he hired to fly his private plane with a 36-24-36 resume and hours to match her flight time. He thought nothing of criminal behavior, and I suppose adultery was the least of his worries.

My world bled ugly colors once again. I was swimming in the middle of a giant cesspool without a life preserver and I was about to get sucked down the drain.

And then, two months after Miles received the target letter, I received the phone call: the FBI wanted to speak with me.

———◆———

You need to cooperate with them if you're going to continue to work there. And you need to work there to still have Debra, your only chance to have a family. I knew what the voice in my head said was true, and I was scared. What would become of my family, my job, my life, if I shifted gears and became a snitch for the FBI? I hadn't done anything wrong. I knew that taking the honest approach would preserve my innocence, but it would also mean disloyalty to my sister. A crossroads had appeared and both thoroughfares were muddy and unpaved.

I found a path that would allow me to live with myself, not lose my sister, and actually squeeze something good out of this mess for her and the kids. It had a lie as its first step.

"Ed and Susan are meeting with the contractor in Minneapolis." The falsehood wasn't too difficult to spit out and Miles bought it. I suppose when someone is under investigation by the Feds, that person tends to be a little conservative about whom they trust because they definitely don't trust the "good guys"—the FBI. My lie was easy to deliver *and* easy to swallow, apparently.

In fact, Ed and Susan, two of Miles' most senior employees, were in Minneapolis (the truth) but not on business (the lie). A few employees had been called in to testify at a grand jury nearly halfway across the country. The case had snowballed against Miles, and he had no idea just how big it had grown. Information that was kept private, details I had about Miles's personal life and habits as well as his behavioral patterns, were transmitted to the FBI. I was privy to only pieces of the investigation. I felt as though I had been swept through a time warp into a bad "B" movie.

"Sit there, Gil. We need you there in case we need clarification," the suit said. I parked myself on the edge of a stained side chair in one corner of the seedy hotel room near the airport.

"It seems that he paid some of his employees handsomely."

"Yes, while some contractors and tradespeople never received their checks," the other suit said, crossing the room. "It looks convenient that the money from their paychecks ended up in an unknown bank account."

"Right, one that Mr. Fischer seemed to have access to," the first suit said, and he began riffling through a stack of papers lying on the table.

"Impressive that he got away with it for so long. Do you think his wife…what's her name again?"

"Deb," I piped in. "Debra."

They both glanced up at me, apparently having forgotten I was still in the cramped hotel room they had turned into investigation headquarters.

"Thank you, Gil. Debra," the first suit said, and he smiled. "What do you know of Debra's involvement? She's your sister, right?"

He straightened the stack of papers and laid them back down on the table. I eyed him for a moment before speaking.

"Debra *is* my sister and she didn't know anything about what Miles was doing. Neither did I. He was a pro at conning everyone in his life, including family."

The suits both nodded, apparently comfortable with my answer. We went on like this for a while. I almost expected someone to hold a spotlight on me while a faceless voice interrogated me for hours on end. But that never happened. Instead, they discussed the case, occasionally glancing my way and saying something like, "Isn't that right, Gil?" or, "Is that how it went down, Gil?" I would generally nod in the affirmative, except when it came to my sister's involvement. She really had no idea what the creep she was married to had been doing throughout their entire marriage. She was a victim, just like me.

We concluded our meeting that afternoon and as we walked out of the hotel, I overheard one of the agents casually state, "This guy's life is a made-for-TV movie." I couldn't have agreed with him more.

Surprisingly, I began to find new confidence as a snitch for the FBI. My life had been loosely woven together with secrets and guilt. Somehow, it became cathartic to expose the dark deceit of a scumbag whose sole design was to hurt someone I cared about. There was no question in my mind. Deb and her children would not fall prey to this con artist any longer. The FBI would make certain that he got his just dues and I would help them, protecting my sister and her kids in the process.

"My goal is to protect the company…and you," I said to Deb one morning after Miles had left the house. I had come by for coffee before work but the clock had my attention as I had to get to a meeting of investors trying to force a sale of the company. Although Miles had always made money for his investors, they sensed that where there was smoke with him—the investigation—there would be fire. The distraction did not help with our conversation. "If investors lose their money or the company falls apart, it's not good for anyone."

I wasn't sure she believed me, but I was resolute. There were forces beyond my actions that would save whatever was left of the company. She didn't understand the mechanics, but I hoped she would trust what I was saying. In reality, Deb had no idea I was working with the FBI, which was the only way I could pull off helping her. It was another secret, another dark fact to keep hidden from her.

"I hope you're right." She dropped her head into her hands.

"There will be a small piece of the reborn company set aside for you. I promise you won't be left with nothing…and four kids to raise. I promise I'll do everything in my power to protect you and the kids."

She thanked me and we parted ways for that day, Deb to the latest exercise craze and me to my purpose.

———◆———

For the next year and a half, we continued this way. I worked hard to keep the seams of the company from splitting apart and reassured Deb that she wouldn't be left homeless when this was all over.

My life was now filled with even bigger secrets, and I was drowning. I needed to do something about the stress that was building or something would give. There was only one option left.

I told another lie.

"I've got to get away for a few days. Everything is getting to me and I need to clear my mind," I announced to Deb and Miles one Tuesday evening.

"Well, that makes sense, Gil. You've been under a lot of pressure too," Deb said, sipping from her glass. Miles sat across the room, enmeshed in his thoughts, drowning reason with scotch and water.

"Yeah, whatever you need to do, buddy," he slurred and polished off another glass.

"Where will you be going?" Deb asked.

"Mexico," I lied. I don't know why I said Mexico but it slid out easily and seemed to work. Deb nodded.

"I'll only be gone for a few days."

"Okay then," Miles said, and the conversation was over.

Two days later, I boarded a plane for New York.

CHAPTER 22

———◆———

THE DAY WAS BRIGHT AND filled with hope as I stepped out of the plane. New York had a bite to the air, even in late spring. I inhaled deeply as I made my way through the airport and onto the curb where I hailed a cab that drove me straight to my father.

"I need your advice," I said. "I'm drowning here, Dad. I'm in way over my head."

He stared at me blankly and shrugged his shoulders. "I've got nothin' for ya, Gil. He's a crook and is going to do time. That's it. Plain and simple."

"Dad," I pushed, "I'm still working for the company. I'm working for the FBI. Deb's stuck in the middle, with nothing except whatever I can squeeze out of this mess for her. I think Miles is bugging my apartment and my car. I'm alone out there with nobody to talk to."

He shrugged again. "She'll land on her feet, as she always does."

I stared at him. Deb truly was just like Dad, always coming out on top and smelling good.

"What would you do?" I asked, hoping this new direction would engage him.

"Nothin'. It's gonna be up to the judge now. Miles is headed for the slammer and Deb's got to make the best of it, raise those kids, and hope they don't turn out like their father."

I stared at him. *What a waste of time this has been.*

"That's it? That's all you're going to say?" I couldn't believe he could be so cold. He knew this was more than I could handle, that my life would probably fall apart again at some point.

Once again, I'm screaming out for help and all he can do is talk about Deb.

"There's nothin' else to say about it, Gil."

End of story. And for another full year, I was left carrying a heavy load, drowning in a sea of corruption without a life preserver.

I made a trip back to New York the following May to finish up with some dangling divorce matters that still hung between Laura and me. It happened to be my birthday that week and I had plans to celebrate. I awoke that morning to a steaming cup of coffee and the New York cityscape spread before me. The hotel had delivered a complimentary copy of the *New York Times* that I carried out to the balcony, placing it on the tiny table next to my coffee cup. It wasn't a bad morning to turn thirty-one, and I smiled in spite of myself. I stretched, took in the scenery for a moment, and then sipped my coffee. For some reason, it tasted particularly good. Taking up the newspaper, I opened it to the front page.

There, in bold letters, my birthday greeting displayed itself in black and white:

SCANDAL HITS AS MAJOR FRAUD INDICTMENT IS LEVIED AGAINST
CALIFORNIA BUSINESSMAN

The *Times* could have followed up with "Happy Birthday, Gil" and it wouldn't have shocked me more, or been any less fitting. Miles' name was plastered all over the front page of the *New York Times* and so was my company's, the one I still worked for, with hope for the success of a new company that would rise up from the ashes of the old one.

Two days later, the company was thrown into involuntary bankruptcy. Miles had kept delaying and delaying and ultimately would never sign off on the deal to save the company. Everything I had labored for to help Deb and her kids unraveled at the seams, undone overnight.

As investors turned against Miles, those who once called themselves "friends" immediately turned against my sister. She jumped on the bandwagon and turned against Miles. Of course, this came with filing divorce papers, protesting her innocence to anyone who would listen. That list had few names on it. I watched her rave, surprised that she felt compelled to portray herself as a victim to the point of sainthood. Deb definitely was a victim but she was no saint.

She turned to me in desperation to validate her position. I stayed loyal through our conversations, though I grew weary. I'd heard it before and would hear it again. I had tried to help her, done everything I could think of, but she wanted more from me. I had nothing left to give except the truth. I guessed this was the time to deliver that one last thing.

"Gil, I don't know what to do." Deb's voice came in huffs over the receiver as I grabbed my luggage from the baggage carousel. I could hear her try to stay focused. She inhaled deeply. "There's nothing left. Nothing. I don't know…" Her voice cracked and she broke off.

Thirty minutes later, I was in Deb's kitchen. *You know you have to tell her the truth. It's as painful as ripping a Band-Aid off—hurts for a minute, then it's over.*

"It's not as simple as that," I said out loud.

"I'm sorry?" Deb replied. She turned back to fixing sandwiches for us both. Fortunately, she was distracted and had missed my comment. I decided to change the subject.

"Don't you have anything in the house? Something for a 'rainy day,' so to speak?" That was the wrong thing to say, so I tried levity. "It's pouring now, Deb." It didn't work. I heard her take measures to control her breath.

"No, nothing…maybe three-hundred and fifty dollars and some change in my wallet… I charge everything and the office pays the bills. I have nothing, Gil. Miles managed to leave my name off the investments. I don't even have rights to this house." She waved her arms.

"The courts will consider your and the kids' best interests, as well as the needs of investors. Miles has done some nasty stuff over the years and that's part of what the trial will determine." I waited for her to defend him, but she didn't.

She needed my help.

I sucked in a breath and told her my last secret.

"I've been working with the FBI, Deb," I blurted out, "so I could help you and the kids."

She was silent for a while, processing what I'd just said, so I remained quiet until she decided to speak.

"You've been doing what?"

"I've been an informant for the FBI, but things didn't go as I'd planned. They've had me gather information and share what I know about Miles and his illegal business dealings," I said, trying to be as direct as possible. While I didn't want to hurt Deb, I decided the best course of action was to be honest, for a change. She'd find out sooner or later anyway.

I knew she was crying now. I could hear a soft sob occasionally whenever she took another breath. This was my only blood sibling, my sister. Fatigue washed over me.

She made some pretty selfish decisions when we were little, remember that, Gil? I couldn't fault her for it. She ended up in this mess because she'd never been taught. We were the product of our parents' dysfunction, their divorce, and the choice to solidify our separation as brother and sister sealed it. I did what I had to do.

Overnight, she became a broke, single mother of four children. She was left with nothing, except me. Helping Deb and her kids became my life. From that point on, I would help raise them, go to soccer games, coach basketball, teach them to ride a bike...*they* were my family.

Miles went to trial, was convicted, and was sentenced.

"Twenty-five years in prison," the judge stated, then signed a paper and handed it to the bailiff. "This should stand as a warning to corporate personnel and business executives in general who seek to take financial advantage through fraudulent means."

I sat in the courtroom, stone-faced and spent. Thankfully, I had not been called upon to testify against him, despite the fact that I was on the bailiff's list to do so. They had more than enough evidence against him without the complications his family on the witness stand would create. I placed my palm over my chest and whispered a prayer of thanks that I had been spared testifying against my crooked brother-in-law. The scar stung only slightly.

His penance will be for the duration of his lifetime.

"I know," I said silently to the voice in my head that had awakened and refused to be silent.

What makes it worse is that the money he stole was supposed to provide shelter for people who didn't have any.

"It's the narcissism," I breathed.

It's disgraceful, shaming his wife, children, family, employees, investors, and anyone else who was involved with him. The victims still live with the consequences of his crime. The scar began to burn its familiar fire.

"It doesn't go away."

It most certainly doesn't.

There was silence for a moment, and then I exhaled for the first time in years. I'd been busy taking care of Deb and her kids but who was taking care of me? As I realized that somehow once again Deb would find a way to land on her feet and I'd be left with another secret as to why I was now not working for my wealthy brother-in-law after no longer working for my wealthy father, the voice in my head asked the question I still cannot answer.

Why the hell did you move to LA?

I could only respond with silence and grit my teeth against the pain in my chest. It would all go away, eventually…at least some of it would.

The chair is crumbling, literally falling apart as you sit on it. There's nothing you can do except get your act together and move on.

I could barely listen. It was too painful, the words my gut confirmed as truth.

These people, the ones you trust, the ones you believe in and the ones you love, they're all legs on the chair that you choose to sit upon.

But I didn't choose these people! I was born into the mess they call "family."

Oh yes you did! You chose that chair to sit upon. The music of life plays and plays and when it stops, someone is left standing. You chose the chair because you can't face standing on your own.

Truth.

It's easier for you to remain stuck on a broken chair where it's safe than to venture off, easier to remain with something that is crumbling around you than to be left without a chair.

The pain in my scar exploded.

My old, familiar friend had found me once again.

You can do this!

The voice screamed in my head but I didn't believe what it said. I reached my hand toward the knob but my fingers won't obey.

It's too far...too much to ask!

My shaking hand dropped back down to my side. Beads of sweat surfaced on my forehead but I could not wipe them away. I couldn't do anything but stare. Suddenly, my lungs would not expand. Tiny tubes in my chest sucked air into lungs that would not accept it.

Just breathe.

I heard the command and my chest rose forcibly. You see, that is how it's done: just force everything to happen the way it's supposed to. Take care of everyone and everything else first. And remember, you're disposable.

You know you'll never make it out. You know you're trapped inside this place. You might die here.

I shook my head to silence the voice, but it only laughed at me. My breathing continued, faster and with greater force than before, but it still didn't feel right and my head began to swim. I lifted my hand again, this time to my chest where an invisible scar screamed the truth at me—about me. Sweat fell to my wrist as it dripped from my cheek. My other hand wiped my forehead with the back of my sleeve to prevent another unwanted spill of my anxiety. In spite of everything, the expanse widened and I could hear my heart pounding in both ears.

You know you'll never do it. You'll just die instead.

I refused to let this beat me, so I urged my feet to move. First, one step, then the other. I'd moved forward at least two inches, but it wasn't enough. The expanse still overwhelmed. My heartbeat quickened and the air became heavier.

You're not going to make it.

The voice was right all along. Perhaps I would die here. Perhaps this was my destiny all along. My eyes shifted and I blinked back the tears that surfaced. I caught a glimpse of a man out of the corner of my eye. He was frozen, unable to move, a worthless effort to make something of himself. I turned my head to stare at him and he did the same. Our eyes met and I saw sorrow embedded in them. But it's not a man, it's a little boy that I see.

Life doesn't always make sense when you're seven. I went through experiences no child should ever endure. How does a kid face his peers when he can barely face himself? Alone and withdrawn, all I could think about was disappearing from the world. No one was around to shore me up and share the burdens I carried, not then, not now.

The child in the mirror shifted his weight.

Nobody had ever stood up for or protected me. My childlike needs existed, but my parents didn't.

At an age when I shouldn't have had a care in the world, I already had too many. Too ashamed to present my true self to the world, I hid in plain sight. I was still doing it. With my true self as big a secret as one of the many diverse secrets I kept. Protecting the people in the periphery of my existence was the only way I knew to survive. Little did I know then, a course had been set and a lifetime of secrets had officially begun.

I said nothing but stared at myself in the mirror. Indeed, there was sorrow there, sorrow for having failed another day, sorrow for being here in the first place. I blinked the tears away and the boy in the mirror did the same. Was this the culmination of my life? Was I looking at the best I would ever be? My image shook his head.

My father had severed the ties that kept my existence safe. He couldn't take a bullet to protect his family when he was the one behind the trigger. Neglect was my mother's parenting mantra, yet she was afraid I might leave her like my father and sister had. Preventing that was paramount. Blinded by her need to be with a man, she failed to realize when things went awry. That myopic view filtered my own perception of what was "normal" and what was not.

You'll never be normal, not ever, Gil. You'd best accept it as truth.

I turned my face from the boy in the mirror. I couldn't stand to look at him, couldn't bear it, actually. He whispered to me, *"Children learn to identify through their parents."*

Was he actually talking to me? I looked at him again. He stood there, helpless, pleading for me to do something. I knew I couldn't.

"It's not my fault," I whispered back. The boy's eyes spilled tears and he stared back at me.

My parents' divorce had robbed me of security and had left me feeling unsure about my place in the world. I still felt a deep shame that I wasn't a good enough son.

"You're not defective," I said. But I knew the boy had grown up feeling just that. The pool that had filled my already saturated lack of self-worth was overflowing now, and fast. The image of inadequacy that I added to it was rendered as well. I was still the wimpy kid—the kid who didn't make friends easily, the one who was bullied, this time by my father.

I stared at the bruises on the little boy's arms. He covered one with his other hand but his eyes never left mine. Things hadn't changed as I'd aged. I could see that then as I could now, that my new family dynamic made things worse.

Family dysfunction will continue to be the catalyst forcing an otherwise highly intelligent man to live in a state of paralysis, surviving in fear, impacting education, career, and relationships.

The voice in my head spoke the truth. Or was it the boy's voice? I could no longer tell the difference.

By far, yours is not the worst life ever, but it's the worst one for you—a gentle and tortured soul, uneasy in the conflict divorce has brought at every stage of your life. Each time, you get through bizarre situations a little worse for wear. Every time you get close to fitting in, the actions of those you should be able to trust the most knock you back down.

"It's true," I said and wiped the tears from my eyes. The boy in the mirror had mutated into the man I had seen before, and he cried with me. "I'm not like the others in my family who always land on their feet. I am unable to manage the pain of scars that will never fully heal."

You continue time and again to paddle out of your own personal quicksand.

"I find my self-worth in doing for others and never learn to do for myself," I said, sniffing.

Bingo!

I couldn't refute the voices in my head. Surely there were two: the man in the mirror and the little boy who still suffered. Once again, just as I was the only one of my mother or father's kids to have to negotiate two parents, I was the only one living in two worlds.

You're haunted by what you aren't and you'll never fully develop confidence and self-worth to live a full life of achievement.

That was the man's voice, but the child's quickly cut it off.

Those causing the pain are often the people I need for support.

"Divorce leaves victims behind who pay a price that therapy or pills don't always heal." I was beginning to understand. The man's face still looked helpless. Life was not a dress rehearsal. Scarred for life can last a lifetime!

175

Try…just once more.

Much was expected of my generation of Jewish New Yorkers. I couldn't do it anymore. I knew it then, as a child, but refused to admit it. I was merely the collateral damage on the road of my father's life. He got all that he wanted, and I got none of what I needed. Resilience is being able to return to the shape you were once in. I never got to be in a shape to begin with.

The music had begun to play, the kind that sings out when kids play Musical Chairs. I cupped my hands over my ears, unable to hear it.

It's not always musical when families are torn apart and blended, is it?

I didn't know who was talking this time.

"Stop it! Stop!"

Pushing, shoving, scrambling for position in a new family always leaves someone out. You, Gil. Think about it. As parents invest time in the new spouse's kids, more than their own, it happens subtly. Someone else is with their kids more than they are.

"People think stepfamilies are cool and fun, and they can be, for beneficiaries," I said. The music still played and my hands remained tightly held against my ears. The voice wasn't silent, though. It tortured me, still.

Here's the problem, though. Many times, these families occur at someone's expense.

The voice snapped my focus away from the mirror. I had to leave. I would certainly die there, alone, unchanged, a little boy suffering as a grown man. I stared at the doorknob once again and noticed the expanse was deeper. I would never make it. My hand left the side of my head and drifted toward the brass knob, but I could not make my feet follow. The realization that I wasn't going anywhere broke my soul deep inside, and my knees buckled.

I buried my face in my hands and allowed the grief to rise once more.

You're a failure and you know it. You'll never make it outside. You'll never leave. You're a prisoner in your own life.

"Stop it." The words choked me as they passed through my throat. "Please stop."

Yet, I knew there was truth to what the voices said. I was a casualty of my own fate, unable to function in the world. It was true; I would never be more than what I saw in the mirror—a tortured child trapped in an adult male's body.

I surrendered once more to what I had become and my body curled into that ball on the floor. This was where I would be for the rest of my life. This was my destiny.

"Once, I had a life in spite of you," I gasped.

PART TWO

CHAPTER 23

———◆———

DESTINY HAS A WAY OF putting two unsuspecting people on a collision course aimed directly at a cataclysm. Roller coasters do too. They ease out from the starting gate, not knowing where the next hill or drop will come. I love roller coasters, even though I fear the unexpected. That's sort of how I met Sandi.

I started the day leaving the security of home, unsure of what the highs or lows might be. Anticipation fueled that morning and hope was its companion. Something great was about to take place, and I could feel it.

The sun blinked through a cloud-speckled sky as I strapped on my rollerblades. Countless tan bodies strolled or skated along the sidewalk, the pavement illuminated to alabaster in the sunlight in stark contrast to the deeply bronzed skin of people employing it.

My eyes were drawn to the magnificence of the blue ocean just beyond. Venice Beach, where I was now living, was crowded with people, and yet the sparkle of the water blanketed the entire scene with serenity.

"Oh!"

Her voice was gentle though shaken. I hadn't seen her coming straight toward me and our bodies collided.

"I'm so sorry," I said and offered my hand to help her up. "I didn't see you."

"That's okay." She whimpered slightly, accepting my hand. "I guess I didn't see you either."

She stood upright and our eyes met. I couldn't prevent the smile that made its way across my face.

"My name is Sandi."

STOP! It's another lie. Why do you tell it this way?

I shook my head and shrugged. "That's the cover story we tell everybody," I said to no one.

It never happened, not that way at least. I wish that it had, but the truth is sometimes harder to face than romantic kismet that supposedly happens on a summer day at Venice Beach. The truth of our meeting doesn't change fate's role. Somehow, tumultuous events changed both of our lives. An unexplained, unseen, and unsolicited force demanded we meet. We call it Fate.

Call it whatever you'd like, Gil, but it doesn't change the truth. "I know, I know," I said to myself and noticed my fingers rested over my heart.

I dropped my hand, wanting to silence the voice in my head that refused to allow a pleasant illusion. The voice went still and the fantasy faded. In its place rose images of what had really transpired the day I met Sandi.

"Meeting the love of your life in a mental hospital is not the story you want to tell when you're making new friends or you're at your kids' back-to-school night," I said. I had already established the ability to keep secrets. Our meeting had just become the next one, a story kept safely tucked away.

Our chance encounter was indeed a crash. Our lives were both in upheaval. I was on the verge of a nervous breakdown and I knew I needed help. My dad refused to be involved, brushing me off as if my presence in his life was a mere annoyance. I decided the best way to get support would be to check myself into a hospital. I'd always made it a priority to have great insurance, so I was able to go to an upscale hospital, although I had no idea what it would do for me.

The facility took on the appearance of a dormitory with apartments that ran the length of two floors. A central dining area connected to a gathering room for group activities and therapy. Several private offices linked to a larger conference room with a single rectangular oak table. The "residents" were never allowed in this wing of the hospital that was used primarily for physicians and hospital donors. Behind the consultation rooms, located just outside a grand foyer, double French doors opened onto an enclosed garden with patio and tables. Everywhere was silence. A massive twelve-foot wall, hidden by shrubbery meticulously trimmed in the shape of diamonds and phallic symbols, surrounded the entire common area, giving the illusion of privacy. Everyone who visited the gardens knew it was designed to prevent "escapees" from bolting before discharge.

The setting couldn't have been better to meet my future wife.

Because the psychiatric unit held patients who had voluntarily admitted themselves, there were few rules. No lockdown here. The patients were allowed to move about freely, although no one was permitted to leave the grounds. Despite the twelve-foot wall reminding its inhabitants that escape was *verboten*, the facility had a sense of rather relaxed supervision.

I had been assigned to one of the numerous rooms wrapped within the hospital's brick-and-mortar structure. None of the rooms matched the décor created for the public eye. My room was no different. There was a simple twin bed on either side of one room, a basic dresser with a nightstand next to it. Down the hallway, another set of rooms had been remodeled to create a tiny gathering area with a standard television and VCR. Stacks of donated tapes lined a rag-tag bookshelf that desperately needed dusting but never received attention. Rows of folding chairs were scattered around a large sofa and one overstuffed, stained chair. TV trays lined the edge of the wall, one or two still upright from the previous night's activities. A record player sat forgotten in one corner alongside several books with missing covers and curled edges. The room was a haven for patients who sought refuge in its anonymity. I could see that this would be my favorite place.

Mornings found me eating breakfast in the refectory with several other early risers. The food was surprisingly good and mealtimes were nearly as enjoyable as the intervals of solitude I found in the private gathering room. Group therapy took place soon after breakfast was over. Of course, my counselor scheduled a daily session in one of the consultation rooms just before lunch and I would often stroll through the gardens on my way to the dining hall for the second meal of my day, right after he dismissed me.

Afternoons were the day's highlight. "Free time" was awarded to "good patients" who could handle a few hours unsupervised. I fit that category and generally chose to spend midafternoons in the private patient gathering area. Basketball or art therapy provided a diversion from TV and movies. I was decent at basketball and found the sport a welcome relief from my thoughts. Friendly interaction only lasted while patients played games or hung out and disappeared the minute "lights out" was announced, around ten p.m.

Sandi had frequented the hospital many times, but I didn't know that the first time I saw her. She was being admitted as I finished lunch and was headed toward the garden on my way to the gathering room. I paused for a moment and watched as the receptionist checked in her belongings. Sandi's face was peaceful in spite of the tears that she wiped with the back of her hand now and then. I could tell she was there of her own choosing, just as I was, but her anguish was obvious, at least to someone who recognized distress with the slightest change of expression. Reading through a person's façade had quickly become a hobby in my first twenty-four hours at the hospital, and I already prided myself on recognizing countenances before the professionals did. Like everyone else there, this beautiful woman was in torment.

She smiled and signed her name at the bottom of a paper, then pushed it back across the counter. Sandi may have sensed me watching her because she glanced my way just as I darted behind one of the diamond-shaped bushes. She turned back to the receptionist and an orderly named Steve stepped forward, taking her belongings to show her down the hallway. I assumed they were going to her room and decided to follow. Steve had been decent to me when he'd escorted me to my room the day before. I felt that he wouldn't care if I trailed behind.

She was "normal" looking, just like me—different from many other hospital residents. She looked cut straight from central casting for Southern California. She was an athletic, beautiful, beach-blonde with lanky legs and stunning blue eyes.

They turned down the hallway beside the stairwell that led to the female patients' floor. I walked to the base and watched as she disappeared above me, Steve talking to her the entire time as if they had known each other for years. I walked back to the gardens and disappeared into my solitude.

When Sandi walked into the hospital and into my life, everything changed. Most days, we could be found side by side in the garden talking, sharing our struggles, and finding relief in one another's company to soften the severity of our individual pain. Literally every waking minute was spent together. Laughter came easily with Sandi and I found comfort in that because she "got" me. We shared a very similar yet contrasting upbringing.

"You know it's after curfew," one of the nurses said, poking her head into the gathering room.

"Yes," I said smiling.

The nurse didn't seem to mind that we were still up. Sandi snuggled into my shoulder. We talked that night until suddenly she noticed that the moonlight had changed to a glistening amber, the sunrise.

"Come on, let's get out of here," she said, grabbing my hand.

"We can't leave," I said a little confused. I allowed her to pull me down a dark hallway, curious to see what she would do next. "Wait, Sandi...what if we get caught?"

"We won't." She pushed the vertical handle that opened one of the back doors. I half expected an alarm to sound or someone to chase after us, but nothing happened. We slipped outside next to a set of garbage bins and into freedom.

"Coffee's brewing over here," she said, urging me down a side street and into a small café. We ducked inside and ordered our drinks, eyeing each other, truant kids from a psychiatric hospital. It was a secret that I was happy to keep.

"See now, this isn't so bad, is it?" she said, sipping from her steaming cup.

"It's kinda nice, actually," I responded and scooted a little closer to her. She didn't move away. The horizon was bursting with sunlight.

We talked for nearly an hour, sitting on a stone and mortar wall facing the beach. Soon, music began to play and the merry-go-round started to turn.

Sandi's head snapped in the direction of the carousel near the pier. "Come on," she said again, tugging at my arm. "I want to go for a ride."

We made our way to the gate. I handed the attendant two dollars and Sandi scurried onto the carousel decked with colorfully painted horses and sea creatures.

"You're crazy," I laughed, taking a seat on a black racehorse with a blue and gold harness.

"I'm just fun," she said, tossing her head back to laugh without restraint. The white steed she'd chosen fit her. It was ornately painted with detail only noticeable when the carousel stopped. Sandi was the same, detailed and ornate, hidden in a mass of humanity that whirled and spun on a different plane than hers. My heart flooded with emotion as I watched her glide up and down to the rhythm of the tinkling music as we moved together while the rest of the world stirred to a different tune.

"You're fun and crazy—Pi," I said.

She glanced at me sideways. "Pi?"

"Yup, you're not quite a whole number, just 3.14. Pi."

We looked at each other and burst into laughter.

"Pi fits. Not quite whole but still on the number line."

The nickname stuck. Life was bearable for me now; joy had finally found its way into my soul. We got back without a minute to spare. Morning activities began at nine sharp.

Not long after our escape into our coffee and carousel adventure, the doctor approached me to invite me into his office for an impromptu "chat" after lunch one day.

"I understand you've been spending a great deal of time with one of our residents lately, Gil," he said and leaned back in his leather chair.

"Yes," I answered. The hackles rose on the back of my neck. He was about to deliver bad news and I wasn't ready to hear it, particularly if Sandi was involved.

"You know that's not a good idea."

"Why? What's wrong with socializing with the other patients? I thought that was part of the therapy you encourage here."

He looked at me over a pair of narrow bifocals, and I thought he looked a lot like a hawk peering down on its prey.

"That's true. We do encourage socializing with the other residents here...*all* of the residents, not just one in particular." He reached for a paper and glanced at it for a moment.

I remained silent. Defending myself would only dig a hole. Besides, I'd already decided not to be the one who brought Sandi into the conversation. He finished reading his notes and glanced at me again, this time removing his spectacles with one hand.

"Gil, she's bad news."

"Who?"

"You know who. Sandi Haas. She'll bring you nothing but trouble," he said, broaching the topic I'd hoped to avoid. I was surprised when he said her last name, as if he knew the woman who had soothed my heart better than I did.

"I didn't even know her last name," I said, hoping to relieve his suspicions. "We're just friends."

It didn't work. I heard him sigh and click his tongue just before he concluded the warning. "That proves my point. You don't know this girl, but I do, and she'll bring you nothing but trouble. I'm not allowed to say much about her but I can give you a gentle word of caution: stay away from her!"

I left his office angry for the first time. Sandi Haas had a beautiful and winsome spirit. She brought joy and a sense of peace with her. The physician delivered a confrontation that I viewed as a threat. *Not see her...or else what?* The thought enraged me. *We'll see whether I spend time with Sandi Haas or not! You called me out, Dr. Pentleton. Now let's see what happens.*

I ran into Sandi later that afternoon, grateful that I'd had some time to calm down. She immediately sensed something was wrong.

"What? What is it, Gil?" she asked.

"Sit down and I'll explain what just happened," I said and I joined her on the sofa. As gently as possible, I explained what Dr. Pentleton had said about me staying away from her, leaving out the insulting tone he'd used when speaking directly about her.

"I think they're just getting stressed that we're seeing so much of each other. It's against protocols for people to couple up in here, I guess," I said, shrugging.

"The protocols stink and don't make any sense, particularly if we're not hurting anyone else in the process."

"I agree. We can see each other as much as we want, as long as we're keeping the rules." There. I'd said it and she hadn't flinched.

"Well, we did sneak out, Gil. I just don't want to be viewed as a danger to myself...or others...and put in the involuntary ward of this hospital, if you know what I mean. I've been there," she said with a faraway gaze in her eyes.

"Hanging out isn't a sin," I said. "Breaking rules is something different. Neither of us can afford to get caught breaking rules."

"That's not going to happen," she said. "We'll figure a way around it."

I realized this was not Sandi's first stint in the hospital—she knew the ropes. She obviously had a past, but I didn't see that as a reason to think less of her. The doctor's words continued to bother me and I put my hand over my heart to stop it from racing. *Sandi and you are the same.* The voice in my head awoke. *If he's speaking negatively about Sandi, it would be reasonable to think he had the same opinion of you as well. You have to do something, Gil.*

I knew the voice in my head was right. Who was the doctor to tell me what to do? After all, I was an adult who had voluntarily checked myself in for help, not for babysitting services. I wasn't here for a doctor's opinion about my romantic life.

Good job standing up for yourself Gil...but what is really going on with Sandi? We'd spent countless hours talking about our pasts. Did I miss something?

I'd avoided the question, although I couldn't help but wonder, what did the good doctor mean when he said Sandi was "nothing but trouble"?

———◆———

Sandi's mother, Pamela, grew up in a privileged, but tortured, life in sunny California. Her parents divorced when she was young and both soon remarried. Pamela ended up living with her mother and stepfather in an affluent beachfront community. Her inherent bohemian personality conflicted with the debutante lifestyle her mother wanted for her. As a result, eating disorders took over. In Pamela's early twenties, she was engaged to be married to the son of a prominent homebuilder. Her future in-laws soon learned of Pamela's troubles and the marriage never happened.

Pamela then moved near the UCLA campus in Westwood. One day, a salesman knocked on the door. He was from Germany and like most young foreigners, was eager to experience America. He had set his sights on spending time in New York City, but while he was preparing for his trip in mid-winter, he discovered that California's climate might be a little more hospitable. Naturally, he wanted to stay longer than his budget afforded, so he began selling encyclopedias.

Pamela quickly married her foreign door-to-door salesman and moved to his native Germany. Nine months later, Sandi was born. The family rapidly expanded to include Tarrah, a sister for Sandi. When homesickness set in, they decided to return to the US to be closer to Pamela's family. As the dysfunction between his wife and her mother reached new heights, this relatively young man saw his life flash by in front of him and not long after their return to the US, Sandi's father decided to run. The father of two returned to his native home in Germany. It would be many years before Sandi would see him again.

Distressed with her own life, Sandi's mother ran through a series of marriages, apparently seeking the intact family that eluded her over and over again, despite the numerous children being added to her little flock. The pattern was set for Sandi's childhood environment, including a total of five marriages and subsequent divorces, almost every one with new children born to the family.

Sandi grew up bouncing back and forth between her mother's marriages and homes. She moved to California, Germany, New York, Maryland, and Arizona, all before reaching puberty. As the oldest of four daughters fathered by three different men, Sandi took on the role of mother to her three younger sisters—a lot of pressure for a little girl. Added to the dynamics was her mother's constant struggle with suicide.

Sandi's mother was a teacher, nurturing and compassionate for her impressionable kindergarten students, including those who were handicapped, a special assignment she willingly accepted. She won many accolades, but for some reason, she couldn't or didn't share her teaching skills at home.

I listened for hours as Sandi expressed her sadness, feeling that her mother cared more about her students and being a daughter than she did about her own children. Pamela's role was that of teacher and daughter; mother was tertiary in her resume of life skills.

The chaos in Sandi's life seemed to settle a bit when she took up residence with her grandparents. Sandi spent time with them in the aftermath of her mother's suicide attempts as well as during summer breaks. These were, by all appearances, stable people who provided a secure home environment. Sandi eventually lived with them year-round, graduating from high school, and then the University of Southern California (USC). Ironically, her major was psychology.

"I think I was Grandma's opportunity, her second chance to raise a debutante daughter in a wealthy world," she said one day out of the blue.

We had been talking about our youth and the decisions of others that had shaped our lives. I squeezed her hand and kept quiet, hoping she would open up a little more. She did.

"I think I took to my grandparents' lifestyle more than my mother did," she said. "But that's when everything went downhill. I got into drugs and drinking, and the eating disorder came right along with everything else."

I had a general understanding about the drugs and alcohol but didn't know what to say about the eating disorder, so I offered my silence. It seemed to be the support she needed because the tears began to well and Sandi revealed the darkness that lay inside.

"I was engaged once, Gil," she looked at my face for a reaction. I gave her none. "He was the grandson of the same iconic homebuilder my mother almost married."

"What happened?" I finally asked.

"His family stopped the wedding, imposing their will on my life just as they did on my mother's, treating me just like they did her. They never deserved my mom and they certainly don't deserve me."

"I agree. You're very special and it was definitely their loss, Sandi."

She nodded and tears spilled over her cheeks. I reached up and brushed them off, then kissed the top of her head.

"That's when I tried to kill myself."

Sandi was immediately placed on her first psychiatric hold, a 'fifty-one-fifty,' they call it in the medical field. Simply put, it's an involuntary admission for psychiatric reasons.

Sandi was given a roommate, the granddaughter of the founder and heir to the Avery Candy Company. The roommate's boyfriend was trouble. He would come by and visit too frequently to fit in with hospital policy, and often enough to develop a relationship with the wrong girl. By the time Sandi was released, she and Russell had officially become a couple.

It seemed to me that Russell belonged in the room down the hall, for patients with "inappropriate interaction based on a history of anti-social and borderline personality disorder." I could have diagnosed him myself.

Their relationship continued after her discharge but Sandi's various psychological issues grew worse, along with an escalating substance abuse and another attempted suicide. In desperation, Sandi's mother helped to place her into an eating disorder program at Columbia University Hospital in New York. Unfortunately, it didn't last long. Sandi was promptly kicked out of the program for smoking pot. After that, nobody would take her in, not her mother in New York nor her grandparents in California. Homeless and addicted, she saw no other option but to return to Russell.

By this time, Sandi was a walking pharmacy. She took enormous amounts of medication on a daily basis. Most of the antipsychotic drugs were necessary for normal functioning. Despite her dependency on the medications, Russell convinced her to get off all of them, including birth control.

It wasn't long before Sandi was pregnant. Abortion was never an option, given her grandparents' religious beliefs. Notwithstanding the paralyzing complications of her personal issues, Sandi chose to keep the baby. Subsequently, she married Russell five months into the pregnancy.

When I asked what her marriage was like, she described it with one word: abusive. While she hung on reasonably well for the first year and a half, during which time she'd given birth, things went drastically downhill very quickly, evidenced by several failed suicide attempts and frequent sojourns in local psychiatric hospitals.

Once, shortly after arriving for a visit at her mother's home in New York City, Sandi exchanged pleasantries and handed her one-year old son to a sister. She then turned from them and immediately jumped out a third-story window. Directly in her path, an awning belonging to the local market served as a buffer, catching her body as she plummeted. She experienced major injuries but her life was spared.

For whatever reason, Sandi chose to stay with Russell in California where their chaotic marriage continued its abusive course, splattered with Sandi's additional suicide attempts.

Her last endeavor to receive help came as a voluntarily hospitalization, a rather bold move for Sandi. It was here that fate took hold and placed Sandi in my path.

"Okay, so the cat's out of the bag," I said aloud and began to pace.

CHAPTER 24

——◆——

IT'S COMPLETELY INAPPROPRIATE, GIL, AND you know it.

Why did I ever touch that area lying over my heart today? The voice in my head had been riding my thoughts since the moment I woke up, and it didn't seem ready to quit any time soon, even though it was nearly midday.

A full week had come and gone since my discharge from the psychiatric hospital. I hadn't heard from Sandi and didn't know the best way to contact her. So, I left her to survive alone in that fishbowl called "mental illness." She was safe, at least for the time being, still a resident in the hospital I had just vacated.

"Nothing's happened," I rationalized, knowing I would never win the argument.

Maybe not but she's still married to Russell. That alone makes it improper. You've got more going on with her than just friendship. Admit it!

"You sound boorish and patronizing," I replied, taking the offense. "I never intended to insert myself between Sandi and her husband."

I moved to the window, hoping to distract my thoughts but the voice continued.

Maybe not, but emotionally that's what happened for both of you.

"Even though they haven't divorced yet, she had left Russell mentally before I met her...way before checking into the hospital...our hospital...where we met. How could I know they hadn't divorced yet?"

Clearly, the relationship moved beyond a simple friendship. You're emotionally invested in her now. Falling in love, I would surmise.

He had me there. I grew silent and stared at nothing from the window in my empty one-bedroom apartment in the harbor where I had awakened. I rested my hand back over my heart. It burned there and I could tell the scar was inflamed, even if no one else could see it.

"Please don't say anything more," I whispered.

I don't know why I never concerned myself with Sandi's marital status during our stay in the hospital. I guess there was a part of me—a selfish part—that was okay with becoming involved with a married woman. After all, I'd learned from my father and Debra this was okay!

Really, Gil. It's not your fault. You act on what you know, and thus far in your life, marriage is only an inconvenience when divorce becomes a better option.

"Sandi's marriage was abusive. She spent the whole marriage trying to kill herself!"

Yes, but she is still married.

"I know you're right. I just don't think her erratic behavior reflects what lies in her heart and soul. She's a good person with few coping mechanisms and fewer options," I said, clutching at the pain in my chest.

I'll be still now.

I dropped my hand to my side and felt the tears rise instead. Unbelievably bad things can happen to good people. I'd seen it time and time again in my own life with my own family interactions. Those difficulties are far more complicated than anyone who doesn't experience them directly can understand. I made a vow never to judge anyone.

I understand your reasoning and it's honorable, but Sandi is still a wild card.

"I thought you were going to be quiet, finally," I said, and watched a cat dart across the lawn after an unsuspecting sparrow.

I can't when you're causing yourself such pain. It's my job to help you see reality.

I looked down at the scar on my chest. It was still there; reality was based on individual perception. I couldn't tell whose side the voice in my head was on, really.

"She's an amazing person. I can see that, even though wounds scar the surface."

Of course you can. That's your gift, Gil, your sensitivity to others, to situations that might be unrecognized by those with a coarser spirit.

The cat missed its target and moved off to the cover of a nearby bush, waiting for the next opportunity.

"She checked into the hospital to get away. I knew it even though she didn't admit it. I could sense how closely our histories were linked."

Yet, the differences remained, stark contrasts that taunted the voice in my head the way that bird taunted the cat outside. I wiped my cheek and suddenly, my vision blurred. The cat came into focus and pounced again, this time catching the tiny bird in its claws. I felt the horror at being captured, the same fear that the sparrow must have felt in that same instant.

"She is itching to break free from an ugliness that has its grip on her," I said, and watched the bird struggle.

Neither of you belonged in that institution for many of the same reasons, yet there you both were, voluntary admissions for exactly the same reason… escape from your own demons!

Just as the voice in my head said the word *escape*, the sparrow broke free of the cat's hold. It fluttered for an instant before launching upward, away from the predator's reach.

"That's what forged a bond between us. Both of us are products of our surroundings," I said, and turned from the window.

The voice in my head had no reaction. The cat-and-mouse game of life between Sandi and those who negatively contributed to her behavior created the vise society labeled as "mental illness." I had the same label for the same reasons. I shuddered and walked over to the aquarium in the far corner of the room to watch the ebb and flow of sea creatures.

Yellow tangs and blue striped angelfish moved gracefully across the glass, barely aware that I was observing them from outside their enclosed world. Turtle grass in various lengths swayed and dipped in the water's current, artificially created to mimic the ocean. These creatures thrived, provided someone took care of them. I wondered if I was no different.

Emerging from beneath a craggy coral outcropping, a hermit crab crept across the stone floor and gathered something in its legs. I watched for a moment, wondering if that was the highlight of the crustacean's existence, or if there was more in store. And then, another crab joined it, a blue one with a flatter shell. It moved quicker than the hermit crab, engrossed with its find. Crawling over its mate, the blue crab scurried along the tank glass, perhaps looking for a way out. I was fascinated. Moments later, three additional crabs made their way to where the blue crab scrambled, all of them clamoring for the same outcome, and they were soon entangled with one another. As if on cue, the hermit crab abandoned its item of interest and joined the others in the fray. Suddenly, clusters of saltwater shellfish were engaged in a fight, battling with each other for an unseen goal. One by one, the crabs in the tank clambered over the other, pushing another crab down in an effort to hoist itself up.

I thought of Sandi...and me.

She was at the bottom of a tank, pushed down by those who supposedly loved her. It was clear that her husband was one of them. No one, not her mother, her grandparents, or even the doctors at the hospital, would let her surface for air. The people around her used her as they tried to push themselves upward, just like the crabs, constantly beating her down. These people were suffocating her, and like crabs, refused to let her crawl out of the fish bowl when she wanted to be free. Her only escape came from drugs and alcohol...or death.

I turned from the aquarium and the repulsive crabs held prisoner there. Turning away from the window where I knew a cat waited to pounce on an unsuspecting victim, I walked down the hall to the kitchen and pledged to find a way out for Sandi. I vowed to free us both.

I was unsure what to do.

The next day, there came a knock at my door.

"Sandi!"

She stood in the doorway with suitcases on both sides of her and a duffel bag slung over one shoulder.

"I didn't know where else to go," she said.

"How did you find me?" I was shocked, unable to think as I stared at her on the front stoop, waiting to be invited in.

"I knew from our conversations...I...I looked you up," she stammered. Obviously she was distressed.

"Come in. By all means come in," I said, picking up both suitcases and setting them just inside the foyer.

"Gil, I need a place to stay for a while."

I glanced at her bags and wondered if they contained everything she owned. This was not just a visit. This was a cry for help.

I danced around an answer, stuttering and mumbling, "I gu-es-ss so... I me-a-n, where's all your stuff?"

Her answer came as she turned to look outside at a silver Ford pickup parked at the curb in front of my building. She had come prepared to stay. I didn't know what to do.

This is the last thing you need in your life, Gil.

I knew the voice in my head was right, but someone I cared about needed help. We had our "love at first sight" experience in the hospital and I felt obligated because of it.

You can't seriously consider taking her in.

"Of course, you can stay here," I said.

Gil, Nooo!

———✦———

CHAPTER 25

ORDINARILY, A LOVE RELATIONSHIP STARTS off with a honeymoon phase. Ours was obscure. Even so, we were in love and we couldn't get enough of each other. I knew this was a phase of superficial presentation, showing only the best versions of us to one another. Inevitably, the little flaws and quirks would begin to surface.

Ours was an out of the ordinary relationship from the beginning, though. We met on the psych floor of a hospital, a truly unconventional setting for romance. Our lowest points were the catalysts that caused us to be there, the fuel that fed into our meeting one another. Sandi and I already knew the worst about each other.

Ultimately, the honeymoon phase never really happened. I suppose it was because we understood each other so well. We were an instantly "seasoned" couple. There were no secrets from the get-go and that was refreshing. No secrets...but still a skeleton in a closet.

Sandi was married to Russell...and she had a child. I had a decision to make. Without consulting anyone, I followed my heart and ignored the obvious.

You've made the commitment already, Gil.

So true, another nudge from the voice in my head, but I chose to tune it out this time.

Months would pass before Sandi began to show me her most troubled self. And then one day, my worst fears became reality.

You're getting lost, Gil.

"Stop it! I don't want to hear this!" In truth, I really didn't want to listen. She was important, she needed me, and I wanted to be there for her. I continued to argue with my own judgment. "Finally, here is someone I can see in my life, someone who will stay."

You'll be swept into this woman's pandemonium.

"She wants out of the hole she's dug for herself," I said aloud.

Out of a hole and into a whirlwind of chaos. Is that where you want to be?

I felt the sting across my chest again but refused to acknowledge it. My hand dropped from my heart, and I turned away from the voice in my head.

I thought I was familiar with divorce but I soon found out that hers was not typical. Sandi could not leave her marriage with her child. An attorney's opinion was based on her psychiatric history, a saga that would never allow her to divorce her husband and keep her son by her side.

Sandi's soon-to-be ex-husband, Russell, would allow her to see her son Gabe only within the confines of his home. The tension that had already developed increased as the dynamics of their marriage were revealed. She was mentally ill and Russell had no qualms about using their three-year-old boy as a tool to control Sandi's every move.

Sandi's family did not support their divorce, which was ironic given that they had been adamantly opposed to the marriage in the first place. The rationale for their position was their religion, which eluded all reason, but their money gave them power and influence.

When Russell made the announcement that he was going to kill her, Sandi took a bold step. Surprisingly, she decided on her own that the only option was a restraining order, so she went to the courthouse and got one. Sadly, the opposite occurred when her family's effort to harass Sandi escalated.

I didn't know how to help her.

Fear settled over our relationship, and no matter how hard the police urged her to file a complaint when Russell violated the restraining order, Sandi couldn't do it. Her justification made no sense to me at the time.

"I cannot arrest my son's father," she stated and refused to reconsider.

Not long afterward, she ended up in court. Testimony was given against Sandi, including a recording of the 911 call made less than twelve months previously. The recording was difficult to listen to, but the courts insisted on playing it publically. I sat in the courtroom and heard it for the first time, along with the others:

"Nine-one-one. What is your emergency?"

"I think my girlfriend is in trouble," a female voice said. The recording was scratchy and difficult to hear.

"Where is your girlfriend now?"

Information was exchanged and I recognized the address as Sandi and Russell's home on a crappy side of town. The phone number belonged to her as well. This didn't sound good for Sandi and I felt a familiar vise grab at my gut. Glancing over to where Sandi sat, I saw her back grow rigid as she listened to the recording.

"Please, tell me where she is now."

"She's at home. I just called the house and her little boy answered the phone."

"What did the little boy say that led you to make this call?"

"He's only three so he really doesn't know what's going on. I had a bad feeling. Something's happened. You've got to get someone over here right away."

"I understand, ma'am. We've got patrolmen on their way now."

"It might be too late already…"

"Please calm down, ma'am. Tell me exactly what her little boy said over the phone."

"He said, 'Mommy threw up and now she's sleeping. Daddy's at a baseball game.' I came straight over to her apartment and found her."

"Are you there with her now?"

"Yes. I can't tell if she's breathing."

"Listen very carefully. I want you to put one hand over her chest and watch to see if it rises up and down. Can you do that?"

"Yes."

There was a pause and some shuffling in the background. I assumed Sandi's friend was checking to see if Sandi was breathing. A tiny voice and then a child crying were heard in the background.

"She's breathing, but not very much. There's vomit and shit everywhere!"

"Okay, you say she's breathing?"

"Yes."

"Is that her son I can hear in the background with you?"

"Yes. He's with me. He's okay."

"Good. Keep him close until someone arrives. Is your friend responsive when you speak to her? Have you tried to move her?"

"No."

"Don't move her. The officers should be arriving any moment. Just stay with her and make sure she keeps breathing. I'll stay on the line until they arrive, okay?"

"Yes, okay… Please hurry."

The recording was turned off and testimony continued. It was noted that the friend had called Russell first, asking him to hurry home. Scattered around the bed where Sandi lay unconscious were at least four empty vodka bottles and an array of prescription pills. Testimony was not in her favor.

The hearing ended. Her visitation schedule was arranged and she was allowed two hours of supervised visitation per week. The severity was largely due to the sworn testimony of family and friends, including the 911 recording played during the hearing.

We left in silence. The troubled past Sandi had tried so hard to erase still followed her. I didn't know what to say but offered my support anyway.

Sandi missed her son tremendously. While it was easy to say she deserved what she got, failure to look at *why* she behaved as she did needed to reach beyond the surface.

A few weeks later, Sandi went to spend the weekend with her grandparents. Upon her return Monday afternoon, she told me she had gone to the courthouse that morning and signed away all custody of her son. I looked through the paperwork and saw that she was left with a provision of ten days to rescind her decision.

She's continuing the pattern. It's a function of her family's dysfunction and not being her true self. You know that behavior well, the voice in my head interjected. Maybe so, but I still believed in her and told her I would go to the wall, if needed, to help her find health and gain her son back.

Nine days passed. At the eleventh hour, Sandi changed her mind and rescinded the decision to give up her son. Her family blamed me. In fact, they were furious with me and while they turned on Sandi in the courtroom, their venom with me was intended to hurt. I couldn't understand how the people who had created such chaos in her life could reproduce such a maelstrom for her son…all the while blaming me. She had no one left, no one except me.

———◆———

I had vowed to do everything within my power to make her happy. Sandi's court battles were just beginning, and I couldn't afford an attorney. I needed to come up with another plan, one that didn't cost money. I spent the next several months in law libraries. Before I realized what the hours had done, through default I became Sandi's "attorney." I drafted and filed her legal documents, which was an impressive feat for someone with no legal training.

The saying goes, "Victories are won one battle at a time." Sandi's fight was just that, a daily victory, little by little, coming out the victor in the court battle for her rights as a mother. Her time with Gabe went from two hours of supervised visits a week to four hours, then six, then unsupervised, then an overnight once a week.

I put a tremendous amount of effort into creating the best possible environment for Gabe when he spent the night at our place. Our home was a one-bedroom apartment, so visitors typically took the couch at night. I knew that wasn't acceptable for a little boy so I moved our bedroom furniture into the living room and turned the only available bedroom into his room. He spent only one night a week with his mother, hardly justification to abandon our bedroom. However, I felt that was exactly what should be done. Sandi was appreciative and relieved to have a home environment that would support Gabe's visits. It was a no-brainer for me. I loved Sandi and would do anything for her, which meant doing anything for Gabe.

In spite of her life getting better in so many ways, the court battle continued, taking its toll on everyone and everything in its path, leaving decimated relationships in its wake.

Sandi's thirtieth birthday was around the corner and I decided a party might mend some fences. I invited both of our families. Dynamics proved challenging, particularly the interaction between Sandi's sister Tarrah and my sister Deb. Keeping them apart seemed a better idea than encouraging them to forge a friendship. On their own, both had a way of manipulating us. Together, they'd be unstoppable. The few hours of celebration offered optimism; however, it ultimately didn't provide any new path forward.

I tried to look ahead, but the future appeared bleak and family undercurrents on both sides built up a stew of contention to the point of boiling over. Sandi barely waded through life anyway, so to add the drama wrought by dysfunctional siblings and crippled parental rapport was more than she could handle. I hung in there, clinging to the promise I made to stand by her side.

Then one day she confided in me a secret so foul, even I did not know how to sustain it.

"Russell is raping me."

"He's doing what?" I couldn't believe what I was hearing.

"Well, it's really extortion more than rape," she said, trying to soften the blow. "If I give him sex, he lets me have more time with Gabe."

"What? How long has this been going on, Sandi?" I was incredulous.

I needed to hire an attorney. Her court case had continued without pause, wearing us both down. There were countless hearings and thousands of pages of legal documentation. Her life had been dismantled and dissected by strangers, and all the while, I worked endlessly to be an uplifting positive influence. Through it all, she was being raped.

Her family hurt her in every way possible. Sandi's sister Tarrah took Russell up on his offer of a room in his house, rent-free: his payment, Sandi's pain.

At one court hearing, Sandi passed through throngs of media and walked into the Santa Monica courthouse to see a former football star going through a wrongful death civil lawsuit surrounded by family. His family supported him after a murder; Sandi's family testified against her.

I was the only person who stood up for her, the only one standing up for her son to have equal parents. I understood that Sandi had crossed some major lines as a parent and while nothing condoned her actions, her family's and Russell's treatment of her was at the root of the trouble.

The more I did for Sandi, the more I became the enemy in the eyes of her family. Although I knew I had undermined their control by supporting the rescission of her decision to sign away custody, I was mystified as to what they gained by their stand against me. It was clear that she got healthier when we were together. Perhaps that was the cause of their hatred.

———————

Another year had passed and one evening, I came home to find Sandi sitting on the living room floor. It was her thirty-first birthday. She had phoned her family stating that without their support it was no longer possible to be in each other's lives. The loneliness she felt along with the intensity of the court case brought more stress than she could bear. She was despondent but fortunately, she hadn't tried to end her life…not this time.

Sometimes I would find her passed out, surrounded by empty liquor and pill bottles. It was an uphill battle and I needed help to manage our circumstances. On several such occasions, when I found her passed out on the sofa, I knew it was time to call her psychiatrist. Thankfully, Dr. Parsons guided me through the turmoil in our life, and did so in a manner that didn't harm her court case. There was hope for a light at the end of this very dark tunnel, or so it seemed.

CHAPTER 26

———•———

You can't go home. You can't be the superhero. You can't make it better, not when she's like this.

How could I face the possibility that I would again find her sprawled out, lying unconscious in the middle of an alcohol- and pill-induced coma? It had been six months without an episode like that and I hoped we'd turned a corner. I reached out to grasp the doorknob but couldn't force my hand to take hold of it.

Perhaps this will be the time you won't be able to wake her up. Perhaps she's already dead on the other side of the door right now.

"Those are ugly thoughts," I said aloud, happy to hear my own voice echo back within the confines of the small entryway.

You will be responsible.

Sandi's family would hold me accountable for her death. Even with the many nights I stayed awake, tallying each breath to make sure the count didn't stop, even with all of that, in their eyes I would be responsible if she died.

I shook out my hand and attempted the doorknob again. I really did not know what waited on the other side for me. I didn't know if I could face it…not this night. I was so tired and needed that "chair" to be sturdy, available, and waiting for me. I took hold of the knob, but couldn't force it to turn. I stood there, paralyzed with fear.

You're on your own.

"Maybe so but I'm all she's got," I said again and successfully twisted the knob. This time my hand obeyed and the mechanism gave way. I heard the familiar click as the front door swung open on protesting hinges. My feet wouldn't move. I glanced down at them as if doing so would give a clue as to why.

She's stalked celebrities, remember? You had to bail her out of trouble when she worked at the bookstore because of it. Your family won't tolerate behavior like that, even if you do.

"This isn't about tolerance! It's about kindness and understanding, compassion, which apparently you know nothing about," I nearly shouted and hoped my neighbors hadn't heard.

Compassion doesn't look like a lifeline, Gil. It's not your job to rescue every drowning victim in the sea of sociopathic illness. You're barely staying afloat yourself!

"I can't let her drown. I can't stand by and watch her self-destruct. She's better when she's with me, healthier. I make a difference. I see that when I'm with her."

Do you really think so?

I couldn't answer.

But at what cost, Gil? Think about that before you do anything you'll regret.

Indeed, my family wanted nothing to do with Sandi, so we were on our own. We had no support and nobody to turn to.

Maybe so, but she doesn't believe it. Even though she is stunning on the outside, she can't believe that anyone could love someone like her, want to help her for nothing in return.

"Sandi," I called out through the crack in the door.

I heard shuffling inside the house and hoped it was a good sign. Less than a year earlier, I'd heard the same type of shuffling and found Sandi in the bathroom. She'd apparently been to a clinic. The pregnancy wasn't something she wanted, although in her twisted mind it was the answer to keeping me by her side. She was bleeding heavily and needed some help. I came to the rescue then too, afterward begging her not to lie to me and go off birth control pills.

She promised, but a few months later, it happened again. Obviously, Sandi was not healthy enough to have children and two abortions took place during the past year.

I wasn't sure about the right course of action after the second abortion and decided to up the ante, reassuring her of my commitment to our relationship. Our conversation after that included new boundaries for our sexual relationship. I explained that I would no longer have sex with her—even after we married. I couldn't risk making a child with her until the moment we were ready to assume responsibility for a baby. In spite of the new doctrine, I needed her to believe I would never leave her. Sandi could not physically endure another abortion, and it might hamper our future chance to have children. When I explained it that way, she said she understood and the topic was left to rest.

I advanced into the darkened room a little farther, waiting for my eyes to adjust. I called out again.

"In here."

I heard her voice; it sounded happy. I offered a silent prayer of thanks and closed the door behind me.

"I'm in here," she sang out again.

I made my way through the kitchen and down the short hallway to the dining room.

"In here," she said again.

I rounded the doorway and saw a vibrant Sandi, her eyes lit up. Behind her on the wall in giant lettering, a message had been painted.

Will you marry me?

I stared at the message, dumbfounded. What could someone say to that? My response came without forethought. "When the time is right, I will propose to you, and I *will* marry you."

"Gil?" Her face fell and I could tell she wanted to cry. I took her by the shoulders and smiled.

"Sandi, I want to have children with you. I want to watch you be the mom I know you are," I reassured her. "I made a commitment to you years ago when we began living together that I would never leave. Be patient; when the time is right, I will ask you to marry me."

She seemed satisfied with that answer for the time being.

———◆———

As we began our fourth year together, we moved into a new apartment that had a great bedroom for Gabe.

The judge was tiring of this case and he handed down an edict. "I order you to undergo an independent evaluation for child custody. The court will instruct your evaluator to look into the mental health and parenting practices of each of the parents involved."

I was hopeful there would be relief from the abuse levied by Russell. A court-approved psychiatrist would analyze each parent's life, past and present. The interviews would be conducted with the parents, the child, grandparents, friends, and teachers—anyone close to the child or family. Sandi's psychiatrist would be interviewed at length and though he understood Sandi better than anyone, he somehow would be viewed as biased. Even so, I knew we had taken a step in the right direction and hoped that Sandi would be free from her child's father.

The psychological tests conducted were an intrusion into our personal life and the evaluator's report produced a barrage of conflicting detail.

"Here it is." Hank, Sandi's attorney, pushed a packet across the table to me. "It describes Sandi's behaviors and gives the details of her final evaluation."

I froze, staring at the manila envelope as if it were a cobra ready to strike.

"Here," Hank said again, this time picking it up and handing it to me. "You'll need a copy of this for your files."

"What is it exactly?" I asked, a little nervous to glance down at the typeset blanketing the papers in my hand.

"Just read it. It's pretty self-explanatory. The critical piece is the final evaluation conducted on Sandra."

"I'm not sure…"

"The judge has a copy and you need to know what he's privy to," he said. "Read it when you have some privacy if you don't want to read it now."

My eyes dropped to the two-hundred-page document as her attorney bid farewell and walked down the remaining steps of the courthouse. I caught sight of the words, *mental disorder* and couldn't pull away from reading it further. I flipped around the pages, forward and backward, then forward again.

…severe chronic, probably biologically based mental disorder that was made worse by a chaotic upbringing and extremely dysfunctional family dynamic, a very complicated family history that is relevant to understanding her psychiatric history, a chronic psychiatric condition that will require her to be under the care of a psychiatrist probably for the rest of her life, a psychiatric disorder that is biological in nature, and which will probably affect her behavior and thought process periodically over her lifetime. Her problems are such that she will probably always run the risk of having stress affect her in ways where she could have extremely poor judgment and impulse control…

My eyes began to water. I blinked to clear my vision and continued to read her psychological resume.

…chronic liar, doesn't keep agreements, unusually rebellious, hostile toward rules, resentful of demands made on her, unpredictable and inappropriate behavior, makes maladaptive judgments, persistently seeks excitement and frequently demonstrates seductive and self-dramatizing behavior, short-sighted hedonism with minimal regard for the long-term problematic consequences of her behavior, may appear charming to casual acquaintances but those having more enduring relationships with her…

I would have to finish the rest in private, unable to read the words any longer. Its meaning blurred into nonsense within my overloaded brain. I knew in my gut that even from the brief few paragraphs I'd read, the evaluator's findings were accurate. Her description of Sandi was spot-on. I had seen these traits myself but chosen to ignore them. They did not matter because I loved her and I'd made a commitment to her.

My curiosity was piqued and I hurried to the privacy of my car, anxious to read the balance of the report, particularly the portion that touched on my interview with the psychologist.

She is not likely to endanger her son if she continues to live with Gil and remain in treatment...

I was amazed.

Gil is her only ongoing social support. She has become very dependent upon her relationship with him and therefore, very vulnerable if that relationship should falter. Another aspect, more difficult to explain, is Gil's demonstration of positive regard and respect for her as well as his concrete caring and support; all seems to have enabled her to grow emotionally and act more like an adult than when she associated solely with her family or ex-husband...

I should have been happy to read such a glowing report of my influence on Sandi's well-being, but I felt more pressure than ever before to cut and run. Still, I knew Sandi and Gabe relied heavily on me. For once in their troubled lives, they finally had someone to protect them.

There was one part of the report, an event that I'll never forget and likely never be able to justify. Gabe had been taken alone into a room with the evaluator and was given little figurines to represent each of the people in his life: his mother, his father, grandparents, and so on...including me. He was asked who he liked to do various activities with and who he counted on for things. He was essentially asked to pick people out of a lineup.

I knew it was a setup; in families, children count on each parent differently and at various times. The answers given that day would be different six months later, making the interview entirely obsolete. The same would be true about with whom a child identifies. Things change quickly for children during each phase of their life. Plus, in a marriage, while one parent is doing something with a child, the other parent might be doing something for the family.

I hated that Gabe was a target and forced to go through that biased interrogation. I hated that the system was broken and that I was the only one to recognize it and was even more powerless to help.

———————

It had taken a year to complete the evaluation. The results offered the evaluator's recommendation for custody and visitation, "based on the findings." Theoretically, it gave the appearance of a great system at work, set in place to protect the child with all decisions made "in the child's best interest," as was repeatedly announced throughout the follow-up hearing with the judge. In fact, the process was a complete waste of time and money, tens of thousands of dollars sucked into a void that ultimately only covered the system's back and created more problems than it resolved.

When all was said and done, the final decision was a fifty-fifty split; that is, time shared with both parents equally. In spite of the positive move for custody, none of the problems were resolved between Sandi and her ex-husband or her family. They continued their toxic response to her attempts at a normal life and nothing changed. Sandi's family and Russell continued to double-team her, with Sandi on the short end. Russell took advantage of dysfunctions in Sandi's family and still treated Sandi horribly when they weren't watching.

Looking back, Sandi made a request of the court which, if granted, would have alleviated strife and taken the steam out of the drama. She requested it be ordered that she be given the right to sole decisions made regarding her family. She also requested that Russell be able to do the same with his, which is the way a married couple essentially functions. The evaluator, and thus the court, denied this request. The status quo would remain; Sandi's family could go on operating with no boundaries, thus bypassing her as Gabe's mother.

They continued to interact with Russell to ensure they would get what they wanted from him without any regard for what Gabe and Sandi needed. The dysfunction of their lineage—an adherence to whoever controlled the money—had propagated itself for generations within her family like a malignancy. The sickness raged on and it became obvious it would not stop.

Science has a definition for chaos: the behavior of dynamical systems that are highly sensitive to initial conditions. It has been called the Butterfly Effect. This is, in essence, the principle of chaos. It reminds me of dominoes created from the same polar field, all lined up neatly but spewing energy that repels anything next to it. The result is a cascading collapse of an entire structure: *your life, Gil.* I had no response.

Another hint of repelling forces within both our families came the day Deb's voice crackled by phone with the same kind of intensity. I should have known better when Deb asked me to meet her at Beverly Hills High. Walking the track was her new exercise du jour. I should have known we'd go in circles again. That's all we'd ever done, because we had no foundation for our relationship. We never had corner pieces of the puzzle to anchor us with loyalty. There was no unbreakable bond between brother and sister. We wanted to be close, but it was always one step forward and two steps back with us.

The talk began with her announcement, rather matter-of-factly, that Sandi's sister Tarrah would be moving in with her in exchange for babysitting.

"Don't do this thing, Deb," I begged her. "Everything's at stake for me here."

"Why? What's wrong with me trying to save a few dollars and help someone else in need?"

"First of all, Sandi and Tarrah aren't even speaking with one another. This will damage Sandi's relationship with your kids. She's trouble, Deb. I'm telling you," I said. "You know that Tarrah used to live with Sandi's ex, which caused a lot of problems for Sandi and me. She has no respect for boundaries and there is always turmoil."

"You're being melodramatic again, Gil." Deb was irritated.

"Please, Deb. After everything I've tried to do for you and the kids, please do this one thing for me," I said. "I'm telling you, this will end badly if you go ahead with it."

After a long pause, Deb agreed. "Okay, Gil, if it means that much to you, I promise."

We ended the conversation pleasantly and I felt satisfied that I had saved us from some unwarranted heartache. Chaos had been averted, for now. Perhaps science was wrong when it came to their chaos theories with families.

Less than twenty-four hours later, Sandi's sister was living with Deb.

She'd lied to me, to my face again. Everything was a lie and secrets.

The past five years had been about much more than family dysfunction, pills, and alcohol. I had been navigating a course between my commitment to Sandi and my obligation to my sister and her kids...and my ship was sinking fast.

You're getting in over your head and you don't even know how to surface, Gil.

"I know, I know! But I don't know what to do," I said aloud.

You need to confront someone...something's got to give. You can't keep being a dad to four kids whose biological father's in jail, as well as a rescuer to a troubled sister. Add to that your chosen role to be the mainstay to a psychopath with a kid.

"She's not a psychopath and this conversation's over," I said. I was firm in my resolve and moved away from thinking this way.

Unfortunately, my family dynamics proved science's theory. This seemed to be especially true with Deb. We had managed to be close at one point in our lives but were close no longer. With such self-focus pulling each individual into their own polarizing lives, there would be no room for anyone else's struggle to invade. The concept of loving one another and supporting each other through difficult times did not belong here. Boundaries had been ignored, or perhaps there were no boundaries, as science demonstrates through magnetic forces. My family was a gathering of repelling forces, with Deb and me unable to attract and hold onto each other for any length of time. The domino effect of the Butterfly Chaos theory was real.

Soon afterward, the internal struggle was buried deep inside and subconsciously I began to line up the dominoes that defined my life, polar fields that mirrored one another and repulsed everything around me.

I felt another leg falling away from my chair as my relationship with Deb was slipping away. She preferred what Sandi's sister offered over me, and she chose deceit over truth. Although neither of us realized it at the time, we parted ways on that track.

Sandi's court case raged on. It seemed as though nothing would stop Russell from keeping the battle alive. It had drained me emotionally and financially, and I knew we would have to let go of the attorney. Sandi was all that I had left to call family. There was little I could do except try to intervene. So, I went back to the law libraries. Obtaining a law degree wasn't something I'd planned on. But as fate would have it, I became an expert on divorce law. I again turned out to be Sandi's fill-in attorney. I had to get creative and won rights for her under the Americans with Disabilities Act. This would be her only means to a fair fight.

Fortunately, Sandi kept winning. Nevertheless, the prize seemed to be an additional opportunity to go back to court. Of great concern was how the court battle was affecting Gabe. Fairness was not meant for anyone involved, but most importantly, not for him.

Sandi's mental health was a concern. She was doing great but still operated at less than one hundred percent. And yet, I loved her and still wanted to marry her. I was frustrated because her health was getting so much better, and yet she wasn't healthy enough to have children. Although my biggest dream was to have kids of my own, I had made a commitment to Sandi, knowing it might never happen.

This will be a never-ending battle.

"Yes, I know." My voice was weak after years of talking with her about the dangers of mixing prescription medications with alcohol as a coping mechanism as well as seeing a bright future.

A new course of action is needed.

After six long years of fighting, I wasn't sure there was another course.

CHAPTER 27

—————◆—————

DISTANCE. PUT SOME DISTANCE BETWEEN Sandi and Russell.

Of course!

The decision was made unanimously with Sandi's doctor. Within a few months, we packed our belongings and moved one hour south to Orange County. Inside, a feeling of regret began to develop, moving closer to her family and farther away from mine. Hopefully, this would prove a good decision and not the mistake I was trying to avoid.

We had come up with a new parenting plan for Gabe. The idea was to share time in which Gabe would be with one parent during the school year and the other parent for vacations. The option was given to Russell. Sandi was exhausted and wanted some type of arrangement, any arrangement. It was a first step to create a positive experience for Gabe. The ultimatum was there would be no more fighting. Either we would all agree to this arrangement or we would work to come up with a different one. No more court. This was a dangerous ultimatum to lay down because Sandi would have to stand behind what she said, which would mean she and Gabe might have to pay the price of not being in each other's lives for a while.

I had made one more attempt to bring Sandi and her family together. Surprisingly, they supported our plan and we anticipated familial healing. When Russell found out about Sandi's family's support, he inserted himself in between the reconciliation attempt. As a result, everything we had accomplished came undone. Her family would not back her, and again Russell found no incentive to ensure Gabe had as much time as possible with each of his parents.

Two weeks later, I made plans of a different nature. It had been my hope during the millennial New Year to reach out and ask Sandi's mother for permission to marry her daughter. Not that she was deserving of that honor, but that wasn't my place to judge. She was unavailable, vacationing with Russell and Gabe. The sabotaging had begun dashing any hopes I'd had for some sort of normalcy with family. The chance to speak with Sandi's mother never came again.

———◆———

Several months later, the Butterfly Effect—chaos—showed itself again.

"I don't think I can do it." Sandi was adamant even with the encouragement I'd given her over the past hour. "It's too difficult to be around children when I can't be with my own son."

"I get that, Pi, but I think this will be different. It's a Bat Mitzvah and you love celebrations, right?" I tried to reason with Sandi, but her face told me that I was probably wasting my breath.

Lately, I felt that my life had been robbed, not of material possessions, but of something more valuable, something that could never be replaced: my time. Over the course of seven or eight months, I'd been unable to visit with my sister's kids. All three nieces and my solitary nephew had been the focus of my life for virtually all of my time in California. Then Deb's response to my request about Tarrah took them away from any association with Uncle Gil. The Bat Mitzvah offered a chance to see them again.

"It's at the temple; you know the place," I continued. "In Beverly Hills. There will be a big party afterward, Pi. Think about it." I could hear myself sounding desperate.

"I know it's been a long time since you've seen them, Gil but I don't know…"

I pulled out the last stop. "Please, do this for me."

Sandi caved an hour later, and by evening, we were driving the long stretch on the 405 to the Temple. I could hardly wait. These were *my* kids, *my* family, and I'd missed them terribly. The time lost would never be given back, but this was a new occasion, another opportunity to share time with them, and with Sandi.

We entered the temple hand in hand and my eyes scanned the room. Bright blue and silver drapes flashed from centerpieces and candles, lit in celebration. But it was not the decorations I sought. I looked for small faces that lit up a room, lit up my soul. Those were my quest and I searched desperately to find them.

"There?" Sandi asked and pointed to a table decked with cakes and latkes that rimmed plates picked apart by little fingers.

"Yes!"

I pushed my way through a growing crowd, pulling Sandi by the hand behind me. Their little faces turned up and I heard the words I'd been longing to hear for months.

"Uncle Gil!"

My nephew ran to my side as one niece leapt into my outstretched arms. I dropped Sandi's hand and embraced her, burying my face into her little neck, the scent of honeysuckle lingering in her hair. This was a perfect moment for me.

But not for Sandi.

"I...can't breathe." She backed away from me. I should never have let go of her hand. "I need some air."

In that moment, Sandi turned and made a beeline for the door. I set my niece down and went after her, catching up seconds before she would have crossed the threshold.

"What is it, Pi?" I wasn't sure I really wanted the truth. My gut told me this had more to do with the kids than I really wanted to know. She faced me and, trembling, clasped my hands in her own. The color had drained from her face and she looked like a ghost haloed by the setting sun's rays in the doorway of the temple. It reminded me of Michelangelo's marble statues plastered around a Roman cathedral, only Sandi was no saint. Her grimace told me as much. I tried desperately to calm her down but she began to shake.

"I…this…Jesus!"

"Take a breath, Sandi. You're scaring me," I said and tried to pull her close. If I could shield her with my own body, perhaps she'd calm down.

"Satan is looking and Jesus told me the fish are ready."

I stared at her and felt the color drain from my face. Her eyes darted from the children to the tables to the ceiling, wild eyes, the kind you see in caged animals. Blindly searching for something, they skimmed past me to an invisible being somewhere above the feasting guests.

"There…yes, Jesus. Shabbat is on Thursday. Pour the garden into…a very sad…indeed…chibbit."

Her diction became allusive as she spewed word-salad jargon at everyone, eyes focused on a distant object that no one could see.

"Baby, you're not making sense." I pleaded with her to move outside. I hadn't thought that her first instinct may have been the correct one after all: she didn't belong there. Sandi didn't budge. Her feet were planted firmly in the doorway, preventing anyone from exiting or entering while the doorway continued to encase her with sunlight, a fitting spotlight for someone going mad.

"What's wrong with her?" my niece asked innocently.

"I think she's sick," I answered and tried to catch Deb's eye. As much as I didn't want to create another excuse for distance between the children and me, Sandi was beginning to garner attention, and not the kind I wanted my nieces and nephew to see.

"Salloooo…chu…mmmm…Jesus is here. Jesus is here. Gabe. Gabe."

This was not the place for Jesus, not at a Bat Mitzvah, not in a temple in Beverly Hills, and certainly not the place for Sandi. She broke down, collapsing to her knees. There was little that would calm her as she began to cry hysterically.

"Someone better call 911." I heard the suggestion made from the far side of the room. I tried again out of desperation to take her outside with me but she swung wildly with fists fighting off an unseen foe, fighting off her would-be husband.

"Get the police."

I faced the gathering crowd. "She'll be okay, really. She's just not feeling well all of a sudden," I said and caught a glimpse of my sister's foreboding stare.

"Get her out of here before you ruin everything," Deb said softly, but I knew everyone else had heard.

"I've got this." I put my arms around my thrashing girlfriend who called out to Jesus to save her.

Carrying her to the car was a bigger challenge than I had anticipated. Sandi stood five feet six inches. She was wily, and her 117 pounds surged with the strength that comes from pure adrenaline. Indeed, she fought for her life and did not recognize the man she battled as her protector. I had no other choice but to force her into the car and escape the event I'd hoped would bond my ties to those children I loved.

As I drove home with her, wild eyes skirted objects she thought she saw outside the window. It was clear I had a choice to make.

———◆———

"Don't even think of marrying her!" Dad said as I grabbed a coffee with him the next morning. The day had sprung to life with the scent of orange blossoms and eucalyptus, typical for a summer day in Southern California, but Dad never noticed. He was heading to the airport for his flight back east and had little time to notice. "Everyone is done with her destroying your life! Find yourself a nice Jewish girl. Live the life you're supposed to live."

"Dad, the details are different, but she's me, if you haven't noticed. I ended up in the same place she did."

"If you marry that shiksa, we're done."

That was the last thing Dad said before he left that day.

Sandi needed a lot of sleep after an episode like that. As I watched TV late that night, a film came on that I'd seen a dozen times before. I watched it again, a military film in which a guy is falsely accused of something and if convicted, he'll spend the rest of his life in the brig. He refused to cut a deal that would get him home in six months because he believed his commitment to his military unit came first. He wouldn't do it because he said he lived by a code: Unit. Corps. God. Country.

I had made a commitment to Sandi and although I was warned of the danger ahead in making it an official union, for all intents and purposes, we were already married. I had already gone back on my commitment to Laura. I wasn't going to do that again, even though choosing Sandi meant that I would lose my family.

The TV blared as the sergeant's lawyer adamantly defended her client in court. The actress was marvelous as she refused to accept the judge's overruling of her objection and fired back at him that she "strenuously objected"!

Well, I too had strenuously made a commitment to Sandi a long time ago, to the point that I had argued that I didn't need a Jewish divorce in negotiations with Laura. I knew she needed a "Jewish Get"—a traditional, amicable Jewish annulment with no strings attached—because she, like everyone else in my clan, would never even think of marrying someone who wasn't Jewish.

Sandi would be my family. She needed me and I needed her.

———◆———

The sun dropped rapidly beyond the horizon while the rain saturated all hopes for a peaceful twilight. I stood at the window and watched the last ray descend below the outline of buildings marking the edge of the city. Rivulets of water ran down the windowpane. I brushed the back of my hand against my face as a tear trickled down.

Was our connection made for the wrong reason? I didn't have the answer and my inner voice was silent. People with unresolved emotional baggage meet at convenience stores every day. They move on with happy, productive lives, so why couldn't I?

With marriages failing in every socioeconomic group, just how and where we met didn't seem to be the issue. In fact, we were probably more honest with each other than most couples because of it. Few people meet in a psych hospital where their secrets are exposed—at least, most of them.

Did I do the right thing? Did I cover for her? I wasn't sure. All I knew was that I loved her with all my heart, worked incredibly hard to allow her son to enjoy both parents, and I wanted to protect her. Still, it felt like we failed. I was supposed to be Sandi's protector, her knight in shining armor, the one to rescue her, but this battle with her family was a war I couldn't win.

Give yourself a break, Gil. On one hand, you are proud of all you had done to help her discover a beautiful life, and rightly so. She has been given a life that she otherwise would not have enjoyed. My conscience had awakened.

"Yes, but many men would be embarrassed to be with a woman who didn't have custody of her child. Most men would have quit on her a long time ago," I said aloud.

Well, you're not most men and didn't do that.

"I feel as though I failed her," I said again, hoping the voice in my head would respond with more comforting words. My only answer was a guilty feeling.

While the outcome with Sandi's son was not what either of us had wanted, it was what we'd been given, another storm to weather. We were a team. But a team is only as strong as its weakest member. With sadness, I wondered about the truth to myself. It was time to talk to someone.

"You're the weakest link, Gil." I stepped away from the window.

———◆———

"You have some issues you are struggling with internally, Gil."

Well really? What kind of an answer is that?

"That's the reason I'm sitting on your couch," I said. I gave Phil an insincere smile that I sensed he could somehow see even with my back turned. Dr. Phil Parsons was Sandi's psychiatrist. While it could be reasonably said I would have been better off speaking to someone independent of Sandi, I always felt Phil understood more than any other doctor did exactly what I was going through with Sandi and her family.

I hadn't spoken with him in a while and decided to make the phone call without a lot of forethought. Fortunately, his secretary had been able to pencil me in for a thirty-minute session. He was an hour away in Los Angeles but was amenable to squeezing me in—another advantage to speaking with him. It was short but under the circumstances, I took what I could get.

"Let's see if we can figure out what the cause of your distress is, Gil."

I doubted he could do that in just a half hour and glanced at the clock on the wall to be certain we had that much time left. Twenty-three minutes. Well, it would have to do.

"Deep-seated feelings of failure are surfacing, worse than ever before," I said trying to give a CliffsNotes version of my concerns.

"Why do you think you're feeling this way?"

Seriously? Did this guy remember me or read my file? Had he even been listening for the last five minutes? I cleared my throat of the sarcasm lodged there and smiled again.

"It falls back to feeling as if I am unable to do my job as a man. I mean, I didn't protect Sandi and that makes me feel inadequate. Besides that, her family despises me."

"Why?"

I stared at him, trying to figure out how to answer as succinctly as possible.

"There's really no good reason. I guess it all stacks up to years of being told that I am a bad person, that I was never good enough.

Being told something like this so frequently only compounds one's belief that it's true, doesn't it, doc?"

He smiled and glanced down at his folded hands.

"Not always. The broken casualties of divorce often shadow truths. You've lived that principle all of your life, Gil. Miraculous, really, that one man has been able to accomplish so much against all odds."

The compliment did not make my stomach stop twisting on itself, nor did it dissipate the self-doubt that followed me.

"I guess, from an outside perspective, it seems ridiculous that I've stayed with her, but I love her, and I made a commitment to her." I said it more to myself than to him.

"I'm sure you do, Gil. Society is an unfair peer. Its dictates don't allow for a mother such as Sandi to make a decision to not participate in her child's life if not afforded a fair and equitable means of doing so."

Rather wordy but I understood where he was going and was grateful that he had an idea of where I was.

"Our fickle society operates in a way that suggests a day here and there with your child is reason alone to accept it as a viable plan for life. In many circumstances, such as your own, it is not."

"I don't know what to do. Sandi faces health issues that become more serious when she's not treated appropriately. I don't see how it is unwise for Gabe to witness his mother being treated as a first-class citizen, for him to have two equal parents. Instead, the courts continue to insist the 'best interest of the child' is served," I said, but could not contain the sarcasm in my voice.

He began to drum his pencil on the desk. I glanced at the clock. Only seven minutes left.

"It's not. But you know very well that society, and our legal system, doesn't always take the wisest approach. It's your task, together, to find a way to make your future livable, even positive."

It was the chicken and the egg. I had spent years treating Sandi the way she deserved to be treated and had seen what it did for her.

I had also witnessed her treated disrespectfully by Russell and her family when she interacted with them and had seen how that affected her health. There was so much more to this situation than appeared on the surface.

"She's been getting healthier. Even during the most brutal times, she's been able to decrease her medication and get healthier. She had so many emotional issues, but it seemed like I made it better just by loving her. I am not trying to take credit. I just gave her the love and support she needed. I devoted my life to Sandi and did all in my power to make her happy. That's what you do for someone you love," I said. My voice sounded hopeless.

"No doubt you're Sandi's rock."

I left his office with a sense of duty and little improvement in my self-esteem. I had reached a point where there wasn't much else I could do.

Sandi had begun volunteering for a therapy practice that used horseback riding to help disabled people. Also, the horse I leased for Sandi was close by. I had hoped that environment would help her, and it seemed to work. She was able to be her playful whimsical self. Everyone loved her. Nobody could tell anything was wrong underneath. Out of hundreds of volunteers, she received a volunteer of the year award and was written about in the paper.

In spite of everything, her suffering was a daily struggle. Holidays were even worse.

Perhaps it was time to ask Sandi to share my last name. Perhaps that one act would give her the feeling of belonging to a family. Because ours was not a typical relationship, I knew my proposal couldn't be typical. I went to a jeweler and had a diamond ring designed in the shape of the pi symbol. It represented her nickname and was perfect.

I asked Pi to marry me on March 14th—3/14—and she said yes.

Feeling more pressure than ever, a secret refused to stay hidden. While Sandi flourished, I struggled. The most humiliating, difficult secret I would ever keep began to take over my life. Sandi had been spending a great deal of time at the stables, volunteering as well as riding the horse she loved, both of which were great therapy. One day, I decided to join her. The afternoon was perfect, sunny and warm. The air was crisp and filled with the fragrances of pine and autumn leaves. I had no thought of tribulations but rather, focused on the wonderful day.

Upon returning home, we began to settle into the evening, and prepared for a relaxing end to a memorable day together. Suddenly, the voice took hold and I was overcome with panic.

What happened in the bathroom at the stable?

What? What are you talking about? I said silently to myself. My hand darted to that place over my chest where my heart beat rapidly beneath the sudden burn of my scar.

You used them today, earlier. Remember? The small bathroom with three stalls. What did you do while you were in there?

"I didn't do anything! Leave me alone!" My palms grew clammy.

You did something. You know you did. Did you hurt something? Kill someone, maybe?

"No!" I screamed. I couldn't have done anything so evil, so blatant. The voice had to be wrong! I couldn't breathe. My heart was pounding and I could literally feel its pace through my shirt, drenched now with sweat.

You killed someone, you know it. Killed someone! Killed!

"No! No, I didn't. Stop it! *Stop!*"

I believed in my soul that I would never be capable of hurting another living being but I could not stop the panic. The thought circled its lethal loop in my head, not the voice in my head but something else, a voice that surfaced from the panic taking control of my body.

"There was no one else in the bathroom," I said aloud. The panic continued its influence and I began to feel dizzy.

You're a bad seed, Gil, the person Sandi's family says you are.

"No... I'm not capable of hurting anyone. I'm afraid of my own shadow." My voice came out in wheezy gasps.

I knew I couldn't return to the stables to check my own handiwork. I might get caught. So, I decided to attempt distraction by watching the news. Surely, if someone had been murdered inside a stable's bathroom, it would be on the news. Sandi joined me on the sofa, feigning interest in the headlines broadcast from the announcer but her focus remained on me. I ignored her inquisition and kept my eyes glued to the TV set.

The hour came and went, local and national news followed by sports and weather, with no mention of a cold-blooded killer on the loose who chose his victims in a stable bathroom. I was safe. There was no blood on my hands today.

"What's wrong with you, Gil?" Sandy asked, eyeing me.

"Nothing," I replied and shook my head for emphasis.

Just to be certain, I rose from the sofa and washed twice before returning to Sandi's side.

CHAPTER 28

———◆———

MY HANDS TREMBLED AS I lifted the page to examine the doctor's notes.

"Severe anxiety disorder"

The diagnosis was printed all over my youthful file and I knew it had surfaced its ugly head again. It had developed once before. "A method to control your surroundings" was the explanation given to me in one therapy session. "It is a cycle of illness designed to prevent debilitating panic attacks but in doing so only causes more by needing to feel in control when things feel so out of control."

Well, its horrific methods worked. I would go on to spend every single day of my life since then living with fear. Even though I knew better—knew the truth, I'd live with the belief that because so many people treated me badly, I must be a bad person. Only bad people rehearsed their day, looking for evidence of heinous crimes committed by their own hands. This constant fear led to the next phase of my mental illness: Obsessive Compulsive Disorder.

Leaving the house in the morning became a process. I would empty my pockets individually and take out every piece of paper, including dollar bills and credit cards, cleaning out my wallet in order to be sure nothing would be written there that could incriminate me. I would then put everything back, although I might be forced to start the process over again if I didn't proceed in the correct order. Getting dressed became even more debilitating. While I had no system to pick out which shirts to wear, inherently I knew some were okay and others were not. I would dress, undress, turn my pants, shirt, and socks inside out to make sure there wasn't anything hiding in them, and then get dressed again.

My life had been overtaken with paranoia. Sandi had assumed the role of supporter. She found a way to laugh about it with me but underneath the mirth, my illness took a major toll on both of our lives. Often, she would watch me check and recheck my pockets countless times, then gently direct my attention to my folly.

"What in God's name are you looking for?" she chuckled.

I knew the repetitive behavior was aberrant and a major issue. Eventually, I could pull my focus away and laugh for a moment with her.

The panic attacks continued but didn't occur as much in public places, such as a coffee shop. I drew comfort in my ability to return and check for damage done even though I knew there was none. Places that were not as easy for me to return became the bigger problem. If I stayed in a hotel located out of town, it would take a tremendous amount of time for me to check out of a room because I wouldn't be able to return there. I would live with paralyzing fear about what could be written on any given piece of paper, incriminating evidence of something I might have done.

It's almost the end of the day. Have you checked? You know it will be two full days before you can return. Check again. There has to be something… It's Friday, you know. Check again.

The voice was incessant and Fridays became the most difficult days for me. Generally, Fridays meant the working week had ended and the weekend had begun. When most people celebrated, I would panic, waiting anxiously for Monday to arrive. Leaving an office on Friday afternoon, I knew I would have to face the weekend wondering if I'd left something incriminating. It caused so much anxiety that I began avoiding *any* office building on Fridays. The fear became overwhelming and I avoided any places or scenarios that could potentially cause these panic attacks. I felt safest when I was with another person, but then I came to the conclusion that such proximity would allow knowledge of my possible wrongdoing. Soon, I was unable to work. Indeed, the problem had taken over my life.

Medication didn't help. It seemed our culture had become so accustomed to popping some pill or another to make everything better; that was how it was supposed to work. However, medication and therapy didn't always work, not for me, not the way I'd hoped. Sandi became my only remedy. She was the only person I trusted, and I was *not* embarrassed about myself when I was around her.

I saw firsthand how volunteering at Happy Trails had helped her and I wondered if that could happen for me. We began every day together as a couple, working with disabled people. It was humbling and gave me new perspective.

My own problems became small in comparison to the struggles others faced. Happy Trails helped us gain a new outlook and both of us became better people because of it. We loved volunteering, and I found enormous comfort in being there with Sandi. She was almost always in sight, and with that came a tremendous sense of safety and security.

One night, after a great day at the stables, we watched an episode of our favorite show, which that week happened to be about a brilliant surgeon who suffered from OCD. Sandi and I were in awe because the doctor's character was a perfect imitation of me. We laughed and cried when he was mired in "a loop," with repetitive behavior one moment followed by supreme intellect the next. I watched "myself"—my own thirty minutes of fame—without ever leaving the sofa.

———◆———

Time to move on, Gil. You've become accustomed to the breaking legs of that toppling chair. Move on.

Life had a way of throwing me off balance and I was learning to lean with every shove. I didn't know if I would find joy. I stayed with my secrets, lost in the shuffle of narcissistic people and the pains of a little boy who still longed for an intact home.

Then one day, I threw life a curve ball and finally realized my heart could smile.

The happiest day of my life found me in a courthouse in San Diego. Sandi and I were alone and had just been pronounced "man and wife." It was a simple, beautiful wedding for a couple who loved one another—the only two people in attendance.

It goes without saying that nobody goes into a marriage planning to divorce. Every couple anticipates "forever" and "till death do we part." Sandi and I approached marriage even more earnestly because of the trials we had been through.

"I believed that I was put on earth with a purpose," I said to my reflection in the mirror. The razor remained steady in my hand as I used it against the stubble that had sprung up during the night. "I've never had dreams of being an astronaut or politician. My aspiration has always been to be a husband and a father."

Your ambition blinds you.

I finished shaving and walked away. Today was not the day I'd be bogged down with an analysis of my problems. Maslow's pyramid had disappeared from the mirror years ago and I had no desire to bring it back. "Life is good for me now."

Is it really?

Luckily, Sandi's health held steady. She was well and happy, volunteering at Happy Trails. It was obvious she had turned her life around, and I was proud of her. However, I lived in fear because I knew Sandi's success, and by extension mine, would only last as long as she remained in a positive, healthy mental state.

Is it really that good?

I ignored the voice and began to dress for the day but reminiscent thoughts continued.

"You can't walk on eggshells your entire life, Gil," my sister had said many years ago. The comment continued to play through my head as I realized the norm for my life was indeed to "walk on egg-shells." I lived life with a ticking time bomb labeled "mental illness." In truth, I lived in constant fear that the illness waited to find my wife and make her sick again.

Internal struggle is something you hide well.

That was true. While friends and acquaintances on the outside viewed us as a happy-go-lucky couple and our marriage as endearing, we struggled with more than just the typical newlywed issues that pop up within the first year or two of marriage. My anxiety disorder, Sandi's mental health, both of our extended families' toxic dynamics created a laundry list that went on and on.

"You're making much more of this than it is," I said, pulling on a pair of socks.

Look at your health. It continues to degenerate and you struggle to maintain working.

Another truth; I'd obtained an insurance license and was trying to begin a career, while Sandi tried to get beyond just functioning free from medication and suicidal thoughts. It was taking a toll on me.

"I'm fine," I lied. I walked out the bedroom door and into my life.

Seven years had passed from the time we met before real stability was beginning to take hold. While we were able to create a supportive environment for raising children, I knew we weren't ready yet. Sandi kept pressuring me, saying, "We will never be ready" and "Having a family of our own would heal you, Gil."

I knew she was right. I wanted kids.

The clock is ticking, Gil. What if you can't get pregnant?

"We'll adopt."

How would you be able to adopt with Sandi's past and now with your health being what it is?

We couldn't wait too long. So many what ifs—so much to fear.

My biggest concern was alleviated. All our cards were on the table. The decision to postpone building our family had been the topic of countless discussions. We agreed upfront that divorce was not going to be an option for us, a non-negotiable condition to bringing children into the world. The cycle of broken families and broken lives ended with us. Sandi and I talked continually and extensively about our backgrounds over the course of our relationship. I needed to be certain that our marriage would be a lifetime commitment so that our children would never experience divorce. Without that assurance, I risked passing down my horrible childhood.

Remember the Wednesday night dinners with your dad? I hated those!

I refused to take anyone else along that path, particularly my children. Simply put, I didn't want to have kids if divorce was an option.

Included in our discussions was Sandi's son, Gabe. When he turned eighteen and had a legal right to make his own decisions, he would be able to finally step out from underneath his father's umbrella, and we would reengage as a family. In the meantime, Sandi needed to put away the past to enjoy a happy present and a promising future. Our ability to thrive as a couple was exacerbated by divorce. Sandi needed to look forward to what we would have, rather than fret over what we didn't.

"We've made a vow to break the chain of dysfunction and never allow our children to experience a repeat of our pasts."

It was the best encouragement I could muster.

CHAPTER 29

———◆———

MORNINGS CAME VERY EARLY FOR Sandi and me. Every day began with coffee together while we watched the news. Three days after Sandi's thirty-fifth birthday, we witnessed the events of 9/11 on a nationwide broadcast. It was a beautiful, clear, autumn morning. We were enjoying the pleasant aftermath of a surprise party I'd thrown for Sandi's birthday the night before, sipping coffee, and chatting. In that instant, our joy dissipated and I flashed back to a time when I worked in the World Trade Center with my dad. Suddenly, I became worried about his safety. I knew he could be in the vicinity of the attack. I tried to call but couldn't reach him. Much later, days after telephone service had been reestablished, my father finally called back.

"Yeah, I'm okay. We were up at our country home. It was horrific though. I'll never get over it," he said, his voice hesitating between sentences.

"No one will, Dad. I was really worried about you," I responded.

"Yeah, well. I'm fine."

"Why didn't you try to call sooner? It's been difficult, wondering whether you were alive or dead."

"I just did. Probably because I called Debra that afternoon to tell her I was okay."

The statement drilled deep into my emotional memories as a child. Deb was always his first priority, not me. Of course he would call her, and then get around to me when he had time.

I glanced across the room at my wife in the kitchen, washing our coffee cups at the sink. All thoughts of my father disappeared. Sandi was my wife, my real family. I was approaching forty and her biological clock was ticking, as was my deepest fear: the possibility that we might not get pregnant.

We decided then and there that it was time to begin our future as parents.

It didn't take long for Sandi to get pregnant with our first daughter. When she broke the news, I was excited to become the kind of father that I'd never had and happy for us, but happier for her. This was her chance to be the mother she wanted to and could be.

Our joy was taken away all too soon with news that five months' pregnant Sandi would never recover from.

"It's been so long, Sandi. Years? Something like that," Vanessa said casually over lunch one day.

The café where the two friends had decided to reunite overlooked the harbor. Seagulls called from below, foraging through abandoned belongings of beach dwellers as they surfed or played in the summer sun. Both women smiled in satisfaction as they observed the activities of the people.

"This place is magnificent," Sandi said. "Thanks for making the arrangements, Vae."

"Of course! We needed to catch up and I can't think of a better way to do it than over seafood at the harbor."

"Well, I'm glad we finally did. There's so much that's happened since Gil and I got married."

"I know, Sandi. I'm so sorry about your mother," Vanessa said innocently.

"What do you mean?"

"I read her obituary a few weeks ago and I wanted to call you but didn't get the chance. It must be hard for you."

Sandi sat motionless in her chair, a blank stare holding back tears. She swallowed and after a few moments was finally able to speak. "Yes, thank you, Vae."

They left the lunch; Sandi's food remained untouched. She drove home in a stupor, unable to process the news she'd just received. Her mother was dead? No one had told her. Sandi was devastated. She wasn't even invited to the funeral. Her family remained toxic and brutal in their association with her.

"Don't waste your time," I suggested. "They don't deserve your loyalty."

That's the pot calling the kettle black.

Another truth: though Sandi was my first priority, I still pined for my family.

Her mother had been dead for over a month and she had just received the news. Part of my role as husband was to comfort her, but I didn't know how to do that under the circumstances. So, I just held her that evening and let her cry in my arms.

Neither of us slept that night as grief overwhelmed each of us for different reasons.

———◆———

"I want to attend a women's Bible study group," Sandi announced one day a few weeks later.

"What's that?" I asked.

"It's a dozen or so women who get together once a week to talk about life. I haven't been to church in a lot of years, Gil. I was disillusioned by the disconnect between what I was taught in church and what really went on in my family. But we're going to have our family now and I want it to be a part of our life."

"Go for it," I replied. What could I say? She needed support and maybe this group would provide it. There was a bigger picture that needed to be acknowledged. Religious differences couldn't get in the way, so I stuffed down my Jewish background and supported her move back to Christianity.

The experience proved to be a good investment of Sandi's time. She made friends and continued to weave healthier people into her life. I was pleased and eventually met one of her new friends, Ashley. I couldn't help but encourage Sandi's budding relationship with her; she was a decent woman and I wanted their friendship to continue. I met Ashley's husband. Everett was a good man, a good fit for Ashley. We hit it off right away and before too long, the four of us became great friends.

I was invited to a presentation given by the church. Sandi wanted me to go, using her "what've ya got to lose?" argument. I was always on the losing side of that.

You're almost forty; this will be the first church you've ever walked into.

It seemed a bit daunting but sitting in a room with a bunch of enthusiastic Christians wasn't as difficult as I'd first thought it might be…strange, but not unbearable.

"Believers will have eternal salvation. The only way to heaven is through Jesus."

I shifted in my chair and crossed my legs, bouncing one foot up and down.

Are you really buying into this, Gil?

I wondered if the speaker had heard the voice in my head. I bit my lip and stared at the lady seated across from us. The lady's glance darted from behind glasses that rested nearly on the tip of her nose. She looked from Sandi to me, then back down to her book. I didn't know what a "believer" was and couldn't understand what anyone was saying. So far, Christians seemed like a cult.

Whose God is he talking about? Yours? Mine? I thought and pinched my lips together so that the words wouldn't escape. My hand had found its way to the scar resting over the place on my chest where my heart beat strongest. I don't know how it got there but touching it reminded me of the burn beneath and I knew I would soon hear the voice in my head, the one lying deep within my heart.

The word is "believer" and it means someone who believes in Jesus, being part of a list, so to speak, of the only people who will be allowed into heaven.

I still didn't comprehend what the voice was saying but I seemed to grasp the concept. The lady leaned back in her chair and crossed her arms. I slid down in mine, hoping to be as small as possible. Maybe she and Sandi would stop looking at me.

Yes, Gil. The Christians call you a non-believer. You're heading down a path that will change the course of yours and Sandi's future for the rest of your lives.

"Believing in Jesus will bring me peace?" I whispered to the voice in my head, remembering what Sandi had said about my health. "This doesn't happen very much where I come from." Lines formed between my eyes and Sandi leaned forward in her chair. I slunk down further into mine. My chest hurt.

"What's wrong, Gil?" she whispered in my ear.

"Nothing," I whispered back.

"Well, stop fidgeting and try to be quiet," she said and shifted again in her chair, smiling a fake grin at the man up in front.

I understand you are skeptical, Gil. The voice in my head wouldn't leave me alone. Sitting still would be impossible.

"Stop bothering me!"

Sandi shushed me and nudged me with her elbow.

Please understand, Gil. I am just trying to help you.

The lady sitting across from us pushed the glasses up her nose and glared at me.

"She can't hear you, can she?" I asked the voice in my head.

Christians don't understand that you've been told the exact opposite of this for the past forty years. What an impact a decision to join them would have for you. You trust Sandi, but maybe you shouldn't trust the rest of 'em.

"Well, what else am I supposed to do? She's my wife and she wants this."

Another round of nasty looks followed by "Shh!" came my way. The voice ignored my question and continued on, using words that I normally wouldn't understand. But for some reason, when they were spoken by the voice in my head, I understood everything. Sandi pushed to the edge of her chair and sat very straight. She drummed the tip of one finger on the edge of her knee. Apparently, fidgeting was contagious. The lines deepened in her forehead and I could tell she was guessing that I wasn't buying it. The man at the podium rustled some papers lying on top and spoke without even looking up.

It's fallout from the peoples' decisions. What they do today will affect the rest of their lives...and into eternity.

"Amen!" The man at the pulpit smiled.

Sandi stood up and began to clap with the rest of the people gathered in the room. "It's over," she said. "We can go now." The lady across from us stood up too.

"It's obvious from what you're saying that you have no idea about what really goes on in Jewish families." My voice rose higher as the whispering became audible. Sandi grabbed her purse with one hand and my hand with the other.

"What are you babbling about, Gil?" she asked, irritated. "You can't hold still for one hour?"

"Sorry, Sandi," I said and trailed along with her.

"Come on," she said and pulled me out the door. I glanced at the lady who'd sat across from us. She was staring with her arms crossed. I think Sandi was embarrassed but she didn't stop walking and wouldn't let go of my hand until we got to the car. We made good time back to the house, only speaking once in a while, mainly to ourselves.

I decided not to answer, even though the voice kept asking the same questions over and over again. *Who do they think they are? Christians can't tell you you're not going to heaven, and Sandi's a part of it. How do they think you'll cope? Who do they think they are?*

Over the next few months, I went to church a handful of times and was surprised to hear people reading from the Old Testament. I decided to read the Bible and soon found myself hungering for more religion in my life. As best as I could tell, the Jewish people in my life didn't seem to be living according to The Old Testament. Interestingly, the Christians didn't seem to be living according to The New Testament either. The premise of God, to honor marriage and family, was present in both books, which was significant for more than just religious reasons.

A baby was soon to be born, joining Sandi and me. There was the bigger picture to consider and it included our child.

———◆———

Several months later, after a Sunday dinner with Everett and Ashley, we made our way to the car, bidding them good night and making plans for another dinner soon. I opened the door for a very pregnant Sandi, who struggled, moving into the now tiny space that was her seat on the passenger side. I took my place next to her in the driver's seat, glanced over, and saw that her expression had changed from one of joy to one of despair.

"What's wrong, Pi?" I asked and put one hand on her knee.

"I think the baby's coming," she said and looked up into my eyes, then beamed. An enormous grin crossed her face!

The drive to the hospital happened almost without my knowing; wildly inconsistent thoughts filled my head as my heart pounded. I was going to be a daddy!

"Sandi, you will never miss one single day of your baby girl's life!" It was the very first thing I said the moment Danielle was born at 2:08 p.m. the next day. Tears welled up as I gazed down on the beautiful face, swaddled in a pale yellow and pink blanket, sprinkled with the outlines of bunnies.

"She's absolutely beautiful, Pi. I'm so happy for you!"

"She's amazing," Sandi said. She couldn't tear her eyes away.

Danielle was born on a Monday. She was perfect, untainted by a world that had been unfair to her parents.

Hers will be a life free from the neglect and loneliness that I have endured.

"She is my daughter, my precious responsibility, and I mean to make certain to protect her and her mother," I whispered in response to my thoughts.

You'll be a good daddy, Gil. You know what the results of a destructive, toxic family can be, which makes you powerful against repeating the pattern.

The voice was right. My chest was full but there was no pain over the scar on my chest. I smiled; there was no argument from me.

"The Bears are playing the Dolphins," I said to Danielle a few hours after she was born. She slept peacefully in my arms, unaware of the television broadcasting the football game overhead. "You're going to love watching football with me." My heart was full as I cuddled her, glancing at her sleeping mother, peaceful in the bed next to where we sat.

This is your perfect moment, Gil.

"Yes, this is the moment I've dreamt about for almost forty years," I said aloud to my sleeping family.

Time passed quickly and our little girl grew into a toddler before we realized it. Our friendship with Everett and Ashley blossomed as well; their influence over our little Danielle became invaluable. We had been friends for more than a year, and they had become more than just acquaintances. Our two families were together for all of the important days of the year; a good portion of our time was spent with them, and they had become our extended family, so to speak. Our daughter didn't have aunts, uncles, cousins, or even grandparents. It seemed only fitting to ask Ash and Ev to be godparents.

We spoke about how, if anything ever happened to us, we wanted them to take care of our children. The title of godparents was way more than a symbolic gesture to us. They were honored by the request and didn't hesitate for a moment to accept. Sandi and I would both sleep a little more soundly that night.

"But you said 'children,' Gil," Ashley said, raising one eyebrow.

I exchanged a smile with Sandi before answering.

"Yes, I did in fact. Sandi's due in six months," I said, and Everett jumped up from the table, nearly knocking over our glasses, to shake my hand.

"That's just great, buddy! Just great!"

"I should have figured something was up when Sandi filled her glass with water instead of wine like the rest of us," Ashley added.

Sandi tipped her glass in a mock toast.

"You are more than friends," I said, and raised my glass, offering a proper toast. "To our family, the closest family we have ever known and loved. So many of my happiest memories are of our two families together. From inside jokes to the practical ones played on each other, to you being present for so many of the first things Danielle has done as well as being the only ones who know about the funny origin of my nickname for her."

We tipped our goblets together and expressions of love followed. I was so thankful they had come into our lives and even more grateful that they wanted to serve as godparents to our children.

Nearly six months to the day, and sixteen months after Danielle was born, our second daughter, Leigh was born. She was the perfect addition. I couldn't imagine falling in love all over again with another baby girl but that's exactly what I did. Danielle was a big sister and she was crazy about the idea, so protective and gentle with her baby sister. My life was complete. We decided to give Leigh a middle name. The choice was not made easily. Our daughter deserved more than just a name from a book. It was decided to name her Ashley, after her godmother. The names flowed, a beautiful tribute to a beautiful woman and dear friend.

Leigh's birth was another "Godly" moment for me. My Jewish family wasn't part of my life and Sandi's reconnection with Christianity meant more and more to both of us because of the family we'd created with Ashley and Everett.

I had previously only lived in New York City and Los Angeles. Now we lived one hour south of LA. Here, in Mega-Church Alley, I was a fish out of water and among the four of us, I was the odd man out—the Jew.

"Christianity is all about being selfless and giving," Sandi explained.

That's all you've ever been to Sandi, so living that way won't be anything new to you.

"I guess this is supposed to be a Godly way of life, as opposed to a worldly way of life," I responded, unsure whether it was to Sandi or the voice in my head.

"Exactly," she replied.

It will be different and you can finally be accepted for who you are, rather than what you are not.

It was a good point.

"It's the same God the Jewish faith worships, after all. I don't know what the issue is," Sandi said. It sounded so rational that I couldn't argue.

So, I declared my leap of faith into the world of Christianity on Christmas Day in Ashley and Everett's home. They had given me a Bible that day with a heartwarming inscription written by Ashley. It was one of the most meaningful gifts I'd ever received.

My health was getting better already. I still walked on eggshells though, worrying about Sandi's health. Once again, tucked away with my precious toddler, wife, and our newest addition sleeping soundly in my arms, I experienced a feeling of being complete. I felt a lingering sense of shame lift from my life.

Our lives together had unfolded with joy, more than either of us dreamed was possible. I thought that it would last forever. Of course, the rain falls soon after the sun shines brightest.

CHAPTER 30

—◆—

SANDI APPROACHED ME WITH TEARS in her eyes.

"I miss Gabe," she said. The girls were asleep in the next room, our family tucked in for the night. Sandi always opened up to me during these brief hours in the evening when we had some privacy, so I knew she needed to talk.

"I do too," I said and waited for her to begin.

"The girls are so lucky. They have what Gabe will never have."

"What's that?" I urged.

"Parents who love him, who live in the same household, and are all about making his life happy…safe…peaceful."

I didn't know how to answer her because she was right. Gabe was a victim of a divided home, something I could not imagine for my own daughters. I couldn't imagine the new pain Sandi must be experiencing. She wanted to re-engage with her son but it wasn't as simple as it sounded. We had our children to consider now. I was conflicted about how to support my wife. I couldn't risk Sandi becoming sick again by reconnecting with the people who were the source of her sickness to begin with. Her family had always acted in toxic ways, and there was nothing to indicate that she would be treated appropriately as Gabe's mother. Should I risk her being treated poorly by "kinfolk" or keep her safe without the dysfunctional people we called "family"?

I felt agonizingly alone because those now in our life hadn't known Sandi years ago and so they didn't understand my angst over what appeared to them a seemingly simple decision.

Sandi's health had continued to improve.

Recently, she was offered an opportunity to train to become a part-time instructor in an exercise program. Sandi didn't believe she could pull it off, but I knew she could and encouraged her to try. She became a great teacher with the eventual opportunity to buy a franchise. That offer fell through, but the idea of Sandi running her own company was invigorating.

Again, Sandi didn't believe she could do this and again, my belief in her gave her the confidence to try. We put money into the venture and I helped her start the company. It never became a source of much income but that didn't matter; Sandi loved it. The effort paid off when a look of accomplishment crossed her face. She was proud of herself and happy, which is all that I ever wanted for my wife.

"What do you want to do?" I asked, knowing there was no support outside of these walls. Gabe came from a different set of circumstances with different players each vying for a piece of him. It was a game for Russell and he played it well, leaving Sandi always on the defensive with Gabe as the sacrificial pawn.

"Let's try."

"Okay," I said hopefully, but doubt clouded my optimism. Without the threat of going to court, we could be walking blindly into another ambush of Sandi's health.

We made contact two weeks later, and tried to pull Gabe into our life, but everyone again found their customary dysfunctional places with Gabe as the tool to injure Sandi. Ultimately, the events took a toll on Sandi. While she did not outwardly become self-destructive in the same way she had years ago, her lack of coping still caused wounds that would not easily heal. I tried to intervene and she turned her anger on me.

"I don't get it, Pi," I said one day trying to break the tension between us.

"Don't call me that…not now!"

"Why are you so angry with me? I've had your back through all of this," I countered.

"Well, you take your pain out on the ones you love," was her response. Her rationale made no sense, and I was taking the brunt of it.

"I get that you need to take your frustration out on someone, maybe even turning on the ones you love. But you can't take your life's pain out on me. Not again," I said. "I can't pay the price for your family again."

The vise took hold but I stood my ground. We had daughters to think about now and I couldn't be the only one holding this family together. We both knew what we were signing up for from Day One of marriage and of parenting. There were no excuses, not anymore. All the cards were on the table from the beginning and this is what we vowed to do, "for richer or poorer, in sickness and in health, for better or for worse…till death do us part."

She refused to talk to me after that.

"No one will ever love you the way Gil does…you know that, don't you?" Vanessa glanced over her coffee at Sandi and waited for a response.

I had just walked into the house and neither woman sensed my presence yet. I decided to remain a secret and stole silently down the hallway toward the bedroom, waiting just within earshot to hear Sandi's reply.

"Yes, I know," Sandi said, and took a sip.

Her voice had that too-familiar melancholy about it and my gut started to squirm. The vise would soon return and I didn't want to admit that its presence meant bad things ahead for Sandi and me.

"Then why are you…"

I wondered the same thing. My life as a father and husband was something that made me proud. I had spent years trying to do right by my wife. I was taking care of her and the girls as best I could, doing everything possible to make their lives easier, more peaceful, and pleasant.

I took pride in my ability to be the kind of husband that Sandi deserved and an amazing dad to both of my girls, to be there every step of the way, feeding them, changing diapers, rocking them to sleep, involved in every aspect of their lives as babies. Sitting on the sidelines as a spectator dad was the farthest thing from what I had become. I made sure I witnessed their first steps. I read to them, taught them how to ride a bicycle, played soccer with them, took them to parks and beaches on lazy Saturdays. The list seemed endless; I wasn't just their "birth father," I was their daddy.

You know what's happening, don't you?

"No! I won't believe it," I said aloud.

No! This was not happening. I refused to accept it and told the voice so again.

Mission impossible. The vise cinched itself around my heart this time and the scar flared.

Evidence bore out my theory. My health had been improving, but began to suffer again as Sandi took her pain out on me. Worse than ever this time, because with two toddlers she knew she couldn't take any out on herself. I got it all and then some. The eggshells stayed underfoot with Sandi's health always in the back of my mind.

The Fujiwhara effect is a phenomenon said to occur no more than once in fifty years. It is a perilous event, a maelstrom so rare that experts cannot accurately identify it until it's too late, often putting lives at stake. A trifecta of cold against heat with the added bonus of raging tempests equals the perfect recipe for something now known as the "Perfect Storm."

I should have been able to predict the perfect storm headed my way the day Sandi walked into the kitchen and announced, "Something's up with Ashley."

"What do you mean, 'something's up with Ashley'?" I asked. My attention was focused on making a sandwich.

"I don't know exactly, but I can tell something's up." Sandi grabbed her keys and headed for the car.

I didn't make much of it even though the two of them had been making more than the normal amount of small talk lately. I figured it was nothing more than the usual gossip that happens at the nail salon or over lunch. I heard the car pull out of the driveway and sat down to eat. I would hear about it later.

At about the same time Sandi pulled into the parking lot of the Italian Bistro just three doors down from the church, Ashley pulled up and hopped out of her car.

"I've been dying to eat here since last summer. Why don't we do this more often?" Sandi said and hugged her friend. Ashley was less receptive. A cool glance at Sandi implied this was not a lunch date that included warm affection.

"I'm bored with Everett," Ashley admitted after they had been seated and served coffee.

"Bored? How can you be bored, Ashley? He's a wonderful husband," Sandi countered.

Ashley clutched Sandi's hand. "That's just it. He's too nice. And boring because of it, I guess."

Sandi remained silent. A wave of foreboding washed over her as she stared at an empty coffee cup. Lifting her eyes to meet Ashley's, Sandi found her voice, although it refused to sound strong.

"What are you going to do?"

"I don't know but I can't just keep on pretending that I'm happy, that our marriage is satisfying," Ashley said. She set her coffee cup down with enough force that it echoed in the tiny restaurant. A few eyes glanced their way, then the diners quickly returned to their meals.

"Have you talked to Everett about this?"

Ashley's look suggested an answer that didn't sit favorably with Sandi.

"I mean, Ashley, you've been happily married for more than ten years to the man. He deserves to know how you feel."

"He knows. I don't have to tell him," Ashley snapped, the words sounded as bitter as the unsweetened coffee.

"You're family. What can Gil and I do to help? We don't want to see either of you suffer," Sandi offered.

"Too late for that."

Tears filled Sandi's eyes as she met Ashley's.

"I've got to go. Thanks for lunch." Ashley kissed Sandi on the cheek and walked out of the restaurant.

When Sandi returned, she gave me the news. My stomach dropped. *This is bad!* I knew the tides had changed for Ashley and Everett. My gut told me so, but I couldn't put my finger on exactly what had happened.

"Maybe they just need time," I said, but both Sandi and I knew what that meant. Ashley had started down the same course she'd navigated so many times before. The winds of time were not her friend when it came to marriage, and her pattern was continuing with Everett.

"This is her third marriage, Gil. She's making a huge mistake," Sandi voiced the obvious.

"I'll talk to Everett," I offered, but I knew it wouldn't make a difference. The trouble was Ashley and her loose definition of commitment.

"They're the godparents of our girls, Gil. What'll we do?"

"Well, we're not going to assume the worst. Nothing drastic has happened yet. Most marriages face problems and the couple works through it, rides out the storm, so to speak." My voice sounded more hopeful than sure.

"I hope you're right," Sandi said.

She beat me to the idea to meet with Ashley again. I prayed that something would dispel the clouds that hung over Everett and Ashley, but I had little hope.

Sandi's lunch with Ashley proved my hunch correct.

"Marriage is like that. One day it's bliss and the next, the doldrums set in. But it's no reason to give up," Sandi said, sipping from her wine glass.

"Perhaps that's true for most marriages but not for mine. He's just boring!"

"How can you say that, Ashley? He's a good man. The other guys you married were nowhere near as stable as Everett is, and you have two kids together."

"They were fun!"

Sandi took another sip and hoped her tears wouldn't spill into the crystal. With little emotion, Ashley dug into the panzanella spread over the gold-encrusted china. Fine linen, soft violins, and authentic Italian cuisine did little to lift Sandi's spirits. She hoped the wine would do its job and dull the pain.

"According to you, they put themselves first, Ash. That is something Everett will never do." Ashley shook her head and refused to comment, so Sandi continued. "He does everything he can to make you happy. I mean, a trip to New York City for your fortieth birthday just this year. Not many husbands—"

"A lot of husbands take their wives on trips. The others couldn't afford it, that's all."

"But that's my point, Ashley! Everett could afford it and you only had to say that's what you wanted and it was done. Now you're complaining he doesn't do enough?"

"I'm not complaining, just stating a fact. He's not a fun guy to be married to. The mortgage, the bills, the kid's expenses, and even the timeshare—everything else comes first. Where's the fun? We have no money for excitement."

Sandi returned home from lunch barely able to speak. Little in the way of comfort seemed to help but I slipped my arm around her shoulders and pulled her close anyway.

"If this happens, things for us will never be the same," she said. "They are choosing to abandon everything they love, including us. Has Ashley given any thought to how this will affect us?"

I didn't know what to say.

Sandi went on. "The thing that amazes me is how flat she is about it all. I mean, she didn't even balk when I called her out on the New York trip."

"That's cold," I joined her lament. "He gives her a vacation and she decides he's not good enough?"

"Exactly! She's timed it right too. The magic ten-year mark just hit so if she leaves him she'll get half of his hefty pension as well."

"Do you really think that's what she did?" I asked, incredulous.

The look Sandi gave me was all the answer I needed. Our lives would change. We had spent every holiday together, everyone's birthdays, church together every Sunday with lunch afterward—it would all come to an end.

"And who will be our kids' godparents? I certainly wouldn't want Ashley raising them...not now, anyway."

"Let's hope we're wrong." I pulled Sandi closer, almost afraid to let her go.

———◆———

Over the next few weeks, Sandi's conversations with Ashley became more frequent and any remaining hope faded. As Ashley grew colder to her husband, the heat turned up between them, and tempers flared. I prayed for them...for us. How would we handle it one more time, the very thing that had crippled us our entire lives, divorce within our family? These were people we called family and the devastation would be just as great as if they were blood relatives.

A few weeks later, right after Leigh's second birthday, Sandi came home from her visit with Ashley and confirmed the outcome.

"They're getting a divorce." Sandi announced through tears.

As if on cue, thunder rumbled outside and rain began to pour. The perfect storm had found its way into our lives. Losing Sandi's family, losing my family, and now, losing the family we created, our church family, so to speak…I wondered if it was more than we could handle.

"I can't believe it!" A wave of nausea hit as I considered the impact this would have on my daughters, their godchildren. I began to pace. Even though I knew there'd been trouble, the words still sent a shock wave from my spine to my gut. Everett and Ashley had the perfect union. I had been certain that divorce would never rear its ugly face in that marriage.

"I told her I couldn't support her decision. It's just not right," Sandi said. She was adamant.

"You know your stand on this will damage your relationship with her?"

She turned a sour look on me, half angry, half sad, before answering. "Of course I do!"

"Okay."

Weeks later, they were still not on speaking terms. Sandi had made her point. Her position didn't damage the relationship, it destroyed it. The fallout would have the same effect as a nuclear explosion wiping out anything of value within reach, including relationships. My mind whirled, a tornado of thoughts, impressions, and sheer panic, all of which dug into my instinct stronger than I had the constitution to allow. Ashley's dysfunction was a cancer eating away at Sandi's relationship with her, and I feared it might eventually eat away at her bond with me.

"What happens for Ashley and Everett now?" I asked one day. The topic had been weighing on both our minds.

"That's up to Ashley," Sandi said. "But I'm finished with the mess she's caused in her own life and the garbage they preach at the church about 'loving one another' and 'marriage is holy'…all that crap."

"You don't mean that, Sandi. You're not going to give up on everything you value just because you don't agree with her decision."

"You support their divorce?" She leveled a stare at me that would stop a panther in his tracks.

"Of course not!" I countered, and she eased back a bit. "I just don't want to see you throw away the baby with the bathwater."

"I don't know what you mean, Gil. I'm not throwing anything away. I'm just done with believing in futility and dreams. I'm done with this Christian crap!"

"Can't you see this is more than just the drama surrounding a bad decision? It's about destroying families!" I began to pace, hoping to temper the emotions that would remove any credibility from what I wanted to say. Men who cry aren't taken seriously.

"It's all wishful thinking. This whole Christianity thing is just stories, parables, and promises that never materialize. Divorce is the result." She was close to tears.

"You don't mean that." I pulled her into my arms.

"Ashley and Everett have broken a promise to us as well, Gil. How can we believe that they'll do right by their godchildren, our little girls? How can we believe anyone in that church will do right by us?"

She had a point and I had nothing for an answer. Our little girls were facing loss of a treasured relationship with people I had taught them to trust. I couldn't imagine the destruction these cataclysmic events would cause. It was more than I could face. Instead, I held Sandi and prayed we would wake up from this nightmare.

"I don't know, Sandi," I finally muttered, and deep down, I felt that my wife was right.

A few more weeks passed with the turmoil that follows the aftermath of an unplanned disaster. Church had become unbearable. I hung back near the rear of the chapel one sunny morning, and watched as my wife walked down the aisle in search of a place for us to sit. My little girls straggled along behind their mother, innocent and unaware the wake they trailed simmered up with unseen danger to their godparents continued presence in their lives. Sandi was isolated while Ashley relished the comforts given to her by fellow "saints." It was evident that our children's Christian godmother simply had no further need for my wife's friendship. She had plenty of friends in the church who supported her, even if her divorce didn't match their stated values. The friendship would never recover.

Another trifecta moved before my eyes. My wife, my daughters, and I were pulled into another family's frenzy of failing hope, and Christianity did not throw us a remedy or a lifeline. Once more, I found myself in a broken family with a separation that resembled my broken family of childhood in the Jewish community.

The hypocrisy was more than Sandi could bear. Too soon, in the aftermath of the loss of our closest friends, Sandi's lifestyle turned inward on itself and she began to step away from the one we had chosen to live together. Our life as a Christian family was supposed to be safe and secure, so I believed, the true path that would bring our family peace and unending love. That didn't happen. The tide that divided our friends threatened to divide us as well. Sandi walked away from the church and never looked back.

As loved ones limped away, I stood by and watched the people around me, wondering what had happened to the hope I'd built upon friends who had captured my heart and my trust. Now surrounded by more dysfunction and chaos, I asked myself, "What the heck have I signed up for? I thought this was supposed to be different?"

Look around you, Gil. The loss is tremendous and you're the only one who seems to notice. I was dumbfounded but wasn't going to quit...not yet. The aftermath of devastation is overwhelming to most. My wife and I were no exception.

If perhaps you had seen the storm on the horizon and had somehow braced yourselves against it, your friends too, do you think they'd still be married and would have remained friends?

I had no idea, honestly.

Just like the perfect storm that had taken the *Andrea Gail*, the survivors of this land-based storm would be few. Lives would be forever changed because of the decisions made by our dearest friends. Our own recovery looked bleak as I watched Sandi move away and build her rage toward me—a familiar, dangerous course.

I turned my face to the horizon and prepared for the worst.

CHAPTER 31

———◆———

OUR DEAR FRIEND, GIL…

The page lay flat, without wrinkles or creases that come with frequent use. The page had been fingered, although it still had that crispy sound most pages that are gilded along the edge make as they're turned. I didn't want to hear the sound again. I couldn't. So, I simply stared at it.

He truly does hear our prayers and is faithful to answer.

I felt the air being sucked from my lungs. "No…not now…not from this." The words stuck in my throat as I tried to force myself to relax. My eyes wouldn't leave Ashley's meticulous penmanship.

Well, He obviously didn't answer your prayers, did he, Gil? What's that about?

"Stop it!" My lips only mouthed the words. Without thinking, my hand lifted to the place over my heart where I knew a scar would be inflamed—a scar that no one else could see but me. I had to pull my glare from that book, to break free from its hold, but I couldn't get my eyes to obey my will.

It's not your will be done, Gil. Isn't that obvious. Nothing is your will.

I tried to blink but couldn't. A tiny drop of water fell onto the page. It must have come from me…from my eyes, perhaps?

He has heard your prayers and is already at work on your behalf.

I watched helplessly as the ink bled from the 's,' the one at the end of 'prayers.' My prayers, the words Ashley had written for me. The 's' smeared the crisp page as the tear settled. It was almost symbolic and as if to prove it, the book toppled from the table. I must have jarred it when I clutched the table. I think I was falling but I'm not sure; all I knew was that my chest hurt and I could not breathe.

"Help me."

There's no one to help you now, Gil. Don't you see that? 'Prayers' are answered for everyone else, not for you. It's obvious.

I looked around for someplace to sit, any place.

"I think I'm going to pass out..." I could hear the words form in my head but there was no sound from my lips, only the ringing in my ears that had begun sometime, before the book had fallen, I think.

I was in a tunnel. Or was that my life? I couldn't tell. Everything suddenly became distant as I fell into that narrow space reserved for the moment before you lose consciousness. I gasped. This was too familiar, too much like my reality. I was isolated from everything around me but no one knew it, just like no one knew I was about to slip away now. My eyes drifted once again to the book. Perhaps there would be an answer on its pages. At least, that's what I'd been told.

As you wait on Him for the answer that He will increase your faith and guard your heart from unbelief.

"Your answer was to divorce, Ashley. His answer was to believe in Him, to believe in the vows you made when you married Everett. The only thing that's happened to decrease my faith and open my heart to unbelief has come from you!"

Are you being dramatic again, Gil?

I swallowed in an attempt to clear the ache squeezing my chest and blocking my breath. My body screamed that something was wrong and my rational senses confirmed it.

"No!" I said aloud. My eyes wandered back to the page.

And bless him with patient endurance.

"Me? Bless me with patient endurance? Ha! Where was your endurance, Ashley?" My body began to quiver. The truth was too painful to bear. She had abandoned the very ethics she had preached to me and who would be the one to suffer for it, really? It was my task to sort through the values that mattered and the ones that could be discarded when life became too difficult; and still she preached to me about God.

Did Ashley think about that when she told you to turn to God?

"I don't know...please..."

I grasped at the table but it was too far from my reach, too far down the tunnel. I couldn't get to it. There was nothing for me, nothing but isolation. I could feel myself pulled further into the darkness.

Don't pass out, not here. You're without a chair to break your fall. You're always without a chair. Ashley and Everett gave you that book, that promise that they'd always be there for you. But they lied. It's all a lie.

"Stop...please have compassion and just stop."

It will never stop. The hypocrisy will always be there. Can't you see that? Even now, the two people who you trusted the most preached to you to follow God's will, but they don't follow it. They never intended to follow it... not really. The laws of the gospel are for everyone else, not for Everett and Ashley, not when it's inconvenient or uncomfortable. It's only for you...just you, Gil.

"But I can't..."

People you trust, people who preach at you, even people who give you gifts, like that Bible there. They all lie about what's truth and what makes life convenient. Abandonment has a valid reason; divorce does too. Just because it's written in the Bible, that holy of holy books, it doesn't mean anything. Not really, not when it makes life inconvenient.

My eyes dropped to the book lying on the floor. The crisp clean pages were crumpled and some of the words were smeared. I'd done it. I'd knocked the Bible from its resting place and shed tears over the ink. I'd been the one who damaged it.

But you have to, Gil. It's in your conscience to live by the rules, to honor truth, and that's why you're alone and always will be. Those who pledge their loyalty and love to you, they are the ones who never lived up to their promises. They bailed on each other, on your little girls, on you, Gil. They are the ones who damaged everything and you take the fall for it, because you believe in truth. What a waste.

I looked back at the Bible lying askew on the floor. It was damaged, just like me. Words had been inscribed on its pages, just like my life. I had been given promises. But all of it was blurred...forgotten. I felt the room spin as the realization of it all hit once more.

They've pulled another leg from the chair that you thought was yours. Will you have a soft place to fall, with friends, family, or promises? You're always the one without a chair, Gil.

I surrendered and watched as the ground came up to meet me. The last thing I saw was Ashley's handwriting:...*With all our love...*

Mercifully, the darkness took hold before I saw the rest.

———•———

CHAPTER 32

THE SUN DIPPED BELOW THE watery horizon as I took Sandi's hand in mine. Danielle jumped up and down with excitement as she watched the waves lap against the beach.

"This is where it is?" Danielle asked and clasped her hands together.

"Over there, *liebchen*." Sandi pointed to a white building with a peaked red rooftop and flower-filled boxes lining the front porch. I was always startled at her easy use of the German term of endearment.

"You speak German so well," I said.

She smiled and shrugged. I could sense something boiling under the surface.

"Always very impressive, Pi," I said. "You'll have to teach the girls."

"My mother, you know. She would have loved this school," Sandi said a little too casually as she followed Danielle onto the stoop. Placing her hands around her eyes, she peered through the glistening window into the empty schoolroom beyond the glass.

"I love it, mommy!"

Sandi's father was German. She was born in Germany. They had been estranged for most of her life and she seemed to search for anything to do with his culture.

"The founder is German," Sandi said absently. "It might be good for the girls to learn German too."

My heart sank. There was the dark key to her sulking of late. The connection between the German-born founder of this school and her father was a little too close for comfort. Add to that, the painful detail of Sandi's mother having been a teacher, and we had another trifecta for trouble building.

"Are you okay?" I put my arm around her.

"Of course I am. Why wouldn't I be?"

Something was amiss. I suspected it had more to do with the heavy grief Sandi still felt for her mother's passing. She never received closure, never got to say good-bye, didn't even know about the funeral. My best guess was that Sandi yearned for some connection to her parents, both of them. Perhaps this school facilitated the link in her mind.

Sandi took Danielle by the hand and led her to the side of the building.

"Guess what! They teach sign language here too. That's what my mother taught. You'll be able to learn it with the other children who go here."

I watched my daughter jump up and down again, then glanced down at our baby, still sleeping comfortably in the stroller. A chill ran down my back. We were in for some rough times ahead. I could feel it.

I had received my license to sell insurance a few years back, but my health got in the way of turning it into the career I had hoped for. Still, I was presented an offer to start an insurance agency, partnering with an agent I knew who wanted to come out of retirement. He had been very successful and I was flattered when he picked me to join him. With Sandi's support, in time I could provide well for my family.

Nothing more was said that day and Sandi acted as if the whole idea was perfectly normal. As always, my love for Sandi, as well as my fear that she would get sick again should she not be in a "happy" place, led me to act against my gut. As a result, the girls were now scheduled to attend a private school we could not afford.

Within a few weeks, Danielle started school at the very exclusive and expensive private establishment, although I was leery about her attending. Private school in Pacific Beach was not what I wanted for the girls. Quickly it became a source of contention between Sandi and me, no matter that we couldn't keep up financially with the private school's social circle. There it was, the third element of the trifecta!

As tension mounted, my health and business suffered and the debt to the school grew. Sandi couldn't see the problem inherent in continuing with private schooling for the girls; the school was more important than anything else. Sandi began volunteering at the school and in time, she wiggled her way into a part-time teaching job without any formal training or credentials. Unfortunately, what may have been a positive opportunity for her became a negative influence on our lives. Once again, to others this seemed like an awesome decision, but they didn't know Sandi the way I did.

The conversation was sour before it began. I kept my eyes glued to the back of Sandi's head, hoping she'd at least turn to face me, but she never did.

"Well, to me it seems that the school is more about you than it is about our daughters' education." It was a brave statement and my gut gnawed uncomfortably after the comment had left my lips.

"That's ridiculous! I only want what's best for the girls," she replied, her focus lowered to the sink where her hand feverishly washed dishes in suds at least an inch high. I could tell she was tense, although she maintained a casual tone in her voice as she spoke.

"What I mean is, I think that this is more about your connection to your parents." Only silence rose from the sink, so I continued. "I mean, I don't blame you. You never really got closure when your mom died and your culture is—"

"Stop!" She turned to face me and I saw a look on her face that I hadn't before. Suddenly, Sandi's eyes grew dark and I knew I would never see the light return to them again. She had turned into the one she never wanted to resemble: her mother, a teacher with kids from multiple marriages who cared more about being a daughter than a mother.

—————

Over the next few years, I watched as Sandi became more and more emotionally tied to the school—and even though we looked picture perfect in all we did together, less and less involved with our family and me. Something had changed. Everything was about the school and Sandi.

She's using the girls' education as a cover.

I couldn't hear that, not now. I shut down the voice in my head for the time being, but it wouldn't stay quiet long.

Barbara, my business partner Joel's wife, who was Sandi's mother's age and who Sandi confided in from time to time, took a chance and approached Sandi. "Honey, you're ripping your family apart chasing after your mother's ghost. She isn't here in the school. You've got to find closure with your mother some other way."

It didn't help, and Sandi resented Barbara for the comment. The whole situation reminded me of each time I sought resolution with my father. Every year or two I'd make contact, wishing without reason to that something would change. That was a hard lesson learned over and over again, just like Sandi was learning, or so I'd hoped. But I was wrong. Neither of us would learn the lessons taught from self-centered parents. And still we would continue to reach out...one more time.

After nearly six rings, Dad answered the phone. His voice sounded older than last time I heard it, yet it still carried the same edge I remember as a child.

"How are you doing, Dad?" I asked, expecting a polite and vague response.

"I've had two heart attacks and I had major surgery just a month ago."

I didn't know what to say and felt my throat tighten.

He paused for a moment, letting the silence between us settle before speaking again. "Gil? Is that you?"

"Uh, yeah, Dad, it's me. Listen, I don't want it to be like this anymore," I said without thinking.

"What are you talking about? Be like what?"

"No more distance. No more lengthy periods of time before we speak to one another again. I haven't seen you in ten years. You've never met your granddaughters." I couldn't stop. "I want us to be close, for you to get to know them. You're their grandfather, for heavens' sake."

There was a long pause before either of us said anything. I could feel tears wash over my cheeks, but I didn't bother to wipe them. When he finally spoke, his voice was hard, low.

"Look, Gil, this is how it is. This is how things are between us. I'm not the dad you've always wanted, and I won't be any different kind of grandfather for your girls either. And you're not the son I wanted. I'm embarrassed when my friends talk about their sons' accomplishments and I have nothing to say about you."

Ouch. Ignore it, Gil.

"You've been a great father for Carole's kids and for Debra. And a great grandfather for their kids. I've always been on the outside looking in at all the fun things you do with your family. You're eighty. This can't be how it ends between us, Dad?" My voice failed me.

"Yup, this is it. This is how it ends."

I hung up. I couldn't speak, not even to say good-bye.

That night, life moved forward as it always did, void of my father and the girls' grandfather. I kissed Sandi as she walked in the door and invited her to have dinner, a quick meal I'd put together before the girls got ready for bed. She sat down at the table and smiled at the girls but didn't eat. I assumed she was tired after a long day and wanted to help her relax a little.

"Go get your pajamas on and I'll be in to read you a story before bed," I said to our daughters and watched as they hopped down from their chairs, skipping hand-in-hand into their bedroom.

"Okay, Daddy," they said in unison. When they were gone, I turned my full attention to my wife.

"You seem beat today. Was it a rough day?" She said nothing so I continued. "Those sneakers you had your eye on are still on sale. Why don't you go pick them up tomorrow? You're on your feet all day. They'll really make a difference."

"Okay, Gil, if that's what you want." She wasn't engaged, although she was speaking. I needed her support and decided the small talk wasn't working.

"I spoke to my father today. Dad had a heart attack this month. Actually, he's had a couple, and a major surgery also." I wiped a tear and continued. "I've always had a glimmer of hope things would change between Dad and me, but it couldn't be any clearer today that they never will. I'll probably never ever see him again."

She glanced at me with vacant eyes for just a moment and said flatly, "I want a divorce."

CHAPTER 33

THEY SAY THAT EARTHQUAKES HAPPEN when a fault shifts somewhere, usually creating a large gaping fissure in the earth's surface. My marriage had just taken a direct hit and the shift would be irreparable.

I sat at the table dumbfounded, unable to speak. I was so shocked and hurt by her response. I said some things, expressed a few feelings, and decided to go for a walk. I didn't want to look at Sandi after what she had said. Her timing sucked. I couldn't believe she'd picked that moment to say it.

When I rounded the corner, headed back to my house, the police car was already parked at the curb. Glaring blue and red lights flashed rhythmically, illuminating the entire street. Every neighbor was staring at the front of our home, wondering what was going on.

"You've got to be kidding me!" I said aloud, though no one heard me. I walked up to one of the officers and asked what the problem was. He politely asked my name and what business I had at the home. I explained that I lived here and belonged to the family inside.

Nearly every couple develops a keen understanding of how to push each other's buttons, and some methods are more formidable than others are. "Divorce" was my nuclear button. That single word caused more pain in my heart than anything else. Explaining that concept to a police officer would be difficult.

"Your wife said you wanted to kill yourself," he said and I heard his radio squawk. The officer ignored it and stared me down, waiting for an answer.

"I made an off-hand comment to that effect," I admitted, then quickly added, "Do I look like someone who is going to commit suicide?"

You just didn't know what to say in response…it's as simple as that. You don't want to make Sandi look bad by telling this stranger what she said when you told her about your father.

It was true. My kneejerk reaction after Sandi pushed that button was to hit her with full impact, so I said the nasty word, "suicide" which conjured up hurt feelings about her mother.

I went on to explain that my dad had just suffered two heart attacks. I was feeling stressed, said the wrong thing, and went for a walk to clear my head. The officer seemed to understand where I was coming from and nodded.

A few minutes later, he left with his partner and the neighborhood went dark again. I made my way inside and found Sandi sitting with Barbara. She didn't look up and I could tell she was crying. They were in a heated emotional conversation that I didn't want to interrupt, but I wasn't going to let it ride in silence, not here. So I stood in the doorway and listened.

"Do you really want a divorce?" The question was gentle and Barbara's eyes moved to meet mine. I had called Joel while I was walking, not knowing where to turn, which maybe wasn't such a bad idea. Barbara had driven over to be with Sandi sometime between that call and the police officers' arrival.

Sandi shook her head. "No."

"Then you've got to stop saying that to Gil, sweetie. It sounds like you've been saying this a lot since you started working at the school. It's causing too much pain for the both of you. It's a tender spot. His

Achilles' heel, so to speak. You're pushing his buttons and hurting yourself at the same time." Barbara spoke softly.

Her advice was the same advice given to me by her husband moments earlier on the phone.

"You're pushing each other's buttons," he'd said, as if the solution were a simple fix.

I said nothing and studied Sandi's face. I was sure she would say exactly what she knew everyone wanted to hear for that moment. Barbara made eye contact again, a silent *agree with me on this, Gil.*

"You don't really want to kill yourself, now do you, Gil?" Barbara said in her reassuring voice.

I said nothing, didn't respond, and kept my eyes on my wife. She glanced at me and I could tell her light had gone out once again.

"There, see? Gil was just saying that to hurt you. He doesn't mean it. You are both just having a bad day," Barbara announced and prepared to leave. "I tucked in the girls and they were asleep before the cops got here."

So she had rushed over as soon as I'd called Joel. Thankfully, her intervention had spared the girls any drama. Sandi blew her nose and muttered a soggy, "Thank you" as Barbara made her way to the door.

"Joel and I will check in on you both tomorrow. Try to sleep. This will blow over by morning," she said, and walked out of the house, problem solved.

We said nothing to each other that night. I sensed there would be no going back from the damage that had been done. Our psyches couldn't handle such damage. The next morning, I rose early. I left before Sandi or the girls were up and immediately placed a call to Dr. Parsons.

"You can't push back, Gil," he said. His words stuck with me.

I counseled with him over the next few months and tried to retain the rational advice he offered as the situation escalated. "Take the healthy approach, but remember, you don't have to be a punching bag for her bad behavior either."

What the hell did that mean? I was supposed to decipher exactly how to be solid in a crumbling relationship with a volatile woman who oozed a screwy mental health status quo that prodded her outbursts.

I decided the only way to honor myself and hold it together was to promise myself to never again push back, or drop any bomb using the word "suicide." Mostly, I didn't want to answer to the police on a dark evening. It was a good MO and during the next several months, I kept my feet gingerly walking over the eggshells that cropped up every time Sandi said the "D" word, which was often. Her classic follow-up was, "I didn't really mean that. I just don't know how to handle marriage. I love you, Gil!"

I could hear a shell begin to pop every time that came out of her mouth. So I kept mine shut and tiptoed out of the conversation, as despite our family appearing so close-knit and fun-loving to others, Sandi slowly tiptoed out of my life.

"Did you threaten to kill yourself, Mr. Belmont?"

The officer was dressed in full uniform and I could see his bulky Kevlar jacket peeking underneath his pressed shirt.

"Yes, I said the words, but no. She knows exactly why I said them and the context I said them in," I said.

I didn't invite him inside and he didn't ask to come in. The neighbors were already at their windows, but I didn't care. *Why does she have to pick after dark to bring the cops here?* I glanced at the flash of red and blue illuminating the front of my neighbor's house.

"Well, your wife made the call and said you were serious about harming yourself, said you'd threatened it before, which I see here in our records," he said.

"That's a lie," I responded. "She got angry after I told her I was going to pull our girls from their private school tomorrow and put them in a public school. She kept saying she wanted a divorce and I told her that moving the kids to a new school would be the next step."

"Why does she want a divorce?" he asked, and glanced at a notebook in his hands.

What kind of a question is that?

"I don't know. She says it all the time. She also asked me to go get ice cream with her and our little girls. Did she tell you that too?"

"No."

"Why would she threaten divorce, ask me to join her for ice cream, offer to bring some back instead, and then call the cops to say I was threatening suicide? Why would anyone act that way unless they had problems themselves?" I almost let out "mental illness" but kept my word selection under scrutiny. With everything Sandi was, she didn't need me to label her as mentally ill. She was doing a great job of that herself.

"Well, Mr. Belmont," the officer said, and he paused a little too long. "You have two choices. You can either come willingly with me and we'll have a doctor take a look at you...or you can go involuntarily and I will place you on a seventy-two-hour hold."

"A 51-50?" I was shocked. I'd heard the term before, used in Sandi's past but never understood the depth of what that meant. It was clear that Sandi did and obviously knew what she was doing.

"If the doctor releases you, it will be within about ten minutes. When that happens, you can let your wife know that if she ever does this again, she'll be charged with filing a false complaint."

I had no choice. I gathered my things, locked the door, and walked down the sidewalk to the patrol car that still flashed its lights with an armed officer sitting inside. This was going to be a long night, no matter what. The ER would be the first obstacle; just getting through triage was always the biggest hurdle.

"Is there anyone you want to call first?" the Emergency Department's nurse asked me. She handed a wall phone to me. I thanked her, and immediately called Dr. Parsons.

"She called me after she'd already phoned the police, Gil," Phillip said in his professional therapy voice.

"Interesting that she didn't get in touch with you before, to get your advice, just as I always did. Interesting, she's so quick to make sure that I'm taken away, so quick to advance her own interests. I always called you rather than an ambulance in order to protect her, to protect her court case, Phillip, and you know it," I replied. I was furious. I covered for her so many times when she was drunk and had abused pills. So many times. I was scared of what would happen if I didn't call an ambulance, but I had always trusted in Dr. Parsons to help her, help us both through the immediate event so it would never hurt her in court. The tables had turned; this could hurt me if we ever ended up in court.

"Please wait over there," the nurse said, motioning to a vacant chair in the crowded waiting room. Apparently, I wasn't "urgent" and would have to wait.

It's a good time to reflect. Think about things, Gil. Remember when you were doing all her legal work? There was that one time when you had no choice but to call for an ambulance because she was in such bad shape after yet another round of booze and prescription medication.

I remembered. It was early in the morning and she ended up being released from the hospital early in the evening. As her "lawyer," I would continually write on her legal paperwork that she had never spent a night in the hospital since leaving Russell, which was technically true, but omitted the fact that she had been in the hospital. That would have destroyed her court case at the time.

You covered for her then. There's no one covering for you.

"I covered for her because her drug and alcohol abuse was in response to the abuse she was suffering from Russell and her family," I whispered. There were a lot of people whispering to themselves in this place, so I fit right in. "No, her response wasn't appropriate but she and her son shouldn't lose each other because she couldn't handle being treated poorly by those people."

Thinking back over the past few months, it made total sense to me. Sandi had begun to push certain friends away. I had to do something. I knew it. Barbara and Joel didn't visit anymore and rarely called to "check up on" us. The isolation that hovered over our circumstances was prime for what she'd just done to me. I should have seen it coming, but this was something I never dreamed she would be capable of.

You're making excuses for her again.

"Maybe." I cleared my throat and realized my therapist had gotten back on the phone. "Sorry, Phillip. This place is really busy," I added trying to cover for myself.

"Well, uh, let me make a few calls and I'll see what I can do," Phil said and quickly hung up.

That was the last I heard from him for the next eighteen hours. On Monday, the day I had arranged to meet with the public school administrators, the doctor finally showed up.

"Sorry about the confusion. Dr. Parson's message got lost," he said.

I was so angry I could barely speak but I knew that showing any emotions other than "calm and cooperative" would earn me a longer stay in the hospital. I'd been in the psych unit for more than eighteen hours, and no one noticed. Sandi was good and she knew how to play this game. Her timing was meticulous: a Sunday night when doctors are generally not around. She knew I wouldn't be released in time to make my appointment with the school officials, and the reason for my no-show would not help in any argument I could make about changing schools if Sandi and I ended up in court to face off against one another. I took a deep breath.

"No worries. I know you get busy and things get messed up sometimes," I said and smiled.

Our conversation went forward pleasantly. He asked what happened and I explained. In ten minutes, I was released with the diagnosis of:

Marital and financial issues—not requiring mental evaluation.

That was generous. As I was handed my belongings, he said, "You really never should have been brought here."

I could have told him that eighteen hours ago.

I returned home to a very strained environment that grew tense with the aftereffects of my hospital "visit." Sandi took no responsibility for it. Within weeks, the letter from my medical insurance carrier arrived denying coverage for my hospital "hold" because it was "not medically necessary." The bill was enormous, and worse than that, the stamp "51-50" would now appear on my health record.

Ironically, only three days earlier, the restriction placed by the Medical Information Bureau for the only hospital stay I'd ever had—fifteen years ago, when I'd met Sandi—had been removed from my health records. Sandi's manipulation wiped out fifteen years of waiting for a "clean record" and branded me once again as mentally unstable to life insurance companies. In the realm of life insurance, I couldn't get covered, which meant I couldn't protect my family.

All those years you worked so hard to look out for Sandi. Look where it's gotten you. You were so upset when you first applied for life insurance and were turned down because of that voluntary hospitalization you thought was so smart.

"At the time, I was so worried she'd be at the mercy of Russell and her family if anything ever happened to me." The argument was moot.

And, when you were turned down again after the girls were born, you were heartbroken because you knew you couldn't count on relatives to help watch over your family if anything ever happened to you.

"That's exactly why I hadn't sought more help for my issues, because I had to keep my record clean and look out for my family's best interests," I argued back.

My point exactly. Look where it's gotten you.

A hole opened up and I could feel myself fall into it. Despite years of effort to maintain a healthy, normal life for my wife and daughters,

Sandi's antics had obliterated everything we had worked for, and she'd done it in just one night.

You're a life insurance agent without life insurance, unable to tell clients the truth when they ask you about the coverage you carry for your own family.

Always more secrets to keep.

I needed help and needed it fast.

When God closes a door, He opens a window.

"That's an odd comment to end this argument with," I said aloud. No one heard me. It seemed they never did. I thought about the saying, as the voice remained silent. I had heard it said before and realized that even my trap doors had been welded shut. I needed to find that open window and decided to look within the church. Not that long ago, it had been a big part of our lives.

———◆———

Sarah was the counselor who had shown interest in Gabe's situation years ago when Sandi and I were desperate for help. My circumstances seemed as desperate as any I'd faced before and Sarah seemed to be the next best step. A brief session with her revealed much about the interaction Sandi and I had had as a couple many years ago.

"It was 'crisis of the moment' counseling, Gil. You both were in distress and we focused on the immediate problems regarding Gabe," she said, matter-of-fact. "Sandi quit the day Gabe wasn't able to come down for the week he was supposed to because Russell sent him away with her family. You've never done any serious, in-depth marriage counseling."

Perhaps that was the problem. We weren't trained to be marriage partners, let alone parents. How could I expect positive results without background knowledge of what that would entail?

"That makes sense," I said and looked down at the hands folded in my lap. They had been through so much in the short years of my life. I hadn't even hit fifty yet, but my hands looked old, tired.

"Listen, Gil. I'm not taking on any new clients at this time but... come in with Sandi and I'll work with you both. You're important to me, and your marriage matters. Let's see if I can help you address some of the inherent problems."

I looked at her with gratitude. "Thank you."

"Good. Make arrangements with my secretary and I'll work you in." She escorted me to the door and then paused. "Oh and Gil, don't take the girls out of the school just yet. I think the less 'waves' you make right now, the better." My face must have betrayed my thoughts because she quickly added, "Don't misunderstand me; I don't think the school is a good idea at all. In fact, I'm thinking just the opposite. That place is an unhealthy environment for your family."

"Then why keep the girls in there?" I asked. I was rather confused and wanted to keep up with her logic but anger was getting in the way.

"Gil, you've already seen the lengths she'll go to. Take some time to address the issues. Let's get through some counseling and see what happens next."

I shook my head and my eyes dropped again. Gently, she placed her hand on my shoulder. "Is this the hill you want to die on, Gil?"

Sandi refused to go see Sarah. To make matters worse, she insisted that she wanted nothing to do with Sarah because she had been part of the church that silently watched Ashley leave Everett. Sandi didn't believe in church anymore.

She was right.

Nevertheless, I knew Sarah was our best hope. I went home to pick my battles in this developing war.

A few days later, Phillip spoke with Sandi and encouraged her to seek counseling as well. It was a known fact that I had been to see Sarah for advice and that I planned to return. Sandi was next to follow, although convincing her to do so was a challenge. Phillip had his work cut out for him.

"I don't need any more therapy!" Sandi insisted, as Phillip broached the subject. "I've had more therapy than you or Sarah will have in a lifetime!"

"It's not about us, Sandi. This is about you and your marriage," Philip said, attempting to pull her back on track. "Both of you made some significant mistakes. Gil is the only one who's paid a price, though."

"That's not true!"

After that, Sandi became distracted, distant. I felt as though I was living with a ghost. She'd adamantly refused to go to any counseling session, leaving me holding the therapy "ball" with no one on my team.

You're crossing a boundary here, Gil.

"You don't have to tell me," I said quietly. "This is nuts!"

Think about this. You can't go back and 'un-ring the bell.' You'll never be able to undo what you're about to do.

"Look, I know what I'm doing."

In desperation, I looked at her email. Our passwords were the same, so it would be easy to get in, though it would be hard to cross a line that was not part of my character.

When I opened Sandi's account up and began scanning through the list of emails, I stumbled across something that didn't seem real. I blinked my eyes and read it again. There was no mistaking to whom the email was addressed or what the message contained:

| Helene | 7:43am | ★ |
| Re: Miss you already | Yesterday | |

Who exactly was "Helene" and what was Sandi doing writing to her? I scrolled the cursor over her name and hesitated, ready to click the email open.

"There are at least twenty more emails between Sandi and this *Helene*." I could barely spit out her name. "And I want to know why Sandi is writing to her!"

Why? Why do you want to know?

"Because…" I really had no answer. There was only the vise that gripped my insides, warning me something was wrong. "Because my gut tells me there's more to these than just an innocent email to a friend…someone I've never heard of before, by the way."

Listen to your instincts, Gil.

Without thinking any more about it, I clicked on the email and watched the words spring to life on the laptop screen.

Sandi wrote to Helene:

Helene	10:52pm

I've missed you more than you'll ever know. The days drag between seeing each other in private and casually in the hallways. Please, help me find a way to make this less of the struggle than it is. Maybe when you get back from Catalina…

What was Sandi saying?

There will be some free time for us after school on Friday. Find some way to slip out, if even for just an hour, and I will meet you in our usual place. I need to be with you. Need to feel your arms around me and feel the tenderness of your soul again…

An affair!

I couldn't stomach anymore. I clicked off the computer. It was clear that Sandi had taken a road I did not know existed. She was having an affair with someone named Helene! I couldn't swallow, my mouth having gone dry in spite of the tears that welled in my eyes. I needed to get away from the computer, away from my life for a moment, and think.

Isn't Helene a woman's name?

I'd heard the name *Helene* before. Where? Catalina? This was familiar and I needed to figure it out.

Think, Gil. Catalina...school...Helene...

"Helene Garner!" The teacher? Miss Helene? That's where I'd heard the name before. She was to be Danielle's teacher this coming year, the teacher who had taken Leigh's summer camp class to Catalina just last month! I had met with her during parent-teacher orientation only six or seven weeks ago! I felt a wave of nausea hit. Suddenly, the walls began to cave in and I could barely hear the sounds of the city outside.

Don't pass out, Gil.

I rushed to the bathroom. I forced myself to take a breath but it was too late. Retching took away most of the anxiety for the next five minutes but then it hit again, this time as the image of Mrs. Garner flooded my mind.

You know this woman.

She was old enough to be Sandi's mother. Nausea hit again and I couldn't get oxygen into stiffening lungs. The air around me grew thinner. My ears began to ring. Blindly, I began to walk with arms outstretched, just to prevent a fall.

Maybe a glass of water. Try that.

"I'm going to pass out," I whispered to no one, knowing I was the only one awake, trusting that some invisible being would help. I glanced around the living room, looking for anywhere that would break a sudden fall. The ringing in my ears increased to the sound that a trumpet makes when playing its highest note. My heart picked up its pace, percussion to accompany the wailing inside my head. I reached out both hands for any place to sit down, but they were left empty.

Still...no chair.

I placed a call first thing the next morning. "Sarah? I've got a serious problem!" I tried to keep my voice under control as I addressed the therapist who suddenly held the last vestiges of hope for our marriage. I tried not to sound desperate over the receiver. "A big... *big* problem."

"Gil?"

"Yes, oh, sorry. Yes, it's me, Gil. Can you talk?"

"Well, not really, not right now," she said, pausing.

I took that as my cue. "This is serious, Sarah. Sandi's having an affair!"

Silence followed. "Look, we can get through this. We need to set up an appointment—"

"With another *woman*!" I screeched.

Another pall of stillness followed, during which I heard a meek, "Oh dear," from the other end. I could tell Sarah was chewing gum because I could hear it, her jaw moving fast as she sat quietly with the revelation.

"She's my daughter's teacher, Sarah! I'm definitely taking the girls out of that school!"

Finally, Sarah spoke. "I understand this is upsetting Gil, but ask yourself once more, is this the hill you want to die on?"

"I'm already dead."

CHAPTER 34

I HAD NO IDEA WHETHER Sandi would ever agree to see Sarah and hoped something would come along to persuade her. Maybe just calling her out on the affair. I could barely think of what that meant. Something else surfaced. Actually, it was someone else: Dr. Parsons

"Gil, I spoke with Sandi and I finally got through to her. I told her I thought it would be best for you, Sandi, and your daughters to do what it takes to act like a married couple standing still, doing nothing to push you two apart, and allow the marriage counselor to guide you both forward with full effort to understand what is wrong, with a desire to fix what's wrong rather than destroy it."

"Are you kidding?" I was incredulous yet relieved.

"Look, I'm putting it in writing and sending it to both of you so it's clear." He paused then added, "She agreed."

"Wow, Phil! Thank you. What happened?"

"I've known her a long time, Gil. I reminded her of a few things she might be able to fool others with but couldn't hide from me. This has gone on long enough. It was a very matter-of-fact chat."

I hung up the phone and called our counselor.

"Great news, Gil," Sarah said, when I finally got hold of her. "Make an appointment for some time after the first week in August and I'll see you then."

"But Sarah, that's two weeks away!"

"I'm out of town for a week and my schedule fills up weeks in advance. This is the best I can do, Gil."

I hung up the phone and faced the next two weeks with little hope. I turned to Dr. Parsons again and again, as Sandi continued to poke and prod, looking for an argument. My skepticism continued throughout the entire waiting period.

Two weeks later, Sandi and I sat side by side in Sarah's office.

"You have to commit to working through some of these issues, Sandi. If you want to see improvement in your marriage and to avoid divorce, it's going to take some intensive work…and of course, time," Sarah said, as gently as possible.

"I don't want to avoid divorce, *Saa-rah!*" The sarcasm and disrespect in her voice set my teeth on edge. I glanced at Sarah who only smiled, appearing unruffled by Sandi's tone.

"I see," she replied and sat back in her chair. "Well, if that's your intent, then, I'll make a pact with you. Look, I am confident that I can help you both. But I'm not going to be available for the next month. I'm away on vacation."

One month?

As if she heard my thoughts, she continued. "I know, a full four weeks sounds terribly long, but I'll make a deal with you."

"It's impossible, Sarah! We need help now!" I said.

"Hear me out, Gil." She waited for a response, but I gave her none so she went on. "Wait for me to come back from my out-of-town obligations a month from now, and I will spend however long you need to get through this crisis." she said. "Promise me that you won't do anything rash."

"Okay," I said, still reeling from the news that my therapist would be out of town for nearly four weeks.

"No filing any legal papers, no moving out, nothing that would take you closer to a divorce."

"Yeah. Okay," Sandi said.

"A deal?" I interjected, rolling my eyes.

"Yes! And here it is," Sarah's eyes trained on Sandi. "If you'll give a full one hundred percent effort toward fixing the issues within your marriage, and if at the end of a year of therapy you still want a divorce, I will help you get that divorce. And you know how adamantly I am against divorce as a solution to marital problems!" Sarah said a little too confidently.

"What?" I started to protest but Sarah held her hand up to silence me.

"It's fair, Gil," Sarah said, and shot me a "work with me on this" look. I couldn't respond, which she took as agreement.

We left that session with a year of therapy planned and Sandi certain of divorce. I wasn't sure where I'd gone wrong.

The entire idea of marriage sat like a stone with Sandi. She'd never stopped asking for a divorce and I knew she hadn't stopped seeing Helene. However, the idea that maybe I knew about her illicit affair might have been enough motivation to wait at least one month to start marriage counseling, even if she had no intention of staying married.

———◆———

The first day of school brought the excitement of a fresh new year and our first therapy session a day later gave me renewed optimism. The session began with a discussion about what we'd done right. I was grateful for that until I realized the direction Sarah was taking. My gut stayed locked in the vise until the knotted feeling became a simple inconvenience. I was losing control of my life again and didn't know how to stop the insanity. Sandi felt right at home in this type of turmoil so I was odd man out...again.

"The point is," Sarah said and I snapped to attention. "You both know more about one another than most couples. You two already had your cards on the table, so to speak. There were no surprises when you signed up for this. You met in the hospital, after all."

"There was for me," Sandi said. "I didn't expect him to be sick and not be able to make enough money for the life I deserved. I was supposed to marry the grandson of one of the wealthiest families in the county, the biggest homebuilder there is!"

"Every time you compare me to another guy, you forget that you were nothing like the 'other girl'! I mean, I never expected... Oh, what's the use?" I said.

Sarah raised both hands to stop the argument.

"Look," she said. "Many marriages with as many or more problems than you're facing have made it. They simply made the choice to stay the course, through thick and thin, and they kept working at it."

"Yeah, but we're not a typical couple," Sandi said.

"No you're not. Remember that other couples with fewer problems than you're facing have also decided to call it quits. Prematurely, in my opinion," she added and eyed Sandi.

"With good reason, most likely," Sandi chimed in.

"Perhaps. The point is..." Sarah said, and I knew she was preparing to close out our session for that day because she always said that in conclusion. "The point is, that it's not about what your problems are, it's about who you are."

Profound! Really? You could have said the same thing, Gil, and saved a month of going through hoops to get therapy!

I left that day more frustrated than before.

As Sandi became more distant, I found myself becoming more and more suspicious. Before long, I became a person I despised: a snoop.

Early morning, when Sandi would leave the house for her run, I would begin my quest to find something, anything. I picked through her belongings, rifled through emails, and sorted through her private things. I found my behavior sordid, and still I couldn't stop myself!

This is about Danielle's teacher. You can't let it go!

"No! I can't!" I shouted back under my breath inside the quiet house, as I picked through the pockets of Sandi's favorite jeans.

It's become an addiction with you.

"Yup, well, I didn't plan on a wife who decided to be unfaithful to me with a woman. Our daughter's teacher, no less!" I could feel my breathing increase as my heart started to pound against my ribcage.

Calm yourself, Gil.

I sat down on the edge of the bed and scanned the room. There had been nothing found inside her jeans pocket except additional guilt to add to my already full cache. I glanced at my hands; they felt dirty. Life was muddy once again and I didn't like the soot clinging to my sordid behavior.

"I don't like this either. I'm just trying to figure out what's going on with my daughter's teacher."

Sandi was shifting her routine, doing things out of the norm. Every little nuance suggested infidelity and I could barely stand it.

"I found sexually explicit text messages on her phone yesterday sent to Helene Garner." My voice echoed against the walls and I felt as empty as the room where I sat. I glanced down and saw the corner of a piece of pink paper sticking out from beneath the bed. Instinctively, I reached for it, pulling it up to eye level. It was a letter.

Don't do it, Gil.

My eyes disobeyed the voice in my head and scanned the note written in Sandi's handwriting.

...you have been the finest liplocking lesbian therapist best friend ever. Talk about a complete therapeutic program! Helene, you have opened your heart to it all. These feelings for you have really put me through the wringer.

I wiped my eyes, barely able to read the words. What was Sandi doing to us? How could she say these things to someone like this? My eyes dropped once again to the paper and I read on.

...These feelings for you have really put me through the wringer. I'm sure it's been a pain in the ass for you like, you must have bad karma or must just be an angel of love!

I tucked the letter back into its place under the bed, so overwhelmed and hurt by the things I'd read. It was written the way a schoolgirl would write to her first crush. None of it made any sense. I walked out of the room and into the rest of my home, nowhere to sit comfortably, no place to feel peace.

It was only the second week of school and it felt like this would be the longest year of my life. The second week of therapy was the only thing to give me hope.

During the second session, Sandi quit therapy. Sarah convinced Sandi to come back the following week but her attitude remained defiant and she quit again. This went on for two more weeks; Sarah made bargains while Sandi remained defiant, quit, and then came back the next week. Though counseling had begun, we still hadn't had a counseling session.

September had flown by and I soon faced a big meeting that Joel and I had with some prospective new agents we needed in place before the end of the year because the tumbling economy was crippling our business. I walked down the stairwell and into the kitchen the day of my meeting. Sandi hadn't touched her breakfast and had set out only three plates. My girls, busy with their waffles, glanced up at me with syrupy smiles. I saw the pain behind the grins.

"Hi, daddy."

"Good morning, my two princesses," I said, kissing each one of them on the head. I glanced at Sandi and took my place at the table.

"Aren't you going to eat?" I asked.

Sandi busied herself with the contents of her purse and began to look for the car keys. Her eyes never made their way to the table where our daughters and I ate breakfast without her.

"I've got something to do this morning. Will you please drive the girls?"

"Why can't you take them?" I asked, curious as to the source of her urgency.

"I just can't, Gil. They love spending time with you and they love it when you take them to school, anyway."

I had no response for her comment because there was so much truth wrapped up in the lie she'd just told. I did love being with my girls, and I cherished every moment with them. I agreed.

Sandi took off with a skip in her step and said nothing more. Minutes later, I had rescheduled my meeting and was loading my daughters into the car. Their giggles floated across the seat and circled the inside of the sedan. I wondered how much of their mother's deceit they had witnessed, how much they understood, and what they made of it.

After kissing them good-bye at school, I headed to my meeting and began to think more about Sandi's behavior earlier that morning. Something was up and her way of not answering questions glossed over the quick exit she made at breakfast. I drove past an ATM and thought about stopping for cash. Then, it hit me…

The big deposit went in yesterday. Our rent is due tomorrow.

Turning the steering wheel in the opposite direction, I went directly to our bank. As I pulled into the parking lot, I saw Sandi's car. She anxiously paced in front of the bank, waiting for its doors to open.

"Wow, what a coincidence," I said.

To say she was startled would be an understatement. Her eyes widened and I watched her do that thing with her lips just before she calmed herself, readying to put on a good act.

"Oh, hi, Gil," she said. "I'm just going to grab some money for the school bill."

"I see. You know we don't have money for that right now," I said.

She was cool as a cucumber and spit out lies with ease. "Oh, yes, well I forgot to tell you that I've got money coming from a dividend, a late distribution because of a paperwork snafu from my mother's account that somehow I wasn't supposed to get after she cut me out of her will. I'll put the money back into our account with that on Friday."

"You should wait until the money comes and then pay the school," I said. "We used most of that money for the school in the first place and that was a mistake. We still couldn't afford it and still owe them money."

Sandi reached a hand to my arm and kissed my lips. I didn't know what to do.

"Gil, everything's going to be fine. I've got it handled. We're gonna start doing well with therapy now. Our marriage will get back on track. I'm sorry for everything. Do you know how much I love you?"

I stood still for a moment, taking in the hugs and kisses, comfort I hadn't felt in months. As I went to my car, Sandi entered the bank.

When we began our therapy session that night, we didn't mention the events of the morning. Sandi was sweet and I was grateful. We sat next to one another on chairs placed close together. Sarah walked purposefully across the room and took her seat.

"How's it been this week?" she asked.

I opened my mouth to speak but heard Sandi's voice instead.

"I'm back together with my family. I've leased my own apartment and am moving out next week," she said.

Sarah leaned forward in her chair, her eyes darting to mine, and back again to Sandi. "Well, now that's a surprise. I didn't know you had plans to move out on your own, Sandi. Our agreement—"

"I didn't know either," I said. "What are you saying, Sandi? What about our agreement?"

"You know me by now, Gil, I don't keep agreements," she snapped.

I stared at her and wondered what had become of the promise to fulfill a year of therapy, and the woman who vouched for the change in our marriage this morning, then followed it with a kiss? I knew immediately where the money had gone and that it would never be returned. She was very calculated and good at saying exactly what needed to be said in order to get her way. I was the sap who wanted to believe her.

You were her pawn in a plan to keep the school funded and the girls in attendance.

"Why did you agree to these sessions for a year if you planned to move out? That was one of our conditions." I felt my face flush.

"Gil's got a point, Sandi. You're going back on your word. That is completely unacceptable at this point," Sarah said, her face pinched.

I waited for Sandi's response but she gave none. She shrugged her shoulders. She just needed to get through September. That was her goal. I'd look awful pulling the girls out of school once it had begun and more important, the upheaval would be too chaotic for my daughters. Sandi knew I wouldn't do that to them. The situation had quickly spiraled out of control. Tension filled the room so thickly, I could barely breathe. The session ended, and I followed my wife out. We parted ways to separate cars and the beginning of separate lives.

———•———

CHAPTER 35

"Give Sandi a couple of months to cool down...a little space," Sarah said over the phone the next day.

"Excuse me?"

"Gil, we can work together. Sandi will need time to work through some issues. Then we will be able to establish some new rules."

"What about holding her accountable? How about making her answer to the decision to break our agreement?"

"You heard her, Gil, she doesn't keep agreements. She's been getting away with it all of her life. She doesn't care about breaking an agreement, with you or me or anyone else. Trying to hold her accountable will leave me with no chance to help with your marriage."

This didn't make sense to me, but I accepted Sarah's judgment as a professional.

Over time, Sarah worked with us to figure out an acceptable parenting schedule. The girls alternated two days at a time between Sandi and me. But nearly as soon as the plan was in place, Sandi began to shift the arrangements. The girls were brought back to me at five in the morning, and other odd times at random. Their schedules were inconsistent, and the dysfunction escalated. I could tell that my daughters felt the stress of our tug-of-war, and I felt helpless. There were no boundaries left for Sandi to cross; she had obliterated them all, claiming she "didn't want to be controlled." I called it mutual respect.

I wanted off the roller coaster ride but I didn't know how to do it. Sandi still didn't know that I was cognizant of her affair. That was the last tool in my belt and since therapy had never really begun, I would have to keep this well hidden, ready for retrieval in a moment's notice whenever Sarah said it was the right time. The longer this brewed inside me, the bigger this issue became. That woman was still my daughter's teacher.

The insanity didn't seem to have an end. Barely able to function as I drove my girls to school and in fear of running into the "other woman," I discovered I was on the outside of a very toxic whirlpool, being sucked into its center situation by situation. I soon learned that Sandi had branched out—her manipulative ways reaching to others.

Without mutual respect or even simple communication, co-parenting with Sandi became impossible. When I told Danielle we couldn't afford a birthday party for her at American Girl in Los Angeles, Sandi talked to a divorced grandmother of one of Danielle's classmates, gained her sympathy, and manipulated her into paying for a party without me in attendance. Disneyland had always been a special place for our family. We lived thirty minutes away and had annual passes. We went there for all four of our birthdays each year, and had created so many special family memories. Sandi got the same grandmother to purchase annual passes for Sandi and the girls so that new memories could be created without me.

Sandi sold a half-story to other well-to-do parents, who told her of their separations and became the newest targets for Sandi's manipulation. Sadly, these victims never recognized how little their situation had any resemblance to our dynamics or finances.

Sandi also didn't hesitate to gain the sympathy of people she knew through her role at the school: manipulating school advisors, shutting me out of traditions, and always playing the victim. No one seemed to see Sandi for who she was. They never knew the Sandi who I nurtured back to health, though still so damaged inside. This scared me and repulsed me at the same time. My relationships with other parents became uncomfortable.

Sarah tried unsuccessfully to get us to resume counseling. We would make an appointment, and then on the day of our scheduled time, Sandi would cancel it. It would take weeks to get another appointment, and Sandi would cancel again the day of. This went on for months. Sandi would say she would only meet with Sarah if I gave her money for this or that. She'd get what she wanted and cancel again.

I watched as our daughters became the trappings for Sandi's constant manipulation of others. Even our pediatrician was duped into writing prescriptions for psychiatric medications for Sandi so that she could avoid accountability with Dr. Parsons. I had no other choice but to pull back, which I did in a big way. I slowly withdrew from the toxic behaviors Sandi was so engulfed in. I stopped paying the pediatrician, and he stopped writing prescriptions.

In desperation, Sandi cloaked herself in conspiracy and made whatever deal she had to in order to get what she wanted, this time with Dr. Parsons. Phil explained that as a matter of professional obligation, he would only write prescriptions again if she went to therapeutic marriage counseling. Sandi made an appointment with Sarah, got her prescription, and then canceled the appointment. Phil, because he actually was her psychiatrist, was now compelled to keep writing her prescription—another broken agreement with no accountability for Sandi. I covered my eyes with rose-colored glasses to believe these deals would work, but they never did.

On Christmas, the girls were with me. Sandi agreed to come by for the day. Our time together went well until Sandi announced that she had been spending a great deal of time with her ex-husband, Russell, along with our daughters. She ended up leaving abruptly. Understandably, the kids were very upset.

I called Sarah right after the holiday weekend and followed up with an unscheduled visit to her office. She said she had been in touch with Sandi already. Barely able to speak, I hardly knew where to begin with this newest "nugget" added to her growing list of deceit.

"Calm down, Gil," Sarah said as I paced in front of her desk. "I spent a great deal of time explaining to Sandi just how inappropriate this is and how confusing her behavior will be for your girls, as well as how she owes it to all four of you to quit playing games, begin counseling, and only have people in her life who support fixing her marriage."

"Well, now she wants to take the girls and go see a movie with him! This is the man who beat her, raped her, and made her life a nightmare! She's told everyone this for years, including you, Sarah."

"I understand. Please sit down, Gil. You're going to wear a rut into my carpet."

I sat in the closest chair and balled my fists. Sarah followed, sitting a cautious distance from me.

"Thank you," she said, her voice too calm for my comfort. "Sandi promised me that she wouldn't do this anymore. She knows that she's out of control."

I couldn't speak, couldn't hear anything Sarah was saying. The scar on my chest had been carved this moment by a knife and it seemed to drive itself too close to my heart.

You still don't get it, do you? They'll never hear what you're saying, never understand what you're feeling, or witness anything you're experiencing. You are alone...solitary...a lone soldier who is fighting for a cause that no one else recognizes.

"That's not true," I said aloud.

Sarah stopped mid-sentence. "Oh but it is true, Gil. She knows... she just chooses a different path than yours and needs to understand where it will take her."

Nowhere near your path.

I left soon afterward, my mind whirring and my pulse pounding against the knife-carved scar that nobody knew was embedded into my chest.

A week later, the scene in Sarah's office repeated itself.

"She's been out with the girls and Russell again. Now she's asked to take our daughters to Big Bear Lake with another older woman, who's a teacher at the school!"

"What did you say?" Sarah was trying to divert my anger. It didn't work. I glared at her and let out my response without checking the sarcasm in my voice.

"What do you think, Sarah? This is Leigh's teacher now."

"I assume you refused."

"I absolutely refused. There was no way she would be taking my daughters out of town with a different lesbian lover."

My response to her request was a simple, "No."

I still hadn't told Sandi that I knew about her affair.

Sarah nodded and we talked a little further about the "next steps."

No next steps came to pass, and nothing changed. That left little in the way of actively changing her behavior. It became evident that sitting by and waiting for Sandi to snap into "responsible conduct" with an "appropriate lifestyle" while bound within her "still-married" state to me would never happen. Sandi continued to take the girls with her when she spent time with Russell, and she took the girls to Bear Lake.

People were telling me to go to court and get a formal legal order.

"She doesn't keep agreements so then I'll be in the crappy place of having to call the cops on my wife. This isn't the hill I'm gonna die on."

Did you just say those words? It's becoming your mantra now.

"Besides, I won't take my wife to court. I've seen what it did to her when Russell did that to her."

Something drastic had to take place and happen soon!

"Intervention. I think that's the best course of action," Sarah said over the phone. She apparently had taken time to speak with Dr. Parsons, who'd known Sandi for more than twenty years.

"When?"

"Immediately," Sarah said, without hesitation. Obviously, the plans were well underway. Her voice was serious. "The goal is to help Sandi see things through a different set of glasses other than her own and see just how she has rewritten history and devalued your marriage. Let her discover just what her actions are doing to your children."

The intervention was a colossal disaster.

The pattern continued to run the same course: negotiating, planning, scheduling, and abandoning plans, then meeting to begin the process all over again. As predictable as the cycle had become, I still believed that perhaps with a little more time and another chance, Sandi would come around.

Sarah's phone number remained on my speed dial and I used it frequently, hoping to stay in line with "doing things right." Any negative outcome wouldn't be because of something *I* did. How incredibly altruistic and unbelievably naive on my part! I followed Sarah's advice on when, and when not, to meet Sandi's demands. Mostly, I catered to accommodating her ridiculous schedule with the girls and, of course, money!

You still believe it will save your marriage.

"I don't have a choice." My response sounded weak.

And still, you won't take Sandi to court to get a formal order.

The voice in my head had warned me about codependency many times but I barely heard it. I heard nothing but Sandi's misrepresentations and Sarah's call for a "new plan." Finally, the voice in my head gripped the vise and turned it, screaming at the same time, *enough!*

CHAPTER 36

SANDI EMAILED THE RE-ENROLLMENT FORMS to me, documents required for the next school year. It was February and we'd been doing a dance around tuition and counseling since September. I made the phone call.

"What do you mean, you're not going to sign the forms? How can you do this, Gil?" Sandi was in a state of panic. I no longer cared.

"I'm not signing them."

"Gil, don't you get it? The girls won't be able to go to this school next year if you don't sign the forms this week."

I heard hysteria building in her voice. "I'm not willing to put my girls in a private school that I haven't been able to afford, placing them in an environment that fosters..." I stopped myself just in time. I had still not told Sandi that I knew about her affair with Miss Garner.

"Fosters what, Gil?"

"Never mind. I'm not willing to sign the damn forms."

"You have to, Gil! It's the girls we're talking about here!"

That was the last straw. I was done with the cost of the tuition and done with the cost of Sandi's choices as well as her lesbian lover. I was not going to continue paying for her affair. Something inside me snapped.

"I have my reasons...good reasons," I said, my voice suddenly cool and calm.

"What are you talking about, Gil?"

Hesitating, unsure whether to reveal the secret I'd kept from her for so many months, I held my tongue. Agonizing silence was my only comfort as I had swallowed her secret and kept still day after day, watching my girls walk into the school where the horror began and my wife made the decision to commit adultery. I'd kept all that I knew quiet, waiting for just the right moment, counseling frequently with Sarah about the right time to confront Sandi.

"I'll explain in Sarah's office, whenever you're ready," I said.

She lingered for a moment before she agreed to meet. "Gil, it's going to take three weeks to get an appointment with Sarah!"

I wavered. Was there still a chance to save our marriage? Signing those papers was the only chance at this marriage being saved, and that was my goal. As much as I wanted the girls out of the school, this wasn't the battle I wanted to end our marriage over. Once again, this wasn't the hill I was going to die on.

I agreed to sign the paperwork and Sandi agreed to long-term marriage counseling with Sarah. We made another "first" appointment with Sarah.

Two weeks later on the morning of the appointment…Sandi canceled. I saw her at the school.

"You know you're not going to do anything, Gil," Sandi threatened me. And her eyes became dark. Emotion had fled her very being and I saw nothing but emptiness behind her stare.

"I'm sorry, Sandi," I said and walked away.

I wasn't sure what I felt sorry for when I said those words. Perhaps it was sorrow for the course her life had taken and the way her destiny had shaped itself. Perhaps it was just sadness because I knew I would follow through this time. I would talk to the school principal about the affair and open a new set of grievances that would fester for the rest of her life. Whatever the reason, my heart felt heavier than I ever remember before. Gone was the voice. The voice in my head remained silently observant.

The day after Sandi canceled with Sarah, I met with the principal.

"Do you know how long this has supposedly gone on?" she asked from behind a simple but very orderly desk. My thoughts drifted to another time when I sat in front of such a desk, and the dean of my college faced me with concern etched in the lines around his eyes. I wondered if Mrs. Portman would be as gentle. I decided she probably wouldn't.

"There's no 'supposedly' in that sentence, Mrs. Portman," I said as respectfully as I could. "This has gone on for at least seven months."

She leaned back in her chair and regarded me with severity. I returned her stare and waited for a response.

"Mr. Belmont." She paused just long enough to make a statement with my name. "Our staff is well above reproach here. Miss Garner is no different, I can assure you." I held back and allowed her to continue. "In all my years in education, I have never heard of such travesty being levied so inhospitably against one of our own."

Her use of the language caused my anger to flare. "I realize this is probably new to you, Mrs. Portman, but a neglectful response to inappropriate behavior by a third party is nothing new to me. I am more than happy to take this to the school board if you are unwilling to handle it."

Her eyes narrowed and her face blanched slightly. My threat hit its mark, for the moment.

"I think I can handle this, Mr. Belmont," she hissed. "Of course, I will need to speak with Miss Garner and get her position on the whole affair."

"Of course. And yes, it is an *affair* you will want to inquire about, with all parties involved."

Her eyes darted back to mine. Again, a direct hit. My play on words had not missed its intended target. I left knowing I'd taken the first step in the right direction.

A day later, Mrs. Portman called me, apologizing on behalf of the school for "indiscretions and inappropriate actions" that had caused me distress throughout the past year. The day after that, I was back at school for a meeting with Ms. Helene Garner and her principal. The knots that began to twist on my stomach never ceased to turn, even after we'd taken our seats in Mrs. Portman's office. I turned to stare at the woman who had stepped between my wife and me. Unable to return my glare, she kept her eyes trained on Mrs. Portman, who sat stoically behind her mask of authority.

"Thank you both for your time," Mrs. Portman began as she looked at Helene and me. "We have some rather grave issues to discuss this morning. There have been allegations levied against you, Helene." She glanced at Miss Garner briefly to take in her response. Miss Garner gave none. "Mr. Belmont, I will turn this over to you…"

Hate filled my eyes as I stared at her for one last moment before turning my attention to my briefcase. I'd come prepared. Stacks of printed emails, phone records, even numerology readings that Sandi charted to see "how compatible" she and Helene were. Soon, papers covered the small table that lay between Helene Garner and me. Mrs. Portman shifted in the seat next to mine and sorted through documents, occasionally glancing up at Ms. Garner or me. A moment of interruption came when a soft knock sounded on the office's closed door.

"Sorry I'm late," an administrator announced and walked in without invitation.

"No worries. We were just getting started," Mrs. Portman said and she motioned to a set of vacant seats lining the other end of the table. The administrator moved deeper into the cramped room and was followed by another, the school's owner, close at her heels. "Janice," Mrs. Portman said, with a slight smile.

"This is evidence that an inappropriate relationship developed between Ms. Garner and my wife," I said finally.

"I want to say something in my defense," Ms. Garner said.

Mrs. Portman sat back in her chair, mouth open as she listened, the others absorbed to the point of paralysis. I felt the room close off and my composure spin. I grasped the edge of my chair to gain a sense of balance.

"Sandi was the aggressor. I tried to keep our association professional… I didn't want even to be friends but she wouldn't back down. *Sandi's* the one who sent the explicit messages, not me!" She waved her hand over the incriminating stack of papers.

"Did this go as far as an intimate…a sexual relationship between you two?" the owner asked with gravity.

"No. Not even close," Ms. Garner said. "But Sandi wanted to take it that far. I wouldn't go there but I felt sorry for her because she seemed so fragile, so I just kept the friendship going."

I believed Helene Garner was lying about her involvement, but could barely take it in because the truth of what she said about Sandi rang true, particularly her artful skill with manipulation. It hit me squarely and I could barely breathe.

"Are you sure there was nothing…intimate…between you two, ever?" Mrs. Portman said.

"Nothing…never! I tried to break off our friendship after a while, but Sandi was emotionally both vulnerable and volatile. I thought I was helping her but it got more and more uncomfortable. That's one reason I didn't stay at the Christmas party last year."

Mrs. Portman nodded. The others noted her acknowledgement. Mrs. Portman said, "There's a report here from our receptionist that you mentioned being afraid."

"A report from the receptionist here?" the administrator asked.

"Yes, Daphne Williams," Mrs. Portman clarified. "She works for the school and is a friend of yours, isn't she, Helene?"

Helene nodded, "Yes. I told Daphne that if anything bad happened to me, she should be aware that I was being stalked."

"Sandi was stalking you?" I blurted out. I knew this was probable but didn't want to believe it. It felt as if my life had been lived in a dream for the past year. I had no idea Sandi had done anything like that, although it made sense.

"I would go out to get my newspaper in the morning and there she was, jogging by. I would go out to eat with my husband—"

Ms. Garner has a husband? The voice in my head awakened and I quickly pulled a hand away from my burning chest.

"…or maybe go to my favorite spot at the beach and there Sandi was. It was creepy," she said.

This isn't new behavior for her, Gil. She did the same thing with the famous actress when she worked in the bookstore. Remember what is written in her files. I knew it was truth, and classic Sandi behavior. How could I have missed this?

"I see that there have been multiple contacts made from Sandi to the school, insisting that your daughters attend, and looking for ways to cover the cost. It was one of the reasons she sought employment with us. I'm sure you're aware of this, Mr. Belmont." Mrs. Portman directed her attention to me.

Before I could answer, the administrator cut in. "It appears Mrs. Belmont may have an unhealthy obsession with this school."

I could see the uneasiness behind her comment.

Then the owner's daughter chimed in, "I believe her dress, when she's come to pick up the girls or help in the school," the owner stated, "…seems rather risqué and the music she plays around the children is not…within school standards."

I was flabbergasted. There was little I had to do to build my case. Sandi had single-handedly destroyed her own reputation just by being herself.

"The school's lawyers have been advised on this." Mrs. Portman said, glancing down at something on her desk. "This is definitely something we need to address right away. However, policy doesn't allow for employee termination during the active school year."

"Moreover, it's my understanding that we were advised we have no grounds for termination because the relationship continued between Mrs. Belmont and Ms. Garner voluntarily," the administrator added and glanced at Helene. "This is in spite of your claims that the relationship continued against your wishes. You allowed it to continue, so it puts a different color on the entire affair."

I didn't think the administrator realized the depth of what she'd just said and found myself smiling at her choice of words. I looked at Ms. Garner, whose face had flushed.

"At this point, our next course of action will be to give written warning to Mrs. Belmont with immediate probation," Mrs. Portman stated. "Helene—Ms. Garner, you will need to notify Sandi in writing that she is not to have contact with you from this date forward, unless that's already been done?" She glanced at Ms. Garner, who nodded. "Good. I'll let the attorney know you've taken care of this piece."

"Is that all?" I said, and immediately wished I'd kept my mouth shut. The past hour had turned into a meeting about Sandi's employment, with no reference to my marital concern. All discussion about Ms. Garner's participation in the destruction of my family had apparently fallen through the administrative cracks.

"I've already contacted your wife, Mr. Belmont, and explained to her exactly what is going on. That's all that's within my power. My instructions to her were very clear, that she is in no way to contact Ms. Garner ever again," Mrs. Portman said, then turned her focus to Ms. Garner. "Should either of you breach this agreement, one or both of you will be dismissed for sexual harassment. Do I make myself clear?"

Ms. Garner frowned, but nodded. I wondered if Sandi understood the implications of the school's boundaries.

Unlikely.

CHAPTER 37

———◆———

THE SCHOOL ADMINISTRATION WAS TRUE to its word. Sandi was placed on probation. Additionally, her summer hours were cancelled. It was a token consequence; however, it seemed as if maybe somebody was finally holding Sandi accountable for her actions, and I felt some relief at the idea. She'd been told that the school hadn't in forty years been forced to confront any of their teachers with inappropriate behavior. Sandi had made her mark on the school.

Fortunately, Ms. Garner had admitted to crossing boundaries that had never been approached before in the history of the school's existence. While I appreciated her candidness, I couldn't forgive her. I knew she was under heavy scrutiny and probably speaking in half-truths, but I didn't care. Most likely, Ms. Garner had thrown Sandi under the bus but I didn't care about that either. The only people I cared about now were my daughters. I wanted to protect my family.

Now that the skeletons had been wrenched from Sandi's closet, people rushed from the wings to give me free advice. Most thought I should go to court seeking sole custody. This wasn't a battle I wanted to fight…not yet…not ever!

I had a long conversation with Mrs. Portman in private and she agreed to shred the re-enrollment documents for next year with a provision that I be given a few weeks to change my mind. They needed to know what vacancies they had to fill; there was a waiting list to get into the school, after all. She also said Sandi's employment could continue. She wanted everything to work out okay, if that's what our family wanted.

Behind that conversation, Sarah let me know that Sandi had called in hysterics and wanted to go to counseling right away.

"Of course she did," I said to myself.

The meeting somehow took place at Sarah's office within the week. Sandi wanted to get a signature on the forms. As she walked into the office, she glared at me, but I could see the panic behind her eyes. We took our seats, the same ones we'd taken months earlier when the goal was a happier marriage. *Ironic.* The thought went unchecked and I turned my attention to Sarah instead.

"Welcome, Gil, Sandi. We're here to consider a statement that Gil has prepared so the school issue can get resolved once and for all. Are you willing and able to listen to what he has to say, Sandi?"

She nodded.

"Go ahead then, Gil, and let's remember the rules of this venue, that Gil be allowed to say everything he has to say before Sandi replies. Of course, you will be given the same courtesy, Sandi, and Gil will respect your time to speak." Sarah nodded at me, to signal that I had everyone's attention. I paused for a moment and turned to face my wife.

"Sandi, it's been difficult throughout the past ten months, particularly when I had to be at the girls' school. We've made several attempts to bring the marriage together through counseling, only to have you cancel again and again." I paused and looked at her.

"Is this why we're here?" Sandi asked.

Sarah held up one hand. "Go on, Gil."

"You've been desperate to get my signature on the forms for the girls' school, which I refused to do. For good reason."

"There's no good reason for—"

"Sandi, please. It's Gil's turn. You know the rules."

Sandi muttered that she was sorry and I picked up where I'd left off.

"You hoped Sarah would somehow convince me to sign the papers but even so, you always cancelled our meetings..."

Sandi stood up. "I did no such thing!"

"Sandi, please sit down and let Gil finish," Sarah said again, placing a hand lightly on Sandi's arm. Sandi returned to her seat, eyes trained on me.

"Go ahead, *Gil*," Sandi said, hitting my name with venom.

Before we met, Sarah had advised that I take the time to write my position on different issues, the most specific being the situation with the school. I had followed her advice and sat down in front of a blank sheet of paper one afternoon as dark clouds made their way across an otherwise blue sky. *Fitting*, I thought at the time. Those clouds flashed across my mind as I began to read what I had written aloud.

"Thus far I have agreed to send the girls to this school because it means so much to you, my wife. If I continue to be married to you, and not just in name only, I will continue to agree to send the girls to this school because it means so much to you. Being married includes living together again and sharing family experiences. Because of the way the school, you, and our marriage have intersected, if our marriage does not continue, I will not find the school a comfortable place for me to support. Your wants will no longer be a priority and I will find it best for our daughters and for myself to have a fresh start elsewhere."

"Sandi, Gil's concerns about the intersection with the school were written in love. He spoke his truth, which appears to be supported by external evidence," Sarah said.

"Well, that's what Gil says, but there are a lot of people who back me up," Sandi replied.

"This isn't about who is right or has the greatest number of people behind them. This is about your relationship with Gil, your marriage, your daughters, and your commitments."

"What about Gil?" Sandi asked, and flipped her hand in my direction.

Sarah had a look of exhaustion written on her face. "Sandi, you continue to want to use me to get what you want with the school rather than use me to fix and continue your marriage."

Sarah had let me know beforehand she didn't have any more time in her schedule or gas in her tank to just go round in circles with Sandi.

After a moment of reflection, Sarah said, "It's apparent that my efforts are ineffective for you at this point. I would recommend you both seek out another counselor. I have a friend who might be able to put a fresh set of eyes on this. Another option could be a therapy group for couples I'm starting up, if you are interested."

No resolution and the time extension to decide about school enrollment was almost up. Nothing had changed. I still faced the same battle.

———————●—————————

Within days, I found myself sitting near Sandi in a new therapist's office discussing old issues.

"I've spoken with Sarah with your permission," said Joannie. She was younger than Sarah but seemed equally as experienced as her marital therapist colleague.

"I'm not going to spend an additional ten months going in circles. I will only work with you if you move back home, Sandi. This separation is hurting everyone and not helping your girls. I need you both to be active participants in a marriage-counseling program," she stated, rather matter-of-factly. There would be little room for argument with Joannie.

"I'm not ready," Sandi said. "I need more time to decide whether this is what I want to do. I need space."

I glared at her in disbelief, unable to see the woman I had met so many years ago, the woman who planned our family with me, created our children with me. Here sat an imposter.

"Then you've made the decision for everyone, Sandi. I wish you and Gil well and will take your name off my schedule. Best of luck to you."

That was the end.

"Sandi, we've been doing this dance for ten months and we still haven't had a single marriage counseling session," I said, my soul crushed a bit more.

"Don't worry Gil, we'll find another counselor. And we still have the group Sarah's running. Please, don't do anything rash about school. Everything is going to work out with us," Sandi said. As we walked away from the therapy office, she reached for my hand and I felt my resolve soften. A long hug and kiss followed. *Gil!*

"Sandi, the truth is that the school wants to help, but the economy has taken its toll there too. They can't afford to hold a spot that we may not use."

"We're going to find a marriage counselor, and I will come home before the start of the school year. I just need a little more time."

"It's got to be a reasonable amount of time before the school year starts, Sandi, and if you don't come home, I will rescind my signature, as the school knows. I want this in writing from you!"

A few days later, I signed the papers.

Three weeks in, Sandi stopped showing up for the group, but swore she was still keeping her agreement and coming home soon. Controlling the only thing I could, I set out to finish the remaining ten weeks in couple's group therapy by myself. One night, it was so painful being there with the other couples that I couldn't take it anymore and walked out in the middle of the session. I made it as far as the bottom of the stairs, with a hand outstretched to the front door.

You're quitting? You're throwing in the towel and assuming the mantle of "quitter"?

"No." With that, I turned around, walked up the stairs, and back into the room. I was not a quitter!

Sadly, while I was doing everything possible to save our family, my daughters were suffering. Sandi assured the girls she would move back home Easter weekend, but it never happened. She then would become "unavailable" for nearly ten days at a time, never once inviting the girls to stay with her. On the occasions she would take the kids, her pick-up time was at odd times, only to drop them off hours later, never keeping the girls for the time they had planned. It was a roller coaster of lies and manipulation, and she was not only putting me through this, but more importantly, she was putting the girls through it.

The subject of our daughters' schooling kept rearing its ugly head. The day before my birthday, I received a call. Tears muffled the voice on the other end. Danielle was in distress.

"Mommy wants us to go to our school and you don't," Danielle said through sobs.

Apparently, Sandi had been talking to the girls.

"Slow down, honey. What did Mommy say?" I asked

"She said you don't want us to go to school, but she does," Danielle repeated, and sobbed again.

I gathered my thoughts and tried to reassure my daughter that she would be okay, school would be okay, and that she needn't worry about it any further.

I contacted Sandi immediately. She presented a new set of promises, very convincingly, and I bought into her rhetoric. As I hung up the phone, I began the preparations for Sandi's imminent return home.

But time and again she never showed.

Danielle began to have signs of separation anxiety. She'd complain of stomachaches and headaches and refused to attend school. I consulted with Sarah and she advised me to avoid putting pressure on her. My daughter needed nurturing, not pressure, something I understood too well. Fortunately, the school kept in close contact with me, supporting me as I guided Danielle through her difficulties.

Soon, I received a call from the school about an issue with Leigh. She'd refused to participate in field trip activities at the beach, something completely out of character for her. Sandi was aware of the problem but was unwilling to get involved. I seemed to be the only parent on duty while my daughters struggled through the end of the school year.

"Daddy, my class is going on an end-of-the-school-year overnight field trip to Joshua Tree. I need you to be one of the parents who chaperones," Danielle said, on the verge of tears.

"Of course I'll go, sweetie," I said. I dreaded the thought of two solid days with the lip-locking lesbian therapist best friend ever, Ms. Garner, but this was for my daughter and not about the home-wrecker or Sandi.

I made it to the end of June, bruised and beat up, but intact. One thing became clear as we met the end of this academic calendar:

Finis!

A sigh of relief escaped my lips as I met the girls for the last time at the school's front doors, knowing I would never have to see that place again if Sandi didn't keep her word. My resolve was set—I would not be fooled into another year. Summer would be a break from school, but not from Sandi's childish behavior.

CHAPTER 38

———◆———

SANDI AND I MADE A plan that she would return home in August. The girls were suffering and this was the best course of action, or so I thought.

Week after week, the stories and delays mounted. The magic date for her arrival never seemed to materialize, in spite of the many loving texts and phone calls received from her promising to do so. She continued to encourage me not to lose faith, and not to do anything with the girls' enrollment.

You believe too intently that she will really return…that your family will be intact. It's blind faith and you never learn, Gil.

"I still believe her." I didn't believe the words that fell from my mouth.

They're all lies, Gil. Sandi is good at telling you exactly what you want to hear, and you are good at believing it.

"She means it this time. She said she loves me. This discussion is over." The vise hit my gut as soon as I said it. She just needed a little more time. I wanted to believe that so badly. Absently, I touched the scar on my chest. It burned again. I could hardly stand it.

You'll find out, Gil.

I dropped my hand. The vise grew tighter every time the voice in my head spoke and I didn't want to feel pain any longer. I looked at the boy in the mirror and wanted to run away. So I left the home I'd prepared and went for a walk.

You know you won't go far, Gil. She might actually follow through this time—it's the hope that keeps you glued to the falsehoods of your life.

Finally, the actual day had arrived. A clear blue and sunshiny Saturday.

"You know, Mommy is coming home today."

Danielle and Leigh jumped up and down in place, clapping their hands, and making plans for what they wanted to do when she arrived. After a long discussion about something to do with baking cookies, the girls waited impatiently on the front stoop, watching for Sandi to drive up.

"You don't deserve this," I whispered to the backs of their heads. Watching them through the screen door, I flashed back to my own days as a little boy waiting with eyes glued on the street for my dad to return home.

Neither did you. The thought sent chills down my spine. I rushed to check my phone just to make sure there was nothing foreboding in a text.

A single message flashed, waiting to be read. It had been sent only a few minutes ago from Sandi:

Can't make it today. Have to pick up one of the school's employees from the airport. Reschedule for Tuesday? Hug the girls for me.

My gut wrenched and the back of my throat soured. Immediately, I sent a reply text:

How can you do this again? The girls are waiting for you.

I included a photo of them sitting on the porch just for emphasis. Maybe that would tug on her icy heartstrings.

You know how it goes. They look so cute!

I set the phone down and tried to think of a way to break the news to the girls. It wasn't in me to do this again. The phone chimed.

One last request. I need your help moving my things back home. We'll get a truck. It'll be fun!

I looked up from my phone and glanced at the girls and blinked back the tears.

The following day was filled with phone calls discussing whether or not we needed this or that piece of furniture.

"Oh, and I'm taking the girls tomorrow night. It will be their last night in the apartment. You know how that is, Gil." Sandi's voice sounded a little too bubbly for my comfort.

"This isn't right, Sandi. You know it. This is going to hurt the girls."

"Actually, I've made some special plans for our last night. They'll be fine, trust me."

"That's not what I'm talking about and you know it, Sandi. The separation is damaging everyone. How can you do this when…"

"Okay, well, see you tomorrow." She hung up without another word.

Of course, the special plans and the last night in the apartment were a ruse. Another postponement. I knew exactly what it meant and what she was up to. Sandi needed to delay just one more week until September and the start of school.

"You're a cunning woman, Sandi," I said aloud in response to the text she had just sent. The phone glared back at me. "Your lies have run their course, and so has my naïveté."

———◆———

The next day, I rescinded my signature at the school and my decision was accepted. I had been clear from the start. Sandi retaliated by keeping the girls.

You're in breach of our agreement. This is insane, Sandi. The girls are supposed to be home by now.

The text went unanswered, just like my six previous phone calls. I'd left messages—I knew she was getting them and hoped the text would prompt some kind of response.

Your marriage is over, Gil.

I shook my head, refusing to hear the words I knew were true.

Sandi has taken away your role as husband. All that you have now is your role as father, and even that's pretty weak.

I was paralyzed with fear. How could this be happening? Would the kids ever come back home?

You know the answer to that, Gil.

"She'll bring them back. She just needs time to cool down," I said aloud, but the voice in my head wouldn't listen. I wasn't going to start a legal battle over our daughters. "I'm sure we can work something out as soon as Sandi comes to her senses."

I knew it wasn't true. There hadn't been any custody orders this past year. We voluntarily shared custody as an agreement between us.

She's broken your agreement. How much more are you going to let her get away with before you wake up and smell the roses, Gil? They're dying and stink of decayed marriage vows and wormy commitments.

"Well what am I supposed to do? Call the police?"

Maybe…

Calling the police to report my daughters missing—taken by their mother and never returned—would only lead to the Department of Child Protective Service being involved. I didn't want that!

"Have a little patience, Gil. She's hot under the collar about the school. You knew that she would be," I said to myself, trying to sound convincing.

You know the outcome. The scar burned and I felt the air grow thin.

"Well, at least the school is no longer an issue." The rationalization also stunk and I knew it. I had relied all along on their policy of needing both parents' signatures. They did not have that, and they never would.

I decided to give Sandi some space to take her anger out on me. This also allowed me a minute to take a breath.

"Time. I just need some time to let this mess breathe a little and work itself out." Again, I didn't believe my own rationalization.

Only one option remained: public school. My girls could attend one of two public schools based on the school district where Sandi and I each lived. I wasn't going to make an issue out of which one Sandi wanted. I'd give her that. Yes, I had a preference, and it wouldn't have been Sandi's choice, but as long as they weren't attending the private school, I would not complain.

Two weeks later, the phone rang.

"Hey, Gil. Meet me at Apple Pie Station. Let's get something to eat. The girls miss you. Take them back home with you from there."

My heart pounded and I gathered my things. Apple Pie Station was the girls' favorite restaurant. Maybe Sandi's heart had softened. As I drove the short 16 miles to the restaurant, I prayed this would be a turning point for us all.

No one was there.

I waited for fifteen minutes before sending a text.

I'm here. I'll get a table and order an appetizer.

Sandi never showed up.

I finished the zucchini sticks that had grown cold and got up to leave. Just then, a stranger approached me.

"Are you Gil Belmont?"

I stared at him blankly and nodded my head.

"Good," he said and smiled. My skin began to crawl as I watched his eyes grow dark.

"You've been served." He handed me an envelope. "My job's done here." As he turned to leave, I noticed his blazer was rumpled on the backside. He'd likely been sitting in his car for a while, watching me.

"Wait!"

He turned to look at me. Stubble blanketed his chin and he looked like he needed a drink just to get through the next hour.

"Yeah?"

"Who are you?"

He smiled at my question and dropped his hands into his jacket pockets. "That's not important. What's important is in your hand. Good luck, brother."

I watched him walk out of the restaurant and fought back the need to retch. Zucchini sticks on an empty stomach were a bad idea, especially when a stranger takes the place of my family, delivering papers I didn't want to read.

"You okay?"

The voice startled me. I looked and saw my waitress staring at me.

"No...I...I don't think so."

She put her hand on my shoulder. "Sit down and I'll bring you some coffee." Her eyes dropped to the envelope in my hand. "Take your time with that," she added, glancing between my face and my hand.

I did as she suggested and sat back down in the booth I'd just gotten up from. Within minutes, she'd brought a steaming cup of coffee and set it down in front of me, along with a slice of their famous Apple Crisp Pie.

"Thanks." I couldn't make eye contact as I blinked back tears.

With trembling hands, I opened the envelope and pulled out legal documents. Sandi had petitioned for divorce. Adding insult to injury, the filing date was 5 months old. All the while, I believed her when she said she wanted to come home. Once again, I had been played.

Why are you shocked, Gil? She doesn't know how to tell the truth. You've been swimming in her wake for years. The quagmire she leaves behind stinks and you're the one left to clean everything up. So, why would you be surprised at this?

I couldn't answer the question. I guess I really wasn't surprised. I looked at the pie. "Such a waste."

The pie or your belief system?

"That's not fair." I decided to save one and took a bite of the pie. It had no taste and only made it more difficult to fight the tears.

Something doesn't make sense. This still doesn't get her the school.

"True. She can't get the girls into the school. That's one battle I've won...right?"

The waitress glanced at me. Maybe I was talking too loudly. I took another bite of pie to shut myself up.

Your chair is collapsing, Gil. Time to get up now, abandon the chair, and move on.

"Can I get you more coffee?"

I looked at my cup that was untouched and filled to the rim.

"Look, I don't know what that guy did to you," the waitress said, smiling as she sat in the seat opposite mine, "but you look like a decent guy and I've got a break right now if you need an ear."

I sighed and looked up at her. The tears had already spilled onto my cheeks. She didn't flinch but waited for me to answer.

"I don't know what awaits me, absent from Sandi and the kids. I have no concept of what a divorce will bring."

"Are those the papers?"

I nodded.

"I've been there. It's painful at first, but once you get away from a bad marriage, life gets better."

How does she know it's a bad marriage?

"Yeah, sure."

"When I left Chris, he disappeared for a while, then came back to get money or bug me or something. I'm not sure what. But the kids were affected. They always are. It's hardest on them."

"Yeah."

"This is probably a blessing in disguise. Look at it that way. You'll be fine. How's the pie?"

"Yeah."

"Okay, well, hang in there, mister. Things always work out."

No they wouldn't. She had no idea what she was talking about. No, I would do better to stay where I had been for so many years—hiding within the security that comes with familiarity, with my family, no matter how broken that place may be. Things don't work out, not always.

You're living proof of that, Gil.

"Yeah."

I threw down a tip and left my daughters' favorite restaurant for the last time.

CHAPTER 39

SHE KEPT THE KIDS WHILE serving the divorce papers to allow time to assess your mental health, Gil. I couldn't believe what my eyes were telling me as I read her declarations. *Isn't it obvious? Sandi's playing the mental health card.*

"Are you kidding me?" I said to myself, bewildered and amazed at the pot calling the kettle black. If this were really about a mental health issue, Sandi could have called Phil or Sarah ahead of time, but they wouldn't have bought her lie. Rather, she played a hoax behind the cover of concern.

Why are you so shocked, Gil?

"I don't know who she is anymore."

She's back in the only place she knows how to function.

"With all those people who treated her so poorly? I don't understand."

There was no answer. Even my conscience didn't seem to have a comeback. The hearing would be held in two months. She'd requested that I see my daughters only four days a month. The whole situation felt surreal.

My heart began to race and I could feel my airway constrict. "How can I go two months without seeing my girls? Should I file an emergency court action?" I wheezed. Suddenly, the room began to spin and the familiar burn of a scar no one knew was there consumed me. I looked into the mirror and saw the little boy staring back at me, cheeks wet with tears. "Why couldn't I bring myself to handle this six months ago when everyone told me to?" The little boy just shook his head.

She's not giving you a choice. She's pulled your chair and you're still looking for it.

The scar flared, and my head swam. I reached out for support, but my hands found only empty space. The fall happened quickly. The pain that wracked my body next, that wracked my soul, was greater than any injury sustained before.

"Divorce was the one thing we swore to each other we'd never do. I can't drag her through the mud in court, no matter what she's done to me. I won't do that to my daughters." The voice belonged to me, but I didn't recognize it. I curled into a ball and lay still, willing my body to die the way my spirit had done.

A litigated divorce is far worse for a child than divorce itself. Sandi has forgotten what Gabe went through, but you haven't.

"How can I go two months without seeing my girls? What should I do?"

I sat alone in our bedroom that night and cried.

I couldn't help but wonder if she told me the truth about her first marriage and her family years ago. I wondered if she really was the damsel in distress, or if she was actually the damsel causing the distress.

Gil, turn it off. Let's not go down this road tonight.

"But I accepted and loved Sandi unconditionally. I make limitless sacrifices for someone I love…it's how I do things. I was willing to give up my dream of having kids when she was too sick to get pregnant and didn't know that she would ever get better. I was committed to Sandi even through that!"

Gil, it's 2:00 a.m. Enough!

I grabbed a pen and paper, deciding that a list might help. Folding the paper in half created two columns. I began to write the reasons I never should have married, or had kids, with her:

Mental illness
Dishonesty
Inability to have kids
Family who doesn't support either of us

So far so good.

Lie
Cheat (with a woman)
Con
Cunning

The pen stopped as I stared at the list.

You have no boundaries when it comes to Sandi.

"Obviously. I was able to do Superman-like things for Sandi others might not have been able to. Her life is a million times better the day after she left than the day before we met. My sensitivity gave me the strength to…"

Why does that matter now? You did what you did—right or wrong, the truth doesn't matter. Nobody cares about truth when it comes to divorce. That should have been obvious from Sandi's first divorce.

The pen began to write something—almost on its own.

I'm a rescuer.

The words stung. There was the truth. I had allowed myself to fall in love with Sandi because I believed in what she could be. She was a better person than her circumstances, and her son deserved a better life with his mom. I loved the possibility of Sandi. It was pretty obvious who was flawed.

"But we were already in love by the time I realized how damaged she was. It was so easy to love her, but almost impossible to care for her. Another man would have run far away. My heart ached with Sandi's pain and I ran toward her…to be her hero."

Stop it. Go to bed. No one is listening Gil. Stand still!

"Along the way, I became embarrassed of myself. I caved under pressure to find a way to fix all the hurts from her past. I thought I could make sure she never got sick again. I guess it just kept triggering my neuroses. I was never embarrassed to be with her when others would have been ashamed to be with a mother who had no custody of her son. I'm proud nobody saw my wife's weaknesses after we moved. Now, though, mine were on full display. Now, we were part of a social circle. Now, money and appearance mattered more than me."

Like with your father?

That one stung. I shifted my weight and took a deep breath. The scar had to stay quiet...I couldn't take another day of its pain. Not today.

Gil, stop talking. No one cares.

"While we were together, Sandi lived by a very different set of values—good ones—a good life. Despite our hardships, she became healthier than she had ever been, accomplished more than she ever had, and we had a wonderful family. Now *that's* truth!" I knew it was only part of a bigger picture and shifted my weight again.

No one cares about the truth, Gil. When are you going to get that through your thick head!

"I even stood up to her own family for her. I defended and vouched for her as a mother when no one else in the world would."

Gil, enough! She's not listening. No one is listening.

"I knew her family controlled her son and this was the only way to have Gabe back in her life. What about that?"

There was no answer, only darkness, a mercy that came from somewhere, taking my consciousness with it as the tears wet my pillow and I eventually fell asleep.

CHAPTER 40

———◆———

DAYLIGHT BROUGHT A NEW RESOLVE. As I stood from the emotional fetal position that had become my life, a different person faced me in the mirror. Still, I chose not to fight. There would be no court battle, no lawyer. Instead, I would choose patience—the only choice my values and naïveté provided. In the meantime, I figured that Sandi would just enroll the girls into the Pacific Beach public school near her. Hopefully she'd come to her senses before two months passed.

A week later, I realized I was wrong.

The twenty-four-hour notice for an emergency court hearing on the first day of school arrived without fanfare. I panicked, but only for a moment. That was all it took.

Find a good lawyer

I'd written it down, even though I had suspicions—based on all I'd been through with Sandi's first divorce—about how court would work. The experience was daunting at best, but I faced it, marched into my lawyer's office and my future—a new Gil.

Almost as soon as I entered his office, I froze. The very room reeked of acumen and success. Cathedral ceilings hovered over scratched wood flooring where antique desks and bookcases, stuffed with an assortment of books, welcomed those who dared to enter. Hardcover books' bindings were dusted and stacked in some pre-arranged order. And while the room appeared recently cleaned, sunlight filtered through streaked windows, highlighting dust motes in the light. The whole place smelled of musty oak and paper.

"Once you've been served with a notice, there's not much you can do, Gil. In any case, she's noticed you for an ex parte hearing tomorrow."

My face must have conveyed confusion because Lloyd paused briefly before handing me additional documents. He was my lawyer and was good at the craft. Tapping his pointer finger on the middle of the stack, he responded with one simple sentence meant to explain everything. "It's the process used to file for emergencies."

"I told you on the phone, Lloyd, that I'm very well aware of what it is. I've been through her first divorce already. I know exactly how this game works." My cheeks were the color of homegrown tomatoes. He showed me the documents but I'd already read the notice. It didn't matter what the print said. The whole thing had been well planned, and I was trapped.

"Tomorrow is the first day of school, at what was supposed to be their former school." I was furious.

My attorney said nothing.

She purposefully manipulated the court date. Her goal: to get a judge to overrule my refusal to sign for the girls' school admission. That guarantees a place for them in class.

"What are we going to do about this? It's all a con to get what she wants at my expense," I stated, eying the attorney who stared at me with a pinched look.

Finally, Lloyd spoke. "The challenge lies in the timing of this hearing. Typically, the normal due process, which would afford each party the appropriate amount of time to make individual pleas to the court, is suspended." My attorney still seemed intent on delivering his speech.

"Lloyd." I attempted to calm my voice. "I said I'm well aware of how this works. She shouldn't even be let in the front door of the court-house because the only emergency is the one she's manufactured.

That's not what's going to happen, though. The court will hear arguments regarding the school, even though this fight isn't really about what school the girls attend. It's about how we resolve problems. We didn't resolve problems during marriage. We had no marriage counseling. It's no surprise we didn't resolve the school issue during a separation."

My standby had always been, "There's Sandi's way or hell to pay." The ugly truth had surfaced and the joke was on me. "Hell to pay" was how we resolved problems, unless I caved. I wasn't about to cave now.

Though Sandi could prove charming to others, she was next to impossible with me, particularly when she showed no regard for anyone but herself. My quip had turned dark; the meaning was ominous and prophetic. A dysfunctional family court system stood ready, able, and willing to help her out.

Remember her psych evaluation, Gil. There is no emergency; you know that. She's Sandi.

"Yeah, but she made me promise to agree to the school...agree, or there would be no chance for our marriage," I argued.

It's called emotional blackmail, Gil. You may have acted in good faith but you were really just paying a toll by making agreements to be in marriage counseling, to address the school issue, to be a family. Extortion of the heart. Your heart, Gil.

"Maybe."

Are you kidding? She lied, cheated, and manipulated her way from February to September without ever walking through the front door of a counselor's office for a real marriage counseling session. She will stop at nothing to coerce the court to buy into her "emergency."

"You make it sound so hopeless," I said, fighting back the vise gnawing at my gut.

You know the truth but you cannot face it.

The attorney kept his eyes glued to the documents on his desk. I couldn't swallow reality as it bubbled to the surface after so many years of pushing it down. I had to keep smothering truth in order to believe lies. Those were easier to digest. I could live with lies.

"Lloyd." My attorney finally glanced up at me. "The judge's usual response to an ex parte is to leave the status quo, which in this case would be to leave them in the school they were in last year, and issue an Order Shortening Time so it can't be said later that I wasn't ultimately given a somewhat appropriate amount of time to respond. Don't let the judge take the easy way out and put the girls back in the school where they were for the meantime while scheduling a hearing for two weeks from now. The damage will be done! We all know this is the game they play—what they do when someone didn't notice it properly in the first place. She didn't have the moral fiber to schedule a properly noticed hearing. She should be turned away at the front door. She gamed the system."

"You can't assume—"

"Don't let them issue an order shortening time! Don't play the game, Lloyd!" I couldn't let him buy into the lies as well. I'd forgotten, though, that he made his living swimming in these waters.

He gathered the documents into fine stacks and clicked open his briefcase. "We'll discuss that tomorrow in the courtroom."

"I won't be there, Lloyd. For this type of hearing my presence isn't required and you can represent me."

My attorney stopped and stared at me. "Gil, it's going to look a lot better if the judge sees you and realizes that you are a sophisticated, upstanding gentleman."

"Agreed. But I've already violated my boundaries in hiring you, and that's only because I had no time to think this through. My wife and I slept in the same bed for fifteen years. I can not and will not sit with her at opposing ends of a courtroom table."

He lifted his chin and regarded me. The circles under his eyes deepened. "Gil, then why did you hire me?"

"I panicked. I ignored my values."

We parted ways and I didn't hear from him for twenty-four hours. The phone rang and neon writing scrolled the caller ID Lloyd across a tiny screen.

"The court allowed the girls start at the private school because that's where they were last year. The judge shortened time for a hearing, allowing us action. If you can produce a witness from the school to testify to the school's policy requiring both parents' signatures, the girls will be removed mid-month."

How could I pull the girls out of school two weeks into it? What kind of father does that to his girls? The damage was done.

Adding insult to injury, I discovered the school administration had now conveyed to Sandi a slightly different acceptance policy than they had to me. Sandi had been working hard to become chummy with the school staff and administration over the past few years and with a potential scandal on their hands, they found it more advantageous to align with Sandi. Apparently, now, a student who obtained both parents' consent *or* had a court order was their new requirement for admission. On the surface, this seemed innocuous because court orders are law. The opposite appeared to be the case. I soon learned that the school was not a party to an action between two parents and did not have to obey any order made by the court. Simply put, the school had the right to accept the girls without both our consents. I relied on their policy as stated to me over and over again for the past eight months and they deviated from it, devastating my family in the process.

Bottom line: Sandi should have acted with integrity—but she didn't. Typical.

I sat alone in my girls' room that night. The first day of school should have been an exciting time. This one was a tragedy.

Schools are supposed to teach your children morals and values. They are supposed to be an example of honesty and responsibility. This school failed you, Gil. It enabled your wife to lie, cheat, and manipulate her way into her own agenda. They enabled a different kind of marriage, one that replaced your marriage with a new union to the school.

"Sandi has never been held accountable for anything! By anyone!" The cat yawned and rolled over. Fortunately, she didn't awaken to my rant.

It's heartbreaking to watch a school put their and your wife's interests ahead of what's best for your daughters. Sadly, they elected not to adhere to their stated policies, something that you relied upon.

"There are plenty of other places our daughters could have received a wonderful education. There are lots of people in the area who could afford this private school and choose not to have their kids there."

Obviously, whatever your daughters have gained from that school, they've lost exponentially more!

I had no argument and stared at a picture of my innocent babies asleep in their beds, completely unaware of how the course of their lives had been carved out for them, cruelly, by a selfish, narcissistic mother. They would never know.

The court hearing regarding the school was continued into the latter part of September with the custody arrangements to be decided then as well. I remained in conflict and reluctantly began to prepare for a hearing. My brain felt like it was playing a ping-pong game with my heart. It was just after midnight and I began to draft a response.

Behind her beauty hides multiple psychological disorders and numerous suicide attempts. At times charming and sincere, this femme fatale trails cunning and narcissism in her wake. However, cunning gifts her with the ability to shift into a chameleon, manipulating anyone who benefits her.

So far, so good. Only I wasn't convinced. If I couldn't convince myself, it was likely the courts wouldn't be convinced either.

The court doesn't care about the truth beneath the façade of deceit spouses turned litigants put forth. Her family paid for an attorney. Their goal: to get

Sandi sole custody and make you virtually nonexistent in your daughters'
lives. It was payback time in their eyes. I stood up for Sandi years ago when
they wouldn't and that set off a tumultuous feud between us.

It was torturous for me to deal with the hate I felt from her family.
They wouldn't support her to end a marriage she behaved unhealthily in, but now they were only too happy to help end this one. And
they would mock, humiliate, distort, and lie about painful experiences in my life, all of which happened because of all I did for Sandi
while she was in so much pain over how they treated her. This, to try
and take my kids away from me, to make me a scapegoat in order
to reunite their family on their terms. How sad that someone who
cried a million tears over things done to her, things so harmful to her
health and to her relationship with her son, would do the same thing
to someone else, especially to me.

Gil, she's not listening. No one is listening.

This will continue to get very ugly. Who are you going to be? Decide now.
What's it gonna be?

I had no answer, no recourse. My world had completely crashed
down around me. Sandi's first divorce had exhausted me physically,
emotionally, and financially. There was so much pressure suddenly
thrust upon me that I got sick from it.

I didn't have the physical, emotional, or financial strength for
Sandi's second divorce.

I also didn't have any support system—literally none—just as
Sandi and I had had none in dealing with all we'd had on our plate.

Again, I began to write.

After forty years battling isolation, secrecy, and rejection, and after sacrific-
ing my health and family to triumph for Sandi, having fulfilled my life's dream
to have the family I wanted more than anything, the only one I ever trusted
betrayed me. Sandi returned to her past. After a four-decade battle with
divorce, I have no strength left for the one divorce that will destroy me like
none other, and affect me the most. Knocked down for the count, my dream,
my precious, priceless, and irreplaceable dream, is gone.

Again, I wasn't convinced.

Stop editorializing Gil! They don't care. What's it gonna be? Decide!

The voice was relentless. After decades of being traumatized by everyone else's drama along with the trauma from other people's divorces, I had nothing left to give by the time I got to the one that mattered most: my own. I couldn't handle it. I didn't have the money or the heart for this battle. My well had run dry.

"Damn it, forty years after my own parent's divorce, the conflicts that grew out of it are still unresolved, causing me pain and heartache."

I had no will left to fight.

The decisions compounded the problems. Lloyd would be no use in figuring out this mess. I had to find someone completely different—something the opposite of Lloyd.

CHAPTER 41

———◆———

"INDEED, YOU HAVE A FAMILY here. A congregational family. A family built on the church…"

Too many times, I'd heard this pastor preach the same message—that my extended family could be found in the church. Did they mean it? I wondered as I stood there, staring at the carved oak door. Perhaps these people are only acquaintances.

"Who knows."

The whole idea of living like this—with no family of any kind—felt overwhelming.

I found myself standing outside the church where we, along with Ashley and Everett's family, used to spend every Sunday. I sipped on coffee and berated myself for even considering going inside. Still, this church had represented everything I had been longing for. It had been my fresh start. This was to have been my new home—the place I would find myself, the place where I could stop hiding. That had brought a sense of hope never experienced before. Now it only brought pain and here I was, looking for a hiding place.

I couldn't walk in. There were couples and families and I couldn't find a place where I would belong. These kinds of people go to church. People like me don't.

I couldn't bring myself to go in.

I sat on the patio and cried. At least I was still on the church's grounds, but my public display made others uncomfortable. Why did a grown man who cried in a churchyard make people cringe? Wasn't this place supposed to be different?

"You need to go in."

But I couldn't. This was as far as I could go.

An hour later when people filed out of the service, I was still in the same spot.

"Your Mets are doing good—stats show they're probably headed to their best year," Nathan said. I had no idea why he was saying this to me but I figured he knew why because he seemed to know every-thing. Nathan was a scholar. I'd met him a few years earlier and we'd discussed theology over coffee a handful of times. I'd always felt a good connection with Nathan. Maybe it was because he was a Jew who believed in Jesus. "I was the guest speaker today," he said and placed a hand on my shoulder.

"Yeah, I guess…maybe." I tried to act liked I cared.

"You don't really care about how the Mets are doing this year, do you?" Nathan glanced at me and moved ahead with the conversa-tion. There was promise in this; I could tell because I was standing there with one of the most respected men in the community who noticed my pain and he wasn't walking away. *Another new start.* The idea sounded good, so I allowed it to play repeatedly in my head. I forced a smile and sipped the coffee again.

I told Nathan what background I could get out in somewhat coherent sentences. *It feels like it takes a book to answer basic questions.* Nevertheless, I quickly got to my present dilemma.

"Filing a response to participate in this type of ugliness, particu-larly because I wouldn't do battle against someone I loved, makes my stomach turn. A beautiful fifteen-year relationship has been reduced to a legal process that allows two people who once loved each other to tear one another down. I don't get it. I never will."

Nathan said nothing.

"Participating in a court battle with Sandi, allowing a judge to oversee our children, devalues everything we had worked for. It's just not right. The 'professionals' in the justice system don't know our daughters, can't possibly love them, and certainly won't make sacrifices for them. None of them will ever lose sleep over my precious little girls."

He placed a hand on my shoulder again. "Life isn't fair."

I looked at him and there was genuine concern in his eyes. "I'm going to be fine, really Nathan." Secretly, I hoped he would leave.

"Of course you are. It just takes time…and a lot of faith."

"I believe I would win at the hearing, but ironically, I don't want to. I don't want to hand the keys to our daughters' lives over to strangers. She did that with Gabe. I think that would be the biggest loss."

Nathan nodded. His moment to divulge great wisdom—anything that would make the pain go away—was now. I waited. He simply handed me a Bible instead.

"I've got jury duty tomorrow or else I'd go through it with you, but it's probably better that you search for yourself. There, you'll find the strength to move forward."

"Nathan…" I didn't know how to respond.

"I'll make sure you're settled, Gil." Nathan pointed at the heavens, inspecting nothing in particular. "I'll call you tomorrow evening."

"Come on, Nathan." His wife, Judy, had arrived at our meeting five minutes or so earlier and thankfully, had remained a spectator. Unknowingly, she had come to my rescue because what Nathan was saying didn't sit well with me. Maybe it showed in my face.

"Let's give Gil a chance to think." She winked at me and pulled Nathan's arm, urging him toward their car.

From my seat at a patio table, I watched them cross the massive lawn that ended at the general public parking lot. When I finally saw their car's taillights turn from the church grounds and head toward the main highway, I turned my back on them and faced the Bible.

"What on earth is he talking about?" I said as my mind wandered off again. I had nothing else to do today and nowhere else to be, so I opened the book.

I sat on that patio and read for hours about marriage and divorce, from the dueling rabbinical factions and the origins of irreconcilable differences thousands of years ago, to the early church fathers, to Luther and Calvin's beliefs, which have been stretched so far beyond their intent to narrowly reform, they wouldn't recognize it today if they tripped over it.

"Am I understanding this correctly?" I asked myself more than once.

The Bible itself seemed to be a story of marriage—one big love story—God's vows to us and ours to him. Apparently, marriage is the ultimate illustration of a relationship with God, and the answer to when it's okay to divorce your spouse is when God stops forgiving you for all your weaknesses, shortcomings, and failures—when God divorces you.

It seemed to go without saying that some situations would test the outer boundaries of this thesis. However, it seemed clear to me that God would always bless separation for safety's sake.

Another disclosure was that Christians are not supposed to use secular courts for civil matters, because generally speaking, those are not in alignment with the Bible. Yes, God calls on followers to do as a court says; however, God provides clear instruction where there is conflict between God's directives and man's authority. There was no question.

"Obey God rather than human beings! Better you be cheated than to participate." The words felt clean and for the first time, clear.

I continued to read and clarity revealed itself in the words.

"Grace isn't about forgiveness. It is about reconciliation. When we sin, we are out of alignment with God. He doesn't kick us to the curb. He gives grace so that we may realign with Him. Grace is for reconciliation, not remarriage!"

I voiced my thoughts and continued to gain insight. For years, I'd sat in this church and never heard any of this. *Half the people in this church are on second or third marriages.*

"Am I understanding it correctly?" I asked myself again.

I found that God separated from the Jews—not divorced—but waited for reconciliation with His chosen people. God granted salvation to the Gentiles. They should live in such a counter-cultural way that God waited, hoping the Jews would become jealous and want what the Gentiles had.

Ironically, the only ones I'm jealous of now are the Jews. I feel punished by God for my exposure to Christianity. It's now clear to me why ninety-nine percent of the people I come from don't believe in what Christians say about how to get to heaven.

I gazed up at the same heavens Nathan had gazed up at earlier. The bright full moon had obviously given me light to read. I looked at my phone. It was four a.m.! An eternity had passed with my focus glued elsewhere.

As I stood up, I felt my head and heart collide. Immediately, the story of King Solomon and two mothers fighting over the same baby came to mind. This was the first story I had learned from the Bible— from Sandi—as she cried endlessly during the years of litigation surrounding her first divorce.

Both women make arguments to the King as to why the baby in question is hers—leaving King Solomon to resolve to which woman the baby actually belonged. After much consideration, he demanded a sword—declaring the only way to solve this problem was to cut the baby in half. Each woman could take her half of the infant and go in peace. As the proposition was announced, the first woman agreed that killing the baby was an acceptable outcome. The second woman cried out—begging the King not to harm the baby. She would allow the other woman to keep the child, sacrificing her own desire just to let the baby live. King Solomon, after witnessing both women's reactions, handed the baby to the second woman. "For she must be the true mother because she would rather give him up than let him be harmed." Only a true parent would make such a sacrifice.

I arrived home as the sun was coming up and headed for the shower. I glanced at the mirror on my way and was shocked to find written on it:

Romans 12:2. Don't copy the behavior and customs of this world, but let God transform you into a new person by changing the way you think. Then you will learn to know God's will for you, which is good and pleasing and perfect.

I was too tired to think, so I shrugged it off. After my shower, I decided to take a second look. Gleaming on the mirror, something new had been written.

Prov 1:15. My child, don't go along with them! Stay far away from their paths.

I would certainly need some rest before I meet with Nathan later.

———◆———

"Yes, I found..." I stopped. I couldn't say it. Nathan was intrigued. I realized anything that I would say about the words in the Bible being in alignment with what I was feeling would sound ridiculous. So, I changed course. "I'm supposed to follow Ashley and Everett's lead—do divorce the way everyone else does."

Nathan cocked his head. "What are you saying, Gil?"

"I'm just supposed to do things the way the world does them and accept that God forgives us and loves us."

There it was. I'd said exactly the opposite of what I'd come here to say, the exact opposite of the words I'd seen on the mirror.

"Hmm." Nathan turned to gaze at the menu. Chinese food seemed to interest him more than my remarks did.

I couldn't bear the silence, so I stated the obvious. "I've come to the conclusion you wanted me to, and now we can get down to eating."

Nathan looked up. "Is that all you wanted to say, Gil?"

I nodded. "I think so."

"All right. We'll have to agree then—just because it says something in the Bible, it doesn't mean that's the way we do things today. God forgiving us, as well as God loving us, is all that matters. Right?"

My jaw dropped.

"Will that work for you?" Nathan's tone took an edge.

"Absolutely!" the waitress added, waving as she bolted toward the kitchen door.

I stared at her, then turned to look at Nathan. It's been said that the definition of insanity is to repeat the same actions while expecting different results. In less than five minutes, I'd completely done an about-face with my own plans. I was sure God would stamp my forehead with the moniker "Insane" in big, red letters.

"That was easy." Nathan motioned for service. "But I suspect that wasn't the original conversation you planned to have, was it?"

"No. I'm not sure what just happened." My stomach clenched. Smells of soy and fish sauce assaulted me and I fought back the urge to vomit.

You didn't tell him, did you?

I shook my head. There was no way I could tell Nathan about the mirror, not yet, but I'd found courage enough to tell him about my limitations. After forty years of secrets and disappointments, I'd found strength—even though my belief system clashed with how things were done. At least now my heart happened to be aligned with God's heart—at least when it comes to marriage.

Nathan called off the waitress as she was heading toward us. His expression pinched, and I could tell something else bothered him. Perhaps my comments were falling on deaf ears.

"Do you understand, Nathan?"

He said nothing, so I gave him silence and waited for him to collect his thoughts. After all, there was still a chance that if Nathan could just have a little more time, he would understand what I was trying to say. The Bible says what it says, and we do things the way we do them. Maybe he wanted me to have the time—time for everything in my head to switch back to the way it was a few minutes earlier. *Let it go now.*

But I couldn't.

I snapped. "I gotta go. I'll be more than happy to meet with you another time, Nathan."

It would be better to walk away than to further engage in an empty conversation. I feared the only outcome could be that somehow Gil was wrong and the Church was right. I couldn't listen to that one more time.

"We're not finished, Gil. You've got some rethinking to do."

"The game the church plays with divorce seems no better than the game the lawyers play," I said over my shoulder as I headed for the door.

I could feel Nathan glaring at me as I pushed open the door. Tiny bells tinkled at the movement, announcing my exit. Mostly, they drowned out Nathan' final comment.

"Come back, Gil. We're not through yet."

CHAPTER 42

———•———

"WHAT WAS HE SAYING AS I was leaving?"

Your frustration comes from the cost to be Jewish as nothing—it was given to you. Your having paid such a big price to be Christian means nothing to those for whom it cost nothing to be Christian. It's an unfair, hypocritical dichotomy.

I let the thought sink in as I stared at a father and son skipping rocks across the lake. This should have been a peaceful place, filled with the smell of young pines and honeysuckle. I inhaled, hoping the scents of nature would fill my soul the way angst had flared my scar after meeting with Nathan.

It costs us nothing to be Jewish in this day and age, while it cost those who lived during the Holocaust everything. Even today, those who live in Israel fear things we take for granted—things like walking into a supermarket.

I glanced down at the bag of peanuts sitting next to my soda and felt a familiar twinge of guilt.

It cost nothing to be Christian nowadays either. Think of those around the world who fear for their lives just by attending church or opening a Bible.

"Your frustration is about where the two meet. Things not generally understood by Christians whose only expense is to live godly, rather than worldly!"

The father and son walked away. Perhaps they heard me. Perhaps they too were offended by my comments. I didn't care.

Just then, my phone rang. I glanced down and saw Nathan's name flashing in green and black letters. I decided to take the call and clicked on Answer with trembling fingers. My gut clenched for the third time that day.

"I'm glad you took my call, Gil." He didn't pause for my response but continued without taking a breath. "In court this morning, I told the lawyers that if I found out the plaintiff or defendant was Christian, I would automatically vote against that person for being in this civil court in the first place. I was dismissed from jury duty, just so you know."

Again, Nathan didn't pause for my response. "Who's your hero, Gil? Do you remember a childhood hero, a ballplayer maybe? Do you even have a hero, Gil?"

"Rosa Parks is my hero. I don't know why. Maybe because she was misunderstood too—still, she took a stand. The truth is that Rosa Parks didn't set out to do anything spectacular that day. She was just being herself. It was raining and she just couldn't go to the front of the bus to pay and then back outside, walking to the rear entrance one more time. She simply had the courage to be not as the world was, but as it should be. Who is your hero, Nathan?"

"My hero is the great Rabbi Hillel, who said, 'If not you, then who? If not now, then when?'"

It suddenly became clear to me that this was to be my King Solomon moment. "I cannot appear in a courtroom to fight against my wife over our daughters, which means I automatically lose. There will be no ugly five-year battle like there was with Gabe." This wasn't a sudden decision, even though it sounded that way—it was my DNA speaking.

"Gil, standing up for God this morning didn't cost me any-thing I couldn't afford, or for that matter, wanted. I didn't want jury duty."

"I'm not doing this because God says so, Nathan. This is just me being me, and God happens to see it the same way as I do."

Now I didn't pause.

"Change never occurs by maintaining the status quo and it never happens without pain, suffering, and persecution. I'm not trying to change the world, Nathan. I'm just trying to do what I can with mine."

Without my involvement, the court would become a rubber stamp for Sandi's requests. I would have four days per month with my daughters and, of course, the infamous Wednesday Night Divorced Dad's Dinners. The most important aspect of these two little girls' lives would, in the time it took to slam a gavel, be reduced to rubble. The victims—our daughters—were forgotten. The chain Sandi and I set out to break fifteen years ago had wrapped itself around our family. A chaotic divorce would shape another generation.

By default, according to the judge, I would go from being a father whose priority was to spend time with his kids to the standard "dad package," becoming virtually nonexistent in their lives, except for a granted opportunity to visit with my daughters four days per month.

My daughters wouldn't get to be with their dad for even half of the time they deserved. They wouldn't be allowed to share their first date, a trip for ice cream, or a chance to play math games with stuffed animals with their dad. No more angel hair and cereal parties with me.

I loved putting a daily schedule on my desk so that I could visualize just where each one was whenever I paused for a cup of coffee. I loved setting my phone to go off at the time they were born on their birthday to cherish that very moment annually. I loved always taking their call and nobody else's while in a meeting, to hear the little voice on the other end say, "Hi, daddy." Those moments seemed more purposeful and good, more important than climbing a corporate ladder. That moment when she saw her first convertible and observed that it had "none lid"—such an innocent response—deserved pause and notice.

We've had so many funny memories: assembling a stroller; assembling toys and having parts left over. I've been the one person in the world my daughters could count on. I was their rock. I was the one who reminded them at least ten times in the morning to get out of bed to get ready for school, to go over spelling words, and to eat green bagels every St. Patrick's Day. I taught them how to make a bed in the morning and read stories with them at night.

Joy came from an ice cream cone after school, the playground and the park, homework completed together, sharing nicknames they loved but were embarrassed to say in front of their friends, telling knock-knock jokes, the countdown each night of the week until a birthday, watching Christmas movies together for weeks before Christmas, deciding when to put up the tree and just how to do it.

"That's what will happen."

According to the judge, you're no longer considered "Daddy," Gil.

"Yeah, that's apparent. But I can't be forced to watch as some other guy eventually steps into my daughters' lives and becomes the 'dad' for ninety percent of their time."

"You'll always be the only father they ever have."

Time spent together is where bonds are built and memories created.

"A father in name only. That's not me! My daughters as just some obligation like my father treated me. That's not me! I won't stoop to that level. I didn't wait until I was forty to have kids for this." No one was around to hear my rant, and I wouldn't have cared if anyone had been.

"Okay, I hear the depth of your love for your daughters. It's highly emotional, I feel for you, Gil. But emotions aside, what are you saying?"

Nathan's questions burned as fiercely as my scar did, and I could not ignore it. My answer came quickly. Again, it wasn't so much a decision as it was a personification.

"I cannot participate in being anything less than the father I am."

There was shock behind his silence. He didn't understand—he never would.

I know. Ironic, isn't it? All those 'Godly people' will judge me in worldly ways.

With Sandi, there was no negotiating, at least not in good faith, not without leverage. I could not be a father with less than full participation in my daughters' lives—that included decisions that would be made about their school. Their current school was a place I vowed never to set foot in again. So long as they went there, I was for all intents and purposes, not their father. A child does not go to a school where their father does not want them to go. At least that was my position.

"You're not the least bit confused anymore, are you?" Nathan's question seemed odd, but he was right.

Something had changed inside of me. I carefully reviewed my thoughts about what I would do and what I wouldn't. I knew who I was and what I wouldn't become as a father. "We all have to be realists, Nathan. It's part of life."

Nathan didn't dissent. Maybe he was actually listening.

"However, when it comes to my daughters, our family, and myself as a parent, I'm an idealist, and proud of it. Kids get one childhood. Parents get one opportunity to enjoy it. It's not a dress rehearsal. I am a dad who has been actively involved in my family since the first moment my children were born. I have always been a dad who never spent a day without them in it. Those girls are my life, and I cannot handle being a visitor or a token presence. It would be hard enough for me to be a half-time dad. A four-day-a-month dad is not who I am." My voice sounded as strong as my resolve.

"Go on." Nathan seemed keenly interested.

"Having dinner with my daughters for two hours on Wednesday night is not what I do. Those types of mandatory dinners are some of the worst memories of my childhood. I will not repeat the same experience for my own children."

"Okay…so once more, what are you saying?" Skepticism edged his voice.

Again, the question burned as fiercely as the scar, and again I could not ignore it. My final moment of clarity happened in an instant and this time it was a little easier to digest.

"I will neither lie to my girls by endorsing their mother's version of the truth, nor will I tell them mine. This will make speaking on the phone difficult at best. It will put them in the middle." Nathan still didn't comprehend what I was trying to say.

"We're not pen pals or phone friends anyway. I'd rather my daughters be mad at me, if that's what happens, than to confuse them. The truth will bear them out, but I won't be party to a tug o' war."

There it was. Another trifecta. Another Perfect Storm!

Nathan was speechless for just a moment. "You know what this means, Gil?"

I nodded.

Adhering to my limitations, my positions, values, and boundaries would box me into a corner. Divorce can rob me of marriage and family, but it can't rob me of who I am. I vowed to always protect Sandi and in the moment of Danielle's birth, I promised Sandi that she would never miss a day of her girls' lives—and I meant it.

My conscience was stilled. For once, the voice was silenced. I peered out onto the lake and in the reflection, saw a man.

"Yes."

EPILOGUE

THE SUN WARMED HIS FACE as he lifted his chin, eyes closed, toward the sky. This brought comfort, warmth. It almost felt like compassion but it was only heat from the sun. Where was the human compassion in his life?

Gil walked toward the fountain that spouted water in all directions. Little children danced and splashed in the spray—complete innocent bliss. He had never known what that felt like—his childhood had been robbed of that one unique gift given to innocent children. It seemed to happen the day his parents divorced.

He sat quietly and observed the children as they played in the fountain. A smile crossed his lips as he watched them. At least half of these kids would be spared the pain he went through. The rest would face the broken homes that came from divorce—just like him—and now, his daughters.

Everyone will be okay. That's what they say. But you're different, Gil. The voice was unwelcome and broke Gil's revelry. *You don't look the same as anyone else and society knows it. You're better to stay in hiding.*

It had been ten months since Gil had last ventured outside and he was beginning to wonder if he should have stayed put.

"No one asked you." Gil didn't care this time who heard him.

It's the best decision because there are no simple answers. Every time someone discusses family, you have no answer. Every time someone asks that question of a divorced dad...

"Oh yeah? So, what's that?"

You know full well what it is, but if you need to hear it again, then here you go: 'So, Gil...how often do you get to see your kids?' Now what's the answer?

"I hate that question. It's insulting and ridiculous!"

Of course you do, but that doesn't absolve you from an answer—even one that you choose to keep to yourself.

"So, I guess I'm the villain here?" Gil could feel irritation bubble from somewhere deep inside. He picked up a rock and tossed it against a tree.

Apparently society thinks so.

"Yeah, well, society can just..."

You're the one who has no family or friends left. You're the one who keeps pissing off people by being real with how divorce has destroyed your life. It's all part of society, Gil.

Gil stared at the fountain.

"I can't stay in hiding. I turn on the TV and watch as almost every commercial and every show makes some reference to family." He tossed another stone, this time a little harder, and watched as bits of bark splintered from where it hit. Gil flinched. "I can't even watch the news anymore because nearly every story weaves in support of family. Then there are the holidays. Those are the worst, the big and small ones. I used to cherish them all. Now they only cause pain. I can't wait for them to be over. But that only starts the clock moving toward the next one. Add in birthdays and anniversaries—there's something all the time. The days and weeks leading up to each event—those are more torturous than the actual day."

You don't know whether to go out, so you stay solitary—in your own prison. You go out and face a world you're not a part of. You don't belong anywhere. Inside or out, the phone doesn't ring.

"Yes, exactly. And on this day, the poison I chose was the warmth of some much needed sunshine." He picked up another rock but couldn't find the strength to throw it.

"Gil, may I have a word with you, please?"

Gil jumped.

A pretty blonde with matching shoes and handbag stepped forward. It was Olivia. We were friends with her and her husband at the stables years ago. She was always up on the latest gossip.

"Oh, Olivia. You startled me. Of course. Sit down. How are you?"

"Well, fine, I guess." She glanced down at the sidewalk—something Gil recognized meant that she was lying. He stayed quiet and waited for her to put together her thoughts. "I...I just want to know what the problem is." Her eyes lifted to meet his and there was a different emotion behind them—not sadness, not pain, perhaps contempt?

"What problem?"

"With you. These were kids you longed for, yet ultimately abandoned in the name of integrity and what appears to be a little self-righteousness."

Gil paused. He had expected others to voice their irritation with his path, but never Olivia.

Completely abandoned my children! What are you saying? How dare you use that word to describe me!

"Look, Olivia." Gil sighed and dropped the rock in his fist. "Abandoning your kids is something that happens when a person walks away from his family. That isn't me. I'm so sick and tired of these one-stop-shop labels."

"It's not a label, Gil...just an observation."

Great, my life is a living hell and I have to defend myself again.

"Tell me, are all single moms alike? Is a widow the same as a career welfare mom? Is a poor divorced mother who was left by her husband the same as a wealthy divorced mom who left her husband? Is a victim of domestic violence the same as someone who just wasn't happy—someone who didn't want to do the work to fix her marriage? Someone like...oh...Sandi?"

"Okay, well, then you're trying to *be right* instead of *choosing right*."

"Whose definition of *'right'* are you using, Olivia? Who decided you're supposed to do divorce a certain way?" The image of his daughters' tear-stained faces flashed in Gil's head. "I don't know if my decisions are right or wrong. I just know I shouldn't be put in the position to have to make them."

He locked eyes with Olivia.

"Don't find me right or wrong, Olivia. Look at me and notice what you really see—it's the unpleasant effects of decades of treating divorce like a common cold. You have an emotionally driven response because you, like practically everyone else, have experienced divorce through your parents, yourself, your siblings, or someone else in your extended family. Stop viewing it as normal. It's a dysfunction. You devalue marriage when you devalue pain associated with the loss of it."

"I understand you have problems, Gil, but then so does everyone else," Olivia interjected. She shifted her weight. "The rest of us don't go around 'stirring the pot,' as it were."

"I'm not 'stirring any pot,' Olivia. I'm just speaking the cold hard truth of my circumstances. People seem to need to twist my words into whatever makes them feel comfortable. You're being another armchair therapist judging and opining like it's the lightning round of a game show—and you have all the answers to everyone else's problems!"

"Gil...I..."

"Oh, I can do that with your problems too. In fact, I can line up everyone I know and solve all their problems in ten seconds each because they're not my problems and I've never walked a day in their shoes."

"Then I'll say it another way, Gil. You exonerated yourself from doing the best thing, not only for yourself, but for your own children."

"That explains a lot."

"What does?"

Gil shook his head. How could he explain that for over a year, he had been receiving venomous responses from everyone he tried to talk with. He'd shared his pain in confidence, which was immediately followed by vicious character assassinations intended to harass him. Mostly, the attacks were designed to force him to get with the program and do a divorce the way it was *supposed* to be done.

Gil took a deep breath.

"First of all, the best thing for everyone would have been for Sandi to do the work to fix our marriage. Yeah, I owned fifty percent of the condition of my marriage, but I own no part of its destruction, or of the destructive nature of it. Unfortunately, my daughters' childhood ended the moment Sandi left. So, we're not talking about the best thing, Olivia, you're talking about finding some sort of right answer on the wrong road, which isn't always possible."

Olivia stood and faced him. "I don't know why I'm wasting my time talking to you, Gil. You haven't done anything different than your own dysfunctional parents did. How did you give your kids a good divorce?"

It's the response, Gil. What else did you expect…concession?

"There are things my kids will not be able to do and I would never criticize them for it, to begin with. Encouragement for kids is standard. Assisting each one to find her passion and pursue it. We all aim to foster courage, principles, and integrity in our offspring. I am no different. I *was* committed to being a married father because that's what I could do. And I did a great job at it too!"

"You're being self-righteous again."

"Look, I signed on to be a fulltime dad in a fulltime marriage. I am not a good 'divorced dad.' I don't have any of the tools or the support system necessary to be a good divorced dad. I don't have the heart to be one. If a pregnant woman decides she doesn't have the wherewithal to be a parent and gives her baby up for adoption, she is looked upon as courageous and selfless. I, on the other hand, somehow, am a scoundrel…and I don't get to move on, to find joy. For me, it would have been better, less painful, to have never loved at all, than to have loved and lost."

Olivia cocked her head to one side and blinked. "Your message is loud and clear, Gil. And wrought with great empathy for yourself, but...I'd hoped you'd finally step up and shed the dysfunction you'd been steeped in for a lifetime to break the cycle. You didn't! You let me down. I'm disappointed in you!"

Gil shook his head. "Well, you're not the only one, I can assure you. 'Scarred for life' isn't just a catchy phrase. No, 'scarred for life' really can last a lifetime."

"But others do go through hard times, Gil. You're not the only one," she said, and crossed her arms as if that sealed her statement. "You seem comfortable clinging to your role as victim."

Her comment was snide, and Gil felt the sting.

"Bad behavior is constantly rewarded these days, and somehow victims are a problem. When did we start looking at victims who are not able to overcome their circumstance in a lesser light than victims who have? I'm not some bitter, angry ex-husband. I have the courage to say I'm a victim and it's about time you stop denying my reality. No, Olivia, of course I'm not comfortable with it. In fact, I'm very uncomfortable."

"Well, you're pissing everyone off—people won't put up with your antics for long."

Gil sighed. He was getting nowhere and arguing would not improve his station. Besides, each day brought more confirmation that society needed him to be the villain so it could perpetuate the current culture where "dad's third wife" and "mom's boyfriend" roll off the tongue as easily as we breathe. He forced a grin. "Okay, Olivia."

"What is it about you that creates such dissidence?"

Gil had heard enough. "Is there anything I can say that you will listen to? Because if not, then there really is no point in continuing this conversation." Gil stood and looked at Olivia eye to eye.

"Probably not."

"Well then, have a nice day, Olivia." Gil started to walk away. Suddenly, he glanced back. "One last thing, Olivia. How many times have you said, 'My marriage, my family is everything to me and I couldn't survive without them?' We've all said it. I'm not saying you meant it any less than me, but those aren't just idle words to me."

Gil walked away, leaving her standing alone on the sidewalk. Even the solitude of home paled in comparison to the nagging voice in his head. Nevertheless, a change of scenery still would be good, or so he thought.

He ducked into a bookstore that had disappeared between the crack of a mega one-stop shopping center and a theater. Competition for attention seemed moot, so the owners did little to make it stand out, except for the Open sign in the front window.

"The perfect place to disappear," Gil said as he crossed the threshold.

"Indeed it is!" The voice came from behind a cluttered counter. No one stood there, which made Gil wonder if he'd been hearing things. "Bookstores are always a great place to get lost."

A face popped up near the cash register and Gil turned to see a roly-poly man in his sixties wearing spectacles and a brilliant blue vest. He smiled.

"I meant..." Gil stopped mid-sentence and pretended to scan a row of shelves on the opposite end of the store.

"Lookin' for nonfiction, eh?"

"Yes...yes, that's exactly what I'm looking for. Over here, is it?" Gil pointed to the back. He chose not to wait for an answer but instead strode with long steps away from the clerk.

"There's a section on Historical Figures back there you might like," the clerk shouted after him.

"Probably not." Gil made a sharp left into a stack of shelves. Books had been crammed into every available space, filling that part of the store with a musty aroma. Dust motes danced in token slivers of sunlight that escaped through a dingy window near the ceiling. Gil found an old leather chair and settled into it, making himself as small as possible. To one side, a tiny end table supported the only lamp he'd seen. Its light paled against the sunlight but still illuminated a stack of books left behind by the last person seated there. He reached over and picked up the topmost novel and scanned the cover.

As if fire burnt the tips of his fingers, he suddenly dropped the book. Staring down at the cover, Gil felt his throat close off and the air flee his lungs. He couldn't breathe—but he couldn't take his eyes off it either. Lying face-up, the title blared at Gil: *Resilience Is Relative.*

The first page spoke of the Greek warrior Achilles. He was given special powers when his mother submerged him as a baby in the River Styx. This was supposed to make him invincible. The legend continues that his mother missed Achilles' heel in the dunk because she held him by it and forgot the spot beneath her hand, apparently. After Achilles went on to be a great warrior, winning countless battles and fighting foes with ferocity, he met death when an arrow lanced the part of his body his mother forgot to protect—his heel.

Gil identified with the great warrior.

We all have that one thing that weakens us, makes us vulnerable to defeat. Superman has his kryptonite. For some it's vanity; for others, food; and for others, power. You have an Achilles' heel, Gil—divorce!

It's easy to opine—you should fight for your kids or be labeled as abandoning them without assigned visits. Everyone lives in his own Pandora's box. Sandi knew beforehand, even though you've dealt with much in life, divorce was your weakness—something you would never be able to handle. She had her arrow and knew where to hit your heel.

"It's the Civil War my father drafted me into all over again." Gil continued, though no one was present to listen—no one except the voice in his head. "Brooklyn. General George Washington had the courage to take a not-so-popular path and retreat toward a revolution."

But your kids want to know you're fighting for them.

"If you need to label me, call me what I am, a Conscientious Objector, and try to understand my pain. In wartime, those with deep moral convictions were given alternative ways to participate in what they morally objected to."

Gil couldn't contain himself. He quickly bought the book and hurried home.

———◆———

That's it Gil! There is still another course of action.

Gil exhausted his list of options. He sighed and waited.

While you cannot be nonexistent in your own life, you can make a difference in others' lives. You can be the force that recognizes the toxic acceptance of the role the status quo plays. Divorce is society's answer, but now you know better and you can make the difference, Gil. You have experience and now you have a purpose!

The voice in Gil's head spoke gently this time but he didn't believe what it said.

Be present, Gil. Come back to the moment and see your life for what it is.

Gil reached his hand toward the doorknob but his fingers wouldn't obey. "It's too far...too much to ask." His hand fell back to his side, trembling. Beads of sweat rose over his forehead that he wiped with the back of his hand.

Just breathe.

Time to force everything to happen the way it's supposed to. The game of musical chairs had begun, that Gil had been playing without realizing it wasn't the usual game. In this version, it looked much different after the final round...

The music had stopped and everyone had been seated, everyone except Gil who stood alone, without a chair. At fifty, Gil had lost everyone and everything—family, friends, faith, career, reputation, and time, the legs to his chair. He was left with a life of secrets, embarrassment, hiding, loneliness, and shame. He was back to looking out the window at the world passing by, a spectator of life appearing smart, talented, and capable...but just too broken inside.

———◆———

"I'll do it this time—make it out." Gil looked at the man staring back at him in the mirror. The boy gazed through the grown man's eyes but there was something different about him—something had changed within—a resolve not seen before had surfaced.

He shook his head and silenced the voice, though it still laughed.

Gil realized long ago that he'd been chasing that elusive chair, always hoping to find a place to sit, to find peace in his life, to live with hope, and to relish the joy that comes from belonging. He would never belong, he knew it now, but somehow it didn't matter. The only thing that mattered was getting outside, making a difference for others, finding a way to purge the illness that was consuming the lives of families all around him. Divorce couldn't win.

He looked again at the mirror and saw that secrets no longer dwelt there. Nothing was there...just the man with the little boy's eyes in an empty room.

You'll always be the one without a chair.

"Where will I find the strength?" Gil said, turning again to the mirror. There it was.

> *"If you love the truth, you'll trust it—that is, you will*
> *expect it to be good, beautiful, perfect, orderly, etc., in*
> *the long run, not necessarily in the short run."*

> —Abraham Maslow

Join the online Without A Chair book club discussion.
http://davidschel.com

Learn about Kids Against Divorce, the organization founded
by author David Schel.
http://kidsagainstdivorce.org

 Kids Against Divorce
GIVING CHILDREN A VOICE

Made in the USA
Columbia, SC
11 April 2018